Dear Readers,

Many years ago, when I was a kid, my father said to me, "Bill, it doesn't really matter what you do in life. What's important is to be the *best* William Johnstone you can be."

I've never forgotten those words. And now, many years and almost 200 books later, I like to think that I am still trying to be the best William Johnstone I can be. Whether it's Ben Raines in the Ashes series, or Frank Morgan, the last gunfighter, or Smoke Jensen, our intrepid mountain man, or John Barrone and his hard-working crew keeping America safe from terrorist lowlifes in the Code Name series, I want to make each new book better than the last and deliver powerful storytelling.

Equally important, I try to create the kinds of believable characters that we can all identify with, real people who face tough challenges. When one of my creations blasts an enemy into the middle of next week, you can be damn sure he had a good reason.

As a storyteller, my job is to entertain you, my readers, and to make sure that you get plenty of enjoyment from my books for your hard-earned money. This is not a job I take lightly. And I greatly appreciate your feedback—you are my gold, and your opinions *do* count. So please keep the letters and e-mails coming.

Respectfully yours,

WILLIAM W. JOHNSTONE

JOURNEY OF THE MOUNTAIN MAN

THE FIRST MOUNTAIN MAN: CHEYENNE CHALLENGE

PINNACLE BOOKS
Kensington Publishing Corp.
http://www.kensingtonbooks.com

PINNACLE BOOKS are published by

Kensington Publishing Corp.
850 Third Avenue
New York, NY 10022

All Kensington Titles, Imprints, and Distributed Lines are available at special quantity discounts for bulk purchases for sales promotions, premiums, fund-raising, and educational or institutional use. Special book excerpts or customized printings can also be created to fit specific needs. For details, write or phone the office of the Kensington special sales manager: Kensington Publishing Corp., 850 Third Avenue, New York, NY 10022, attn: Special Sales Department, Phone: 1-800-221-2647.

Pinnacle and the P logo Reg. U.S. Pat. & TM Off.

ISBN-13: 978-0-7860-1898-7
ISBN-10: 0-7860-1898-4

First Pinnacle Books Printing: April 2007

10 9 8 7 6 5 4 3 2 1

Printed in the United States of America

JOURNEY OF THE MOUNTAIN MAN
7

THE FIRST MOUNTAIN MAN:
CHEYENNE CHALLENGE
275

JOURNEY OF THE
MOUNTAIN MAN

It is only the dead who do not return.
—Bertrand De Vieuzac

Dedicated to: James Albert Martin

1

"I didn't think you had any living relatives, except for your sister?"

"I didn't either. But then I forgot about Pa's brother. He was supposed to have gotten killed at Chancellorsville, back in '63. I guess this letter came from his kids. It would have to be; it's signed Fae Jensen."

"I wonder how they knew where to write?" Sally asked. "Big Rock is not exactly the hub of commerce, culture, and industry."

The man laughed at that. The schoolteacher in his wife kept coming out in the way she could put words together.

It was 1882, in the high-up country of Colorado. The cabin had recently been remodeled: two new rooms added for Louis Arthur and Denise Nicole Jensen. The twins were approaching their first birthday.

And the man called Smoke was torn between going to the aid of a family member he had never seen and staying at home for the birthday party.

"You have to go, Smoke," Sally spoke the words softly.

"Gibson, in the Montana Territory." The tall, wide-shouldered and lean-hipped man shook his head. "A long way from home. On what might be a wild goose hunt. Probably is. I don't even know where Gibson is."

Sally once more opened the letter and read it aloud. The handwriting was definitely that of a woman, and a woman who had earned high marks in penmanship.

Dear Cousin Kirby,

I read about you in the local paper last year, after that dreadful fight at Dead River. I wanted to write you then, but thought my brother and I could handle the situation ourselves. Time has proven me incorrect. We are in the middle of a war here, and our small ranch lies directly between the warring factions. I did not believe when this range war was started that either Mr. Dooley Hanks or Mr. Cord McCorkle would deliberately harm us, but conditions have worsened to the point where I fear for our lives. Any help you could give us would be greatly appreciated.

Respectfully, your cousin
Fae Jensen

"Have you ever heard of either of those men, Smoke?"

"McCorkle. He came into that country twenty years or more ago. Started the Circle Double C. He's a hard man, but I never heard of him riding roughshod over a woman."

"How about this Dooley Hanks?"

Smoke shook his head. "The name sort of rings a bell. But it isn't ringin' very loud."

"When will you be leaving, honey?"

He turned his brown eyes on her, eyes that were usually cold and emotionless. Except when he looked at her. "I haven't said I was going."

"I'll be fine, Smoke. We've got some good hands and some good neighbors. You don't have to worry about me or the babies." She held up the letter. "They're blood kin, honey."

He slowly nodded his head. "I'll get things squared away

around the Sugarloaf, and probably pull out in about three days." He smiled. "If you just insist that I go."

She poked him in the ribs and ran laughing out of the room.

"That's him," the little boy said to his friend, visiting from the East. "That's the one ever'body writes about in them penny dreadfuls. That's Smoke Jensen."

Smoke tied his horse to the hitchrail in front of the Big Rock Guardian and went inside to speak with Haywood Arden, owner and editor.

"He sure is mean-lookin'," the boy from back East said. "And he really does wear them guns all whopper-jawed, don't he?"

The first thing Haywood noticed was Smoke wearing two guns, the left hand .44 worn butt forward for a cross-draw, the right hand .44 low and tied down.

"Expecting trouble, Smoke?"

"Not around here. Just getting used to wearing them again. I've got to take a trip, Haywood. I don't know how long I'll be gone. Probably most of the spring and part of the summer. I know Sheriff Carson is out of town, so I'd be beholden if you'd ask him to check in with Sally from time to time. I'm not expecting any trouble out there; Preacher Morrow and Bountiful are right over the ridge and my hands would fight a grizzly with a stick. I'd just feel better if Monte would drop by now and then."

"I'll sure do it, Smoke." He had a dozen questions he'd like to ask, but in the West, a man's business was his own.

Smoke stuck out his hand. "See you in a few months, Haywood. Give Dana my best."

Haywood watched the tall, broad-shouldered, ruggedly handsome man stroll up the boardwalk toward the general store. Smoke Jensen, the last mountain man. The hero of dozens of dime novels. The fastest gun in the West. A man who never wanted the title of gunfighter, but who at sixteen years of age was taken under the tutelage of an old he-coon named Preacher. The old mountain man had taught the boy well, and the boy had grown into one of the most feared and respected men in the West.

No one really knew how many outlaws and murderers and gunslingers and highwaymen had fallen under Smoke's thundering .44's. Some said fifty, others said two hundred. Smoke himself didn't really know for sure.

But Haywood knew one thing for a fact: if Smoke Jensen had strapped on his guns, and was going on a journey, it would darn sure be interesting when he reached his destination.

Interesting and deadly.

The next morning Smoke saddled a tough mountain-bred horse named Dagger—the outline of a knife was on the animal's left rump—checked his canvased and tied-down supplies on the pack horse, and went back into the cabin.

The twins were still sleeping as their father slipped into their rooms and softly kissed each child's cheek. He stepped back out into the main room of the cabin—the den, as Sally called it. "Sally, I don't know what I'm riding into this time. Or how long I'll be gone."

She smiled at him. "Then I'll see you when you get back."

They embraced, kissed, and Smoke stepped out the door, walking to the barn. With the pack horse rope in his left hand, Smoke lifted his right hand in farewell, picked up the reins, and pointed Dagger's nose toward the north.

Sally watched him until he was out of sight, then with a sigh, turned and walked into the cabin, quietly closing the door behind her.

Smoke had dressed warmly, for it was still early spring in the high lonesome, and the early mornings and nights were cold. But as the sun touched the land with its warming rays, he would shed his heavy lined jacket and travel wearing a buckskin jacket, made for him by the squaws of Indian friends.

He traveled following a route that kept the Rocky Mountains to his left and the Medicine Bow Mountains to his right. He crossed the Continental Divide and angled slightly west. He knew this country, and loved it. Preacher had first shown this country to him, back in the late sixties, and Smoke had fallen in love with it. The columbine was in early bloom, splashing the countryside in blue and lavender and white and purple.

Smoke's father, Emmett Jensen, was buried at Brown's Hole, up near the Utah line, in the northwest corner of Colorado. Buried lying atop thousands and thousands of dollars in gold. No one except Smoke and Preacher knew that, and neither one of them had any intention of spreading it about.

Old Preacher was in his early eighties, at least, but it had filled Smoke with joy and love to learn that he was still alive.

Cantankerous old billy-goat!

On his third night out, Smoke made camp halfway between Rabbit Ears Pass and Buffalo Pass, in the high-up country of the Rockies. He had caught some trout just before dusk dropped night on the land and was frying them in a dollop of lard when he saw Dagger's ears come up.

Smoke set the frying pan away from the flames, on a part of the circle of stones around the flames, and slipped back a few feet from the fire and put a hand on his Winchester .44.

"Hallo, the fire!" the voice came out of the darkness. "I'm friendly as a little wolf cub but as hongry as a just woke-up bar."

Smoke smiled. But his hand did not leave his Winchester. "Then come on in. I'll turn no hungry man away from a warm fire and a meal."

The stranger came out of the brush, keeping one hand in view, the other hand tugging at the lead rope which was attached to a reluctant donkey. "I'm aheadin' for the tradin' post on the Illinois," he said, stripping the gear from the donkey's back and hobbling the animal so it could graze and stay close. "Ran slap out of food yesterday and ain't seen no game atall."

"I have plenty of fish and fried potatoes and bread," Smoke told him. "Spread your blanket and sit." Smoke poured him a tin cup of coffee.

"Kind of you, stranger. Kind. I'm called Big Foot." He grinned and held up a booted foot. "Size fourteen. Been up in Montana lookin' for some color. Got snowed in. Coldest damn place I ever been in my life." He hooked a piece of bread and went to gnawing.

"I run a ranch south of here. The Sugarloaf. Name's Jensen."

Big Foot choked on his bread. When he finally got it swallowed, he took a drink of coffee. *"Smoke* Jensen?" he managed to gasp.

"Yes."

"Aunt Fanny's drawers!"

Smoke smiled and slid the skillet back over the flames dumping in some sliced potatoes and a few bits of some early wild onions for flavor. "Where'bouts in Montana?"

"All around the Little Belt Mountains. East of the Smith River."

"Is that anywhere close to Gibson?"

"Durn shore is. And that's a good place to fight shy of, Smoke. Big range war goin' on. Gonna bust wide open any minute."

"Seems to me I heard about that. McCorkle and Hanks right?"

"Right on the money. Dooley Hanks has done hired Lanny Ball, and McCorkle put Jason Bright on the payroll. I reckon you've heard of them two?"

"Killers. Two-bit punks who hire their guns."

Big Foot shook his head. "You can get away with sayin' that, but not me. Them two is poison fast, Smoke. They's talk about that Mex gunhawk, Diego, comin' in. He's 'pposed to be bringing in half a dozen with him. Bad ones."

"Probably Pablo Gomez is with him. They usually double-team a victim."

"Say! You're right. I heard that. They gonna be workin' for Hanks."

Smoke served up the fish and potatoes and bread and both men fell to it.

When the edges had been taken off their hunger, Smoke asked, "Town had to be named for somebody . . . who's Gibson?"

"Well, it really ain't much of a town. Three, four stores, two saloons, a barber shop, and a smithy. I don't know who Gibson is, or was, whatever."

"No school?"

"Well, sort of. Got a real prissy feller teachin' there. Say! His name's Jensen, too. Parnell Jensen. But he ain't no kin to you, Smoke. Y'all don't favor atall. Parnell don't look like nothin'!"

Parnell was his uncle's middle name.

"But Parnell's sister, now, brother, that is another story."

Smoke dropped in more lard and more fish and potatoes. He sopped up the grease in his tin plate with a hunk of bread and waited for Big Foot to continue.

"Miss Fae would tackle a puma with a short switch. She ain't no real comely lass, but that ain't what's keepin' the beaux away. It's that damn temper of her'n. Got her a tongue you could use for a skinnin' knife. I seen and heared her lash out at that poor brother of her'n one time that was plumb pitiful. Made my old donkey draw all up. He teaches school and she runs the little ranch they got. Durnest mixed-up mess I ever did see. That woman rides astraddle! Plumb embarrassin'!"

Big Foot ate up everything in sight, then picked up the skillet and sopped it out with a hunk of bread. He poured another cup of coffee and with a sigh of contentment, leaned back and rolled a smoke. "Mighty fine eats, Smoke. Feel human agin."

"Where you heading, Big Foot?"

"Kansas. I'm givin' 'er up. I been prowlin' this country-side for twenty-five years, chasin' color. Never found the motherlode. Barely findin' enough color to keep body and soul alive. My brother's been pesterin' me for years to come hep work his hog farm. So that's where I'm headin'. Me and Lucy over yonder. Bes' burro I ever had. I'm gonna retire her; just let 'er eat and get fat. You?"

"Heading up to Montana to check out some land. I don't plan on staying long."

"You fight shy of Gibson, now, Smoke. They's something wrong with that town."

"How do you mean that?"

"Cain't hardly put it in words. It's a feel in the air. And the people is crabby. Oh, most go to church and all that. But it's . . . well, they don't like each other. Always bickerin' about this and that and the other thing. The lid's gonna blow off that whole county one of these days. It's gonna be unpleasant when it do."

"How about the sheriff?"

"He's nearabouts a hundred miles away. I never put eyes on him or any of his deputies. Ain't no town marshal. Just a whole bunch of gunslicks lookin' hard at one another. When they start grabbin' iron, it's gonna be a sight to see."

Big Foot drank his coffee and lay back with a grunt. "And I'll tell you something else: that Fae Jensen woman, her spread is smack in the middle of it all. She's got the water and the graze, and both sides wants it. Sharp tongue and men's britches an' all . . . I feel sorry for her."

"She have hands?"

"Had a half a dozen. Down to two now. Both of them old men. Hanks and McCorkle keep runnin' off anyone she hires. Either that or just outright killin' them. Drug one young puncher, Hanks's men did. Killed him. But McCorkle is not a really mean person. He just don't like Hanks. Nothin' to like. Hanks is evil, Smoke. Just plain evil."

2

Come the dawning, Smoke gave Big Foot enough food to take him to the trading post. They said their goodbyes and each went their own way: one north, one east.

Smoke pondered the situation as he rode, trying to work out a plan of action. Since he knew only a smattering of what was going on, he decided to go in unknown and check it out. He took off his pistols and tucked them away in his supplies. He began growing a mustache.

Just inside Wyoming, Smoke came up on the camp of half a dozen riders. It took him but one glance to know what they were: gunhawks.

"Light and set," one offered, his eyes appraising Smoke and deciding he was no danger. He waved toward the fire. We got beef and beans."

"Jist don't ask where the meat come from," a young man said with a mean grin.

"You talk too much, Royce," another told him. "Shut up and eat." He looked at Smoke. "Help yourself, stranger."

"Thanks." Smoke filled a plate and squatted down. "Lookin' for work. Any of you boys know where they're hirin'?"

"Depends on what kind of work you're lookin' for," a man with a long scar on the side of his face said.

"Punchin' cows," Smoke told him. "Breakin' horses. Ridin' fence. Whatever it takes to make a dollar."

Smoke had packed away his buckskin jacket and for a dollar had bought a nearly wornout light jacket from a farmer, frayed at the cuffs and collar. He had deliberately scuffed his boots and dirtied his jeans.

"Can't help you there," the scar-faced man said.

Smoke knew the man, but doubted the man knew him. He had seen him twice before. His name was Lodi, from down Texas way, and the man was rattlesnake quick with a gun.

"How come you don't pack no gun?" Royce asked.

Smoke had met the type many times. A punk who thought he was bad and liked to push. Royce wore two guns, both tied down low. Fancy guns: engraved .45 caliber Peacemakers.

"I got my rifle," Smoke told him. "She'll bang seventeen times."

"I mean a short gun," Royce said irritably.

"One in the saddlebags if I need it. I don't hunt trouble, so I ain't never needed it."

One of the other gunhands laughed. "You got your answer, Royce. Now let the man eat." He cut his eyes to Smoke. "What be your name?

"Kirby." He knew his last name would not be asked. It was not a polite question in the West.

"You look familiar to me."

I been workin' down on the Blue for three years. Got the urge to drift."

"I do know the feelin'." He rose to his boots and started packing his gear.

These men, with the possible exception of Royce, were range-wise and had been on the owlhoot trail many times, Smoke concluded. They would eat in one place, then move on several miles before settling in and making camp for the night. Smoke quickly finished his beef and beans and cleaned his plate.

They packed up, taking everything but the fire. Lodi lifted his head. "See you, puncher."

Smoke nodded and watched them ride away. To the north. He stayed by the fire, watching it burn down, then swung back into the saddle and headed out, following their trail for a couple of miles before cutting east. He crossed the North Platte and made camp on the east side of the river.

He followed the Platte up to Fort Fred Steele, an army post built in 1868 to protect workers involved in the building of the Union Pacific railroad. There, he had a hot bath in a wooden tub behind a barber shop and resupplied. He stepped into a cafe and enjoyed a meal that he didn't have to cook, and ate quietly, listening to the gossip going on around him.

There had been no Indian trouble for some time, the Shoshone and the Arapahoe were, for the most part, now settled in at the Wind River Reservation, although every now and then some whiskeyed-up bucks would go on the prowl. They usually ended up either shot or hanged.

Smoke loafed around the fort for a couple of days, giving the gunhands he'd talked with ample time to get gone farther north.

And even this far south of the Little Belt Mountains, folks knew about the impending range war, although Smoke did not hear any talk about anyone here taking sides.

He pulled out and headed for Fort Caspar, about halfway between Fort Fetterman and Hell's Half Acre. The town of Casper would become reality in a few more years.

At Fort Caspar, Smoke stayed clear of a group of gun-slicks who were resupplying at the general store. He knew several in this bunch: Eddie Hart, Pooch Matthews, Golden. None of them were known for their gentle, loving dispositions.

It was at Fort Caspar that he met a young, down-at-the-heels puncher with the unlikely handle of Beans.

"Bainbridge is the name my folks hung on me," Beans explained with a grin. "I was about to come to the conclusion that I'd just shoot myself and get it over with knowin' I had to go through the rest of my life with everybody callin' me Bainbridge. A camp cook over in the Dakotas started callin' me Beans. He didn't have no teeth, and evertime he called my name, it come out soundin' like Beans-Beans. So Beans it is."

Beans was one of those types who seemed not to have a care in the world. He had him a good horse, a good pistol, and a good rifle. He was young and full of fire and vinegar . . . so what was there to worry about?

Smoke told him he was drifting on up into Montana. Beans allowed as how that was as good a direction as any to go, so they pulled out before dawn the next day.

With his beat-up clothes and his lip concealed behind a mustache and his hair now badly in need of a trim, Smoke felt that unless he met someone who really knew him, he would not be recognized by any who had only bumped into him casually.

"You any good with that short gun?" Smoke asked.

"Man over in Utah didn't think so. I rattled my hocks shortly before the funeral."

Now, there was two ways to take that. "Your funeral or his?"

"He was a tad quicker, but he missed."

'Nuff said.

On the third night out, Beans finally said what he'd been mullin' about all day. "Kirby . . . there's something about you that just don't add up."

"Oh?"

"Yeah. Now, to someone who just happened to glance over at you and ride on, you'd appear to be a drifter. Spend some time on the trail with you, and a body gets to thinkin'."

Smoke stirred the beans and laid the bacon in the pan. He poured them both coffee and waited.

"You got coins in your pocket and greenbacks in your poke. That saddle don't belong to no bum. That Winchester in your boot didn't come cheap. And both them horses are wearin' a brand like I ain't never seen. Is that a circle double snake or what?"

"Circle Double-S." As his spread had grown, Smoke had changed his brand. S for Smoke, S for Sally. It was registered with the brand commission.

"There ain't no 'S' in Kirby," Beans noted.

"Maybe my last name is Smith."

"Ain't but one 'S' there."

"You do have a point." Beans was only pointing out things that Smoke was already aware of. "How far into Montana are you planning on going?"

"Well," Beans grinned, "I don't know. Taggin' along with you I found that the grub's pretty good."

"You're aware of the impending range war in Montana?"

"There's another thing that don't ring true, Kirby. Sometimes you talk like a schoolteacher. Now I know that don't necessarily mean nothin' out hcre, but it do get folks to thinkin'. You know what I mean?"

Smoke nodded and turned the bacon.

"And them jeans of yours is wore slick on the right side, down low on the leg. You best get you some other britches or strap that hogleg back on."

"You don't miss much, do you, Beans?"

"My folks died with the fever when I was eight. I been on my own ever since. Goin' on nineteen years. Startin' out alone, that young, a body best get savvy quick."

"My real name is Kirby, Beans."

"All right."

"You didn't answer my question about whether you knew about the range war?"

"I heard of it, yeah. But I don't hire my gun. Way I had it figured, with most of the hands fightin', them rich ranchers is gonna need somebody just to look after the cattle." He grinned. "That's me!"

"I'd hate to see you get tied up in a range war, Beans, 'cause sooner or later, you're gonna have to take a stand and grab iron."

"Yeah, I know. But I don't never worry about bridges until I come to them. Ain't that food about fitten to eat?"

* * *

They were lazy days, and the two men rode easy; no reason to push. Smoke was only a few years older than Beans—chronologically speaking; several lifetimes in experience—and the men became friends as they rode.

Spring had hit the high country, and the hills and valleys were blazing in God's colors. The men entered Johnson County in the Wyoming Territory, rode into Buffalo, and decided to hunt up a hot bath; both were just a bit on the gamey side.

After a bath and a change of clothes, Smoke offered to buy the drinks. Beans, with a grin, pointed out the sign on the barroom wall: "Don't forget to write your mother, boys. Whether you are worth it or not, she is thinking of you. Paper and inveelopes free. So is the picklled eggs. The whiskey ain't."

"You got a ma, Kirby?"

"Beans, *everybody* has a mother!" Smoke grinned at the man.

"I mean . . . is she still alive?" He flushed red.

"No. She died when I was just a kid, back in Missouri."

"I thought I smelled a Missouri puke in here." The voice came from behind them.

Smoke had not yet tasted his whiskey. He placed the shot glass back on the bar as the sounds of chairs being pushed back reached him. He turned slowly.

A bear of a man sat at a table. Even sitting down he was huge. Little piggy eyes. Mean eyes. Bully was invisibly stamped all over him. His face looked remarkably like a hog.

"You talking to me, Pig-Face?" Smoke asked.

Big Pig stood up and held open his coat. He was not wearing a gun. Smoke opened his jacket to show that he was not armed.

Beans stepped to one side.

"I think I'll tear your head off," Big Pig snorted.

Smoke leaned against the bar. "Why?"

The question seemed to confuse the bully. Which came as

no surprise to Smoke. Most bullies could not be classified as being anywhere close to mental giants.

"For fun!" Big Pig said.

Then he charged Smoke, both big hands balled into fists that looked like hams. Smoke stepped to one side just at the last possible split second and Big Pig crashed into the bar. His bulk and momentum tore the rickety bar in half and sent Big Pig hurling against the counter. Whiskey bottles and beer mugs and shot glasses were splintered from the impact. The stench of raw whiskey and strong beer filled the smoky barroom.

Hollering obscenities and roaring like a grizzly with a sore paw, Big Pig lumbered and stumbled to his feet and swung a big fist that would've busted Smoke's head wide open had it landed.

Smoke ducked under the punch and sidestepped. The force of Big Pig's forward motion sent him staggering and slipping across the floor. Smoke picked up a chair and just as Big Pig turned around, Smoke splintered the wooden chair across his teeth.

Big Pig's boots flew out from under him and he went crashing to the floor, blood spurting from smashed lips and cuts on his face. But Smoke saw that Pig was a hard man to keep down. Getting to his feet a second time, Pig came at a rush, wide open. Smoke had already figured out that the man was no skilled slugger, relying on his enormous strength and his ability to take punches that would have felled a normal man.

Smoke hit him flush on the beak with a straight-from-the-shoulder right. The nose busted and the blood flew. Big Pig snorted away the pain and blood and backhanded Smoke knocking him against a wall. Smoke's mouth filled with the copper taste of blood.

Yelling, falsely sensing that victory was his, Pig charged again. Smoke dropped to his knees and drove his right fist straight up into the V of Big Pig's legs.

Pig howled in agony and dropped to the floor, both hands cupping his injured parts. Still on his knees, Smoke hit the man on the side of the jaw with everything he could put into the punch. This time, Big Pig toppled over, down, but still a hell of a long way from being out.

Spitting out blood, Smoke got to his feet and backed up, catching his breath, readying himself for the next round that he knew was coming.

Big Pig crawled to his feet, glaring at Smoke. But his eyes were filled with doubt. This had never happened to him. He had never lost a fight; not in his entire life.

Smoke suddenly jumped at the man, hitting him with both fists, further pulping the man's lips and flattening his snout.

Pig swung and Smoke grabbed the thick wrist with both hands and turned and slung the man, spinning Big Pig across the room. Pig crashed into the wall and went right through it, sailing across the warped boardwalk and landing in a horse trough.

Smoke stepped through the splintered hole in the wall and walked to the trough. He grabbed Big Pig's head and forced it down into the water, holding him there. Just as it appeared the man would drown, Smoke pulled the head out, pounded it with his fists, then grabbed the man by his hair and once more forced the head under water.

Finally, Big Pig's struggling ceased. Smoke wearily hauled him out of the water and left him draped half in, half out of the trough. Big Pig was breathing, but that was about all.

Smoke sat down on the edge of the boardwalk and tried to catch his breath.

The boardwalk gradually filled with people, all of them staring in awe at Smoke. One man said, "Mister, I don't know who you are, but I'd have bet my spread that you wouldn't have lasted a minute against old Ring, let alone whip him."

Smoke rubbed his aching leg. "I'd hate to have to do it again."

Beans squatted down beside Smoke. When he spoke his

voice was low. "Kirby, I don't know who you really are, but I shore don't never want to make you mad."

Smoke looked at him. "Hell, I'm not angry!" He pointed to the man called Ring. "He's the one who wanted to fight, not me."

"Lord, have mercy!" Beans said. "All this and you wasn't even mad."

Ring groaned and heaved himself out of the horse trough.

Smoke picked up a broken two-by-four and walked over to where Ring lay on the soaked ground. "Mister Ring, I want your attention for a moment. If you have any thoughts at all about getting up off that ground and having a go at me, I'm going to bust your head wide open with this two-by-four. You understand all that?"

Ring rolled over onto his back and grinned up at Smoke. One eye was swollen shut and his nose and lips were a mess. He held up a hand. "Hows 'bout you and me bein' friends. I shore don't want you for an enemy!"

3

The three of them pulled out the next morning, Ring riding the biggest mule Smoke had ever seen.

"Satan's his name," Ring explained. "Man was going to kill him till I come along. I swapped him a good horse and a gun for him. One thing, boys: don't never get behind him if you've got a hostile thought. He'll sense it and kick you clear into Canada."

There was no turning Ring back. He had found someone to look up to in Smoke. And Smoke had found a friend for life.

"I just can't handle whiskey," Ring said. "I can drink beer all day long and get mellow. One drink of whiskey and I'll turn mean as a snake."

"I figured you were just another bully," Beans said.

"Oh, no! I love everybody till I get to drinkin' whiskey. Then I don't even like myself."

"No more whiskey for you, Ring," Smoke told him.

"Yes, sir, Mister Kirby. Whatever you say is fine with me."

They were getting too far east, so when they left Buffalo, they cut west and crossed the Bighorn Mountains, skirting north of Cloud Peak, the thirteen-thousand-foot mountain rearing up majestically, snow-capped year round. Cutting south at Granite Pass, the men turned north, pointing their horses' noses toward Montana Territory.

"Mister Kirby?" Ring asked.

"Just Kirby, Ring. Please. Just Kirby."

"OK . . . Kirby. Why is it we're going to Montana?"

"Seeing the sights, Ring."

"OK. Whatever you say. I ain't got nothin' but time."

"We might find us a job punchin' cows," Beans said.

"I don't know nothin' about cows," Ring admitted. "But I can make a nine-pound hammer sing all day long. I can work the mines or dig a ditch. There ain't a team of horses or mules that I can't handle. But I don't know nothin' about cows."

"You ever done any smithing?" Smoke asked.

"Oh, sure. I'm good with animals. I like animals. I love puppy dogs and kitty cats. I don't like to see people mistreat animals. Makes me mad. And when I get mad, I hurt people. I seen a man beatin' a poor little dog one time back in Kansas when I was passin' through drivin' freight. That man killed that little dog. And for no good reason."

"What'd you do?" Smoke asked him.

"Got down off that wagon and broke his back. Left him there and drove on. After I buried the little dog."

Beans shuddered.

"Dogs and cats and the like can't help bein' what they are. God made them that way. If God had wanted them different, He'd have made 'em different. Men can think. I don't know about women, but men can think. Man shouldn't be cruel to animals. It ain't right and I don't like it."

"I have never been mean to a dog in my life," Beans quickly pointed out.

"Good. Then you're a nice person. You show me a man who is mean to animals, and I'll show you a low-down person at heart."

Smoke agreed with that. "You born out here, Ring?"

"No. Born in Pennsylvania. I killed a man there and done time. He was a no-good man. Mean-hearted man. He cheated my mother out of her farm through some legal shenanigans. Put her on the road with nothin' but the clothes on her back. I come home from the mines to visit and found my mother in the poor farm, dying. After the funeral, I looked that man up and beat him to death. The judge gimme life in prison."

"You get pardoned?" Beans asked.

"No. I got tired of it and jerked the bars out of the bricks, tied the guard up, climbed over the walls and walked away one night."

"Your secret is safe with us," Smoke assured him.

"I figured it would be."

They forded the Yellowstone and were in Montana Territory, but still had a mighty long way to go before they reached Gibson.

Smoke and Beans had both figured out that Ring was no great shakes when it came to thinking, but he was an incredibly gentle man—as long as you kept him away from the whiskey. Birds would come to him when he held out his arms. Squirrels would scamper up and take food from his fingers. And he almost cried one day when he shot a deer for food. He left the entrails for the wolves and the coyotes and spent the rest of the journey working on the hide, making them all moccasins and gloves.

Ring was truly one of a kind.

He stood six feet six inches and weighed three hundred pounds, very little of it fat. He could read and write only a little, but he said it didn't matter. He didn't have anyone to write to noways, and nobody ever wrote to him.

At a small village on the Boulder, Smoke resupplied and they all had a hot bath. Ring was so big he made the wooden tub look like a bucket.

But Smoke had a bad feeling about the village; not about the village itself, but at what might be coming at them if they stayed. Smoke had played on his hunches before; they had kept him alive more than once. And this one kept nagging at him.

After carefully shaving, leaving his mustache intact, he

went to his packhorse and took out his .44's, belting them around his lean hips, tying down the right handgun. He carefully checked them, wiping them clean with a cloth and checking the loads. He usually kept the chamber under the hammer empty; this time he loaded them both up full. He stepped out from behind the wooden partition by the wooden tubs and walked into the rear of the store, conscious of the eyes of Beans and Ring on him; they had never seen him wear a short gun, much less two of them, one butt forward for a cross draw.

"Five boxes of .44's," Smoke told the clerk.

"You plannin' on startin' a war?" the clerk said, sticking his mouth into something that didn't concern him.

Smoke's only reply was to fix his cold brown eyes on the man and stare at him. The clerk got the message and turned away, a flush on his face.

He placed the ammunition on the counter and asked no more questions. Smoke bought three cans of peaches and paid for his purchases. He walked out onto the shaded porch, Ring and Beans right behind him. The three of them sat down and opened the peaches with their knives, enjoying a midmorning sweet-syruped snack.

"Don't see too many people wearin' twin guns thataway," Beans observed, looking at Smoke's rig.

"Not too many," Smoke agreed, and ate a peach.

"Riders coming," Ring said quietly. "From the south."

The men sat on the porch, eating peaches, and watching the riders come closer.

"You recognize any of them?" Smoke tossed the question out.

Beans took it. "Nope. You?"

"That one on the right is Park. Gunfighter from over in the Dakotas. Man next to him is Tabor. Gunhawk from Oklahoma. I don't know the others."

"They know you?" Ring asked.

"They know of me." Smoke's words were softly spoken.

"By the name of Kirby?"

"No."

The five dusty gunhands reined up and dismounted. A ferret-faced young man ducked under the hitchrail and paused by the porch, staring at Smoke. His eyes drifted to Smoke's twin guns.

The other gunhawks were older, wiser, and could read signs. They were not being paid to cause trouble in this tiny village, therefore they would avoid trouble if at all possible.

The kid with the acne-pocked face and the big Colts slung around his hips was not nearly so wise. He deliberately stepped on Smoke's boot as he walked past.

Smoke said nothing. The four older men stood to one side, watching, keeping their hands away from the butts of their guns.

Ferret-face laughed and looked at his friends, jerking a thumb toward Smoke. "There ain't much to him."

"I wouldn't bet my life on it," Park said softly. To Smoke, "Don't I know you?"

Smoke stood up. At the approach of the men, he had slipped the leather hammer-thongs from his guns. "We've crossed rails a time or two. If this punk kid's a friend of yours, you might better put a stopper on his mouth before I'm forced to change his diapers."

The kid flushed at the insult. He backed up a few yards, his hands hovering over the butts of his fancy guns. "They call me Larado. Maybe you've heard of me?"

"Can't say as I have," Smoke spoke easily. "But I'm glad to know you have a name. That's something that everybody should have."

"You're makin' fun of me!"

"Am I? Maybe so."

"I think I'll just carve another notch on my guns," Larado hissed.

"Yeah? I had you pegged right then. A tinhorn."

"Draw, damn you!"

But Smoke just stood, smiling at the young man.

Two little boys took that time to walk by the store; perhaps they were planning on spending a penny for some candy. One of them looked at Smoke, jerked a dime novel out of the back of his overalls, and stared at the cover. He mentally shaved off Smoke's mustache. His mouth dropped open.

"It's really him! That's Smoke Jensen!"

All the steam went out of Larado. His sigh was audible. He lifted his hands and carefully folded them across his chest, keeping his hands on the outside of his arms.

Beans and Ring sat in their chairs and stared at their friend.

"You some distance from Colorado, Smoke," Tabor said.

"And you're a long way from Oklahoma," Smoke countered.

"For a fact. You headin' north or south?"

"North."

"I never knowed you to hire your guns out."

"I never have. It isn't for sale this trip, either."

"But you do have a reputation for buttin' in where you ain't wanted," Park added his opinion.

"I got a personal invitation to this party, Park. But if you feel like payin' the fiddler, you can write your name on my dance card right now."

"I ain't got nothin' agin you, Smoke. Not until I find out which side you buckin' leastways. McCorkle or Hanks?"

"Neither one."

The gunslicks exchanged glances. "That don't make no sense," one of the men that Smoke didn't know said.

"You got a name?"

"Dunlap."

"Yeah, I heard of you. You killed a couple of Mexican sheepherders and shot one drunk in the back down in Arizona. But I'm not a sheepherder and I'm not drunk."

Dunlap didn't like that. But he had enough sense not to pull iron with Smoke Jensen.

"You was plannin' on riding in with nobody knowin' who you were, wasn't you?" Tabor asked.

"Yes."

"Next question is why?"

"I guess that's my business."

"You right. I reckon we'll find out when we get to Gibson."

"Perhaps." He turned to Beans and Ring. "Let's ride."

After the three men had ridden away, toward the north, one of the two gunhands who had not spoken broke his silence.

"I'm fixin' to have me a drink and then I'm ridin' over to Idaho. It's right purty this time of year."

Larado, now that Smoke was a good mile away, had reclaimed his nerve. "You act like you're yeller!" he sneered.

But the man just chuckled. "Boy, I was over at what they's now callin' Telluride some years back, when a young man name of Smoke Jensen come ridin' in. He braced fifteen of the saltiest ol' boys there was at that time. Les' see, that was back in, oh, '72, I reckon." He looked directly at Larado. "And you bear in mind, young feller, that he kilt about ten or so gettin' to that silver camp. He kilt all fifteen of them socalled fancy gunhandlers. Yeah, kid, he's *that* Smoke Jensen. The last mountain man. Since he kilt his first Injun when he was about fifteen years old, over in Kansas, he's probably kilt a hundred or more white men—and that's probably figurin' low. There ain't nobody ever been as fast as he is, there ain't never gonna be nobody as fast as he is.

"And I know you couldn't hep notice that bear of a man with him? That there is Ring. Ring ain't never followed no man in his life afore today. And that tells me this: Smoke has done whipped him fair and square with his fists. And if I ain't mistaken, that young feller with Smoke and Ring is the one from over in Utah, round Moab. Goes by a half a dozen different names, but one he favors is Beans.

"Now, boys, I'm a fixin' to have me a drink and light a shuck. 'Cause wherever Smoke goes, they's soon a half a dozen or more of the randiest ol' boys this side of hell. Smoke draws 'em like a magnet does steel shavin's. I had my say. We partin' company. Like as of right now!"

* * *

Down in Cheyenne, two old friends came face-to-face in a dingy side-street barroom. The men whoopped and hollered and insulted each other for about five minutes before settling down to have a drink and talk about old times.

Across the room, a young man stood up, irritation on his face. He said to his companion, "I think I'll go over there and tell them old men to shut up. I'm tared of hearin' them hoot and holler."

"Sit down and close your mouth," his friend told him. "That's Charlie Starr and Pistol Le Roux."

The young man sat down very quickly. A chill touched him, as if death had brushed his skin.

"I thought them old men was *dead!*" he managed to croak after slugging back his drink.

"Well, they ain't. But I got some news that I bet would interest them. I might even get to shake their hands. My daddy just come back from haulin' freight down in Colorado. You wanna go with me?"

"No, sir!"

The young man walked over to where the two aging gunfighters were sitting and talking over their beers. "Sirs?"

Charlie and Pistol looked up. "What can I do for you?" Le Roux said.

The young man swallowed hard. This was real flesh and blood legend he was looking at. These men helped tame the West. "You gentlemen are friends with a man called Smoke Jensen, aren't you?"

"You bet your boots!" Charlie smiled at him.

"My daddy just come home from haulin' freight down to a place called Big Rock. He spoke with the sheriff, a man called Monte Carson. Smoke's in trouble. He's gone up to some town in Montana Territory called Gibson to help his cousin. A woman. He's gonna be facin' forty or fifty gunhands; right in the middle of a range war."

Pistol and Charlie stood up as of one mind. The young

man stared in astonishment. God, but they were both big and gray and gnarled and old!

But the guns they wore under their old jackets were clean and shiny.

"I wish we could pay you," Charlie said. "But we're gonna have to scratch deep to get up yonder."

The young man stuck out his hand and the men shook it. Their hands were thickly calloused. "There's a poke of food tied to my saddle horn. Take it. It's all I can do."

"Nice of you," Pistol said. "Thankee kindly."

The men turned, spurs jingling, and were gone.

The silver-haired man pulled off his boot and looked at the hole in the sole. He stuck some more paper down into the boot. "Hardrock, today is my birthday. I just remembered."

"How old are you, about a hundred?"

"I think I'm sixty-seven. And I know you two year older than me."

"Happy birthday."

"Thankee."

"I ain't got no present. Sorry."

Silver Jim laughed. "Hardrock, between the two of us we might be able to come up with five dollars. Tell you what. Let's drift up to Montana Territory. I got a friend up in the Little Belt Mountains. Got him a cabin and runs a few head of cattle. Least we can eat."

"Silver Jim . . . he *died* about three years ago."

"Ummm . . . that's right. He did, didn't he. Well, the cabin's still there, don't you reckon?"

"Might be. I thought of Smoke this mornin'. Wonder how that youngster is?"

"Did you now? That's odd. I did, too."

"I thought about Montana, too."

The two old gunfighters exchanged glances, Silver Jim saying, "I just remembered I had a couple of double eagles I was savin' for hard times."

"Is that right? Well . . . me, too."

"We could ride back to that little town we come through this morning and send a message through the wires to Big Rock."

The old gunslingers waited around the wire office for several hours until they received a reply from Monte Carson in Big Rock.

"Let's get the hell to Montanee!" Silver Jim said.

4

"I thought you would be a much older man," Ring remarked after they had made camp for the evening.

It was the first time Smoke's real identity had been brought up since leaving the little village.

Smoke smiled and dumped the coffee into the boiling water. "I started young."

"When was you gonna tell us?" Beans asked.

"The same time you told me that you was the Moab Gunfighter."

Beans chuckled. "I wasn't gonna get involved in this fight. But you headin' that way . . . well, it sorta peaked my interest."

"My cousin is in the middle of it. She wrote me at my ranch. You can't turn your back on kin."

"Y'all must be close."

"I have never laid eyes on her in my life. I didn't even know she existed until the letter came." He told them about his conversations with Big Foot.

"This brother of hers sounds like a sissy to me," Beans said.

"He does for a fact," Smoke agreed. "But I've found out this much about sissies: they'll take and take and take, until you push them to their limits, and then they'll kill you."

The three of them made camp about ten miles outside of Gibson, on the fringes of the Little Belt Mountains.

"There is no point in any of us trying to hide who we are," Smoke told the others. "As soon as Park and the others get in town, it would be known. We'll just ride in and look the place over first thing in the morning. I'm not going to take a stand in this matter unless the big ranchers involved try to run over Fae . . . or unless I'm pushed to it."

The three topped the hill and looked down at the town of Gibson. One long street, with vacant lots separating a few of the stores. A saloon, one general store, and the smithy was on one side of the street, the remainder of the businesses on the other side. Including a doctor's office. The church stood at the far end of town.

"We'd better be careful which saloon—if any—we go into," Beans warned. "For a fact, Hanks's boys will gather in one and McCorkle's boys in the other."

"I don't think I'll go into either of them," Ring said. "This is the longest I've been without a drink in some time. I like the feeling."

"Looks like school is in session." Smoke lifted the reins. "You boys hang around the smithy's place while I go talk to Cousin Parnell. Let's go."

They entered the town at a slow walk, Ring and Beans flanking Smoke as they moved up the wide street. Although it was early in the day, both saloons were full, judging by the number of horses tied at the hitchrails. A half a dozen or more gunslicks were sitting under the awnings of both saloons. The men could feel the hard eyes on them as they rode slowly up the street. Appraising eyes. Violent eyes; eyes of death.

"Ring," they heard one man say.

"That's the Moab Kid," another said. "But who is that in the middle?"

"I don't know him."

"I do," the voice was accented. Smoke cut his eyes, shaded by the wide brim of his hat. Diego. "That, amigos, is Smoke Jensen."

Several chair legs hit the boardwalk, the sound sharp in the still morning air.

The trio kept riding.

"Circle C on the west side of the street," Beans observed.

"Yeah." Smoke cut his eyes again. "That's Jason Bright standing by the trough."

"He is supposed to be very, very fast," Ring said.

"He's a punk," Smoke replied.

"Lanny Ball over at the Hangout," Beans pointed out.

"The Pussycat and the Hangout," Ring said with a smile. "Where do they get the names?"

They reined up at the smith's place; a huge stable and corral and blacksmithing complex. Beans and Ring swung down. Smoke hesitated, then stepped down.

"Changed my mind," he told them. "No point in disturbing school while it's in session. We'll loaf around some; stretch our legs."

"I'm for some breakfast," Ring said. "Let's try the Cafe Eats."

Smoke told the stable boy to rub their horses down, and to give each a good bait of corn. They'd be back.

They walked across the wide street, spurs jingling, boots kicking up dust in the dry street, and stepped up onto the boardwalk, entering the cafe.

It was a big place for such a tiny town, but clean and bright, and the smells from the kitchen awakened the taste buds in them all.

They sat down at a table covered with a red-and-white checkered cloth and waited. A man stepped out of the kitchen.

He wore an apron and carried a sawed-off double-barreled ten gauge express gun. "You are velcome to eat here at anytime ve are open," he announced, his German accent thick. "My name is Hans, and I own dis establishment. I vill tell you what I have told all the rest: there vill be no trouble in here. None! I operate a nice quiet family restaurant. People come in from twenty, terty miles avay to eat here. Start trouble, und I vill kill you! Understood?"

"We understand, Hans," Smoke said. "But we are not taking sides with either McCorkle or Hanks. I do not hire my guns and neither does Beans here." He jerked his thumb toward the Moab Kid. "And Ring doesn't even carry a short gun."

"Uummph!" the German grunted. "Den dat vill be a velcome change. You vant breakfast?"

"Please."

"Good! I vill start you gentlemen vith hot oatmeal vith lots of fresh cream and sugar. Den ham and eggs and fried potatoes and lots of coffee. Olga! Tree oatmeals and tree breakfasts, Liebling."

"What'd he call her?" Beans whispered.

"Darling," Ring told him.

Smoke looked up. "You speak German, Ring?"

"My parents were German. Born in the old country. My last name is Kruger."

The oatmeal was placed before them, huge bowls of steaming oatmeal covered with cream and sugar. Ring looked up. *"Danke."*

The two men then proceeded to converse in rapid-fire German. To Beans it sounded like a couple of bullfrogs with laryngitis.

Then, to the total amazement of Smoke and Beans, the two big men proceeded to slap each other across the face several times, grinning all the time.

Hans laughed and returned to the kitchen. "Y'all fixin' to fight, Ring?" Beans asked.

Ring laughed at the expression on their faces. "Oh, no. That is a form of greeting in certain parts of the old country. It means we like each other."

"That is certainly a good thing to know," Smoke remarked drily. "In case I ever take a notion to travel to Germany."

The men fell to eating the delicious oatmeal. When they pushed the empty bowls away, Hans was there with huge platters of food and the contest was on.

"Guten appetit, gentlemans."

"What'd he say?" Beans asked Ring.

"Eat!" He smiled. "More or less."

Olga stepped out of the kitchen to stand watching the men eat, a smile on her face. She was just as ample as Hans. Between the two of them they'd weigh a good five hundred pounds. Another lady stepped out of the kitchen. Make that seven hundred and fifty pounds.

When they had finished, as full as ticks, Ring looked up and said, *"Prima! Grobartig!"* He lifted his coffee mug and toasted their good health. *"Auf Ihre Gesundheit!"*

Olga and the other lady giggled.

"I didn't hear nobody sneeze." Beans looked around.

Ring stayed in the restaurant, talking with Hans and Olga and Hilda and drinking coffee. Beans sat down in a wooden chair in front of the place, staring across the street at the gunhawks who were staring at him. Smoke walked up to the church that doubled as a schoolhouse. The kids were playing out front so he figured it was recess time.

The children looked at him, a passing glance, and resumed their playing. Smoke walked up the steps.

Smoke stood in the open doorway, the outside light making him almost impossible to view clearly from the inside. He felt a pang of . . . some kind of emotion. He wasn't sure. But there was no doubt: he was looking at family.

The schoolteacher looked up from grading papers.

"Parnell Jensen?"

"Yes. Whom do I have the pleasure of addressing?"

Smoke had to chew on that for a few seconds. "I reckon I'm your cousin, Parnell. I'm Smoke Jensen."

Parnell gave Smoke directions to the ranch and said he would be out at three-thirty. And he would be prompt about it. "I am a very punctilious person," Parnell added.

And a prissy sort too, Smoke thought. "Uh-huh. Right." He'd have to remember to ask somebody what punch-till-eous meant.

He was walking up the boardwalk just as the thunder of hooves coming hard reached him. The hooves drummed across the bridge at the west end of town and didn't slow up. A dozen hard-ridden horses can kick up a lot of dust.

Smoke had found out from Parnell that McCorkle's spread was west and north of town, Hanks's spread was east and north of town. Fae's spread, and it was no little spread, ran on both sides of the Smith River; for about fifteen miles on either side of it. McCorkle hated Hanks, Hanks hated McCorkle, and both men had threatened to dam up the Smith and dry Fae out if she didn't sell out to one of them.

"And then what are they going to do?" Smoke asked.

"Fight each other for control of the entire area between the Big Belt and the Little Belt Mountains. They've been fighting for twenty years. They came here together in '62. Hated each other at first sight." Parnell flopped his hand in disgust. "It's just a dreadful situation. I wish we had never come to this barbaric land."

"Why did you?"

"My sister wanted to farm and ranch. She's always been a tomboy. The man who owned the ranch before us, hired me—I was teaching at a *lovely* private institution in Illinois, close to Chicago—and told Fae that he had no children and would give us the ranch upon his death. I think more to spite McCorkle and Hanks than out of any kindness of heart."

Smoke leaned against a storefront and watched as King Cord McCorkle—as Parnell called him—and his crew came to a halt in a cloud of dust in front of the Pussycat. When the dust had settled, Jason Bright stepped off the boardwalk and walked to Cord's side, speaking softly to him.

Parnell's words returned: "I have always had to look after my sister. She is so *flighty.* I wish she would marry and then I could return to civilization. It's so primitive out here!" He sighed. "But I fear that the man who gets my sister will have to beat her three times a day."

Cord turned his big head and broad face toward Smoke and stared at him. Smoke pegged the man to be in his early forties; a bull of a man. Just about Smoke's height, maybe twenty pounds heavier.

Cord blinked first, turning his head away with a curse that just reached Smoke. Smoke cut his eyes to the Hangout. Diego and Pablo Gomez and another man stood there. Smoke finally recognized the third man. Lujan, the Chihuahua gunfighter. Probably the fastest gun—that as yet had built a reputation—in all of Mexico. But not a cold-blooded killer like Diego and Pablo.

Lujan tipped his hat at Smoke and Smoke lifted a hand in acknowledgment and smiled. Lujan returned the smile, then turned and walked into the saloon.

Smoke again felt eyes on him. Cord was once more staring at him.

"You there! The man supposed to be Smoke Jensen. Git down here. I wanna talk to you."

"You got two legs and a horse, mister!" Smoke called over the distance. "So you can either walk or ride up here."

Pablo and Diego laughed at that.

"Damned greasers!" Cord spat the words.

The Mexicans stiffened, hands dropping to the butts of their guns.

A dozen gunhands in front of the Pussycat stood up.

A little boy, about four or five years old, accompanied by his dog, froze in the middle of the street, right in line of fire.

Lujan opened the batwings and stepped out. "We—all of us—have no right to bring bloodshed to the innocent people of this town." His voice carried across the street. He stepped into the street and walked to the boy's side. "You and your dog go home, muchacho. Quickly, now."

Lujan stood alone in the street. "A man who would deliberately injure a child is not fit to live. So, McCorkle, it is a good day to die, is it not?"

Smoke walked out into the street to stand by Lujan's side. A smile creased the Mexican's lips. "You are taking a side, Smoke?"

"No. I just don't like McCorkle, and I probably won't like Hanks either."

"So, McCorkle," Lujan called. "You see before you two men who have not taken a side, but who are more than willing to open the *baile*. Are you ready?"

"Make that three people," Beans's voice rang out.

"Who the hell are you?" McCorkle shouted.

"Some people call me the Moab Kid."

"Make that four people," Ring said. He held his Winchester in his big hands.

"Funf!" Hans shouted, stepping out into the street. He held the sawed-off in his hands.

The window above the cafe opened and Olga leaned out, a pistol with a barrel about a foot and a half long in her hand. She jacked back the hammer to show them all she knew how to use it. And would.

"All right, all right!" Cord shouted. "Hell's bells! Nobody was going to hurt the kid. Come on, boys, I'll buy the drinks." He turned and bulled his way through his men.

At the far end of the street, Parnell stepped back from the open doorway and fanned himself vigorously. *"Heavens!"* he said.

5

"Almost come a showdown in town this morning, Boss," Dooley Hanks's foreman said.

Hanks eyeballed the man. "Between who?"

Gage told his boss what a hand had relayed to him only moments earlier.

Hanks slumped back in his chair. "Smoke Jensen," he whispered the word. "I never even thought about Fae and Parnell bein' related to him. And the Moab Kid and Lujan sided with him?"

"Or vicey-versy."

"This ain't good. That damn Lujan is poison enough. But add Smoke Jensen to the pot . . . might as well be lookin' the devil in the eyeballs. I don't know nothin' about Ring, except he's unbeatable in a fight. And the Moab Gunfighter has made a name for hisself in half a dozen states. All right, Gage. We got to get us a backshooter in here. Send a rider to Helena. Wire Danny Rouge; he's over in Missoula. Tell him to come a-foggin'."

"Yes, sir."

"Where's them damn boys of mine?"

"Pushin' cattle up to new pasture."

"You mean they actually doin' some work?"

Gage grinned. "Yes, sir."

Hanks shook his head in disbelief. "Thank you, Gage."

Gage left, hollering for a rider to saddle up. Hanks walked to a window in his office. He had swore he would be kingpin of this area, and he intended to be just that. Even if he bankrupted himself doing it. Even if he had to kill half the people in the area attaining it.

Cord McCorkle had ridden out of town shortly after his facedown with Smoke and Lujan and the others. He did not feel that he had backed down. It was simply a matter of survival. Nobody but a fool willingly steps into his own coffin.

His hands would have killed Smoke and Lujan and the others, for a fact. But it was also hard fact that Cord would have gone down in the first volley . . . and what the hell would that have proved?

Nothing. Except to get dead.

Cord knew that men like Smoke and Lujan could soak up lead and still stay on their feet, pulling the trigger. He had personally witnessed a gunfighter get hit nine times with .45 slugs and before he died still kill several of the men he was facing.

Cord sat on the front porch of his ranch house and looked around him. He wanted for nothing. He had everything a man could want. It had sickened him when Dooley had OK'd the dragging of that young Box T puncher. Scattering someone's cattle was one thing. Murder was another. He was glad that Jensen had come along. But he didn't believe anyone could ever talk sense into Hanks.

Smoke, Ring, and Beans sat their horses on the knoll overlooking the ranch house of Fae and Parnell Jensen. Fae might well be a bad-mouthed woman with a double-edged tongue, but she kept a neat place. Flowers surrounded the house, the lawn was freshly cut, and the place itself was attractive.

Even at this distance, a good mile off, Smoke could see two men, with what he guessed was rifles in their hands, take up positions around the bunkhouse and barn. A woman—he guessed it was a woman, she was dressed in britches—came out onto the porch. She also carried a rifle. Smoke waved at her and waited for her to give them some signal to ride on in.

Finally the woman stepped off the porch and motioned for them to come on.

The men walked their horses down to the house, stopping at the hitchrail but not dismounting. The woman looked at Smoke. Finally she smiled.

"I saw a tintype of your daddy once. You look like him. You'd be Kirby Jensen."

"And you'd be Cousin Fae. I got your letter. I picked up these galoots along the way." He introduced Beans and Ring.

"Put your horses in the barn, boys, and come on into the house. It's about dinnertime. I got fresh doughnuts, 'bear-sign' as you call them out here."

Fae Jensen was more than a comely lass; she was really quite pretty and shapely. But unlike most women of the time, her face and arms were tanned from hours in the sun, doing a man's work. And her hands were calloused.

Smoke had met Fae's two remaining ranch hands, Spring and Pat. Both men in their early sixties, he guessed. But still leather-tough. They both gave him a good eyeballing, passed him through inspection, and returned to their jobs.

Over dinner—Sally called it lunch—Smoke began asking his questions while Beans skipped the regular food and began attacking a platter of bear-sign, washed down with hot strong western coffee.

How many head of cattle?

Started out with a thousand. Probably down to less than five hundred now, due to Hanks and McCorkle's boys running them off.

Would she have any objections to Smoke getting her cattle back?

She looked hard at him. Finally shook her head. No objections at all.

"Ring will stay here at the ranch and start doing some much needed repair work," Smoke told her. "Beans and me will start working the cattle, moving them closer in. Then we'll get your other beeves back. Tell me the boundaries of this spread."

She produced a map and pointed out her spread, and it was not a little one. It had good graze and excellent water. The brand was the Box T; she had not changed it since taking over several years back.

"If you'll pack us some food," Smoke said, "me and Beans will head out right now; get the lay of the land. We'll stay out a couple of days—maybe longer. This situation is shaping up to be a bad one. The lid could blow off at any moment. Beans, shake out your rope and pick us out a couple of fresh horses. Let's give ours a few days' rest. They've earned it."

"I'll start putting together some food," Fae said. She looked at Smoke. "I appreciate this. More than you know."

"Sorry family that don't stick together."

They rode out an hour later, Smoke on a buckskin a good seventeen hands high that looked as though it could go all day and all night and still want to travel.

The old man who had given the spread to Fae had known his business—Smoke still wondered about how she'd gotten it. He decided to pursue that further when he had the time.

About ten miles from the ranch, they crossed the Smith and rode up to several men working Box T cattle toward the northwest.

They wheeled around at Smoke's approach.

"Right nice of you boys to take such an interest in our cattle," Smoke told a hard-eyed puncher. "But you're pushing them the wrong way. Now move them back across the river."

"Who the hell do you think you are?" the man challenged him.

"Jensen."

The man spat on the ground. "I like the direction we're movin' them better." He grabbed iron.

Smoke drew, cocked, and fired in one blindingly fast move. The .44 slug took the man in the center of his chest and knocked him out of the saddle. He tried to rise up but did not have the strength. With a groan, he fell back on the ground, dead. Beans held a pistol on the other McCorkle riders; they were all looking a little white around the mouth.

"Jack Waters," Smoke said. "He's wanted for murder in two states. I've seen the flyers in Monte's office."

"Yeah," Beans said glumly. "And he's got three brothers just as bad as he is. Waco, Hatley, and Collis."

"You won't last a week on this range, Jensen," a mouthy McCorkle rider said.

Smoke moved closer to him and backhanded the rider out of his saddle. He hit the ground and opened his mouth to cuss. Then he closed his mouth as the truth came home. Jensen. *Smoke* Jensen.

"All of you shuck outta them gun belts," Beans ordered. "When you've done that, start movin' them cattle back across the river."

"Then we're going to take a ride," Smoke added. "To see Cord."

While the Circle Double C boys pushed the cattle back across the river, Smoke lashed the body of Jack Waters across his saddle and Beans picked up the guns, stuffing guns, belts, and all into a gunny sack and tying it on his saddle horn. The riders returned, a sullen lot, and Smoke told them to head out for the ranch.

A hand hollered for Cord to come out long before Smoke and Beans entered the front yard. "Stay in the house," Cord told his wife and daughter. "I don't want any of you to see this."

Beans stayed in the saddle, a Winchester .44 across his

saddle horn. Smoke untied the ropes and slung Jack Waters over his shoulder, and Jack was not a small man. He walked across the lawn and dumped the body on the ground, by Cord's feet.

Cord was livid, his face flushed and the veins in his neck standing out like ropes. He was breathing like an enraged bull.

"We caught Jack and these other hands on Box T Range, rustling cattle. Now you know the law out here, Cord: we were within our rights to hang every one of them. But I gave them a chance to ride on. Waters decided to drag iron."

Cord nodded his head, not trusting his voice to speak.

"Now, Cord," Smoke told him, "I don't care if you and Hanks fight until you kill each other. I don't think either of you remember what it is you're fighting about. But the war against the Box T is over. Fae and Parnell Jensen have no interest in your war, and nothing to do with it. *Leave . . . them . . . alone!*"

Smoke's last three words cracked like whips; several hardnosed punchers winced at the sound.

"You all through flappin' your mouth, Jensen?" Cord asked.

"No. I want all the cattle belonging to Fae and Parnell Jensen rounded up and returned. I'm not saying that your hands ran them all off. I'm sure Hanks and his boys had a hand in it, too. And I'll be paying him a visit shortly. Get them rounded up and back on Box T Range."

"And if I don't—not saying I have them, mind you?"

Smoke's smile was not pretty. "You ever heard of Louis Longmont, McCorkle?"

"Of course, I have! What's he have to do with any of this?"

"He's an old friend of mine, Cord. We stood shoulder to shoulder several years back and cleaned up Fontana. Then last year, he rode with me to New Hampshire . . . you probably read about that."

Cord nodded his head curtly.

"He's one of the wealthiest men west of the Mississippi, Cord. And he loves a good fight. He wouldn't blink an eye to spend a couple of hundred thousand putting together an army to come in here and wipe your nose on a porcupine's backside."

From in the house, Smoke heard a young woman's laughter and an older woman telling her to shush!

The truth was, Louis was in Europe on an extended vacation and Smoke knew it. But sometimes a good bluff wins the pot.

Cord had money, but nothing to compare with Louis Longmont . . . and he also knew that Smoke had married into a a great deal of money and was wealthy in his own right. He sighed heavily.

"I can't speak for Hanks, Jensen. You'll have to face him yourself. But as for me and mine . . . OK, we'll leave the Box T alone. I don't have their cattle. I'm not a rustler. My boys just scattered them. But I'm damned if I'll help you round them up. You can come on my range and look, any wearing the Box T brand, take them."

Smoke nodded and stuck out his hand. Cord looked startled for a few seconds, then a very grudging smile cut his face. He took the hand and gripped it briefly.

Smoke turned and mounted up. "See you."

Beans and Smoke swung around and rode slowly away from the ranch house.

"My back is itchy," Beans said.

"So is mine. But I think he's a man of his word. I don't think he'll go back on his word. Least I'm a poor judge of character if he does."

They rode on. Beans said, "My goodness me. I plumb forgot to give them boys their guns back."

"Well, shame on you, Beans. I hate to see them go to waste. We'll just take them back to Fae and she can keep them in reserve. Never know when she might need them. You can swap them for some bear-sign."

"What about hands?"

"We got to hire some, that's for sure. Fae's got to sell off some cattle for working capital. She told me so. So we've got to hire some boys."

"Durned if I know where. And there's still the matter of Dooley Hanks."

Fae would hire some hands, sooner than Smoke thought. But they would be about fifty years from boyhood.

6

They made camp early that day, after rounding up about fifty head of Box T cattle they found on Cord's place. They put them in a coulee and blocked the entrance with brush. They would push them closer to home in the morning.

They supped on the food Fae had fixed for them and were rolled up in their blankets just after dark.

Smoke was the first one up, several hours before dawn. He coaxed life back into the coals by adding dry grass and twigs, and Beans sat up when the smell of coffee got too much for him to take. Beans threw off his blankets, put on his hat, pulled on his boots, and buckled on his gun belt. He squatted by the fire beside Smoke, warming his hands and waiting for the cowboy coffee to boil.

"Town life's done spoiled me," Beans griped. "Man gets used to shavin' and bathin' every day, and puttin' on clean clothes every mornin'. It ain't natural."

Smoke grinned and handed him a small sack.

"What's in here?"

"Bear-sign I hid from you yesterday."

Beans quit his grousing and went to eating while Smoke

sliced the bacon and cut up some potatoes, adding a bit of wild onion for flavor.

"The problem of hands has got me worried," Beans admitted, slurping on a cup of coffee. "Ain't no cowboy in his right mind gonna go to work for the Box T with all this trouble starin' him in the face."

"I know." Smoke ladled out the food onto tin plates. "But I think I know one who just might do it, for thirty and found, just for the pure hell of it. I'll talk to him this afternoon if I can."

"You got a lot of damn nerve, Jensen," the foreman of the D-H spread told him. "Mister Hanks don't wanna see you."

"You tell him I'm here and I'll wait just as long as it takes."

Gage stared into the cold eyes of the most respected and feared gunfighter in all the West. He sighed, shook his head and finally said, "All right, mister. I'll tell him you insist on seein' him. But I ain't givin' no guarantees."

Hanks and McCorkle could pass for brothers, Smoke thought, as he squatted under the shade of a tree and watched as Dooley left the house and walked toward him. Both of them square-built men. Solid. Both of them in their early to mid forties.

Dooley did not offer to shake hands. "Speak your piece, Jensen."

Smoke repeated what he'd told Cord, almost word for word including the bit about Louis Longmont. Grim-faced, Hanks stood and took it. He didn't like it, but he took it.

"Maybe I'll just wait you out, Jensen."

"Maybe. But I doubt it. You're paying fighting wages Dooley. To a lot of people. You're like most cattlemen, Dooley: you're worth a lot of money, but most of it is standing on four hooves. Ready scratch is hard to come up with."

Dooley grunted. Man knew what he was talking about, all right. "You won't get between me and McCorkle?"

"I don't care what you two do to each other. The area would probably be better off if you'd kill each other."

"Plain-spoken man, ain't you?"

"I see no reason to dance around it, Dooley. What'd you say?"

Something evil moved behind Dooley Hanks's eyes. And Smoke didn't miss it. He did not trust this man, there was no honor to be found in Dooley Hanks.

"I didn't rustle no Box T cattle, Jensen. We just scattered them all to hell and gone. You're free to work my range. You find any Box T cattle, take them. You won't be bothered, and neither will Miss Fae or any punchers she hires." He grinned, and it was not a pleasant curving of the lips. He also had bad breath. *"If* she can find anyone stupid enough to work for her. Now get out of my face. I'm sick of lookin' at you."

"The feeling is quite mutual, Hanks." Smoke mounted up and rode away.

"I don't trust that hombre," Beans said. "He's got more twists and turns than a snake."

"I got the same feeling. See if you can find some of Fae's beef and start pushing them toward Box T graze. I'm going into Gibson."

"You're serious?"

"Oh, yes," Smoke told him. "Thirty and found, and you'll work just like any other cowboy."

The man threw back his head and laughed; his teeth were very white against his deeply tanned face. He tossed his hat onto the table in Hans's cafe.

"All right," he said suddenly. "All right, Smoke, you have a deal. I was a vaquero before I turned to the gun. I will ride for the Box T."

Smoke and Lujan shook hands. Smoke had always heard how unpredictable the man was, but once he gave his word, he would die keeping it.

Lujan packed up his gear and pulled out moments later

riding for the Box T. Smoke chatted with Hans and Olga and
Hilda for a few moments—Hilda, as it turned out, was quite
taken with Ring—and then he decided he'd like a beer. Smoke
was not much of a drinker, but did enjoy a beer or a drink of
whiskey every now and then.

Which saloon to enter? He stood in front of the cafe and
pondered that for a moment. Both of the saloons were filled
up with gunhands. "Foolish of me," he muttered. But a cool
beer sounded good. He slipped the leather thongs from the
hammers of his guns and walked over to the Pussycat and
pushed open the batwings, stepping into the semi-gloom of
the beery-smelling saloon.

All conversation stopped.

Smoke walked to the bar and ordered a beer. The barkeep
suddenly got very nervous. Smoke sipped his beer and it was
good, hitting the spot.

"Jack Waters was a friend of mine," a man spoke, the
voice coming from the gloom of the far end of the saloon.

Smoke turned, his beer mug in his left hand.

His right thumb was hooked behind his big silver belt
buckle, his fingers only a few inches from his cross-draw
.44. He stood saying nothing, sipping at his beer. He paid for
the brew, damned if he wasn't going to try to finish as much
of it as possible before he had to deal with this loudmouth.

"Ever'body talks about how bad you are, Jensen," the
bigmouth cranked his tongue up again. "But I ain't never
seen none of your graveyards."

"I have," the voice came quietly from Smoke's left. He did
not know the voice and did not turn his head to put a face to
it.

"Far as I'm concerned," the bigmouth stuck it in gear again,
"I think Smoke Jensen is about as bad as a dried-up cow pile."

"You know my name," Smoke's words were softly offered. "What's your name?"

"What's it to you?"

"Wouldn't be right to put a man in the ground without his
name on his grave marker."

The loudmouth cursed Smoke.

Smoke took a swallow of beer and waited. He watched as the man pushed his chair back and stood up. Men on both sides of him stood up and backed away, getting out of the line of fire.

"My name's John Cheave, Jensen. I been lookin' for you for nearabouts two years."

"Why?" Smoke was almost to the bottom of his beer mug.

"My brother was killed at Fontana. By you."

"Too bad. He should have picked better company to run with. But I don't recall any Cheave. What was he, some two-bit thief who had to change his name?"

John Cheave again cursed Smoke.

Smoke finished his beer and set the mug down on the edge of the bar. He slipped his thumb from behind his belt buckle and let his right hand dangle by the butt of his .44.

John Cheave called Smoke a son of a bitch.

Smoke's eyes narrowed. "You could have cussed me all day and not said that. Make your grab, Cheave."

Cheave's hands dipped and touched the butts of his guns. Two shots thundered, the reports so close together they sounded as one. Smoke had drawn both guns and fired, rolling his left hand .44. It was a move that many tried, but few ever perfected; and more than a few ended up shooting themselves in the belly trying.

John Cheave had not cleared leather. He sat down in the chair he had just stood up out of and leaned his head back, his wide, staring eyes looking up at the ceiling of the saloon. There were two bloody holes in the center of his chest. Cheave opened his mouth a couple of times, but no words came out.

His boots drummed on the floor for a few seconds and then he died, his eyes wide open, staring at and meeting death.

"I seen it, but I don't believe it," a man said, standing up. He tossed a couple of dollars on the table. "Cheave come out of California. Some say he was as fast as John Wesley Hardin. Count me out of this game, boys. I'm ridin'."

He walked out of the saloon, being very careful to avoid getting too close to Smoke.

The sounds of his horse's hooves faded before anyone else spoke.

"The barber doubles as the undertaker," Pooch Matthews said.

Smoke nodded his head. "Fine."

The bartender yelled for his swamper to fetch the undertaker.

"Impressive," a gunhawk named Hazzard said. "I have to say it: you're about the best I've ever seen. Except for one."

"Oh?"

Hazzard smiled. "Yeah. Me."

Smoke returned the smile and turned his back to the man, knowing the move would infuriate the gunhawk.

"Another beer, Mister Smoke?" the barkeep asked.

"No."

The barkeep did not push the issue.

Smoke studied the bottom of the empty beer mug wondering how many more would fall under his guns. Although he knew this showdown would have come, sooner or later, one part of him said that he should not have come into the saloon, while another part of him said that he had a right to go wherever he damned well pleased. As long as it was a public place.

It was an old struggle within the man.

The barber came in and he and the swamper dragged the body out to the barber's wagon and chunked him in. The thud of the body falling against the bed of the wagon could be heard inside the saloon.

"I believe I will have that beer," Smoke said. While the barkeep filled his mug, Smoke rolled one of his rare cigarettes and lit up.

The saloon remained very quiet.

The barkeep's hand trembled just slightly as he set the foamy mug in front of Smoke.

Several horses pulled up outside the place. McCorkle and Jason Bright and several of Cord's hands came in. They walked to a table and sat down, ordering beer.

"What happened?" Smoke heard Cord ask.

"Cheave started it with Jensen. He didn't even clear leather."

"I thought you was going to stay out of this game, Jensen?" McCorkle directed the question to Smoke's back.

Smoke slowly turned, holding the beer mug in his left hand. "Cheave pushed me, Cord. I only came in here for a beer."

"Man's got a right to have a drink," Cord grudgingly conceded. "I seen some Box T cattle coming in, Jensen. They was grazin' on range 'bout five, six miles out of town. On the west side of the Smith."

"Thanks." And with a straight face, he added, "I'll have Lujan and a couple of others push them back to Box T Range."

"Lujan!" Jason Bright almost hollered the word.

"Yes. He went to work for the Box T a couple of hours ago."

A gunslick that Smoke knew from the old days, when he and Preacher were roaming the land, got up and walked toward the table where Cord was sitting. "I figure I got half a month's wages comin' to me, Mister McCorkle. If you've a mind to pay me now, I'd appreciate it."

With a look of wry amusement on his face, Cord reached into his pocket and counted out fifty dollars, handing it to the man. "You ridin', Jim?"

"Yes, sir. I figure I can catch up with Red. He hauled his ashes a few minutes ago."

Cord counted out another fifty. "Give this to Red. He earned it."

"Yes, sir. Much obliged." He looked around the saloon. "See you boys on another trail. This one's gettin' crowded." He walked through the batwings.

"Yellow," Hazzard said disgustedly, his eyes on the swinging and squeaking batwings. "Just plain yellow is all he is."

Cord cut his eyes. "Jim Kay is anything but yellow, Hazzard. I've known him for ten years. There is a hell of a lot of difference between being yellow and bettin' your life on a busted flush." He looked at Smoke. "There bad blood between you and Jim Kay?"

Smoke shook his head. "Not that I'm aware of. I've known him since I was just a kid. He's a friend of Preacher."

Cord smiled. "Preacher pulled my bacon out of the fire long years back. Only time I ever met him. I owe him. I often wonder what happened to him."

"He's alive. But getting on in years."

Cord nodded his head, then his eyes swept the room. "I'll say it now, boys; we leave the Box T alone. Our fight is with Dooley Hanks. Box T riders can cross our range and be safe doin' it. They'll be comin' through lookin' for the cattle we scattered. You don't have to help them, just leave them alone."

A few of the gunslicks exchanged furtive glances. Cord missed the eye movement. Smoke did not. The gunfighters that Smoke would have trusted had left the area, such as Jim Kay and Red and a few others. What was left was the dregs, and there was not an ounce of honor in the lot.

Smoke finished his beer. "See you, Cord."

The rancher nodded his head and Smoke walked out the door. Riding toward the Box T, Smoke thought: You better be careful, McCorkle, 'cause you've surrounded yourself with a bunch of rattlesnakes, and I don't think you know just how dangerous they are.

7

The days drifted on, filled with hard honest work and the deep dreamless sleep of the exhausted. Smoke had hired two more hands, boys really, in their late teens. Bobby and Hatfield. They had left the drudgery of a hardscrabble farm in Wisconsin and drifted west, with dreams of the romantic West and being cowboys. And they both had lost all illusions about the romantic life of a cowboy very quickly. It was brutally hard work, but at least much of it could be done from the back of a horse.

True to his word, Lujan not only did his share, but took up some slack as well. He was a skilled cowboy, working with no wasted motion, and he was one of the finest horsemen Smoke had ever seen.

One hot afternoon, Smoke looked up to see young Hatfield come a-foggin' toward him, lathering his horse.

"Mister Smoke! Mister Smoke!" he yelled. "I ain't believing this. You got to come quick to the house."

He reined up in a cloud of dust and Smoke had to wait until the dust settled before he could even see the young man to talk to him.

"Whoa, boy! Who put a burr under your blanket?"

"Mister Smoke, my *daddy* read stories about them men up to Miss Fae's house when he was a boy. I thought they was all dead and buried in the grave!"

"Slow down, boy. What men?"

"Them old gunfighters up yonder. Come on." He wheeled his horse around and was gone at a gallop.

Lujan pulled up. "What's going on, amigo?"

"I don't know. Come on, let's find out."

Fae was entertaining them on the front porch when Smoke and Lujan rode up. Smoke laughed when he saw them.

Lujan looked first at the aging men on the porch, and then looked at Smoke. When he spoke, there was disapproval in his voice. "It is not nice to laugh at the old, my friend."

"Lujan, I'm not laughing at them. These men are friends of mine. As well known as we are, we're pikers compared to those old gunslingers. Lujan, you're looking at Silver Jim, Pistol Le Roux, Hardrock, and Charlie Starr."

"Dios mio!" the Mexican breathed. "Those men *invented* the fast draw."

"And don't sell them short even today, Lujan. They can still get into action mighty quick."

"I wouldn't doubt it for a minute," Lujan said, dismounting.

"If I'd known you old coots were going to show up, I'd have called the old folks home and had them send over some wheelchairs," Smoke called out.

"Would you just listen to the pup flap his mouth," Hardrock said. "I ought to get up and spank him."

"Way your knees pop and crack he'd probably think you was shootin' at him." Pistol laughed.

The men shook hands and Smoke introduced them to Lujan.

Charlie Starr sized the Mexican up. "Yeah, I seen you down along the border some years back. When them Sabler Brothers called you out. Too bad you didn't kill all five of them."

"Wasn't two down enough?" Lujan asked softly, clearly in awe of these old gunslingers.

"Nope," Silver Jim said. "We stopped off down in Wyoming for supplies. Store clerk said the Sabler boys had come through the day before, heading up thisaway. Ben, Carl, and Delmar."

Lujan sighed. "Many, many times I have wished I had never drawn my pistol in anger that first time down in Cuauhtemoc." He smiled. "Of course, the shooting was over a lovely lady. And of course, she would have nothing to do with me after that."

"What was her name?" Hatfield asked.

Lujan laughed. "I do not even remember."

The old gunfighters were all well up in years—Charlie Starr being the youngest—but they were all leather-tough and could still work many men half their age into the ground.

And the news that the Box T had hired the famed gunslingers was soon all over the area. Some of Cord McCorkle's hired guns thought it was funny, and it would be even funnier to tree one of the old gunnies and see just what he'd do. The gunfighter they happened to pick that morning was the Louisiana Creole, Pistol Le Roux.

Ol' Pistol and Bobby were working some strays back toward the east side of the Smith when the three gunhawks spotted Pistol and headed his way. Just to be on the safe side, Pistol wheeled his horse to face the men and slipped the hammer thong off his right hand Colt and waited.

That one of the men held a coiled rope in his right hand did not escape the old gunfighter. He had him a hunch that these pups were gonna try to rope and drag him. A hard smile touched his face. That had been tried before. Several times. Ain't been done yet.

"Well, well," the hired gun said, riding up. "What you reckon we done come across here, boys?"

"Damned if I know," another said with a nasty grin. "But it shore looks to me like it needs buryin'."

"Yeah," the third gunny said, sniffing the air. "It's done died and gone to stinkin'."

"That's probably your dirty drawers you smellin', punk," Pistol told him. "Since your mammy ain't around to change them for you."

The man flushed, deep anger touching his face. Tell the truth, he hadn't changed his union suit in a while.

"I think we'll just check the brands on them beeves," they told Pistol.

"You'll visit the outhouse if you eat regular, too," Pistol popped back. "And you probably should, and soon, 'cause you sure full of it."

"Why, you godda—" He grabbed for his pistol. The last part of the obscenity was cut off as Pistol's Colt roared, the slug taking the would-be gunslick in the lower part of his face and driving through the base of his throat.

Pistol had drawn and fired so fast the other two had not had time to clear leather. Now they found themselves looking down the long barrel of Pistol's Peacemaker. The dying gunny moaned and tried to talk; the words were unintelligible, due in no small measure to the lower part of his jaw being missing.

"Shuck out of them gun belts," Pistol told them, just as Bobby came galloping up to see what the shooting was all about. "Usin' your left hands," Pistol added.

Gun belts hit the ground.

"Dismount," Pistol told them. "Bobby, git that rope."

"Hey!" one of the gunnies said. "We was just a-funnin' with you, that's all."

"I don't consider bein' dragged no fun. And that's what you was gonna do, right?"

"Aw, no!"

Pistol's Colt barked and the boot heel was torn loose from the gunny's left boot. "Wasn't it, boy?" Pistol yelled.

On the ground, holding his numbed foot, the gunny nodded his head. "Yeah. We all make mistakes."

"Git out of them clothes," Pistol ordered. "Bare-butted nekkid. Do it!"

Red-faced, the men stood before Pistol, Bobby, and God in their birthday suits.

"Tie 'em together, Bobby. But give them room to walk. They got a long way to hoof it."

The gunny on the ground jerked and died.

The bare-butted men tied, their hands behind their backs, Pistol looped the rope around his saddle horn and gave the orders. "Move out. Head for your bunkhouse, boys. Git goin'."

"What about Pete?" one hollered.

"He'll keep without gettin' too gamy. Now *move!*"

It was a good hour's walk back to the Circle Double C ranch house, and the gunnies hoofed it all the way. They complained and moaned and hollered and finally begged for relief from their hurting, bleeding feet. They shut up when Pistol threatened to drag them.

"Pitiful," Pistol told him. "Twice the Indians caught me and made me run for it, bare-butt nekkid. Miles and miles and miles. With them just a-whoopin' and a-hollerin' right behind me. You two are a disgrace."

Cord stood by the front gate and had to smile at the sight as the painful parade came to a halt. He had ordered his wife and daughter not to look outside. But of course they both did.

The naked men collapsed to the ground.

"Mister McCorkle, my name is Le Roux. They call me Pistol. Now, sir, I was minding my own business, herdin' cattle like I'm paid to do, when three of your hands come up and was gonna put a loop around me and drag me. One of them went for his gun. He was a tad slow. You'll find him dead by that big stand of cottonwoods on the Smith. He ain't real purty to look at. Course, he wasn't all that beautiful when he was livin'. I brung these wayward children back home. You want to spank them, that's your business. Good day, sir."

Pistol and Bobby swung their horses and headed back to Box T Range.

Cord looked at the naked men and their bloody feet and

briar-scratched ankles and legs. "Get their feet taken care of, pay them off, and get them out of here," he instructed his foreman. He looked at the gunslicks on his payroll. "Pete was one of your own. Go get him and bury him. And stay the hell away from Box T riders." He pointed to the naked and weary and footsore men on the ground. "One man did that. One . . . old . . . man. But that man, and those other old gun-fighters over at the Box T came out here in the thirties and forties as mountain men. Tough? You bet your life they're tough. When they do go down for the last time, they'll go out of this world like cornered wolves, snarling and ripping at anything or anyone that confronts them. Leave them alone, boys. If you feel you can't obey my orders, ride out of here."

The gunfighters stared at Cord. All stayed. As Cord turned his back to them and walked toward his house, he had a very bad feeling about the outcome of this matter, and he could not shake it.

"It's stupid!" Sandi McCorkle said to her friend. "They don't even know why they hate each other."

Rita Hanks nodded her head in agreement. "I'm going to tell you something, Sandi. And it's just between you and me. I don't trust my father, or my brothers."

Sandi waited for her friend to continue.

"I think Daddy's gone crazy." She grimaced. "I think my brothers have always been crazy. They've never been . . . well, just right; as far as I'm concerned. They're cruel and vicious."

"What do you think your dad is going to do?"

"I don't know. But he's up to something. He sent a hand out last week to Helena. Then yesterday this ratty-faced-looking guy shows up at the ranch. Danny Rouge. Has a real fancy rifle. Carries it in a special-made case. I think he's a back-shooter, Sandi."

The two young women, both in their late teens, had been

forbidden by their fathers to see each other, years back. Of course, neither of them paid absolutely any attention to those orders. But their meetings had become a bit more secretive.

"Do you want me to tell Daddy about this, Rita?"

"No. He'd know it came from me and then you'd get in trouble. I think we'd better tell Smoke Jensen."

Sandi giggled. "I'd like to tell him a thing or two—in private. He's about the best-looking man I've ever seen."

"He's also married with children," Rita reminded her friend. "But he sure is cute. He's even better looking than the covers of those books make him out to be. Have you seen the Moab Kid?"

"Yes! He's *darling!*"

The two young women talked about men and marriage for a few minutes. It was time for them to be married; pretty soon they'd be pegged as old maids. They both had plenty of suitors, but none lasted very long. The young women were both waiting for that "perfect man" to come riding into their lives.

"How in the world are we going to tell Smoke Jensen about this back-shooter?"

"I don't know. But I think it's our bounden duty to tell him. People listen to him."

"That Bobby's been gettin' all red-eared every time he gets around me," Sandi said. "I think maybe he could get a message to Smoke and he'd meet us."

"Worth a try. We'll take us a ride tomorrow over to the Smith and have a picnic and wait. Maybe he'll show up."

"Let's do it. I'll see you at the pool about noon."

The young women walked to their buggies. Both buggies were equipped with rifle boots and the boots were full. A pistol lay on the seat of each buggy. Both Sandi and Rita could, would, and had used the weapons. With few exceptions, ranch-born-and-raised western women were no shrinking violets. They lived in a violent time and had to be prepared to fight. Although most western men would not bother a woman, there were always a few who would, even though they knew the punishment was usually a rope.

Very little Indian trouble now occurred in this part of Montana; but there was always the chance of a few bucks breaking from the reservations to steal a few horses or take a few scalps.

With a wave, the young women went their way, Sandi back to the Circle Double C, Rita back to D-H. Neither noticed the two men sitting their horses in the timber. The men wore masks and long dusters.

"You ready?" one asked, his voice muffled by the bandana tied round his face.

"I been ready for some of that Rita. Let's go."

8

Silver Jim found the overturned buggy while out hunting strays. The horse was nowhere in sight. He noticed that the Winchester .44 carbine was a good twenty feet from the overturned buggy. He surmised that whoever had been in this rig had pulled the carbine from its boot and was makin' ready to use it. Then he found the pistol. He squatted down and sniffed at the barrel. Recently fired.

He stood up and emptied his Colt into the air; six widely spaced shots. It took only a few minutes for Smoke and Lujan to reach him.

"That is Senorita Hanks's buggy," Lujan said. "I have seen her in it several times."

"Stay with it, boys," Smoke said. "Look around. I'll ride to the D-H."

He did not spare his horse getting to the ranch, reining up to the main house in a cloud of dust and jumping off. "Switch my saddle," he told a startled hand. He ran up the steps to face a hard-eyed Dooley Hanks. "Silver Jim found Miss Hanks's buggy just north of our range. By that creek. Overturned. No sign of Miss Hanks. But Silver Jim said her pistol had been fired. I left them looking for her and trying to cut some trail."

The color went out of Dooley's face. Like most men, his daughter was the apple of his eye. "I'm obliged. Let's ride, boys!" he yelled.

Already, one of his regular hands was noosing a rope.

Within five minutes, twenty-five strong, Dooley led his hands and his hired guns out at a gallop. The wrangler had switched Smoke's saddle to a mean-eyed mustang and was running for his own horse.

Smoke showed the mustang who was boss and then cut across country, taking the timber and making his own trail, going where no large group of riders could. He reached the overturned buggy just a couple of minutes before Dooley and his men.

"Silver Jim cut some sign," Bobby told him. "Him and Lujan took off thataway. Told me to stay here."

Dooley and his party reined up and Dooley jumped off his horse. Smoke pointed to the pistol, still where Silver Jim had found it.

"That's hers," the father said, a horrified look in his eyes. "I give it to her and taught her how to use it."

"Look!" Bobby pointed.

Heads turned. Silver Jim was holding a girl in his arms, Lujan leading the horse, some of its harness dragging the ground.

The cook from the D-H came rattling up in a wagon, Mrs. Hanks on the seat beside him. "I filled it with hay, Boss," he told Dooley. "Just in case."

Dooley nodded.

Smoke took the girl from Silver Jim and carried her to the wagon and to her mother. She had been badly beaten and her clothing ripped from her. One of her eyes was closed and discolored and blood leaked from a corner of her mouth. Silver Jim had wrapped her in a blanket.

"How did you . . . I mean," Dooley shook his head. "Had she been . . . ?"

"I reckon," Silver Jim said solemnly. "Her clothes and . . . underthings was strewn over about a half a mile. Looks like they was rippin' and tearin' as they rode. Two men took her, a third joined them over yonder on that first ridge." He pointed. "He'd been waitin' for some time. Half a dozen cigarette butts on the ground."

"She say who done this?" Dooley's voice was harsh and terrible sounding.

"No, senor," Lujan said. "She was unconscious when we found her."

"Shorty!" Dooley barked. "Go fetch that old rummy we call a doctor. If he ain't sober, dunk him in a horse trough until he is. Ride, man!"

Smoke had walked to the wagon bed and was looking at the young woman, her head cradled in her mother's lap. He noticed a crimson area on the side of her head. "Bobby, bring me my canteen, hurry!"

He wet a cloth and asked Mrs. Hanks to clean up the bloody spot.

"Awful bump on her head," the mother said, her voice calm but the words tight.

"For sure she's got a concussion," Smoke said. "Maybe a fractured skull. Cushion her head and drive real slow, Cookie. She can't take many bumps and jars."

Smoke and his people stood and watched the procession start out for the ranch. Dooley had sent several of his men to follow the trail left by the rapists. "Bring them back alive," he told them. "I want to stake them out." He turned his mean and slightly maddened eyes toward Smoke. "Ain't that what you done years back, Jensen?"

"That's what I did."

The man's gone over the edge, Smoke thought. This was all it took to push him into that shadowy, eerie world of madness.

"They're going to find out what we didn't tell them Smoke," Lujan said. "The trail leads straight to Circle Double C Range."

"And one of them horses has a chip out of a shoe. It'll be easy to identify," Silver Jim said.

Smoke thought about that. "Almost too easy, wouldn't you think."

"That thought did cross my mind," the old gunfighter acknowledged, rolling a cigarette.

"I better get over there." Smoke swung into the saddle and turned the mustang's head.

He looped the reins around the hitchrail and walked up to the porch, conscious of a lot of hard eyes on him as he knocked on the door.

A very lovely young woman opened the door and smiled at him. "Why, Mister Jensen. How nice. Please come in."

Smoke removed his hat and stepped inside the nicely furnished home just as Cord stepped into the foyer. "Trouble, Cord. Bad trouble." He looked at Sandi.

"Go sit with your mother, girl," the father said.

Sandi smiled sweetly and leaned up against the wall, folding her arms under her breasts.

Cord lifted and spread his big hands in a helpless gesture. "Boys are bad enough, Smoke, but girls are impossible."

Smoke told them both, leaving very little out. He did not mention anything about the chipped shoe; not in front of Sandi. Nor did he say anything about the trail leading straight to Circle C Range.

"I've got to get over there," Sandi said, turning to fetch her shawl.

"No." Smoke's hard-spoken word stopped her, turning her around. "There is nothing you can do over there. Rita is unconscious and will probably remain so for many hours. Dooley is killing mad and likely to go further off the deep end. And those who . . . abused Rita are still out there. Your going over there would accomplish nothing and only put you in danger."

She locked rebellious eyes with Smoke. Then she slowly nodded her head. "You're right, of course. Thank you for pointing those things out. I'll go tell Mother."

Smoke motioned Cord out onto the porch where they could talk freely, in private. He leveled with Cord.

"Damn!" the man cursed, balling his fists. "If the men who done it are here, we'll find them and hold them for the law . . . or hang them," he added the hard words. "No matter what I feel about Hanks himself, Rita and my Sandi have been friends for years. Rita and her momma is the two reasons I haven't gone over there and burned the damn place down. I've known for years that Dooley was crazy; and his boys is twice as bad. They're cruel mean."

"I've heard that from other people."

"It's true. And good with short guns, too. Very good. As good and probably better than most of the hired hands on the payroll." He met Smoke's eyes. "There's something you ought to know. Dooley has hired a back-shooter name of Danny Rouge."

"I know of him. Looks like a big rat. But he's pure poison with a rifle."

Cord looked toward the bunkhouse, where half a dozen gunhands were loafing. "Worthless scum. I was gonna let them go. Now I don't know what to do."

Smoke could offer no advice. He knew that Cord knew that if Dooley even thought his daughter's attackers came from the Circle Double C, he would need all the guns he could muster. They were all sitting on a powder keg, and it could go up at any moment.

A cowboy walked past the big house. "Find Del for me," Cord ordered. "Tell him to come up here."

"Yes, sir."

"You want me to stick around and help you?" Smoke asked.

Cord shook his head. "No. But thanks. This is my snake. I'll kill it."

"I'll be riding, then. If you need help, don't hesitate to send word. I'll come."

Smoke was riding out as the foreman was walking up.

Smoke rode back to the site of the attack. His people had already righted the buggy and hitched up the now calmed horse.

"I'll take it over to the D-H," Smoke offered. "I've got to get my horse anyway."

"I'll ride with you," Lujan said.

"What are we supposed to do?" Silver Jim asked. "Sit here and grow cobwebs? We'll all ride over."

Bobby had returned to chasing strays and pushing them toward new pasture.

The foreman of the D-H, Gage, met them halfway, leading Smoke's horse. "You boys is all right," he said. "So I'll give it to you straight. Don't come on D-H Range no more. I mean, as far as I'm concerned, me and the regular hands, you could ride over anytime; but Dooley has done let his bread burn. He's gone slap nuts. Sent a rider off to wire for more gunhands, they waitin' over at Butte. Lanny Ball found where them tracks led to McCorkle Range and that's when Dooley went crazy. His wife talked him out of riding over and killing Cord today. But he's gonna declare war on the Circle Double C and anybody who befriends them. So I guess all bets is off, boys. But I'll tell you this: me and the regular boys is gonna punch cows, and that's it . . . unless someone tries to attack the house. I'm just damn sorry all this had to happen. I'll be ridin' now. You boys keep a good eye on your backtrail. See you."

"Guess that tears it," Smoke said, after Gage had driven off in the buggy, his horse and the horse Smoke had borrowed tied to the back. "Let's get back to the ranch. Fae and Parnell need to be informed about this day."

Rita regained consciousness the following day. She told her father that she never saw her attackers' faces. They kept masks and hoods on the entire time she was being assaulted. Cord McCorkle sent word that Dooley was welcome to come help search his spread from top to bottom to find the attackers.

Dooley sent word that Cord could go to hell. That he believed Cord knew who raped and beat his daughter and was hiding them, protecting them.

"I tried," Cord said to Smoke. "I don't know what else I can do."

The men were in town, having coffee in Hans's cafe.

Parnell had wanted to pack up and go back east immediately. Fae had told him, in quite blunt language, that anytime he wanted to haul his ashes, to go right ahead. She was staying.

Beans and Charlie Starr had stood openmouthed, listening to Fae vent her spleen. They had never heard such language from the mouth of a woman.

Parnell had packed his bags and left the ranch in a huff vowing never to return until his sister apologized for such unseemly behavior and such vile language.

That set Fae off again. She stood by the hitchrail and cussed her brother until his buggy was out of sight.

Lujan and Spring walked up.

"They do this about once a month," Spring said. "He'll be back in a couple of days. I tell you boys what, workin' for that woman has done give me an education I could do without. Someone needs to sit on her and wash her mouth out with soap."

"Don't look at me!" Lujan said, rolling his dark eyes. "I'd rather crawl up in a nest of rattlesnakes."

"Get back to work!" Fae squalled from the porch, sending the men scrambling for their horses.

"There they are," Smoke said quietly, his eyes on three men riding abreast up the street.

"Who?" Cord asked.

"The Sabler Brothers. Ben, Carl, and Delmar. They'll be

gunning for Lujan. He killed two of their brothers some years back.

"Be interesting to see which saloon they go in."

"You takin' bets?"

"Not me. I damn sure didn't send for them."

The Sabler boys reined up in front of the Hangout.

"It's like they was told not to come to the Pussycat," Cord reflected.

"They probably were. No chipped shoes on any of your horses, huh?"

"No. But several were reshod that day; started before you came over with the news. It's odd, Smoke. Del is as square as they come; hates the gunfighters. But he says he can account for every one of them the morning Rita was raped. He says he'll swear in a court of law that none of them left the bunk-house-main house area. I believe him."

"It could have been some drifters."

"You believe that?"

"No. I don't know what to believe, really."

"I better tell you: talk among the D-H bunch—the gun-slicks—is that it was Silver Jim and Lujan and the Hatfield boy."

Smoke lifted his eyes to meet Cord's gaze. Cord had to struggle to keep from recoiling back. The eyes were ice-house cold and rattler deadly. "Silver Jim is one of the most honorable men I have ever met. Lujan was with me all that morning. Both Hatfield and Bobby are of the age where nei-ther one of them can even talk when they get around women; besides he was within a mile of me and Lujan all morning. Whoever started that rumor is about to walk into a load of grief; If you know who it is, Cord, I'd appreciate you telling me."

"It was that new bunch that came in on the stage the day after it happened. They come up from Butte at Hanks's wire."

"Names?"

"All I know is they call one of them Rose."

Lujan came galloping up, off his horse before the animal even stopped. He ran into the cafe. "Smoke! Hardrock found Young Hatfield about an hour ago. He'd been tortured with a running iron and then dragged. He ain't got long."

9

Doc Adair, now sober for several days, looked up as Smoke and Cord entered the bedroom of the main ranch house. He shook his head. "Driftin' in and out of consciousness. I've got him full of laudanum to ease the pain. They burned him all over his body with a hot iron, then they dragged him. He isn't going to make it. He wouldn't be a whole man even if he did."

No one needed to ask what he meant by that. Those who did this to the boy had been more cruel than mean.

Bobby was fighting back tears. "Me and him growed up together. We was neighbors. More like brothers than friends.

Fae put her arm around the young man and held him, then, at a signal from Smoke, led him out of the bedroom. Smoke knelt down beside the bed.

"Can you hear me, Hatfield?"

The boy groaned and opened his one good eye. "Yes, sir, Mister Smoke." His voice was barely a whisper, and filled with pain.

"Who did this to you?"

"One of them was called . . . Rose. They called another one Cliff. I ain't gonna make it, am I, Mister Smoke?"

Smoke sighed.

"Tell me . . . the truth."

"The doc says no. But doctors have been wrong before."

"When they burned my privates . . . I screamed and passed out. I come to and they . . . was draggin' me."

His words were becoming hard to understand and his breathing was very ragged. Smoke could see one empty eye socket. "Send any money due me to . . . my ma. Tell her to buy something pretty . . . with it. Watch out for Bobby. He's . . . He don't look it, but he's . . . cat quick with a short gun. Been . . . practicin' since we was about . . . six years old. Gettin' dark. See you, boys."

The young man closed his good eye and spoke no more. Doc Adair pushed his way through to the bed. After a few seconds, he said, "He's still alive, but just. A few more minutes and he'll be out of his pain."

Smoke glanced at Lujan. "Lujan, go sit on Bobby. Hogtie him if you have to. We'll avenge Hatfield, but it'll be after the boy's been given a proper burial."

Grim-faced, and feeling a great deal more emotion than showed on his face, the Mexican gunfighter nodded and left the room.

Hatfield groaned in his unconsciousness. He sighed and his chest moved up and down, as if struggling for breath. Then he lay still. Doc Adair held a small pocket mirror up to the boy's mouth. No breath clouded the mirror. The doctor pulled the sheet over Hatfield's face.

"I'll start putting a box together," Spring spoke from the doorway. "Damn, but I liked that boy!"

The funeral was at ten o'clock the following morning. Mr. and Mrs. Cord McCorkle came, accompanied by Sandi and a few of their hands. Doc Adair was there, as was Hans and Hilda and Olga. Olga went straight to Ring's side and stood there during the services.

No one had seen Bobby that morning. He showed up at

the last moment, wearing a black suit—Fae had pressed it for him—with a white shirt and black string tie. He wore a Remington Frontier .44, low and tied down. He did not strut and swagger. He wore it like he had been born with it. He walked up to Smoke and Lujan and the others, standing in a group.

"Bobby just died with Hatfield," he told them. "My last name is Johnson. Turkey Creek Jack Johnson is my uncle. My name is Bob Johnson. And I'll be goin' into town when my friend is in the ground proper and the words said over him."

"We'll all go in, Bob," Smoke told him.

The preacher spoke his piece and the dirt was shoveled over Hatfield's fresh-made coffin.

"Cord, I'd appreciate it if you and yours would stay here with Fae and Parnell until we get back."

"We'll sure do it, Smoke. Take your time. And shoot straight," he added.

The men headed out. Four aging gunfighters with a string of kills behind them so long history has still not counted them. One gunfighter from south of the border. Smoke Jensen, from north of the border. The Moab Kid and a boy/man who rode with destiny on his shoulders.

They slowed their horses as they approached Gibson, the men splitting up into pairs, some circling the town to come in at different points.

But the town was nearly deserted. Hans's cafe had been closed for the funeral. The big general store—run by Walt and Leah Hillery, a sour-faced man and his wife—was open, but doing no business. The barber shop was empty. There were no horses standing at the hitchrails of either saloon. Smoke walked his horse around the corral and then looked inside the stable. Only a few horses in stalls, and none of them appeared to be wet from recent riding.

The men gathered at the edge of town, talked it over, and then dismounted, splitting up into two groups, one group on each side of the street.

Smoke pushed open the batwings of the Hangout and stepped inside. The place was empty except for the barkeep and the swamper. The bartender, knowing that Smoke had on his warpaint, was nervously polishing shot glasses and beer mugs.

"Ain't had a customer all morning, Mister Smoke," he announced. "I think the boys is stayin' close to the bunkhouse."

Smoke nodded at the man and stepped back out onto the boardwalk, continuing on his walking inspection.

He met with Beans. "Nothing," the Moab Kid said. "Town is deserted."

"They are not yet ready to meet us," Lujan said, walking up.

"We're wasting time here. We've still got cattle to brand and more to move to higher pasture. There'll be another day. Let's get back to work."

The days passed uneventfully, the normal day-to-day routine of the ranch devouring the men's time. Parnell, just as Old Spring had called it, moved back to the ranch and he and Fae continued their bickering. Rita improved, physically, but she was not allowed off the ranch. And to make sure that she did not try any meetings with Sandi, her father assigned two men to watch her at all times.

Bob Johnson was a drastically changed young man. Bobby was gone. The boy seldom smiled now, and he was always armed. Smoke and Charlie Starr had watched him practice late one afternoon, when the day's work on the range was over.

"He's better than good," Charlie remarked. "He's cursed with being a natural."

He did not have to explain that. Smoke knew only too well what the gunfighter meant. With Bob, it was almost as if the gun was a physical extension of his right arm. His draw was oil-smooth and his aim was deadly accurate. And he was fast . . . very fast.

Old Pat rode out to the branding site in the early morning of the sixth day after Hatfield's burying.

"Hans just sent word, Smoke. Them Waters Brothers come into town late yesterday and they brought a half dozen hardcases with them."

"Hans know who they are?"

"He knowed two of 'em. No-Count George Victor and Three-Fingers Kerman. Other four looked meaner than snakes, Hans said. 'Bout an hour later, four more guns come in on the stage. Wore them big California spurs."

"Of course they went straight to the Hangout?" Charlie asked.

"Waters's bunch did. Them California gunslicks went on over to the Pussycat. McCorkle's hirin' agin."

Smoke cursed, but he really could not blame Cord. Every peace effort he had made to Hanks had been turned down with a violent outburst of profanity from Dooley. And Hanks's sons were pushing and prodding each time they came into town. Sonny, Bud, and Conrad Hanks had made their brags that they were going to kill Cord's boys, Max, Rock, and Troy. They were all about the same age and, according to Cord, all possessing about the same ability with a short gun. Cord's boys were more level-headed and better educated—his wife had seen to that. Hanks's boys were borderline stupid. Hanks had seen to that. And they were cruel and vicious.

"We're gonna be pulled into this thing," Hardrock remarked. "Just sure as the sun comes up. There ain't no way we can miss it. Sooner or later, we're gonna run up on them no-goods that done in Young Hatfield. And whether we do it together, or Young Bob does the deed, we'll have chosen a side."

"I'm curious as to when that back-shootin' Danny Rouge is gonna uncork," Pistol said. "I been prowlin' some; I ain't picked up no sign of his ever comin' onto Box T Range."

"Hanks hasn't turned him loose yet." Smoke fished out the makings and rolled him a cigarette, passing the sack and the papers around. He was thoughtful for a moment. "I'll tell you all what's very odd to me: these gunhawks are drawing fighting wages, but they have made no move toward each other. I think there's something rotten in the potato barrel, boys. And I think it's time I rode over and talked it out with Cord."

"You would have to bring that to my attention," Cord said, a glum look on his face. I hadn't thought of that. But by George, you may be right. I hope you're not," he quickly added, "but there's always a chance. Have you heard anything more about Rita's condition?"

"Getting better, physically. Hanks keeps her under guard at the ranch."

"Same thing I heard. Sandi asked to see her and Dooley said he wouldn't guarantee her safety if she set foot on D-H Range. He didn't out and out threaten her—he knows better than that—but he came damn close. His sons and my sons are shapin' up for a shootin', though. And I can't stop them. I want to, but I don't know how, short of hogtyin' my boys and chainin' them to a post."

"How many regular hands do you have, Cord?"

"Eight, counting Del. I always hire part-timers come brandin' time and drives."

"So that's twelve people you can count on, including yourself and your sons."

"Right. Cookie is old, but he can still handle a six-gun and a rifle. You think the lid is going to fly off the pot, don't you, Smoke?"

"Yes. But I don't know when. Do you think your wife and Sandi would go on a visit somewhere until this thing is over?"

"*Hell,* no! If I asked Alice to leave she'd hit me with a skillet. God only knows what Sandi would do, or say," he added drily. "Her mouth doesn't compare to Fae's, but stir her up and you've got a cornered puma on your hands."

"How about those California gunhands that just came in?"

"I don't trust them any more than I do the others. But I felt I had to beef up my gunnies."

"I don't blame you a bit. And I may be all wrong in my suspicions."

"Sad thing is, Smoke, I think you're probably right."

Smoke left McCorkle's ranch and headed back to the Box T. Halfway there, he changed his mind and pointed his horse's nose toward Gibson. Some of the crew was running out of chewing tobacco. He was almost to town when he heard the pounding of hooves. He pulled over to the side of the road and twisted in the saddle. Four riders that he had not seen before. He pulled his Winchester from the boot, levered in a round, and eared the hammer back, laying the rifle across his saddle horn. He was riding Dagger, and knew the horse would stand still in the middle of a cyclone; he wouldn't even look up from grazing at a few gunshots.

The riders reined in, kicking up a lot of unnecessary dust. Smoke pegged them immediately. Arrogant punks, would-be gunslicks. Not a one of them over twenty-one. But they all wore two guns tied down.

"You there, puncher!" one hollered. "How far to Gibson?"

"I'm not standing in the next county, sonny, and I'm not deaf, either."

"You 'bout half smart, though, ain't you?" He grinned at Smoke. "You know who you're talkin' to?"

"Just another loud-mouthed punk, I reckon."

The young man flushed, looked at his friends, and then laughed. "You're lucky, cowboy. I feel good today, so I won't call you down for that remark. I've killed people for less. I'm Twain."

"Does that rhyme with rain or are you retarded?"

"Damn you!" Twain yelled. "Who do you think you are, anyways?"

"Smoke Jensen."

Twain's horse chose that moment to dump a pile of road apples in the dirt. From the look on Twain's face, he felt like doing the same thing in his saddle. He opened and closed his mouth about a half dozen times.

His friends relaxed in their saddles, making very sure both hands were clearly visible and kept well away from their guns.

"You keep on this road," Smoke told them. "Gibson's about four miles."

"Ah . . . uh . . . yes, sir!" Twain finally got the words out. "I . . . uh . . . we are sure obliged."

"You got any sense, boy, you won't stop. You'll just keep on ridin' until you come to Wyoming. But I figure that anybody who cuts kill-notches in the butt of their gun don't have much sense. Who you aimin' to ride for, boy?"

"Ah . . . the D-H spread."

Smoke sat his saddle and stared at the quartet. He stared at them so long they all four began to sweat.

"Is . . . ah . . . something the matter, Mister Smoke?" Twain asked.

"The rest of your buddies got names, Twain?"

"Ah . . . this here is Hector. That's Rod, and that's Murray."

"Be sure and tell that to the barber when you get to town."

"The . . . barber?" Hector asked.

"Yeah. He doubles as the undertaker." Smoke turned his back on the young gunhands and rode on toward town.

10

Among the many horses tied to the hitchrails, on both sides of the street, the first to catch Smoke's eyes was Bob's paint, tied up in front of Hans's cafe. Smoke looped his reins and went in for some coffee and pie. He wondered why so much activity and then remembered it was Saturday. Parnell sat with Bob at a table. They were in such heated discussion neither noticed as Smoke walked up to their table. They lifted their eyes as he pulled back a chair and sat down.

"Perhaps you can talk some sense into this young man's head, Mister Jensen," Parnell pleaded. "He is going to call out these Rose and Cliff individuals."

Smoke ordered apple pie and coffee and then said, "His right, Parnell. I'd do the same was I standing in his boots."

Parnell was aghast. His mouth dropped open and he shook his head. "But he's just a boy! I cannot for the life of me understand why you didn't call the authorities after the murder!"

"Because the law is a hundred miles away, Parnell. And out here, a man handles his own problems without runnin' whining to the law."

"I find it positively barbaric!"

Smoke ate some apple pie and sipped his coffee. Then he surprised the schoolteacher by saying, "Yes, it is barbaric, Parnell. But it's quick. Don't worry, there'll be plenty of lawyers out here before you know it, and they'll be messin' things up and writin' contracts so's that only another lawyer can read them. That'll be good for people like you . . . not so good for the rest of us. You haven't learned in the time you've been here that out here, a man's word is his bond. If he tells you he's sellin' you five hundred head of cattle, there will be five hundred head of cattle, or he'll make good any missing. Call a man a liar out here, Parnell, and it's a shootin' offense. Honorable men live by their word. If they're not honorable, they don't last. They either leave, or get buried. Lawyers, Parnell, will only succeed in screwing that all up." He looked at Bob. "You nervous, Bob?"

"Yes, sir. Some. But I figure I'll calm down soon as I face him."

"As soon as *we* face *them*, Bob," Smoke corrected. "Yes, you'll calm down. Ever killed a man, Bob?"

"No, sir."

Smoke finished his pie, wiped his mouth with the napkin, and waved for Olga to refill his cup. He sugared and stirred and sipped. "A man gets real calm inside, Bob. It's the strangest thing. You can hear a fly buzz a hundred yards off. And you can see everything so clearly. And the quiet is so much so it's scary. Dogs can be barking, cats fighting, but you won't hear anything except the boots of the man you're facing walking toward you."

"How old was you when you killed your first man, Smoke?" Bob asked.

"Fifteen, I think. Maybe fourteen. I don't remember."

"That must have been a terribly traumatic time for you," Parnell said.

"Nope. I just reloaded 'er up and went on. Me and Preacher. I killed some Indians before that . . . in Kansas I think it was.

Pa was still alive then. They attacked us," he added. "I always got along with the Indians for the most part. Lived with them for a while. Me and Preacher. That was after Pa died. Drink your coffee, Bob. It's about time."

Smoke noticed the young man's hands were calm as he lifted the cup to his mouth, sipped, and replaced the cup in the saucer.

Parnell looked at the men, his eyes drifting back and forth. He had heard from his sister and from the old gunfighters at the ranch that Smoke was a devoted family man: totally faithful to his wife and a loving father. A marvelous friend. Yet for all of those attributes, the man was sitting here talking about killing with less emotion than he exhibited when ordering a piece of pie.

Parnell watched with a curious mixture of fascination and revulsion as Smoke took his guns from leather, one at a time, and carefully checked the action, using the napkin to wipe them free of any dust that might have accumulated during his ride to town. He loaded up the usually empty chamber under the hammer.

Bob checked his Remington .44 and then pulled a short-barreled revolver out of his waistband and checked that, loading both guns full. He cut his eyes to Smoke. "Insurance," he said.

"Never hurts." Smoke pushed back his chair and stood up. "You know these people, Bob?"

"They been pointed out to me." He stood up.

"Their buddies are sure to join them. We're probably not going to have much time for plan-making. At the first twitch, we start shooting. Take the ones to your left. I'll take care of the rest."

"Yes, sir."

"Let's go."

Both men had noticed, out of the corners of their eyes, the horses lining both sides of the wide dusty street being cleared from the line of fire.

They stepped out of the cafe and stood for a moment on the boardwalk, hats pulled down low, letting their eyes adjust to the bright sunlight.

"Your play," Smoke said. "You call it."

"Rose!" Bob yelled. "Cliff! And any others who tortured and dragged Hatfield. Let's see if you got the backbone to face someone gun to gun."

Rose looked out the window of the Hangout. "Hell, it's that damn kid."

"And Smoke Jensen," he was reminded.

"Let's shoot 'em from here," Cliff suggested.

"No!" Lanny Ball stepped in. "They're callin' you out fair and square. If you ain't got the stomach for it, use the back door and cut and run . . . and don't never show your faces around here agin. I've killed a lot of men, and I've rode the owlhoot trail with a posse at my back. But I ain't never tortured nobody while they was trussed up like a hog. I may not be much but I ain't no coward."

Only a few of the other gunhawks in the large saloon murmured their agreement, but those few were the best-known and most feared of their kind. It was enough to bring the sweat out on the faces of Cliff and Rose and the two others who had taken part in the dragging and torture of Hatfield.

When open warfare was finally called by Hanks, Lanny and the few other who still possessed a modicum of honor would back-shoot and snipe at any known enemy . . . that was the way of war. But when a man called you out to face him, you faced him, eyeball to eyeball.

With a low curse, Rose checked his guns and stepped out through batwings, Cliff and the others behind him. It was straight-up noon, the sun a hot bubbling ball overhead. There were no shadows of advantage for either side.

Smoke and Bob had drifted down the boardwalk and now stood in the middle of the street, about ten feet apart, waiting.

Rose and Cliff and their two partners in torture stepped off the boardwalk and walked to the center of the street.

"Rose to my left," Bob said. "Cliff is to your right."

"Who are those other two?"

"I don't know their names."

"You two in the middle!" Smoke called, his voice carrying the two hundred odd feet between them. "You got names?"

"I'm Stanford and this here is Thomas!"

"You take Stanford, Bob. Thomas is mine." Smoke's voice was low.

"You ready?" Bob asked.

"I been ready."

Smoke and Bob started walking, their spurs softly jingling and their boots kicking up small pockets of dust with each step toward showdown.

"You boys watch this," Lanny told the others. "I doubt they's many of you ever seen Jensen in action. Don't make no mistakes about him. He's the fastest I ever seen. Some of you may want to change your minds about stayin' once you seen him."

"I do not have to watch him," Diego boasted. "I am better." He knocked back a shot of whiskey.

Several of the others in the saloon agreed.

Lanny smiled at their arrogance. Lanny might be many things, but he was not arrogant when it came to facing Smoke Jensen. He did not feel he was better than Smoke, but he did feel he was as good. When the time came for them to meet, as he knew it would, it would all come down to that first well-placed shot. Lanny knew that he would probably take lead when he faced Smoke, therefore he would delay facing him as long as possible.

"You shoulda heard that Dunk squall when we laid that hot runnin' iron agin him!" Thomas yelled over the closing distance. "He jerked and hollered like a baby. Squalled and bawled like a calf."

Neither Smoke nor Bob offered any comment in reply.

The loud silence and the artificial inner brightness consumed them both.

There was less than fifty feet between them when Rose

made his move. He never even cleared leather. None of the four managed to get clear of leather before they began dancing and jerking under the impact of .44 slugs. Thomas took two .44 slugs in the heart and died on his feet. He sat down in the dirt, on his knees, his empty hands dangling in the bloody dirt.

Bob was nearly as fast as Smoke. His .44 Remington barked again and Stanford was turned halfway around, hit in the stomach and side just as Cliff experienced twin hammer-blows to his chest from Smoke's Colt and his world began to dim. He fell to the dirt in a slack heap, seemingly powerless to do anything except cry out for his mother. He was still hollering for her when he died, the word frozen in time and space.

"Jesus Christ!" a gunslick spoke from the saloon window. He picked up his hat from the table and walked out the back door. He had a brother over in the Dakotas and concluded that this was just a dandy time to go see how his brother and his family was getting along. Hell would be better than this place.

Smoke and Bob turned and walked to the Pussycat, reloading as they walked. Inside the coolness of the saloon, they ordered beer and sat down at a table, with a clear view of the street.

Neither of them spoke for several minutes. When the barkeep had brought their pitcher of beer and two mugs and returned to his post behind the long bar, Bob picked up his mug and held it out. "For Hatfield," he said.

"I'll drink to that," Smoke said, lifting his mug.

Parnell entered the saloon, walking gingerly, sniffing disdainfully at the beery odor. Smoke waved him over and kicked out a chair for him.

"You want something to drink?" the barkeep called.

"A glass of your best wine would be nice." Parnell sat down.

"Ain't got no wine. Beer and whiskey and sodee pop."

Parnell shook his head and the bartender went back to polishing glasses, muttering under his breath about fancy-pants easterners.

Outside, in the bloody street, the barber and his helper were scurrying about, loading up the bodies. Business certainly had taken a nice turn for the better.

Smoke noticed that Parnell seemed calm enough. "Not your first time to see men die violently, Parnell?"

"No. I've seen several shootings out here. All of them as unnecessary as the one I just witnessed."

"Justice was served," Smoke told him, after taking a sip of beer.

Parnell ignored that. "Innocent bystanders could have been killed by a stray bullet."

"That is true," Smoke acknowledged. "I didn't say it was the best way to handle matters, only that justice had been served."

"And now you've taken a definite side."

"If that is the way people wish to view it, yes."

"I have a good notion to notify the army about this matter."

"And you think they'd do what, Parnell? Send a company in to keep watch? Forget it. The army's strung out too thin as it is in the West. And they'd tell you that this is a civilian matter."

"What you're saying is that this . . . ugly boil on the face of civilization must erupt before it begins the healing process?"

"That's one way of putting it, yes. Dooley Hanks has gone around the bend, Parnell. I suspect he was always borderline nuts. The beating and rape of his daughter tipped him the rest of the way. He's insane. And he's making a mistake in trusting those gunslicks he's hired. That bunch can turn on a man faster than a lightning bolt."

"And McCorkle?"

"Same with that bunch he's got. Only difference is, Cord

knows it. He's tried to make peace with Hanks . . . over the past few weeks. Hanks isn't having any of it. Cord had no choice but to hire more gunnics."

"And now . . . ?"

"We wait."

"You are aware, of course, about the rumor that it was really some of your people who beat and sexually assaulted Rita Hanks?"

"Some of that crap is being toted off the street now," Smoke reminded the schoolteacher. "When Silver Jim and Lujan hear of it—I have not mentioned it to them—the rest of it will be planted six feet under. But I think that rumor got squashed a few minutes ago."

"And if it didn't, there will be more violence."

"Why are we so different, Cousin? What I'm asking is that we spring from the same bloodlines, yet we are as different as the sun and the moon."

"Maybe, Parnell, it's because you're a dreamer. You think of the world as a place filled with good, decent, honorable men. I see the world as it really is. Maybe that's it."

Parnell pushed back his chair and stood up. He looked down at Smoke for a few seconds. "If that is the case, I would still rather have my dreams than live with blood on my hands."

"I'd rather have that blood on my hands than have it leaking out of me," Smoke countered. "Knowing that I could have possibly prevented it simply by standing my ground with a gun at the ready."

"A point well put. I shall take my leave now, gentlemen. I must see to the closing of the school for the summer."

"See you at the ranch, Parnell."

Both Smoke and Bob had lost their taste for beer. They left the nearly full pitcher of beer on the table and walked out onto the boardwalk. Most of the gunnies had left the Hangout, heading back to the D-H spread. Lanny Ball stood on the boardwalk in front of the saloon, looking across the street at Smoke.

"He's a punk," Smoke said to Bob. "But a very fast punk. I'd say he's one of the best gunslicks to be found anywhere."

"Better than you?" Bob asked, doubt in the question.

"Just as good, I'd say. And so is Jason Bright."

Lanny turned his back to them and entered the saloon.

"Another day," Smoke muttered. "But it's coming."

11

Smoke was riding the ridges early one morning, looking for any strays they might have missed. He had arranged for a buyer from the Army to come in, in order to give Fae some badly needed working capital, and planned to sell off five hundred head of cattle. He saw the flash of sunlight off a barrel just a split second before the rifle fired. Smoke threw himself out of the saddle, grabbing his Winchester as he went. The slug hit nothing but air. Grabbing the reins, Smoke crawled around a rise and picketed the horse, talking to the animal, calming it.

He wasn't sure if he was on Box T Range, or D-H Range. It would be mighty close either way. If the gunman had waited just a few more minutes, Smoke might well be dead on the ground, for he had planned to ride in a blind canyon to flush out any strays.

Working his way around the rise of earth, Smoke began to realize just how bad his situation was. He was smack in the middle of a clearing, hunkering down behind the only rise big enough to conceal a human or horse to be found within several hundred yards.

And he found out just how good the sniper was when a

hard spray of dirt slapped him in the face, followed closely by the boom of the rifle. Smoke could not tell the caliber of the rifle, but it sounded like a .44-40, probably with one of those fancy telescopes on it. He'd read about the telescopes on rifles, but had never looked through one mounted on a rifle, only seen pictures of them. They looked awkward to Smoke.

He knew one thing for an iron-clad fact: he was in trouble.

Whatever the gunman was using, he was one hell of a fine rifleman.

Hanks had cut loose his rabid dog: that rat-faced Danny Rouge.

What to do? He judged his chances of getting to the timber facing him and rejected a frontal run for it. He worked his way to his horse and removed his boots, slipping into a pair of moccasins he always carried. The fancy moccasins Ring had made were back at the house.

Smoke eased back to his skimpy cover and chanced a look, cursing as the rifle slammed again, showering him with dirt.

No question about it, he had to move, and soon. If he stayed here, and tried to wait Danny out—if it was Danny, and Smoke was certain it was—sooner or later the sniper would get the clean shot he was waiting for and Smoke would take lead. He'd been shot before and didn't like it at all. It was a very disagreeable feeling. Hurt, too.

Smoke looked around him. There was a drop-off about fifty yards behind him; a natural ditch that ran in a huge half circle, the southeast angle of the ditch running close to the timber. He studied every option available to him, and there weren't that many.

His horse would be safe, protected by the rise. If something happened to Smoke—like death—the horse would eventually pull its picket pin and return to the ranch.

Smoke checked his gun belt. All the loops were full. Returning to the horse, he stuffed a handful of cartridges into his jeans' pocket and slung his canteen after first filling his hat with water and giving the horse a good drink. Squatting down, he munched on a salt pork and biscuit sandwich, then took a long satisfying pull at the canteen. He patted the horse's neck.

"You stay put, fellow. I'll be back." *I hope,* he silently added.

Smoke took several deep breaths and took off running down the slope.

Smoke knew that shooting either uphill or downhill was tricky; bad enough with open sights. But with a telescope, trying to line up a running, twisting target would be nearly impossible.

He hoped.

The gunman started dusting Smoke's running feet, but he was hurrying his shots, and missing. But coming close enough to show Smoke how good he was with a rifle.

Smoke hurled himself in the ditch, managed to stay on his feet, then dive for the cover of the ravine's wall. Now, Danny would have to worry about which side Smoke would pop up out of. Catching his breath, Smoke began working his way around, staying close to the earthen wall. He knew the distance was still too great for his .44, and besides that, he didn't want to give away his position.

Smoke took his time, smiling as the ravine curved closer to the timber and began narrowing as the timber loomed up on both sides. When he came to a brushy spot, Smoke carefully eased out of the ravine and slipped into the timber. His jeans were a tan color, his shirt a dark brown; he would blend in well with his surroundings.

He began closing the distance. Smoke had been taught well the ways of a woodsman; Preacher had been his teacher, and there was no finer woodsman to be found than the old mountain man.

He moved carefully while still covering a lot of ground stopping often to check the terrain all around him. Danny not only looked like a big rat, the killer could move as furtively as a rodent.

Before making his run for it, Smoke had inspected the area on the ridges as carefully as possible—considering that he was being shot at—and kept Danny's position highlighted in his mind.

But Smoke was certain the sniper would have changed positions as soon as he made his run for it. Where to was the question.

He moved closer to where he had last seen the puff of smoke. When he was about a hundred yards from where he thought Danny had been firing from, Smoke made himself comfortable behind a tree and waited, every sense working overtime. He felt he could play the waiting game just as good, or better, than Danny.

He waited for a good twenty minutes, as motionless as a snake waiting for a passing rat. Then the rat he was waiting for moved.

It was only a very slight move, perhaps to brush away a pesky fly. But it was all Smoke needed. Very carefully, he raised his rifle and sighted in—he had been waiting with the hammer eared back—and pulled the trigger. The rifle slammed his shoulder and Smoke knew he had a clean miss on his target.

The gunman rolled away and came up shooting, shooting way fast. Maybe he had two rifles, one a short-barreled carbine or maybe he was shooting one of those Winchester .44-40's with the extra rear sight for greater accuracy. If that was the case, the man was still one hell of a marksman.

Smoke caught a glimpse of color that didn't seem right in the timber and triggered off two fast rounds. This time he heard a squall of pain. He fired again and something heavy fell in the woods. A trick on the man's part? Maybe. Smoke settled back and waited.

He listened to the man cough, hard, racking coughs of pain. Then the man cursed him.

"Sorry, partner," Smoke called. "You opened this dance, now you pay the fiddler."

"You Injun bastard!" the man said with a groan. "I never even heard you come up on me."

Smoke offered no reply.

"I'm hit hard, man. I got the makins but my matches is all bloody. Least you can do is give me a light."

"You're gonna have lots of fire where you're goin', partner. Just give it a few minutes."

That got Smoke another round of cussing.

But Smoke was up and moving, working his way up the ridge to a vantage point which would enable him to look down on the wounded man. If he was as hard hit as he claimed.

The man was down, all right, Smoke could see that. And the front of his shirt was badly stained with blood. But it wasn't Danny Rouge.

It was a man he'd seen riding with Cord's hired guns.

What the hell was going on?

The man had stopped his moaning and was lying flat on his back, both hands in plain sight. He was not moving.

Smoke inched his way down the ridge to just above the gunman. He was dead. He had taken a round in his guts and one in his chest. Smoke had been right: it was a .44-.40, and a brand spanking new one from the looks of it.

It took him a few minutes to find the man's horse and get him roped belly-down across the saddle. He shoved the dead man's Winchester in the boot and led the animal down the ridge to his own horse. His horse shied away from the smell of blood and death, pulling his picket pin, and Smoke had to catch him and calm him down.

Now what to do with the McCorkle rider?

If the gunnies on Cord's payroll were playing both ends against the middle, it would not be wise to just ride over there with one of their buddies draped belly-down across his saddle. On the other hand, Cord had to be notified.

Smoke headed for the Box T. On the way, he ran into

Hardrock and sent him over to the Circle Double C to get Cord.

The old gunfighter had looked close at the dead man.

"You know him, Hardrock?"

"Only by his rep. His name is Black. Call him Blackie. He's a back-shooter. Was."

"Keep this quiet at the ranch. Speak to only Cord."

Smoke rode on over to the bunkhouse and relieved the horse of its burden and saddle, letting the animal water and feed and roll. Fae came out of the house, accompanied by her brother.

Smoke explained, ending with, "Something's up. I think we'd better get set for a hard wind."

"And a violent one," Parnell added, grimacing at the smell of the dead gunny.

"You better get a gun, Parnell," Smoke told him.

"I will not have one of those abominable things in my possession!"

"Suit yourself. But I have a hunch you're gonna change your mind before this is all over."

"Never!" Parnell stood his ground.

"Uh-huh," was all Smoke said in reply to that.

Parnell's sister had plenty to say about her brother. Smoke could but stand in awe and amazement at the words rolling from her mouth.

"I don't understand this," Cord said, after viewing the dead man.

"I didn't think you would. But the big question is this: was the sniper working as a lone wolf, perhaps just to gain a reputation for killing me, or was he part of a larger scheme?"

"Involving the gunhands from both ranches?"

"Yes."

Cord's sigh was loud in the hot stillness of the Montana summer. "I don't know. My first thought is: yes. My next thought is: I've got to get Dooley to talk to me; bury the hatchet before this thing goes any further."

"Forget it," Smoke said bluntly. "The man is crazy. He's kill-crazy. I've heard he's making all sorts of wild claims and charges and plans. He's going to take over the whole area and be king. Keep a standing army of a hundred gunhawks—all sorts of wild talk."

"He's damn near got a hundred," Cord said glumly. "If what we're both thinking is true."

"Close to fifty if they all get together," Smoke added it up.

"And if I go back and fire all of those drawing fighting wages . . . ?" Cord left it hanging.

"We'd know where they stand. And you and your family would probably be safer. But if we're wrong, it would leave you wide open, 'cause for sure the gunnies you fire would just hire on at the D-H."

Cord cursed softly for a few seconds. "I'm stuck between that much-talked-about rock and a hard place."

"Whichever way you decide to go, watch your back."

"Yeah." He looked at the blanket-covered body of the sniper. "What about him?"

"We'll bury him. And don't mention it, Cord. Just let the others wonder what happened—if there really is some sort of funny business going on."

"There is some grim humor in all of this, Smoke. If this thing goes on for any length of time, both Dooley and me will go broke paying fighting wages."

"Maybe that's what the gunhands want. Maybe that's why they're hanging back, for the most part."

Cord shook his big head. It appeared that the man's hair had grayed considerably since Smoke had first seen him, only a few weeks back. "This thing's turnin' out to have more maybe's and what-if's than a simple man can understand."

Smoke motioned for Charlie and Spring to come over. "Let's get him in the ground, boys. Well away from the house and unmarked. Spring, you can have that .44-40. It's a whale of a rifle. Dusted my butt proper," he added.

"I'll go through his pockets," Charlie said. "See if there is some address for his family."

Smoke nodded. "Take his horse and turn him loose. He'll find his way back to the ranch. We'll keep the rig. That'll add even more doubt in the minds of the gunslicks." He turned to Cord. "You 'bout caught up at your place, Cord?"

"Yeah. Why?"

"Pull a couple of your best men off the range. Keep them close by at all times. When you ride, take one of them with you and let the other stay around the house."

"Good idea. But at night I don't worry much." He smiled a father's smile. "Ever'time I look up, the Moab Kid is over there sparkin' my daughter."

Smoke chuckled. "She could do worse. Beans is a good man."

"At first, I told her she couldn't see him. That made about as much impression on her as a poot in a whirlwind. I finally told her to go ahead and see him. She told me that she'd never stopped. Daughters!"

"You keepin' a tight rein on your boys?"

"I'm trying. Lord, I'm trying. I've got them working just as far away from D-H Range as possible. But they told me last night they think they're being watched. Stalked was the word Max used. That gives me an uneasy feelin'."

"It might be wise to pull them in and keep them around the house." He smiled. "Tell you what; do this: Tell the gun-hands to start workin' the range."

Cord thought about that for a moment, then burst out laughing. *"Hell,* yes! That'll make them earn their pay and keep them away from the house."

"Or it'll put them on the road."

The men shook hands and Cord rode back to his ranch. Fae came to Smoke's side. "Now what?"

"We sell some cows to the Army. And wait."

* * *

The buyer for the Army had already looked over the cattle and agreed to a price. When he returned, a couple of days after Smoke's misunderstanding with the sniper, he brought drovers with him. Smoke and the buyer settled up the paperwork and the bank draft was handed over to Fae. The two men leaned up against a corral railing and talked.

"You know about the battle looking at us in the face, don't you?" Smoke asked.

"Uh-huh. And from all indications it's gonna be a real cutter."

"What would it take to get the Army involved?"

"Not a chance, Jensen. The Army's done looked this situation over and, unofficially, and I didn't say this, they decided to stay out of it. It'd take a presidential order to get them to move in here."

It was as Smoke had guessed. All over the fast-settling West little wars were flaring up; too many for the authorities or the Army to put down, so they were letting them burn themselves out. Here, they would be on their own, whichever way it went.

The buyer and his men moved the cattle out and the range was silent.

Smoke wondered for how long?

12

"You tellin' me you're not gonna work cattle?" Cord faced the gunslick.

"I'm paid to fight, not herd cattle," Jason Bright told him.

"You're not being paid to do either one after this moment. Pack your kit and clear out. Pick up your money at the house."

Jason's eyes became cloudy with hate. "And if I don't go?"

"Then one of us is going to be on the ground."

Jason laughed. "Are you challengin' me, old man?"

Cord was far from being an old man. At forty-five he was bull-strong and leather-tough. And while he was no fast gun, there was one thing he was good at. He showed Jason a hard right fist to the jaw.

Flat on his back, his mouth leaking blood, Jason grabbed for his gun, forgetting that the hammer thong was still on it. Cord stomped the gunfighter in the belly, reached down while Jason was gasping for breath, and jerked the gun out of leather, tossing it to one side. He backed up, his big hands balled into fists.

"Catch your breath and then get up, you yellow-bellied pup. Let's see how good you are without your gun."

A dozen gunhawks ran from the bunkhouse, stopping abruptly as Cord's sons, his daughter, his wife, and four regular hands appeared from both sides of the house and on the porch, rifles and sawed-off shotguns in their hands.

"It's going to be a fair fight, boys," Alice McCorkle said, her voice strong and calm. She held a double-barreled shotgun in her hands. "Between two men; and my husband is giving Mr. Bright a good ten or fifteen years in age difference. Boys, I was nineteen when I killed my first Indian. With this very shotgun. I've killed half a dozen Indians and two outlaws in my day, and anytime any of you want to try me, just reach for a gun or try to break up this fight—whichever way it's going—and I'll spread your guts all over this yard. Then I'll make your gunslinging buddies clean up the mess."

She lifted the shotgun, pointing the twin muzzles straight at Pooch Matthews.

"Lord, lady!" Pooch hollered. "I ain't gonna interfere."

"And you'll stop anyone who does, right, Mr. Matthews?"

"Oh, yes, ma'am!"

Jason was on his feet, his eyes shiny with hate as he faced Cord.

"Clean his plow, honey," Alice told her husband.

Cord stepped in and knocked Jason spinning, the gunfighter's mouth suddenly a bloody smear. Like so many men who lived by the gun and depended on a six-shooter to get them out of any problem, Jason had never learned how to use his fists.

Cord gave him a very short and very brutal lesson in fistfighting.

Cord gave him two short hard straight rights to the stomach then followed through with a crashing left hook that knocked the gunfighter to the ground. Normally, Cord would have kicked the man in the face and ended it. No truly tough man, who fights only when hard-pushed, does not consider that "dirty" or unfair fighting, but merely a way to get the fight over with and get back to work. In reality, there is no such thing as a "fair fight." There is a winner and a loser. Period.

But in this case, Cord just wanted the fight to last a while. He was enjoying himself. And really, rather enjoying showing off for his wife a little bit.

Cord dropped his guard while so pleased with himself and Jason busted him in the mouth.

Shaking his head to clear away the sparkling confusion, for Jason was no little man, Cord settled down to a good ol'-fashioned rough-and-tumble, kick-and-gouge brawl.

The two men stood boot to boot for a moment, hammering away at each other until finally Jason had to give ground and back up from Cord's bull strength. Jason was younger and in good shape, but he had not spent a lifetime doing brutally hard work, twelve months a year, wrestling steers and digging post holes and roping and branding and breaking horses.

Jason tried to kick Cord. Cord grabbed the boot and dumped the gunhawk on the ground, on his butt. That brought several laughs from Jason's friends, all standing and watching and being very careful not to let their hands get too close to the butts of their guns.

Jason jumped to his boots, one eye closing and his nose a bloody mess, and swung at Cord. Cord grabbed the wrist and threw Jason over his hip, slamming him to the ground. This time Jason was not as swift getting to his feet.

Cord was circling, grinning at Jason, but giving the man time to clear his head and stand and fight.

But this time Jason came up with a knife he'd pulled out of his boot.

"No way, Jason!" Lodi yelled from the knot of gunslingers. "And I don't give a damn how many guns is on me. Drop that knife or I'll shoot you personal."

With a look of disgust on his face, Jason threw the knife to the ground.

Cord stepped in and smashed the man a blow to the jaw and followed that with a wicked slash to Jason's belly, doubling him over. Then he hit him twice in the face, a left and right to both sides of the man's jaw.

Jason hit the ground and did not move.

Cord walked to a water barrel by the side of the house and washed his face and soaked his aching hands for a moment. He turned and faced the gunslicks.

"I want Jason out of here within the hour. No man disobeys an order of mine. Any of you who want to stay, that's fine with me. But you'll take orders and you'll work the spread, doing whatever Del tells you to do. Make up your mind."

"Hell, Mister McCorkle . . ." a gunhawk said. He looked at the ladies. "I mean, heck. We come here to fight, not work cattle. No disrespect meant."

"None taken. But the war is over as far as I'm concerned. Any of you who want to ride out, there'll be no hard feelings and I'll have your money ready for you at the house."

All of them elected to ride.

"See me on the porch for your pay," Cord told them.

When the last gunslick had packed his warbag, collected his pay, and ridden out, Del sat down beside Cord on the front porch.

"Feels better around the place, Boss. But if them gunnies hire on with Hanks, we're gonna be hard up agin it."

"I know that, Del. Tell the men that from this day on, they'll be receiving fighting wages." He held up a warning finger. "We start nothing, Del. Nothing. We defend home range and no more. I won't ask that the men stay out of Gibson; only that they don't go in there looking for trouble. Send Willie riding over to the Box T and tell Smoke what I've done. He needs to know."

"Sure got the crap pounded out of you," Lanny said, looking at the swollen and bruised face of Jason Bright.

Jason lay on a bed in the bunkhouse of the D-H spread. "It ain't over," he mush-mouthed the words past swollen lips. "Not by no long shot, it ain't."

Dooley Hanks had eagerly hired the gunslicks. He was

already envisioning himself as king. And he wanted to kill Cord McCorkle personally. In his maddened mind, he blamed Cord for everything. He'd worked just as hard as Cord, but had never gained the respect that most people felt toward McCorkle. And this just wasn't right. King Hanks. He sure liked the way that sounded.

"It's just going to make matters worse," Hanks's wife was telling their daughter.

Rita looked up from her packing. "Papa's crazy, Mother. He's crazy as a lizard. Haven't you seen the way he slobbers on himself? The way he sits on the porch mumbling to himself? Now he's gone and hired all those other gunfighters. Worse? For who? I'll tell you who: everybody. Everything from the Hound to the Sixteenmile is going to explode."

"And you think you'll be safer over at the Box T?"

"I won't be surrounded by crazy people. I won't be under guard all the time. I'll be able to walk out of the house without being watched. Are you gong to tell on me, Mother?"

She shook her head. "No. You're a grown woman, Rita. Your father has no right to keep you a prisoner here. But I don't know how you're going to pull this off."

Rita smiled. "I'll make it, Mother." She kissed her mother's cheek and hugged her. "This can't last forever. And I won't be that far away."

"Have you considered that your father might try to bring you back by force?"

"He might if I was going to Sandi's. I don't think he'll try with Smoke Jensen."

The mother pressed some money into the daughter's hand. "You'll need this."

"Thank you, Mother. I'll pretend I'm going to bed early. Right after supper. Then I'll be gone."

After the mother had left the room, Rita laid out her clothes. Men's jeans, boots, a man's shirt. She had one of her brother's old hats and a work jacket to wear against the cold night. She picked up the scissors. Right after supper she would whack her hair short.

She believed it would work. It had to work. If she stayed around this place, she would soon be as nutty as her father and her crazy brothers.

"Peaceful," Cord said to Alice. "Like it used to be."

They sat on the front porch, enjoying the welcome coolness of early evening after the warm day.

"If it will only last, Cord."

"All we can do is try, honey. That's all a mule can do, is try."

"Tell me about this Smoke Jensen. I've met him, but never to talk with at length."

"He's a good man, I believe. A fair man. Not at all like I thought he'd be. He's one of those rare men that you look at and instantly know that this one won't push. I found that out very quickly." His last comment was dry, remembering that first day he'd yelled at Smoke, in Gibson, and the man had looked at him like he was a bug.

"It sounds like you have a lot of respect for the man."

"I do. I'd damn sure hate to have him for an enemy."

From inside the house, they heard the sounds of Sandi's giggling. She was entertaining her young man this evening, as she did almost every evening. The Moab Kid was fast becoming a fixture around the place.

Cord and Alice sat quietly, smiling as they both recalled their own courting days.

Smoke leaned against a corral railing and thought about Sally and the babies. He missed them terribly. One part of him wanted this little war to come to a head so he could go home. But another part of him knew that when it did start, there would be a lot of people who would never go home . . . except for six feet of earth. And he might well be one of them.

Charlie Starr walked up and the men stood in silence for

a moment, enjoying the peaceful evening. Charlie was the first to break the silence.

"I'd like to have seen that fight 'tween Cord and Jason."

Smoke smiled, then the smile faded. "Jason won't ever forget it, though. The next time he sees Cord, Cord better have a gun in his hand."

"True."

They stood in silence for another few moments. Both men rolled an after-supper cigarette and lit up.

"You were in deep thought when I walked up, Smoke. What's on your mind?"

"Oh, I had a half dozen thoughts going, Charlie. I was thinking about my wife and our babies, how much I miss them. And, I was thinking just what it's going to take to blow the lid off this situation here."

"What don't concern me as much as when."

"Tonight."

Charlie looked at him. "What are you, one of them fortune-tellers?"

"I feel it in my guts, Charlie. And don't tell me you never jumped out of a saddle or spun and drew on a hunch."

"Plenty o' times. Saved my bacon on more than one occasion, too. That's what you're feelin'?"

"That's it." Smoke dropped his cigarette butt and ground it out with the heel of his boot. "It's always something you least expect, too."

"I grant you that for a fact. Like that time down in Taos this here woman crawled up in bed with me. Like to have scared the longhandles right off of me. Wanted me to save her from her husband. Didn't have a stitch on. I tell you what, that shook me plum down to my toenails."

"Did you save her?"

Charlie chuckled softly. "Yeah. 'Bout two hours later. I've topped off horses that wasn't as wild as she was."

13

Rita had cropped her hair short, hating to do it, but she had always been a tomboy and, besides, it would grow back. She had turned off the lamp and now she listened at her bedroom door for a moment, hearing the low murmur of her mother talking to her father. The front door squeaked open and soon the sound of the porch swing reached her. She picked up her valise and swung out the window, dropping the few feet to the ground. She remained still for a long moment, checking all around her. She knew from watching and planning this that her guards were not on duty after nine o'clock at night. It had never occurred to her father that his daughter would attempt to run away.

Sorry, Pa, Rita thought. But I won't be treated like a prisoner.

Rita slipped away from the house and past the corral and barn. She almost ran right into a cowboy returning from the outhouse but saw him in time to duck into the shadows. He walked past her, his galluses hanging down past his knees. The door to the bunkhouse opened, flooding a small area with lamplight.

"Shut the damn door, Harry!" a man called.

The door closed, the area once more darkened. But something primeval touched Rita with an invisible warning. She remained where she was, squatting down in her jeans.

"It's clear," a man's voice said.

Rita recognized it as belonging to the shifty-eyed gunslinger called Park. And the men were only a few yards away.

Rita remembered something else, too: she had heard that voice before. The sudden memory was as hot and violent as the act that afternoon. While she was being raped.

Fury and cold hate filled the young woman. Her father's own men had done that to her. She thought about returning to the house and telling her father. She immediately rejected that. She had no proof. And her father would take one look at her close-cropped hair and lock her up tight, with twenty-four-hour guards.

She touched the short-barreled .44 tucked behind her belt. She was good with it, and wanted very badly to haul it out and start banging.

She fought that feeling and waited, listening.

"When?" the other man asked.

"Keep your britches on," Park said. "Lanny gives the orders around here. But it'll be soon, he tole me so hisself."

"I'd like to take my britches off with Rita agin," the mystery man said with a rough chuckle.

And I'd like to stick this pistol . . . Rita mentally brushed away the very ugly thought. But it was a satisfying thought.

"You reckon Hanks is so stupid he don't realize what his boys is up to?"

"He's nuts. He don't realize them crazy boys of his'n would kill him right now if they thought they could get away with it."

Rita crouched in the darkness and wanted to cry. Not for herself or for her father—he had made the boys what they were today, simply by being himself—but for her mother. She deserved so much better.

"It better be soon, 'cause the boys is gettin' restless."

"It'll be soon. But we gotta do it all at once. All three ranches. There can't be no survivors to tell about it. They got to be kilt and buried all in one night. We can torture the widows till they sign over the spreads to us."

"We gonna keep the young wimmen alive for a time, ain't we? 'Specially that Fae Jensen. I want her. I want to show her a shine or two."

"I don't know. Chancy. Maybe too chancy. It's all up to Jason and Lanny."

"Them young wimmen would bring a pretty penny south of the border."

"Transport them females a thousand miles! You're nuts, Hartley."

"It was jist a thought."

"A bad one. Man, just think of it: the whole area controlled by us. Thousands and thousands of acres, thousands of cattle. We could be respectable, and you want to mess it all up because of some swishy skirts. Sometimes I wonder about you, Hartley."

"I'm sorry. I won't bring it up no more."

The men walked off, splitting up before entering the bunkhouse.

Rita felt sick to her stomach; wanted to upchuck. Fought it back. Now more than ever, she had to make it to the Box T. She waited and looked around her, carefully inspecting each dark pocket around the ranch, the barn and the bunkhouse. She stood up and moved out, silently praying she wouldn't be spotted.

Once clear of the ranch complex, Rita began to breathe a little easier. She slung her valise by a strap and could move easier with it over her shoulder. She headed southwest, toward the Box T.

The restlessness of the horses awakened Smoke. He looked at his pocket watch. Four o'clock. Time to get up anyway. But the actions of the horses bothered him. Dressed and armed, he stepped out of the ranch house just as the bunkhouse door opened and Lujan stepped out, followed by the other men. Smoke met them in the yard. They all carried rifles.

"Spread out," Smoke told them. "Let's find out what's spooking the horses."

"Hello the ranch!" the voice came out of the darkness. A female voice.

"Come on in," Smoke returned the call. "Sing out!"

"Rita Hanks. I slipped away from the house about eight o'clock last night. You might not recognize me, 'cause I cut off my hair to try to fool anyone who might see me."

"Come on in, Rita," Smoke told her, then turned to Beans. "Wake up those in the house; if they're not already awake. Get some coffee going. As soon as Hanks finds out his girl is gone, we're going to have problems.

She was limping from her long walk, and she was tired, but still could not conceal her happiness at finally being free of her father. Over coffee and bacon and eggs, she told her story while Fae and Parnell and all the others gathered around in the big house and listened.

When she was finished, she slumped in her chair, exhausted.

"I wondered why the gunnies were holding back," Hardrock said. "This tells it all."

"Yes," Lujan said. "But I don't think they came in here with that in mind. No one ever approached me with any such scheme. And both sides offered me fighting wages."

"I think this plan was just recently hatched, after several others failed. Rita's attack did not produce the desired effect; Hanks didn't attack Cord. Blackie failed to kill me. So they came up with this plan."

Smoke looked at Rita. The young woman was asleep, her head on the table.

"I'll get her to bed," Fae said. "You boys start chowing down. I think it's going to be a very long day."

"Yeah," Beans agreed. "'Cause come daylight, Hanks and his boys are gonna be on the prowl. If this day don't produce some shootin', my name ain't Bainbridge."

Silver Jim looked at him and blinked. "Bainbridge! No wonder they call you Beans. Bainbridge!"

Hanks knocked his wife sprawling, backhanding her. "You knew, damn you!" he yelled at her. "You helped her, didn't you? Don't lie to me, woman. You and Rita snuck around behind my back and planned all this."

Liz slowly got to her feet. A thin trickle of blood leaked from one corner of her mouth. She defiantly stood her ground. "I knew she was planning to leave, yes. But I didn't know when or how. You've changed, Dooley. Changed into some sort of a madman."

That got her another blow. She fell back against the wall and managed to grab the back of a chair and steady herself. She stared at her husband as she wiped her bloody mouth with the back of her hand.

"Where'd she go?" Hanks yelled the question. "Naw!" Dooley waved it off. "You don't have to tell me. I know. She went over to Cord's place, didn't she?"

"No, she didn't," Liz's voice had calmed, but her mouth hurt her when she spoke.

"You a damn liar!" Dooley raged. "A damn frog-eyed liar. There ain't no other place she could have gone."

Outside, just off the porch, Lanny was listening to the ravings.

"This might throw a kink into things," Park spoke softly.

"Maybe not. This might be a way to get rid of Cord and his boys in a way that even if the law was to come in, they'd call it a fair shootin'. Man takes another man's kid in without the father's permission, that's a shootin' offense."

"I hadn't thought of that. You right."

"If she did go to the Double Circle C," Lanny added.

"Where else would she go? Her and that damn uppity Sandi McCorkle is good friends."

"Rita is no fool. She just might have gone over to the

Box T. But we won't mention that. Just let Hanks play it his way."

"I'm gonna tell you something, woman," Hanks pointed a blunt finger at his wife. "I find out you been lyin' to me, I'm gonna give you a hidin' that you'll remember the rest of your life."

"That would be like you," she told him. "Whatever you don't understand you destroy."

"What the hell does that mean?" Dooley screamed at her, slobber leaking out of his mouth, dribbling onto his shirt and vest.

She turned her back to him and started to leave the room.

"Don't you turn your back to me, woman! I done put up with just about all I'm gonna take from you."

She stopped and turned slowly. "What are you going to do, Dooley? Beat me? Kill me? It doesn't make any difference. Love just didn't die a long time ago. Your hatred killed it. Your hatred, your obsession with power. You allowed our sons to grow up as nothing more than ignorant savages. You . . ."

"Shut up, shut up, shut up!" Dooley screamed, spittle flying from his mouth. "Lies, all lies, woman. I'm ridin' to get my kid back. And when I get her back here, I'm gonna take a buggy whip to her backside. That's something I shoulda done a long time ago. And I just might take it in my head to use the same whip on you."

Liz stared hard at him. "If you ever hit me again, Dooley. I'll kill you." Dooley recoiled as if struck with those words. "And the same goes for Rita. But you've lost her. She'll never come back here; don't worry about that. I'll tell you where she's gone, Dooley. She's gone to the Box T."

"Lies. More lies from you. Cord planned with you all on this, and you know it. He's conspired agin me ever since we come into this area. He'd do anything to get at me. He's jealous of me."

His wife openly laughed at that.

Dooley's face reddened and he took a step toward his

wife, his hand raised. She backed up and picked up a poker from the fireplace.

"You were warned," she told him. "You try to hit me and I'll bash your head in."

He stood and cursed her until he ran out of breath. But she would not lower the poker and even in his maddened state he knew better than to push his luck.

"I'll deal with you later," he said, then turned and stalked out the door.

She leaned against the wall, breathing heavily, listening to him holler for his men to saddle up and get ready to ride. She did not put down the poker as long as he was on the front porch. Only when she heard him mount up and the thunder of hooves pound away did she lower the poker and replace it in the set on the hearth.

She walked outside to stand on the porch, waiting for the dust to settle from the fast-riding men. She noticed Gage and several of the other hands had not ridden with her husband.

The foreman walked over to the porch and looked up at the still attractive woman. There was open disgust in his eyes as he took in the bruises on her face.

"I ain't got no use atall for a man who hits a woman," Gage said.

"That's not the man I married, Gage."

"Yeah, it is, Liz. It's the same man I been knowin' for years. You just been deliberately blind over the years, that's all."

"Maybe so, Gage." She sighed. She knew, of course, that Gage had been in love with her for a long, long time. And her feelings toward the foreman had been steadily growing stronger with time. She cut her eyes toward him. "You're not riding with him?"

"Me and the boys punch cows, Liz. I made that plain to him the other day. He still has enough sense about him to know that someone has to work the spread."

"What would you say if I told you I was going to leave him?"

"Then me and you would strike out together, Liz."

She smiled. "And do what, Gage?"

"Get married. Start us a little spread a long ways from here."

"I'm a married woman, Gage. It's not proper to talk to a married woman like that."

"I don't see you turnin' around and walkin' off, Liz."

She looked hard at him. "Mister Hanks and I will be sharing separate bedrooms from now on, Gage. I would appreciate if you would stay close as much as possible."

"I would consider that an honor, Liz."

"Would you like to have some coffee, Gage?"

"I shore would."

"Make yourself comfortable on the porch, Gage. I'll go freshen up and hotten the coffee. I won't be a minute."

"Take your time, Liz. I'll be here."

She smiled. Her hair was graying and there were lines in her face. But to the foreman, she was as beautiful as the first day he'd laid eyes on her. "I'm counting on that, Gage."

14

Cord heard the riders coming long before he or any of his men could spot them. It was a distant thunder growing louder with each heartbeat.

"Load up the guns, Mother," he told his wife. "I believe it's time." He walked to the dinner bell on the porch and rang it loudly, over and over. Del and four hands came on the run, carrying rifles, pistols belted around them.

"Stand with me on the porch, boys. Mother, get your shotgun and take the upstairs."

"I'm up here with a rifle Daddy!" Sandi called.

"Good girl."

Rifles were loaded to capacity. Pistols checked. A couple of shotguns were loaded up and placed against the porch railing.

Thirty riders came hammering past the gate and up to the picket fence around the ranch house, Hanks in the lead.

"I don't appreciate this, Dooley," Cord raised his voice. "You got no call to come highballin' up to my place."

"I got plenty of call, Cord. Where's my daughter?"

Cord blinked. "How the hell do I know? I haven't seen her in days."

"You a damn liar, McCorkle!"

Cord unbuckled his gun belt and handed it to Dell. He swung his eyes back to Hanks. "You'll not come on my property and call me names, Dooley. Git out of that saddle and let's settle this feud man to man."

"Goddamn you! I want my daughter!"

"I ain't got your daughter! But what I will have is your apology for callin' me a liar."

"When hell freezes over, McCorkle!"

Two upstairs windows were opened. A shotgun and a rifle poked out. Sandi's voice said, "The first man to reach for a gun, I kill Lanny Ball." The sound of a hammer being eared back was very plain.

The sounds of twin hammers on a double-barreled shotgun was just as plain. "And I blow the two Mexicans out of the saddle," Alice spoke.

Diego and Pablo froze in their saddles.

"Dooley," Cord's voice was calm. "Would you like to step down and have some coffee with me? You can inspect the house and the barn and the bunkhouse . . . after you tell me your anger overrode your good sense when callin' me a liar."

Hanks's eyes cleared for a moment. Then he looked confused. "I know you ain't no liar, Cord. But where'd she go?" There was a pleading note in the man's voice.

"I don't know, Dooley. I didn't even know she was gone."

But the moment was gone, and Jason Bright and Lanny Ball and most of the others knew it. There would be no gunfire this day.

"The Box T," Dooley said. "Liz wasn't lyin'."

"Dooley," Cord said, "You go over there a-smokin', and if she is there, she's liable to catch a bullet. 'Cause Smoke Jensen and them others are gonna start throwin' lead just as soon you come into range."

"She's my daughter, dammit, Cord!" Some of the madness reappeared.

"She's also a grown woman," Alice called from the second floor.

Hanks slumped in his saddle. The fire had left him . . . for the moment. "She don't want my hearth and home, she can stay gone. I don't have no daughter no more." He looked at Cord. "It ain't over, Cord. Not between us. The time just ain't right. There'll be another day."

"Why, Dooley? Tell me that. Your spread is just as big as mine. I made peace with Fae Jensen. She ain't botherin' nobody. Let's us bury the hatchet and be friends. Then you can fire these gunslicks and we can get on with livin'."

Dooley shook his head. "Too late, Cord. It's just too late." He wheeled his horse and rode off, the gunnies following.

"Did you see his eyes, Boss?" Willie asked. "The man is plumb loco."

"I'm afraid you're right, Willie. Question is, when will it take control of him . . . or rather, when will he lose control?"

"One thing for certain, Boss," Del said. "When he does go total nuts, we're all going to be right smack dab in the big fat middle of it."

"Something is rotten," Cord spoke softly. "Something is wrong with this whole setup."

"Riders coming, Boss," Fitz said.

As the dot on the landscape grew larger, Del squinted his eyes. "Smoke Jensen and the Moab Kid."

Sandi smiled and Alice said, "I'll make fresh coffee."

Beans sniffed the air. "Lots of dust in the air."

"I think Cord's had some visitors," Smoke replied. "Look at the hands gathered around the house."

The men swung down and looped the reins around the hitchrail. Cord shook hands with them both and introduced Smoke to those punchers he had not met.

"Fancy seeing you, Beans," Cord said, a twinkle in his eyes. "It's been so long since you've come callin'. Hours, at least."

Beans just grinned.

"Gather your men, Cord," Smoke told the man. "This is something that everybody should hear."

Cord's three sons had just ridden in. His other four

punchers were out on the range. Everybody gathered around on the porch and listened as Smoke related what Rita had told him.

"Damn!" Max summed it up, then glanced at his mother, who was giving him a warning look for the use of profanity.

"Let's kick it around," Smoke said. "Anybody got any suggestions?"

"Take it to them 'fore they do it to us," Corgill said.

"No proof," Cord said. "Only the word of Rita and she didn't even see the men; just heard them talkin'."

"If we don't do something," Cal said, "we're just gonna be open targets, and they'll pick us off one at a time."

Cord shook his head. "Maybe, but I don't think so. I think they got to do everything all at once. At night. If what Rita says is true—and I ain't got no reason to doubt it—they'll split their people and hit us at the same time. And they can't leave any survivors."

"I've got people bunching the cattle and moving them to high graze," Smoke said. "They'll scatter some, but they can be rounded up. From now on, we stay close to the ranch house."

Cord nodded his head and looked at Willie. "Ride on out Willie. Tell the boys to start moving them up toward summer graze. Get as much as you can done, and then you boys get on back here. We're gonna lose some to rustlers, for a fact. But it's either that or we all die spread out." He glanced at Smoke. "When do you think they'll hit us?"

Smoke shook his head. "Tonight. Next week. Next month. No way of knowing."

Cord did some fancy cussing, while his wife listened and looked on with a disapproving frown on her face. "We may end up taking to the hills and fighting defensively."

"I'm thinking that we will," Smoke agreed.

"You mean leave the house?" Sandi protested. "But they'll just move in!"

"Can't be helped, girl," her father told her. "We can always clean up and rebuild."

"Or just go on over and kill Dooley Hanks," Rock McCorkle said grimly.

"Rock!" his mother admonished.

Cord put a big hand on her shoulder. "It may come to that, Alice. God help me, I don't want it, but we may have no choice in the matter."

"Here comes Jake," Del said. "And he's a-foggin' it."

The puncher slowed up as he approached the house, to keep the dust down, and walked his horse up to the main house, dismounting.

"What's up, Jake?" the foreman asked.

"I just watched about fifteen guys cut across our range comin' from the northeast. Hardcases, ever' one of them. They was headin' toward Gibson."

Alice handed the puncher a cup of coffee and a biscuit, then looked at her husband. He wore an increasingly grim expression.

"The damn easterners talk about law and order," Cord said. "Well, where is it when it comes down to the nut-cuttin'?"

Smoke pulled out his right hand Colt and held it up for all to see. "Right here, Cord. Right here."

"The Cat Jennings gang," Charlie said. He had been to town and back while Smoke was talking with the men and women of the Double Circle C. "He's been up in Canada raisin' Cain for the past few years."

"This here thing is shapin' up to be a power play," Pistol said.

"Yeah," Lujan agreed. "With us right in the middle of it."

"Damn near seventy gunslingers," Silver Jim mused. "And the most we can muster is twenty, and that's stretchin' it."

"One thing about it," Smoke stuck some small humor into a grim situation, "we've sure taken the strain off of a lot of other communities in the West."

"Yeah," Hardrock agreed. "Ever' outlaw and two-bit pistol-handler from five states has done converged on us. And it wouldn't do a bit of good to wire for the law. No badge-toter in his right mind would stick his face into this situation."

"Must be at least a quarter of a million dollars worth of reward money hanging over them boys' heads," Silver Jim said. "And that's something to think about."

"Yeah, it shore is," Pistol said. "Why, with just a little dab of that money, we could retire, boys." There was a twinkle in his hard eyes.

"Now, wait just a minute," Smoke said.

The old gunfighters ignored him. "You know what we could do," Charlie said. "We could start us up a retirement place for old gunslingers and mountain men."

"You guys are crazy!" Lujan blurted out the words. "You are becoming senile!"

"What's that mean?" Hardrock asked.

"It means we ain't responsible for our actions," Charlie told him.

"That's probably true," Hardrock agreed. "If we had any sense, none of us would be here." He looked at Lujan. "And that goes for you, too."

Lujan couldn't argue with that.

"Cat backed up from me a couple of times," Charlie said. "This time, I think I'll force his hand."

Smoke and Beans had stepped back, letting the men talk it out.

"Peck and Nappy is gonna be with him, for sure," Pistol said. "That damn Nappy got lead in a friend of mine one time. I been lookin' for him for ten years. And that Peck is just a plain no-good."

"No-Count George Victor's got ten thousand on his head," Silver Jim mused. "And he don't like me atall."

"Insane old men!" Lujan muttered.

"Well, I damn shore ain't gonna try to stop them." Beans made that very clear. "I ain't real sure I could take any of them . . . even if I was a mind to," he added.

Smoke stepped back in. "You boys ride for the Box T," he reminded them. "You took the lady's money to ride for the brand. Not to go off head-hunting. You all are needed here. Now when the shootin' starts, speaking for myself, you can have all the reward money."

"Same for me," Beans and Lujan agreed.

"Aw, hell, Smoke," Charlie said, a bit sheepishly. "We was just flappin' our gums. You know we're stickin' right here. But Cat Jennings is mine."

"And Peck and Nappy belong to me." Pistol's tone told them all to stand clear when grabbin'-iron time came.

"And No-Count George Victor is gonna be lookin' straight at me when I fill his belly full of lead," Silver Jim said.

Hardrock said, "Three-Fingers Kerman and Fulton kilt a pal of mine over to Deadwood some years back. Back-shot him. I didn't take kindly to that. So them two belongs to me."

"You men are incorrigible!" Parnell finally spoke.

"Damn right," Pistol said.

"Whatever the hell that means," Hardrock muttered.

Fae walked out to join them. "Rita's up, having breakfast."

"How's she feeling?" Smoke asked.

"Aside from some sore feet—she's not used to walking in men's boots—she's doing all right. I think she's pretty well resigned that her father is around the bend. I told her what you said about Dooley saying he no longer had a daughter. It hurt her. But not as much as I thought it would. I think she's more concerned about her mother."

"She should be. There is no telling what that crazy bastard is liable to do," Silver Jim summed it up.

15

He had looked into their bedroom and came stomping out. "Where is all your clothes, Liz?" Dooley demanded, his voice hard.

"I moved them out. I no longer feel I am married to you, Dooley."

"You don't . . . *what?*"

"I don't love you anymore. I haven't for a long time. Years. I cringe when you touch me. I . . ."

He jumped at her and backhanded her, knocking her against a wall. She held back a yelp of pain. She didn't want Gage to come storming in, because she knew that she had absolutely no rights as a married woman. She owned nothing. Could not vote. And in a court of law, her husband's word was next to God's. And if Gage were to kill Dooley during a domestic squabble, he would hang.

She leaned against the wall, staring at Dooley as the front door opened, her sons stomping in.

Conrad, the youngest of the boys, grinned at her. "You havin' a good time while Pa's usin' you for a punchin' bag?"

Sonny and Bud laughed.

Dooley grabbed Liz by the arm and flung her toward the

kitchen. "Git in there and fix me some dinner. I don't wanna hear no more mouth from you."

Liz walked toward the kitchen, her back straight. I won't put up with this any longer, she vowed. I'll follow Rita, just as quickly as I can.

A plan jumped into her head and she smiled at the thought. It might work. It just might work.

She began putting together dinner and working out the plan.

It all depended on what Gage said. And the other hands.

She had gone out to gather eggs in the henhouse. Dooley and her sons had left the house without telling her where they were riding off to. As usual. All the hired guns were in town, drinking. Gage had ambled over, as he always did, to carry her basket. She told him of her plan.

"I like it, Liz. Go in the house and pack a few things while ever'body is gone. I'll get the boys."

She stared at him, wide-eyed. "You mean . . . ?"

"Right now, Liz. Let's get gone from this crazy house 'fore Dooley gets back. Move, Liz!"

She went one way and Gage trotted to the bunkhouse. He sent the only rider in the bunkhouse out to tell the others to meet him at the McCorkle ranch.

"We quittin', Gage?"

"I am."

"I'm with you. And so will the others. Hep me pack up their stuff, will you. I'll tote it to them on a packhorse. How about ol' Cook?"

"He'll go wherever Liz goes. He came out here with them."

The hand cut his eyes at the foreman and grinned. "Ahh! OK, Gage."

Working frantically, the two men stuffed everything they could find into canvas and lashed it on a packhorse. "I'll tell Cook to hightail it. Move, Les. See you at the Circle Double C."

Ol' Cook was right behind Les. He packed up his warbag

and swung into the saddle just as Liz was coming out of the house, a satchel in her hand.

"You want me to hitch up the buckboard, Gage?"

"No time, Cook."

"War, how's she fixin' to ride then? We ain't got no side-saddle rigs."

"Astride. I done saddled her a horse."

Ol' Cook rolled his eyes. "Astride! Lord have mercy! Them sufferingetts is gonna be the downfall of us all." He galloped out.

Gage led her horse over to the porch. "Turn your head, Gage. I don't quite know how I'm going to do this. I have never sat astride in my life."

Gage turned his head.

"You may look now, Gage," she told him.

He had guessed at the stirrup length and got it right. She sure had a pretty ankle. "Hang on, Liz. We got some rough country and some hard ridin' to do."

"Wherever you ride, I'll be with you," she told him, adding, "Darling."

Gage blushed all the way down to his holey socks.

"I'll kill ever' goddamn one of them!" Dooley screamed. "I'll stake that damn Gage out over an anthill and listen to him scream." Dooley cussed until he was red-faced and out of breath.

"This ain't good," Jason said. "I'm beginnin' to think we're snake-bit."

"I don't know." Lanny scratched his jaw. "It gives the other side a few more guns, is all."

"Seven more guns."

"No sweat."

Inside the house, Dooley was still ranting and cussing and roaring about what he was going to do to Gage and to his wife. The men outside heard something crash against a wall. Dooley had picked up a vase and shattered it.

The sons were leaning against a hitchrail, giggling and scratching themselves.

"Them boys," Jason pointed out, "is as goofy as their dad."

"And just as dangerous," Lanny added. "Don't sell them short. They're all cat-quick with a gun."

"About the boys . . . ?"

"We'll just kill them when we've taken the ranches."

"Of course you can stay here, Liz," Alice told her. "And stop saying it will be a bother." She smiled. "You and Gage. I'm so happy for you."

"If we survive this," Liz put a verbal damper on the other woman's joy.

"We'll survive it. Oh, Liz!" She took the woman's hands into hers. "Do you remember how it was when we first settled here? Those first few years before all the hard feelings began. We fought outlaws and Indians and were friends. Then . . ." She bit back the words.

"I know. I've tried to convince myself it wasn't true. But it was and is. Even more so now. Dooley began to change. Maybe he was always mad; I don't know. I know only that I love Gage and have for a long, long time. From a distance," she quickly added. "I just feel like a great weight has been lifted from me."

"You rest for a while. I'll get supper started."

"Pish-posh! I'm not tired. And I want to do my share here. Come on. I've got a recipe for cinnamon apple pie that'll have Cord groaning."

Laughing, the two women walked to the kitchen.

Outside the big house, Cord briefed Gage and the other men from the D-H about the outlaws' plans.

Gage shuddered. "Kill the women! God, what a bunch of no-goods. Well, we got out of that snake pit just in time. Cord, me, and the boys will hep your crew bunch the cattle." He cut his eyes to Del. "You 'member that box canyon over towards Spitter Crick?"

Del nodded. "Yeah. It's got good graze and water that'll keep 'em for several weeks. That's a good idea. We'll get started first thing in the morning. Smoke said him and his boys will be over at first light to hep out. They done got their cattle bunched and safe as they could make 'em."

"I sent a rider over to tell them about y'all," Cord told him. "I 'magine Rita will be comin' over to stay with her momma. Smoke's already makin' plans to vacate the Box T. We both figure that'll be the first spread Dooley will hit, and Smoke ain't got the men to defend it agin seventy or more men."

"No, but them men that he's got was shore born with the bark on," Gage replied. "I'd shore hate to be in that first bunch that tackles 'em."

"They'll cut the odds down some, for sure," Del said. "You know," he reminisced, "I growed up hearin' stories about Pistol Le Roux and Hardrock and Silver Jim . . . and Charlie Starr. Lord, Lord! Till Smoke Jensen come along, I reckon he was the most famous gun-handler in all the West. Hardrock and Pistol and Silver Jim . . . why, them men must be nigh on seventy years old. But they still tough as wang leather and mean as cornered grizzlies. It just come to me that we're lookin' at history here."

"Let's just hope that we all live to read about it," Cord said drily.

"I think they'll try us tonight, Smoke," Charlie said. "My old bones is talkin' to me."

"I agree with you."

"I done tossed my blankets over yonder in that stand of trees," Pistol said, pointing. "I never did like to sleep all cooped up noways. I like to look at the stars."

"We'll all stay clear of the house tonight," Smoke said. "Fill your pockets with ammunition, boys, and don't take your boots off. I think tonight is gonna be interesting."

Bob was in the loft of the barn. Spring and Pat stayed in the bunkhouse, both of them armed with rifles. Lujan was in the barn, lower level. Pistol, Silver Jim, Charlie, and Hardrock were spread around the house. Smoke elected to stay close to the now-empty corral. The horses had been moved away to a little draw; Ring was with them. Beans had slipped into moccasins and was roaming. Parnell was in the house with the women. Rita and Fae were armed with rifles. Parnell refused to take a gun.

About a quarter of a mile from the ranch complex, Beans knelt down in the road and put his ear to the hard-packed earth. He smiled grimly, then stood up. "Coming!" he shouted to Silver Jim, who was the closest to him. "Sounds like a bunch of them, too."

Silver Jim relayed the message and then settled in, earing back the hammer on his Winchester.

Beans was the first to see the flames from the torches the gunnies carried. "They're gonna try to burn us out!" he yelled.

Then the hard-riding outlaw gunslingers were thundering past Beans's position. At almost point-blank range, Beans emptied his six-shooter into the mass of riders, then holstered his pistol and picked up his Winchester. He put five fast rounds into the outlaws, then shifted positions when the lead started flying around him.

Beans knew he'd hit at least three of the riders, and two of them were hard hit and on the ground.

Silver Jim got three clean shots off, with one outlaw on the ground and the other two just hanging on, gripping the saddle horn. Not dead, but out of action.

Bob took his time with his Winchester and emptied two saddles before Lujan hollered, "Another bunch coming behind us, Bob. Shift to the rear."

Smoke stood by the corral, a dim figure in the torchlit night, with both hands full of long-barreled Colts, and picked his targets. His aim was deadly true. He knocked two to the ground and knew he'd hit several more before being forced to run for cover.

A rider threw his torch through a window—only two windows were not shuttered, front and back, giving the women a place to fire from—and the torch landed on the couch. The couch burst into flames and Parnell went to work with buckets of water already filled against such an action. He managed to keep the fire confined to the couch.

The barn was not so lucky. While Lujan and Bob were fighting at the rear of the barn, a rider tossed a torch into the hay loft. That action got him a bullet from Smoke that cut his spine and shattered his heart, but there was no saving the barn. Bob and Lujan fought inside until it became too difficult to see and breathe and they had to run for cover amid a hail of lead.

The small band of defenders of the Box T were now having to fight against range-robbers on all sides. One outlaw made the mistake of finding the horses and thinking he was going to set them free.

One second he was in the saddle, the next second he was on the ground. The last thing he would remember hearing on this earth was a deep voice rumbling, "I do not like people who are mean to nice people."

Huge hands clamped around the man's head and with one quick jerk, Ring broke the gunny's neck and tossed him to one side, his head flopping from side to side. Ring got the rifle from the outlaw's saddle boot, made sure it was full, and waited for some more action.

The area around the ranch house was now brightly lighted from the flaming barn; too bright for the outlaws' taste, for the accuracy of the defenders was more than they had counted on.

"Let's go!" came the shout.

No one bothered to fire at or pursue the outlaws. All ran into the yard to form a bucket line to wet down the roof of the house so sparks from the burning barn could not set it on fire. The men worked frantically, for already there were smouldering spots on the roof.

It did not take long for the barn to go; soon there was nothing left except a huge mound of glowing coals.

The men sat down on the ground where they were, all of them suddenly tired as the adrenaline had slowed.

"Fae!" Parnell said. "Give up this madness. Let us leave this barbaric country and return to civilization."

Fae walked toward him, her gloved hands balled into fists. Her face was sooty and her short hair disheveled and she was mad clear through. When she got within swinging distance she let him have it, giving him five in the mouth and dropping him to the ground.

Parnell lay flat on his butt, blood leaking out of a busted lip looking up at his baby sister. He wore a hurt expression on his face. He blinked and said, "I suppose, Sister, that is your quaint way of saying no?"

Smoke and the others burst out laughing. The laughter spread and soon Fae and Rita were laughing. No one paid any attention to the bodies littering the yard and the areas all around the ranch complex.

Parnell sat up and rubbed his jaw. "I, for one, fail to see the humor in this grotesque situation."

That caused another round of laughter. They were still laughing as Ring walked up, leading several horses, one with the body of the neck-broke outlaw draped across the saddle.

"Crazy folks," Ring said. "But nice folks."

16

"This ain't worth a damn!" Jason summed up the night's action. "Nine dead and six wounded. Couple more nights like this and we might as well hang it up."

"Shore got to change our plans," Lanny agreed. "We should have hit McCorkle first."

"Well, you can bet they all is gonna be on the alert after this night," No-Count Victor said. "Hell, let's just go on and kill that stupid Dooley and his sons and settle for this spread."

"No!" Lanny stopped that quick. "It's got to be the whole bag or nothing. Think about it. You think Cord and Smoke would let us stay in this area, on this spread? And what about Dooley's wife; you forgettin' about her?"

"I reckon so," Cat said sullenly.

Both Jason and Lanny had been admiring Cat's matched guns since he'd arrived. They were silver-plated, scroll-engraved, with ivory grips. Smith & Wesson .44's, top break for easier loading. They both coveted Cat's guns. Both of them had thought, more than once: When this is over, I'll kill him and take them fancy guns.

Honor extended only so far.

A wounded man moaned in restless unconsciousness on

his bloody bunk. Before he had passed out, he had drunk a full bottle of laudanum to ease the pain in his chest. Pink froth was bubbling past his lips. Lung shot, and all knew he wasn't going to make it.

"You want me to shoot him, Jason?" Nappy asked.

"Naw. He'll be gone in a few hours. If he's still alive come the mornin', we'll put a piller over his face and end it thataway. It won't make so much noise."

Smoke stepped out before first light, carrying his rifle, loaded full. It had come to him during the night, and if it came to the range-robbers, the small band of defenders would be in trouble. They could starve them out; a few well-placed snipers could keep them pinned down for days. He hated to tell Fae, but Smoke felt it would be best to desert the ranch and head for Cord's place. If they stayed here, it was only a matter of time before they were overrun.

He looked around the darkness. Before turning in, they had stacked the bodies of the outlaws against a wall of a ravine. At first light, they would go through their pockets in search of any clues to family or friends. They would then bury the men by collapsing dirt over the stiffening bodies. There would be no markers.

Smoke smelled the aroma of coffee coming from the bunkhouse, the good odors just barely overriding the smell of charred wood from the remnants of the barn. Smoke walked to the bunkhouse, faint lanternlight shining through the windows.

"Comin' in," he announced just before reaching the door.

"Come on," ol' Spring called. "Got hot coffee and hard biscuits."

Before Smoke poured his first cup of coffee of the day, he noticed the men had already packed their warbags and rolled their slim mattresses.

"You boys read my mind, hey?"

"Figured you'd be wantin' to pull out this mornin',"

Hardrock said, gumming a biscuit to soften it. He had perhaps four teeth left in his mouth. "What about the cattle?"

Smoke took a drink of the strong cowboy coffee before replying. "Figured we'd drive them on over to Cord's."

"Them no-goods is gonna fire the cabin soon as we're gone," Silver Jim said. "After they loot it." He grinned nastily. "We all allow as to how we ought to leave a few surprises in there for them."

Smoke, squatting down, leaned back against the bunkhouse wall and smiled. "What you got in mind?"

Hardrock kicked a cloth sack by his bunk. The sack moved and buzzed. "I gleamed me a rattler nest several days back. 'Fore I snoozed last night I paid it a visit and grabbed me several. I figured I'd plant 'em in the house 'fore we left, in stra-teegic spots." He grinned. "You like that idee?"

"Oh, yeah!"

"Thought you would. Soon as Miss Fae and that goosy brother of her'n is gone we'll plant the rattlers."

Smoke chewed on yesterday's biscuit and took a swallow of coffee. "You reckon any varmits got to the bodies last night?"

"Doubtful," Charlie said. "Ring stayed out there, close by. Said he didn't much like them people but it wouldn't be fitten to let the coyotes and wolves chew on them. Strange man."

Pistol looked toward the dusty window. "Gettin' light enough to see. I reckon we better get to it whilst it's cool. Them ol' boys is gonna get plumb ripe when the sun touches 'em."

The men put on their hats, hitched up their britches, and turned out the lamps. "I'd hate to be an undertaker," Hardrock said. "Hope when I go I just fall off my horse in the timber."

"By that time, you'll be so old you won't be able to get in the saddle," Silver Jim needled him.

"Damn near thataways now," Hardrock fired back.

* * *

They kept the outlaws' guns and ammunition and put what money they had in a leather sack, to give to Fae. Then they caved in the ravine wall and stacked rocks over the dirt to keep the varmints from digging up the bodies and eating them. By the time they had finished, it was time for breakfast.

Fae and Rita had fixed a huge breakfast of bacon and eggs and oatmeal and biscuits. The men dug in, piling their plates high. Conversation was sparse until the first plates had been emptied. Eating was serious business; a man could talk anytime.

After eating up everything in sight—it wasn't polite to leave any food; might insult the cook—the men refilled their coffee cups, pushed back their chairs, and hauled out pipes and papers, passing the tobacco sack around.

"We're leaving, aren't we?" Fae asked, noticing how quiet the men were.

"Till this is over," Smoke told her. "It's a pretty location here, Cousin, but it'd be real easy for Hanks's men to pin us down."

"They'll destroy the house."

"Probably. But you can always rebuild. That beats gettin' buried here. Take what you just absolutely have to have. We can stash the rest for you. Spring, you and Pat stay here and keep a sharp eye out. We'll go bunch the cattle and start pushing them toward Cord's range. We'll cross the Smith at the north bend, just south of that big draw. Let's go, boys."

The cattle were not happy to be leaving lush grass of summer graze, but finally the men got the old mossyhorn lead steer moving and the others followed. Smoke and Hardrock rode back to the ranch house. Hardrock went to the bunkhouse to get his bag of goodies for the outlaws. Ring had bunched the horses and with Pat's help was holding them just off the road. Spring was driving the wagon. Both Rita and Rae were riding astride; Parnell was in his buggy. He had a fat lip from his encounter with his sister the night past. He didn't look at all happy.

"I'll catch up with y'all down the road," Hardrock told Smoke.

"What is in the sack?" Parnell inquired.

"Some presents for the range-robbers. It wouldn't be neighborly to just go off and not leave something."

Parnell muttered something under his breath about the strangeness of western people while Smoke grinned at him.

The caravan moved out, with Smoke riding with his rifle across his saddle horn. Smoke did not expect any trouble so soon after the outlaw attack the past night, but one never knew about the mind of Dooley Hanks. The man didn't even know his own mind.

The trip to the Smith was uneventful and Spring knew a place where the wagon and the buggy could get across with little difficulty. A couple of Cord's hands were waiting on the west side of the river to point the way for the cattle. Smoke rode on to the ranch with the women and Parnell. Cord met them in the front yard.

"The house and barn go up last night?" he asked. "We seen a glow."

"Just the barn. I imagine the house will be fired tonight." He smiled. "After they try to loot it. But Hardrock left a few surprises for them." He told the ranch owner about the rattlesnakes in the bureau drawers and in other places.

Cord's smile was filled with grim satisfaction. "They'll get exactly what they deserve. Your momma's in the house, Rita." He stared at her. "Girl, what *have* you done to your hair?"

"Whacked it off." Rita grinned. "You like my jeans, Mister Cord?"

Cord shook his head and muttered about women dressin' up in men's britches and ridin' astride. Rita laughed at him as Sandi came out onto the porch. She squealed and the young women ran toward each other and hugged.

"The women been cleaning out the old bunkhouse all mornin', Smoke. It ain't fancy, but the roof don't leak and the bunks is in good shape and the sheets and blankets is clean."

"Sounds good to me. I'll go get settled in and get back with you."

"Smoke?"

He turned around to face Cord. The man stuck out his big hand and Smoke took it. "Good to have you with us in this thing."

"They done pulled out!" Larado reported back to Jason and Lanny. "They moved the cattle toward the Smith this mornin'. I found where they caved a ravine in on top of them they kilt last night. And it looks like the house is nearabouts full of good stuff."

"One down," Lanny said with a grin. "Let's take us a ride over there and see what we can find in the house. If they left in a hurry, they prob'ly didn't pack much."

The range-robbers rode up cautiously, but already the place had that aura of desertion about it. Lanny and Jason were feeling magnanimous that morning and told the boys to go ahead, help themselves to whatever they could find in the house.

A dozen gunnies began looting the house.

"Hey!" Slim called. "This here box is locked. Gimme that there hammer over yonder on the sill." He hammered the lock off while others squatted down, close to him, ready to snatch and grab should the box be filled with valuables. Slim opened the lid. Two rattlesnakes lunged out, one of them taking Slim in the throat and the other nailing a bearded gunny on the cheek and hanging on, wrapping around the gunny's neck, striking again and again.

One outlaw dove through a window escaping the snakes; another took the back door off its hinges. A gunny known only as Red fell over the couch knocking a bureau over. A rattler slithered out of the opened drawer and began striking at the man's legs, while Red kicked and screamed and howled in agony.

Larado ran from the house in blind fear, running into

Lanny who was running toward the house, Lanny fell back into Jason, and all three of them landed in the dust in a heap of arms and legs.

Ben Sabler rode up with his kin just in time to see Red crawl from the house and scream out his misery, the rattlesnake coiled around one leg, striking again and again at Red's stomach.

Ben did not hesitate. He jerked iron and shot Red in the head, putting him out of his agony, and then shot the snake, clipping its head off with deadly accuracy.

The bearded gunny staggered out the door, dying on his feet. Venom dripped from his face. He stood for a moment, and then fell like a tree, face first in the dirt. The rattler sidewinded toward Larado, who jerked out his pistol and emptied it into the rattler.

"Burn this damn place!" Lanny shouted.

"Slim's in there!"

Lanny looked inside. Slim was already beginning to swell from the massive amount of venom in his body. Lanny carefully backed out. "Slim's dead," he announced. "Damn Smoke Jensen. The bassard ain't human to do something lak this."

"I heard that he was from hell, myself," a gunny called Blaine said. He sat his horse and looked at the death house. "I knowed a man said Jensen took lead seven times one day some years back. Never did knock him down. He just kept on comin'."

"That ain't no story," Ben Sabler said. "I was there. I seen it."

Lanny looked at Ben. "I'll kill him. And that's a promise."

"I gotta see it." Ben didn't back down. "I seen his graveyards. I ain't never seen none of yours."

"Hang around," Lanny told him. He turned his back and shouted the order. "Burn this damn place to the ground!"

17

They stood in the front yard and watched the smoke spiral up into the sky, caught by vortexes in the hot air and spinning upward until breaking up.

Parnell stood with clenched fists, his eyes on the dark smoke. "I say now, that was unnecessary. Quite brutish. And *that* makes me angry." He stalked away, muttering to himself.

Fae was on the porch, her face in her hands, crying softly.

"She's a woman after all," Lujan said, so softly only Smoke could hear.

Del worked the handle of the outside pump, wetting a bandana and taking it to Fae.

Fae looked at the foreman, surprise in her eyes, and tried a smile as she took the dampened bandana. "Thank you, Del."

"You're shore welcome, ma'am." He backed off a few feet.

"Lujan," Smoke said. "You and me and Beans. We hit them tonight."

"Sí, señor." Lujan's teeth flashed in a smile. "I was wondering when you would have enough of being pushed."

* * *

By late afternoon, everyone at the Circle Double C knew the three men were going headhunting. But no one said a word about it. That might have caused some bad luck. And no one took umbrage at not being asked along. This was to be—they guessed—a hit-hard-and-quick-and-run-like-hell operation. Too many riders would just get in the way.

When Smoke threw a saddle on Dagger, the big mean-eyed horse was ready for the trail and he showed his displeasure at not being ridden much lately by trying to step on Smoke's foot.

The men took tape from the medicine chest and taped everything that might jingle. They took everything out of their pockets that was not necessary and looped bandoleers of ammunition across their chests. They were all dressed in dark clothing.

Just after dusk, Beans and Sandi went for a short walk while Smoke and Lujan squatted under the shade of a huge old tree by the bunkhouse and watched as Cord left the main house and walked toward them.

He squatted down beside them in the near-darkness of Montana's summer dusk. "Nice quiet evenin', boys."

"Indeed it is, senor." Lujan flashed his smile. His eyes flicked over to Beans and Sandi, now sitting in the yard swing. "A night for romance."

Cord grunted, but both men knew the rancher liked the young man called the Moab Kid. "Sandi would be inclined to give me all sorts of grief if anything was to happen to Beans."

When neither Smoke nor Lujan replied, Cord said, "Three against sixty is crappy odds, boys."

"Not the way we plan to fight," Smoke told him. "They'll be expecting a mass attack. Not a small surprise attack."

Again, the rancher grunted. It was clear that he did not like the three of them going headhunting. "We can expect you back when?"

"Around dawn. But keep guards out, Cord. If we do as

much damage as I think we will, Dooley is likely to ride against you this night."

"I'll double the guards."

Beans and Sandi had parted, with Sandi now on the lamp-lighted front porch. The Moab Kid was walking toward the three men at the tree. Faint light reflected off the double bandoleers of ammunition crisscrossing his chest.

All three men wore two guns around their waist, a third pistol rested in homemade shoulder holsters. They had each added another rifle boot; with two fully loaded Winchester .44 rifles and three pistols, that meant each man was capable of firing fifty-two times before reloading. And each man carried a double pouch over their saddlebags, each pouch containing a can of giant powder, already rigged with fuse and cap.

The men intended to raise a lot of hell at Dooley's D-H spread.

Smoke and Lujan rose to their boots.

Cord's voice was soft in the night. "See you, boys."

The three men walked toward their horses and stepped into the saddles. They rode toward the east, fast disappearing into the night.

The old gunslingers joined Cord by the tree. "Gonna be some fireworks this night," Silver Jim said. "Pistol, you 'member that time me and you and that half-breed Ute hit them outlaws down on the Powder River?"

Pistol laughed in the night. "Yeah. They was about twenty of them. We shore give them what-for, didn't we?"

"Was that the time y'all catched them gunnies in their drawers?" Hardrock asked.

"Takes something out of a man to have to fight in his longhandles. We busted right up into their camp. Stampeded their horses right over them, with us right behind the horses, reins in our teeth and both hands full of guns. Of course," he added with a smile, "that was when we all had teeth!"

* * *

The men rode slowly, saving their horses and not wanting to reach the ranch until all were asleep. They kept conversation to a minimum, each riding with their own thoughts. They did not need to be shared. Facing death was a personal thing, the concept that had to be worked out in each man's mind. None of the three considered themselves to be heroes; they were simply doing what they felt had to be done. The niceties of legal maneuvering were fast approaching the West, but it would be a few more years before they reached the general population. Until that time, codes of conduct would be set and enforced by the people, and the outcome would usually be very final.

The men forded the Smith, careful not to let water splash onto the canvas sacks containing the giant powder bombs. On the east side of the river, they pulled up and rested, letting their horses blow.

The men squatted down and carefully checked their guns, making sure they were loaded up full. Only after that was done did Lujan haul out the makings and pass the sack and papers around. The men enjoyed a quiet smoke in the coolness of Montana night and only then was the silence broken.

"We'll walk our horses up to that ridge overlooking Dooley's spread," Smoke spoke softly. "Look the situation over. If it looks OK, we'll ride slow-like and not light the bombs until we're inside the compound. Lujan, you take the new bunkhouse. Beans, you toss yours into the bunkhouse that was used by Gage and his boys. I'll take the main house." He picked up a stick and drew a crude diagram in the dirt, just visible in the moonlight. "We've got about a hundred and fifty rounds between us all loaded up for the first pass. But let's don't burn them all up and get caught short.

"Beans, the corral is closest to your spot; rope the gates and pull 'em down. The horses will be out of there like a shot. We make one pass and then get the hell gone from there. We'll link up just south of that ridge. If we get separated, we'll meet back at the Smith, where we rested. I don't want to bomb the barn because of the horses in there. Ain't no point in hurtin' a good horse when we don't have to."

Lujan chuckled quietly. "I think when the big bangs go off, there will be no need for Beans to rope the gates. I think the horses will break those poles down in a blind panic and be gone."

"Let's hope so," Smoke said. "That'll give us more time to raise Cain."

"And," Beans said, "when them bombs go off, those ol' boys are gonna be so rattled they'll be runnin' in all directions. I'd sure like to have a pitcher of it to keep."

Lujan ground out his cigarette butt under a boot heel and stood up. "Shall we go make violent sounds in the night, boys?"

The men rode deeper into the night, drawing closer to their objective. It was unspoken, but each man had entertained the thought that if Dooley had decided to strike first this night, Cord would be three guns short. If that was the case, and they were hitting an empty ranch, Dooley would experience the sensation of seeing another glow in the night sky.

His own ranch.

The three men left their horses and walked up to the ridge overlooking the darkened complex of the D-H ranch. They all three smiled as their eyes settled on the many horses in the double corral.

Without speaking, Smoke pointed out each man's perimeter and, using sign language, told them to watch carefully. He gave the soft call of a meadowlark and Lujan and Beans nodded their understanding, then faded into the brush.

They watched for over an hour, each of them spotting the locations of the two men on watch. They were careless, puffing on cigarettes. Smoke bird-called them back in and they slipped to their horses.

"What'd you think?" Smoke tossed it out.

"Let's swing around the ridge and walk our horses as close in as we can," Beans suggested.

"Suits me," Lujan said.

"Let's do it."

They swung around the ridge and came up on the east side of the ranch, walking their horses very slowly, keeping to the grass to further muffle the sound of the hooves.

"They're either drunk or asleep," Beans whispered.

"With any kind of luck, we can put them to sleep forever," Lujan returned the whisper. He reached back for the canvas sack and took out a giant powder bomb, the others following suit.

They were right on the edge of the ranch grounds when a call went up. "Hey! They's something movin' out yonder!"

The three men scratched matches into flames and lit the fuses. Beans let out a wild scream that would have sent any self-respecting puma running for cover and the horses lunged forward, steel-shod hooves pounding on the hard-packed dirt road.

Smoke reached the house first, sending Dagger leaping over the picket fence. He hurled the bomb through a front window and circled around to the back, lighting the fuse on his second bomb and tossing it into an upstairs window. The front of the house blew, sending shards of glass and splintered pieces of wood flying just as Smoke was heading across the backyard, low in the saddle, his face almost pressing Dagger's neck. He was using his knees to guide the horse, the reins in his teeth and both hands filled with .44's.

The upstairs blew, taking part of the roof off just as the bunkhouses exploded. All the men knew that with these black powder bombs, as small as they were, unless a man was directly in the path of one, or within a ten-foot radius, chances of death were slim. Injury, however, was another matter.

The first blast knocked Dooley out of bed and onto the floor. The second blast in the house went off just as he was getting to his feet, trying to find his boots and hat and gun belt. That blast went off directly over his bedroom and caved in the ceiling driving the man to his knees and tearing out the button-up back flap in his longhandles. A long splinter impaled itself to the hilt in one cheek of his bare butt, bringing a howl of pain from the man.

One of his sons fell through the huge hole in the ceiling and landed on his father's bed, collapsing the frame and folding the son up in the feather tick.

"Halp!" Bud hollered. "Git me outta here. Halp!"

Conrad came running, saw the hole in the ceiling too late, and fell squalling, landing on his father, knocking both men even goofier than they already were.

Outside, Smoke leveled a six-shooter and fired almost point-blank at a gunny dressed in his longhandles, boots, and hat—with a rifle in his hands. Smoke's slug took the man in the center of the chest and dropped him.

Dagger's hooves made a mess of the man's face as Smoke charged toward a knot of gunnies, both his guns blazing, barking and snarling and spitting out lead.

He ran right through and over the gunnies, Dagger's hooves bringing howls of pain as bones were broken under the steel shoes.

Lujan knee-reined his horse into a mass of confused and badly shaken gunslicks. He fired into the face of one and the man's face was suddenly slick with blood. Turning his horse, Lujan knocked another gunslick sprawling and fired his left hand gun at another, the bullet taking the man in the belly.

Smoke was suddenly at his side, and both men looked around for Beans, spotting him, and with a defiant cry from Lujan's throat, the two men charged toward the Moab Kid. They circled the Kid, holstering their pistols and pulling Winchesters from the boots. The three of them charged the yard, firing as fast as they could work the levers of their seventeen-shot Winchesters. In the darkness, they could not be sure they hit anything, but as they would later relate, the action sure solved blocked bowel-movement problems any of the gunnies might be suffering from.

The horses from the corral were long gone, just as Lujan

had predicted, stampeding in a mad rush and tearing down the corral gates after the explosion of the first bomb.

"Gimme a bomb!" Smoke yelled over the confusion.

At a full gallop, Beans handed him a bomb and Smoke circled the house, screaming like a painted-up Cheyenne, while Lujan and Beans reined up and began laying down a blistering line of fire. Smoke lit the bomb and tossed it in a side window.

"Let's go!" he yelled.

Screaming like young bucks on the warpath, the three men gave their horses full rein and galloped off into the dusty night. Smoke took one look back and grinned.

Dooley was getting to his feet for the third time when the bomb blew. The blast impacted with Dooley, turning him around and sending him, the door, and what was left of his longhandles, right out the bedroom window. Dooley landed right on top of Lanny Ball, the door separating them, both of the men knocked out cold.

"Lemme out of here!" Bud squalled. "Halp! Halp!"

18

There had been no pursuit. It would take the gunnies hours to round up their horses. But come the dawning, all three men knew the air would be filled with gunsmoke whenever and wherever D-H riders met with Circle Double C men.

Several miles from the house, the men stopped and loosened cinch straps on their horses, letting them rest and blow and have a little water, but not too much; this was no time for a bloated horse.

Smoke, Lujan, and Beans lay bellydown beside the little creek and drank alongside their horses, then sat down on the cool bank and rolled cigarettes, smoking and relaxing and unwinding. They had been very, very lucky this night, and they all knew it.

Suddenly, Beans started laughing and the laughter spread. Soon all three were rolling on the bank, laughing almost hysterically.

Gasping for breath, tears running down their tanned cheeks, the men gripped their sides and sat up, wiping their eyes with shirt sleeves.

"Sabe Dios!" Lujan said. "But I will never see anything so funny as that we witnessed tonight if I live to be a hundred!"

"Man," Beans chuckled, "I never knew them fellers was so ugly. Did you ever see so many skinny legs in all your life?"

"I saw Dooley blown slap out of the house," Smoke said. "He looked like he was in one piece, but I couldn't tell for sure. He was on a door, looked like to me. Landed on somebody, but I couldn't tell who it was, 'cept he wasn't wearing longjohns, had on one of those short-pants lookin' things some men have taken to wearing. Come to think of it, it did sorta resemble Lanny Ball. He had his guns belted on over his drawers."

That set them off again, howling and rolling on the ground while their horses looked at the men as if they were a bunch of idiots.

After a few hours' sleep, Smoke rolled out of his blankets noting that Lujan and Beans were already up. Smoke washed his face and combed his hair and was on his first cup of bunkhouse coffee—strong enough to warp a spoon—when Cord came in.

"I just got the word," the rancher said. "You and the boys played Billy-Hell last night over to the D-H. Doc Adair was rolled out about three this morning. So far there's four dead and two wounded who ain't gonna make it. Several busted arms and legs and heads. Dooley took a six-inch-long splinter in one side of his butt. Adair said the man has gone slap-dab nuts. Just sent off a wire to a cattle buyer to sell off a thousand head for money to hire more gunslicks . . . or rather, he sent someone in to send the wire. Dooley can't sit a saddle just yet." Try as he did, Cord could not contain his smile.

"Hell, Cord," Smoke complained. "There *aren't* any more gunfighters."

"Dad Estes," Cord said, his smile fading.

Smoke stood up from the rickety chair. "You have got to be kidding!"

"Wish I was. They been hiding out over in the Idaho wilderness. Just surfaced a couple of weeks ago on the Montana border."

"I haven't heard anything about Dad in several years. Not since the Regulators ran them out of Colorado."

Cord shook his head. "I been hearin' for some time they been murderin' and robbin' miners to stay alive. Makin' little forays out of the wildnerness and then duckin' back in."

"How many men are we talking about, Cord?"

Cord shrugged his shoulders. "Don't know. Twenty to thirty, I'd guess."

"Then all we're doing is taking two steps forward and three steps back."

"Looks like."

"Did you get a report on damage last night?"

"One bunkhouse completely ruined, the other one badly damaged. The big house is pretty well shot, back and front. Smoke, Dooley has given the word: shoot us on sight. He says Gibson is his and for us to stay out of it."

"The hell I will!"

"That's the same thing everybody else around here told me . . . more or less."

"Well, it was funny while it lasted." Smoke's words were glum.

Cord poured a cup of coffee. "Personally, I'd like to have seen it. Beans and Lujan has been entertaining the crews for an hour. Did Lanny Ball really have his guns strapped on over his short drawers?"

Smoke laughed. "Yeah. That was right before the door hit him."

Both men shared a laugh. Cord said, "Would it do any good to wire for some federal marshals?"

"I can't see that it would. It would be our word against theirs. And they'd just back off until the marshals left, then we'd still have the same problem facing us. If I had the time, I could probably get my old federal commission back . . . but what good would it do? Dooley's crazy; the gunslicks he's buyin' are playing a double-cross and Dooley's so nuts you'd never convince him of it. I think we'd just better resign ourselves that we're in a war and take it from there."

"The wife says we need supplies in the worst way. We've got to go into town."

"Then we'll go in a bunch. This afternoon. We've got to show Dooley he doesn't run the town."

"Sorry, Mister McCorkle," Walt Hillery said primly. "I'm completely out of everything you want."

"You're a damn liar!" Cord flushed. "Hell, man, I can *see* most of what I ordered."

"All that has been bought by the D-H spread. They're coming in to pick it up this afternoon."

"Jake!" Cord yelled at his hand driving the wagon. "Pull it around back and get ready to load up."

"Now, see here!" Leah's voice was sharp. "You don't give us orders, Mister Big Shot!"

"Dooley's bought them," Smoke said quietly. He stood by a table loaded with men's jeans. He lifted his eyes to Walt. "You should have stayed out of this, Hillery." He walked to the counter and dug in his jeans pocket, tossing half a dozen double eagles onto the counter. "That'll pay for what I pick out, and Cord's money is layin' right beside mine. If Dooley sets up a squall, you tell him to come see me. Load it up, Jake."

The sour-faced and surly Walt and Leah stood tight-lipped, but silent as Jake began loading up supplies.

"Grind the damn coffee, Walt," Cord ordered. "As a matter of fact, double my order. That way I won't have to look at your prissy face for a long time."

"I hope Mister Hanks kills you, McCorkle!" Leah hissed the verbal venom at him. "And I hope you die hard!"

Cord took the hard words without changing expression. "You never have liked me, Leah, and I never could understand why."

She didn't back down. "You don't have the mental capability to appreciate quality people, McCorkle . . . like Dooley Hanks."

"Quality people? What in the name of Peter and Paul are you talking about, Leah?"

But she would only shake her head.

"Money talks, Cord," Smoke told him. "Especially with little-minded people like these two fine citizens. They're just like Dooley: prideful, envious, spiteful, hateful . . . any and all of the seven deadly sins." He walked around the counter and stripped the shelf of all the boxes of .44 and .45 rounds. "Tally it up, storekeeper."

Cord walked around the general store, filling a large box with all the bandages and various balms and patent medicines he could find. "Might as well do it right," he muttered.

If dark looks of hate could kill, both Cord and Smoke would have died on the spot. Not another word was exchanged the rest of the time spent in the store except for Walt telling the men the amount of their purchases. All the supplies loaded onto the wagon, both Cord and Smoke experienced a sense of relief when they exited the building to stand on the boardwalk.

"Quality people?" Cord said, shaking his head, still not able to get over that statement.

"Forget them," Smoke said. "They're not worth worrying about. When this war is over, and we've won—and we will win, count on it—those two will be sucking up to you as if nothing had happened."

"What they'll do is do without my business," Cord said shortly.

The men walked over to Hans for a cup of coffee and a piece of pie. Beans and Lujan, with Charlie Starr and his old gunslinging buddies, had dropped into the Pussycat for a beer. There were half a dozen horses wearing the D-H brand, among others, at the hitchrail in front of the Hangout.

"You any good with that six-gun?" Smoke asked the rancher.

"Contrary to what some believe, I'm no fast gun. But I hit what I aim at."

"That counts most of all in most cases. I've seen so-called fast guns many, many times put their first shot in the dirt. They didn't get another shot." Then Smoke added, "Just buried."

They sipped their coffee and enjoyed the dried apple pie with a hunk of cheese on it. They both could sense the tension hanging in and around the small town; and both knew that a shooting was more than likely looking them in the face. It would probably come just before they tried to leave Gibson.

Nothing stirred on the wide street. Not one dog or cat could be seen anywhere. And it was very hot, the sun a bubbling ball in a very blue and very cloudless sky. A dust devil spun out its short frantic life, whipping up the street and then vanishing.

Hilda refilled their cups. "And how is Ring?" she inquired, blushing as she asked.

"Fine." Smoke smiled at her. "He sends his regards."

She giggled and returned to the kitchen.

Smoke looked at Cord as he scribbled in a small tally book most ranchers carried with them. "Eighteen dead," the rancher muttered. "Near as I can figure. May God have mercy on us."

"They'll be fifty or sixty dead before this is over. If Dooley doesn't pull in his horns."

"He won't. He's gone completely around the bend. And you know," Cord said thoughtfully, some sadness in his voice, "I don't even remember what caused the riff between us."

"That's the way it usually is. Your rider who talked to Doc

Adair, he have any idea when Dad Estes and his bunch will be pulling in?"

"Soon as possible, I reckon. They'll ride hard gettin' over here. And I'd be willing to bet they'd already left the wilderness and was waitin' for word; and I'd bet it was Jason or Lanny who put the bug about them into Dooley's ear."

"Probably right on both counts."

Both men looked up as several riders rode into town, reining up in front of the Hangout.

"You know them, Smoke?"

"Some of No-Count Victor's bunch."

"Daryl Radcliffe and Paul Addison are ze zwo in der front," Hans rumbled from behind the counter. "Day vas pointed out to me when day first come to zown."

"I've heard of them," Smoke said. "They're scum. Bottom of the barrel but good with a pistol."

"Maybe ve vill get lucky and day will all bite demselves und die from der rabies," Hans summed up the feelings of most in the town.

They all heard the back door open and close and Hans turned as Olga came to his side and whispered in his ear. She disappeared into the kitchen and Hans said, "Four men she didn't know have hitched dere horses at der far end of town and are valking dis vay. All of dem veering zwo guns."

"Is that our cue?" Cord asked.

"I reckon. But I'm going to finish my pie and coffee first."

"You always this calm before a gunfight?"

"No point in getting all worked about it. Stay as calm as you can and your shootin' hand stays steady."

"Good way to look at it, I suppose." Cord finished his pie and took a sip of coffee. "I hate it that we have to do this in town. A stray bullet doesn't care who it hits."

Smoke drained his coffee cup and placed it carefully in the saucer. "It doesn't have to be on the street if you're game."

"I'm game for anything that'll keep innocent people from getting hurt."

"You ready?"

"As I'll ever be. Where are we going?"

"Like Daniel, into the lion's den. Or in this case, the Hangout. Let's see how they like it when we take it to them."

19

Beans and Lujan and Charlie Starr and his old buddies were waiting on the boardwalk.

"The beer is on me, boys," Smoke told them. "We'll try the fare at the Hangout."

"I hope they havc tequila," Lujan said. "They didn't a couple of weeks ago. I have not had a decent drink in months."

"They probably do by now, with Diego and Pablo hanging around in there. But the bottles might be reserved for them."

"If they have tequila, I shall have a drink," Lujan replied softly, tempered steel under the liltingly accented words.

The men pushed through the batwing doors and stepped inside the saloon. For all but Lujan and Cord, this was their first excursion into the Hangout. The men fanned out and quickly sized up the joint.

They realized before the first blink that they were outnumbered a good two to one. Surprise mixed with irritation was very evident on the faces of the D-H gunfighters. This move on the part of the Circle Double C had not been anticipated, and it was not to their liking. For in a crowded barroom, gunfights usually took a terrible toll due to the close range.

Smoke led the way to the bar, deliberately turning his back to the gunslicks. The barkeep looked as if he really had to go to the outhouse. "Beer for me and the Moab Kid and Mister McCorkle, please. And a bottle of whiskey for the boys and a bottle of tequila for Mister Lujan."

The barkeep looked at the "boys," average age about sixty-five, and nodded his head. "I got ever'thing 'cept the tequila. Them bottles is reserved for my regular customers."

"Put a bottle of tequila on the bar, partner," Smoke told him. "If a customer can see it, it's for sale."

"Yes, sir," the barkeep said, knowing he was caught between a rock and a hard place. But who the hell would have ever figured this bunch would come in *here?*

Smoke and his men could watch the room of gunfighters in the mirror behind the bar, and they could all see the D-H hired guns were very uncertain. It showed in their furtive glances at one another. Smoke kept a wary eye on Radcliffe and Addison, for they were known to be backshooters and would not hesitate to kill him should Smoke relax his guard for just a moment.

Several D-H guns had been standing at the bar. They had carefully moved away while Smoke was ordering the drinks.

"Diego finds out you been suckin' at his tequila bottle," a gunny spoke, "you gonna be dead, Lujan."

"One day is just as good as the next day to meet the Lord," Lujan replied, turning to face the man. "But since Diego is not present, perhaps you would like to attempt to fill his boots, *puerco.*"

"What'd you call me?" The man stood up.

Lujan smiled, holding his shot glass in his left hand. "A pig!"

Radcliffe and Addison and half a dozen others stood up, their hands dangling close to their guns.

The town's blacksmith pushed open the batwings, stood

for a moment staring at the crowd and feeling the tension in the room. He slowly backed out onto the boardwalk. The sounds of his boots faded as he made his exit.

"No damn greasy Mex is gonna call me a pig!" The gunny shouted the words.

Lujan smiled, half turning as he placed the shot glass on the bar. He expected the D-H gunny to draw as he turned, and the man did. Lujan's Colt snaked into his hand and the beery air exploded in gunfire. The D-H gunny was down and dying as his hand was still trying to lift his pistol clear of leather.

Radcliffe and Addison grabbed for iron. Smoke's right hand dipped, drew, cocked, and fired in one smooth cat-quick movement. A second behind his draw, Cord drew and fired. Radcliffe and Addison stumbled backward and fell over chairs on their way to the floor.

The room erupted in gunsmoke, lead, and death as Beans and the old gunhandlers pulled iron, cocked it back, and let it bang.

Two D-H riders, with more sense than the others, jumped right through a saloon window, landing on the boardwalk and rolling to the street. They were cut in a few places, but that beat the hell out of being dead.

The bartender had dropped to the floor at the first shot. He came up with a sawed-off ten gauge shotgun, the hammers eared back, and pointed it at Pistol's head. Cord turned and shot the man in the neck. The bartender jerked as the bullet took him, the barrels of the shotgun pointed toward the ceiling. The shotgun went off, the stock driving back from the recoil, smashing into the man's mouth, knocking teeth out.

Cord felt a hammer blow in his left shoulder, a jarring flash of pain that turned him to one side for a painful moment and rendered his left arm useless. Regaining his balance and lifting his pistol, the rancher fired at the man who had shot him, his bullet taking the man in his open mouth and exiting out the man's neck.

Beans felt a burning sensation on his cheek as a slug grazed him, followed by the warm drip of blood. He jerked out his second pistol and added more gunsmoke and death to the mounting carnage.

Lujan twisted as a slug tore through the fleshy part of his arm. Cursing, he lifted his Colt and drove two fast rounds into the belly of the D-H gunhawk who stood directly in front of him, doubling the man over and dropping him screaming to the floor.

The barroom was thick with gunsmoke, making it almost impossible to see. The roaring of guns was near-deafening, adding to the screaming of the wounded and the vile cursing of those still alive.

Smoke jerked as a bullet burned his leg and another slug clipped the top of his ear, sending blood flowing down his face. He stumbled to one side and picked up a gun that had fallen from the lifeless fingers of a D-H gunslick. It was a short-barreled Colt Peacemaker .45. Smoke eared the hammer back and let it snarl as he knelt on the floor, his wounded leg throbbing.

The old gunfighters seemed invincible as they stood almost shoulder-to-shoulder, hands filled with .44's and .45's, all of them belching fire and smoke and lead. This was nothing new to them. They had been doing this since the days a man carried a dozen filled cylinders with him for faster reloading. They had stood in barrooms from the Mississippi to the Pacific Ocean, and from Canada to the Mexican border and fought it out, sometimes with a tin star pinned to their chests, sometimes close to the outlaw trail. This was as familiar to them as to a bookkeeper with his figures.

Several D-H hired guns stumbled through the smoke and the blood, trying to make it to the boardwalk, to take the fight into the streets. The first one to step through the batwings was flung back into the fray, his face missing. Hans had blown it off with a sawed-off shotgun. The second D-H gunny had his legs knocked out from under him from the other barrel of Han's express gun.

Through the thick choking killing haze, Smoke saw a man known to him as Blue, a member of Cat Jennings's gang of no-goods and trash. Blue was pointing his Smith & Wesson Schofield .45 at Charlie.

He never got to pull the trigger. Smoke's Peacemaker roared and bucked in his hand and Blue felt, for a few seconds, the hot pain of frontier justice end his days of robbing and murdering.

The gunfire faded into silence, broken only by the moaning of wounded gunslingers.

"Coming in!" Hans shouted from the boardwalk.

"Come on, partner," Hardrock said, punching out empties and filling up his guns.

Hans stepped through the batwings and coughed as the arid smoke filled his nostrils. His eyes widened in shock at the human carnage on the floor. Widened further as he looked at the wounded men leaning up against the bar. "I vill get the doctor." He backed out and ran for Doc Adair's office.

While Charlie and Pistol kept their guns on the moaning gunslicks on the floor, Smoke and Lujan walked among them, silently determining which should first receive Adair's attentions and who would never again need attention.

Not in this life.

Smoke knelt down beside a young man, perhaps twenty years old. The young man had been shot twice in the stomach, and already his dark eyes were glazing over as death hovered near.

"You got any folks, boy?" Smoke asked.

"Mother!" the young man gasped.

"Where is she?"

"Arkansas. Clay County. On the St. Francis. Name's . . . name's Claire . . . Shelby."

"I'll get word to her," Smoke told him as that pale rider came galloping nearer.

"She always told me . . . I was gonna turn out . . . bad." The words were very weak.

"I'll write that your horse threw you and you broke your neck."

"I'd . . . 'preciate it. That'd make her . . . feel a bunch better." He closed his eyes and did not open them again.

"I thought you was gonna kiss him there for minute, Jensen," a hard-eyed gunslick mocked Smoke. The lower front of the man's shirt was covered with blood. He had taken several rounds in the gut.

"You got any folks you want me to write?" Smoke asked the dying man.

The gunslick spat at Smoke, the bloody spittle landing close to his boot.

"Suit yourself." Smoke stood up, favoring his wounded leg. He limped back to the bar and leaned against it, just as the batwings pushed open and Doc Adair and the undertaker came in.

Both of them stopped short. "Jesus God!" Adair said, looking around him at the body-littered and blood-splattered saloon.

"Business got a little brisk today, Doc," Smoke told him, accepting a shot glass of tequila from Lujan. "Check Cord here first." He knocked back the strong mescal drink and shuddered as it hit the pit of his stomach.

The doctor, not as old as Smoke had first thought—of course he'd been sober now for several weeks, and was now wearing clean clothes and had gone back to shaving daily—knew his business. He cleaned out the shoulder wound and bandaged it, rigging a sling for Cord out of a couple of bar towels. He then turned his attention to Lujan, swiftly and expertly patching up the arm.

Smoke had cut open his jeans, exposing the ugly rip along the outside of his leg. "It ought to be stitched up," Adair said. "It'll leave a bad scar if I don't."

"Last time my wife Sally counted, Doc, I had seventeen bullet scars in my hide. So one more isn't going to make any difference."

"So young to have been hit so many times," the doctor muttered as he swabbed out the gash with alcohol. Smoke almost lifted himself out of the chair as the alcohol cleaned the raw flesh. Adair grinned. "Sometimes the treatment hurts worse than the wound."

"You've convinced me," Smoke said as his eyes went misty, then went through the same sensation as Adair cleaned the wound in his ear.

"How 'bout us?" a gunfighter on floor bitched. "Ain't we gonna get no treatment?"

"Go ahead and die," Adair told him. "I can see from here that you're not going to make it."

Charlie and his friends had walked around the room, collecting all the guns and gun belts, from both the dead and the living.

"Always did want me a matched set of Remingtons," Silver Jim said. "Now I got me some. Nice balance, too."

"I want you to lookee here at this Colt double-action," Charlie said. "I'll just be hornswoggled. And she's a. 44-.40, too. Got a little ring on the butt so's a body could run some twine through it and not lose your gun. Ain't that something now. Don't have to cock it, neither. Just point it and pull the trigger." He tried it one-handed and almost scared the doctor half to death when Charlie shot out a lamp. "All that trigger-pullin'-the-hammer-back does throw your aim off a mite, though. Take some gettin' used to, I reckon."

"Maybe you 'pposed to shoot it with both hands," Hardrock suggested.

"That don't make no sense atall. There ain't no room on the butt for two hands. Where the hell would you put the other'n?"

"I don't know. Was I you, I'd throw the damn thing away. They ain't never gonna catch on."

"I'm a hurtin' something fierce!" a D-H gunhawk hollered.

"You want me to kick you in the head, boy?" Pistol asked him. "That'd put you out of your misery for a while."

The gunhawk shut his mouth.

Adair finished with Beans and went to work on the fallen gunfighters. "This is strictly cash, boys," he told them. "I don't give no credit to people whose life expectancy is as short as yours."

20

All was calm for several days. Smoke imagined that even in Dooley's half-crazed mind it had been a shock to lose so many gunslicks in the space of three minutes, and all that following the raid on Dooley's ranch. So much had happened in less than twenty four hours that Dooley was being forced to think over very carefully whatever move he had planned next.

But all knew the war was nowhere near over. That this was quite probably the lull before the next bloody and violent storm.

"Dad Estes and his bunch just pulled in," Cord told Smoke on the morning of the fourth day after the showdown in the saloon. "Hans sent word they came riding in late last night."

"He'll be making a move soon then."

"Smoke, do you realize that by my count, thirty three men have been killed so far?"

"And about twenty wounded. Yes. I understand the undertaker is putting up a new building just to handle it all."

"That is weighing on my mind. I've killed in my lifetime,

Smoke. I've killed three white men in about twenty years, but they had stole from me and were shooting at me. I've hanged one rustler." He paused.

"What are you trying to say, Cord?"

"We've got to end this. I'm getting where I can't sleep at night! That boy dying back yonder in the saloon got to me."

"I'm certainly open to suggestions, Cord. Do you think it didn't bother me to write that boy's mother? I don't enjoy killing, Cord. I went for three years without ever pulling a gun in anger. I loved it. Then until I got Fae's letter, I hadn't even worn both guns. But you know as well as I do how this little war is going to be stopped."

Cord leaned against the hitchrail and took off his hat, scratching his head. "We force the issue? Is that what you're saying?"

"Do you want peace, Cord?"

"More than anything. Perhaps we could ride over and talk to . . . ?" He shook his head. "What am I saying? Time for that is over and past. All right, Smoke. All right. Let me hear your plan."

"I don't have one. And it isn't as if I haven't been thinking hard on it. What happened to your sling?"

"I took it off. Damn thing worried me. No plan?"

"No. The ranch, this ranch, must be manned at all times. We agreed on that. If not, it'll end up like Fae's place. And if we keep meeting them like we did back in town, they're going to take us. We were awfully lucky back there, Cord."

"I know. So . . . ?"

"I'm blank. Empty. Except for hit and run night fighting. But we'll never get as lucky as we did the other night. Count on that. You can bet that Dooley has that place heavily guarded night and day."

"Wait them out, then. I have the cash money to keep Gage and his boys on the payroll for a long time. But not enough to buy more gunslicks . . . if I could find any we could trust, that is."

"Doubtful. Must be half a hundred range wars going on out here, most of them little squabbles, but big enough to keep a lot of gunhawks working."

"I've written the territorial governor, but no reply as yet."

"I wouldn't count on one, either." Smoke verbally tossed cold water on that. "He's fighting to make this territory a state; I doubt that he'd want a lot of publicity about a range war at this time."

Cord nodded his agreement. "We'll wait a few more days; neither one of us is a hundred percent yet . . ." He paused as a rider came at a hard gallop from the west range.

The hand slid to a halt, out of the saddle and running to McCorkle. "Saddle me a horse!" he yelled to several punchers standing around the corral. "The boys is bringin' in Max, Mister Cord. Looks like Dooley done turned loose that back-shootin' Danny Rouge. Max took one in the back. He's still able to sit a saddle, but just barely. I'll ride into town and fetch Doc Adair." He was gone in a bow-legged run toward the corral.

Cord's face had paled at the news of his oldest son being shot. "I'll have Alice get ready with hot water and bandages. She's a good nurse." He ran up the steps to the house.

Smoke leaned against the hitchrail as his eyes picked up several riders coming in slow, one on either side helping to keep the middle rider in the saddle. Smoke knew, with this news, all of Cord's willingness to talk had gone right out the window. And if Max died . . . ?

Smoke pushed away from the hitchrail and walked toward the bunkhouse. If Max died there would be open warfare; no more chance meetings between the factions involved. It would be bloody and cruel until one side killed off the other.

"Might as well get ready for it," Smoke muttered.

"All we can do is wait," Adair said. "I can't probe for the bullet 'cause I don't know where it is. It angled off from the entry point. It missed the kidney and there is no sign of excessive internal bleeding; so he's got a chance. But don't move him any more than you have to."

Smoke and several others stood listening as Doc Adair spoke with Cord and Alice.

"His chances . . . ?" Cord asked, his voice tired.

"Fifty-fifty." Adair was blunt. "Maybe less than that. Don't get your hopes up too high, Cord. Have someone close by him around the clock. We'll know one way or the other in a few days."

"Did you get him?" Dooley asked the rat-faced Danny Rouge.

"I got him." Danny's voice was high-pitched, more like a woman's voice.

"Good!" Dooley took a long pull from his whiskey bottle, some of the booze dribbling down his unshaven chin. "One less of that bastard's whelps."

He was still mumbling and scratching himself as Danny walked from the room and stepped outside. Dooley's sons were on the porch, sharing a bottle.

"Did he squall when you got him?" Sonny asked, his eyes bright from the cruelty within the young man.

"I 'magine he did," Danny told him. "But I couldn't hear him; I was a good half mile away." Danny stepped from the porch and walked toward the one bunkhouse that was still usable. With the coming in of Dad Estes and his bunch, tents had been thrown up all over the place, the ranch now resembling a guerrilla camp.

The other gunhawks avoided Danny. No one wanted anything to do with him, all feeling that there was something unclean about the young man, even though Danny was as fastidious as possible, considering the time and the place. He was considerate of his personal appearance, but his mind resembled anyone's concept of hell. Danny was a cold-blooded killer. He enjoyed killing, the killing act his substitute for a woman. He would kill anybody: man, woman, or child. It did not make one bit of difference to Danny. Just as long as the price was right.

He went to his bunk and carefully cleaned his rifle, returning it to the hard leather case. Then he stretched out on the bunk and closed his eyes. It had been a very pleasing day. He knew he'd gotten a good clean hit by the way the man had jerked and then slumped in the saddle, slowly tumbling to the ground, hitting the ground like a rag doll.

It was a good feeling knowing he had earned his pay. A day's work for a day's pay. Made a man feel needed. Yes, indeed.

At the Circle Double C, the men sat, mostly in small groups, and mostly in silence, cleaning weapons. The hands, not gunfighters, but just hard-working cowboys, were digging in warbags and taking out that extra holster and pistol, filling the loops of a spare bandolier. They rode for the brand, and if a fight was what Dooley Hanks wanted, a fight would be what he would get.

The hands who had come over to Cord's side from the D-H did not have mixed feelings about it. They had been shoved aside in favor of gunhawks; they had seen Dooley and his ignorant sons go from bad to savage. There was not one ounce of loyalty left among them toward Dooley. They knew now that this was a fight to the finish. OK. Let's do it.

Just before dusk, Cord walked out to the bunkhouse, a grim expression on his face. "I sent Willie in for the doctor. Max is coughin' up blood. It don't look good. I can't stand to sit in here and look at my wife tryin' to be brave about the whole damn thing when I know that what she really wants to do is bust out bawlin'. And the same goes for me."

Then he started cussing. He strung together some mighty hard words as he stomped around the big room, kicking at this and that; about every fourth and fifth word was Dooley Hanks. He traced the man's ancestry back to before Adam and Eve directly linking Dooley to the snake in the Garden.

He finally sat down on a bunk and put his face in his hands. Smoke motioned the men outside and gently closed the door leaving Cord with his grief and the right for a man to cry in private.

"It's gonna be Katy-bar-the-door if that boy dies," Hardrock said. "We just think we've seen a little shootin' up to now."

"I'm ready," Del said. "I'm ready to get this damn thing over with and get back to punchin' cows."

"It's gonna be a while 'fore any of us gets back to doin' that," Les said, one of the men who had come from the D-H.

"And some of us won't," Fitz spoke softly.

Someone had a bottle and that got passed around. Beans pulled out a sack of tobacco and that went the way of the bottle. The men drank and smoked in silence until the bottle was empty and the tobacco sack flat as a tortilla left out in the sun.

"Wonder how Dooley's ass is?" Gage asked, and the men chuckled softly.

"I hope it's healed," Del said. " 'Cause it's shore about to get kicked hard."

The men all agreed on that.

Cord came out of the bunkhouse and walked to the house, passing the knot of men without speaking. His face bore the brunt of his inner grief.

Holman got up from his squat and said, "I think I'm gonna go write my momma a letter. She's gettin' on in years and I ain't wrote none in near'bouts a year."

"That's a good idea," Bernie said. "If I tell you what to put on paper to my momma, would you write it down for me?"

"Shore. Come on. I print passable well."

They were happy-go-lucky young cowboys a few weeks ago, Smoke thought. Now they are writing their mothers with death on their minds.

That ghostly rider would be saddling up his fire-snorting stallion, Smoke mused. Ready for more lost souls.

"What are you thinking, amigo?" Lujan asked him.

Smoke told him.

"You are philosophical this evening. I had always heard that you were a man who possessed deep thoughts."

Smoke grunted. "My daddy used to say that we came from Wales—years back. Jensen wasn't our real name. I don't know what it was. But Daddy used to say that the Celts were mysterious people. I don't know."

"I know that there is the smell of death in the air," the Mexican said. "Listen. No birds singing. Nothing seems to be moving."

The primal call of a wolf cut the night air, its shivering howl touching them all.

"Folks cut them wolves down," Del spoke out of the darkness. "And I've shot my share of them when they was after beeves. But I ain't got nothing really agin them. They're just doing what God intended them to do. They ain't like we're supposed to be. They can't think like nothin' except what they is. And you can't fault them for that. Take a human person now, that's a different story. Dooley and them others, and I know that Dooley's done lost his mind, but I think his greed brung that on. His jealousy and so forth. But them gunning over yonder. They coulda been anything but what they is. They turned to the outlaw trail 'cause they wanted to. What am I tryin' to say anyways?"

Silver Jim stood up and stretched. "It means we can go in smokin' and not have no guilty conscience when we leave them bassards dead where we find them."

Lujan smiled. "Not as eloquently put as might have been, but it certainly summed it up well."

Cord stepped out on the porch just as Doc Adair's buggy pulled up. The men could hear his words plain. "Max just died."

21

Max McCorkle, the oldest son of Cord and Alice, and brother to Rock, Troy, and Sandi, was buried the next day. He was twenty-five years old. He was buried in the cemetery on the ridge overlooking the ranch house. Half a dozen crosses were in the cemetery, crosses of men who had worked for the Circle Double C and who had died while in the employment of the spread.

Sandi stood leaning against Beans, softly weeping. Del stood with Fae. Ring stood with Hilda and Hans and Olga. Gage with Liz. Cord stood stony-faced with his wife, a black veil over her face. Parnell stood with Smoke and the other hands and gunfighters. And Smoke had noticed something: the schoolteacher had strapped on a gun.

The final words were spoken over Max, and the family left while the hands shoveled the dirt over the young man's final resting place on this earth.

Parnell walked up to Smoke. "I would like for you to teach me the nomenclature of this weapon and the proper way to fire it."

A small smile touched Smoke's lips, so faint he doubted

Parnell even noticed it. "You plannin' on ridin' with us, Cousin."

The man shook his head. "Regretfully, no. I am not that good a horseman. I would only be in the way. But someone needs to be here at the ranch with the women. I can serve in that manner."

Smoke stuck out his hand and the schoolteacher, with a surprised look on his face, took it. "Glad to have you with us, Parnell."

"Pleased to be here, Cousin."

"We'll start later on this afternoon. Right now, let's wander on down to the house. Mrs. McCorkle and the others have been cookin' all morning. Big crowd here. I 'spect the neighbors will be visitin' and such all afternoon."

"Funerals are barbaric. Nothing more than a throwback to primitive and pagan rites."

"Is that right?"

"Yes. And dreadfully hard on the family."

Weddings and funerals were social events in the West, often drawing crowds from fifty to seventy-five miles away. It was a chance to catch up on the latest gossip, eat a lot of good food—everybody brought a covered dish—and see old friends.

"We got the same thing goin' on up on the Missouri," Smoke heard one man tell Cord. "Damn nesters are tryin' to grab our land. Some of the ranchers have brung in some gunfighters. I don't hold with that myself, but it may come to it. I writ the territorial governor, but he ain't seen fit to reply as yet. Probably never even got the letter."

Smoke moved around the lower part of the ranch house and listened. Few knew who he was, and that was just fine with him.

"Maybe we could get Dooley put in the crazy house," a man suggested. "He's sure enough nuts. All we got to do is find someone to sign the papers."

"No," another said. "There's one more thing: findin' someone stupid enough to serve the papers when Dooley's got hisself surrounded by fifty or sixty gunslicks."

"I wish I could help Cord out, but I'm shorthanded as it is. The damn Army ought to come in. That's what I think."

Smoke heard the words "vigilante" and "regulators" several times. But they were not spoken with very much enthusiasm.

Smoke ate, but with little appetite. Cord was holding up well, but his two remaining sons, Rock and Troy, were geared up for trouble, and unless he could head them off, they would be riding into disaster. He moved to the boys' side, where they stood backed up against a wall, keeping as far away from the crowd as possible.

"You boys best just snuff out your powder fuse," Smoke told them. "Dooley and his bunch will get their due, but for right now, think about your mother. She's got enough grief on her shoulders without you two adding to it. Just settle down."

The boys didn't like it, but Smoke could tell by the looks on their faces his words about their mother had hit home. He felt they would check-rein their emotions for a time. For how long was another matter.

Having never liked the feel of large crowds, Smoke stayed a reasonable time, paid his respects to Cord and Alice, and took his leave, walking back to the bunkhouse to join the other hands.

"When do we ride?" Fitz asked as soon as Smoke had walked in.

"Don't know. Just get that burr out from under your blanket and settle down. You can bet that Dooley is ready and waiting for us right this minute. Let's don't go riding into a trap. We'll wait a few days and let the pot cool its boil. Then we'll come up with something."

Fine words, but Smoke didn't have any plan at all.

* * *

They all worked cattle for a few days, riding loose but ready. In the afternoons, Smoke spent several hours each day with Parnell and his pistol. Parnell was very fast, but he couldn't hit anything but air. On the third day, Smoke concluded that the man never would be able to hit the side of a barn, even if he was standing inside the barn. Since they had plenty of rifles, Smoke decided to try the man with a Winchester. To his surprise, Parnell turned out to be a good shot with a carbine.

"You can tote that pistol around if you want to, Parnell," Smoke told him. "But you just remember this: out here, if a man straps on a gun, he best be ready and able to use it. Don't go off the ranch grounds packing a short gun, 'cause somebody's damn sure going to call your hand with it. Stick with the rifle. You're a pretty good shot with it. We got plenty of rifles, so keep half a dozen of them loaded up full at all times."

"I need to go in and get some books and papers from the school."

"I wouldn't advise it, Cousin. You'd just be askin' for trouble. Tell me what you need, and I'll fetch it for you."

"Perhaps," the schoolteacher said mysteriously, and walked away.

Smoke had a feeling that, despite his words, the man was going into town anyway. He'd have to keep an eye on him. He knew Parnell was feeding on his newly found oats, so to speak, and felt he didn't need a baby-sitter. But Smoke had a hunch that Parnell really didn't know or understand the caliber of men who might jump him, prod him into doing something that would end up getting the schoolteacher hurt, or dead.

Smoke spread the word among the men to keep an eye on Parnell.

"Seems to me that Rita's been lookin' all wall-eyed at him the last couple of days," Pistol said. "Shore is a bunch of spoonin' goin' on around here. Makes a man plumb nervous."

"Wal, you can re-lax, Pistol," Hardrock told him. "No

woman in her right mind would throw her loop for the likes of you. You too damn old and too damn ugly."

"Huh!" the old gunfighter grunted. "You a fine one to be talkin'. You could hire that face of yours out to scare little children."

Smoke left the two old friends insulting each other and walked to the house to speak with Cord sitting on the front porch, drinking coffee.

Cord waved him up and Smoke took a seat.

"I'm surprised Dooley hasn't made a move," the rancher said. "But the men say the range has been clear. Maybe he's counting on that Danny Rouge to pick us off one at a time."

"I doubt that Dooley even knows what's in his mind," Smoke replied. "I've been thinking, Cord. If we could get a judge to him, the judge would declare him insane and stick him in an institution."

"Umm. Might be worth a shot. I can send a rider up to Helena with a letter. I know Judge Ford. Damn! Why didn't I think of that?"

"Maybe he'd like to come down for a visit?" Smoke suggested. "Has he been here before?"

"Several times. Good idea. I'll spell it all out in a letter and get a man riding within the hour. I'll ask him if he can bring a deputy U.S. marshal down with him."

"We just might be able to end this mess," Smoke said, a hopeful note in his voice. "With Dooley out of the picture, Liz could take over the running of the ranch, with Gage to help her, and she could fire the gunslicks."

"It sounds so simple."

"All we can do is try. Have you seen Parnell and Rita?"

"Yeah. They went for a walk. Can't get used to the idea of that schoolteacher packin' iron. It looks funny."

"I warned him about totin' that gun in town."

"And I told Rita not to go into town. However, since I'm not her father, it probably went in one ear and out the other. Dooley and me told those girls fifteen years ago not to see one another. Did a hell of a lot of good didn't it? Both those girls are stubborn as mules. Did Parnell get his back up when you warned him?"

"I . . . think perhaps he did. I tell you, Cord, he can get that six-shooter out of leather damn quick. He just can't hit anything with it."

The men chatted for a time, then Smoke left the rancher composing the letter he was sending to Judge Ford. The rider would leave that afternoon. Smoke saddled up and rode out to check on Fae's cattle. As soon as he pulled out, Parnell and Rita left in the buggy, heading for town.

"I shan't be a moment, Rita," Parnell said as they neared Gibson. "I only need to gather up a few articles from the school."

Rita put a hand on Parnell's leg and almost curled his toenails. "Take as long as you like. I'll be waiting for you . . . darling."

Parnell's collar suddenly became very tight.

He gathered up his articles from the school and hurried back to the buggy.

"Would you mind terribly taking me over to Mrs. Jefferson's house, Parnell? I have a dress over there I need to pick up."

"Not at all . . . darling."

Rita giggled and Parnell blushed. He clucked the horse into movement and they went chatting up the main street of Gibson. They did not go unnoticed by a group of D-H gunslicks loafing in front of the Hangout, the busted window now boarded up awaiting the next shipment of glass.

"Yonder goes Miss Sweety-Baby and Sissy-Pants," Golden said, sucking on a toothpick.

"Let's us have some fun when they come back through," Eddie Hart said with a wicked grin.

"What'd you have in mind?"

"We'll drag Sissy-Britches out of that there buggy and

strip him nekkid right in the middle of the street; right in front of Pretty-Baby."

They all thought that would be loads of fun.

Golden looked at an old rummy sitting on the steps, mumbling to himself. "What the hell are you mumbling about, old man?"

"I knowed I seed that schoolteacher afore. Now it comes to me."

"What are you talkin' about, you old rum-dum?"

" 'Bout fifteen year ago, I reckon it was. Back when Reno was just a sandy collection of saloons and hurdy-gurdy parlors. They was a humdinger of a shootin' one afternoon. This kid come riding in and some hombres decided they'd have some fun with him. In 'bout the time it'd take you to blink your eyes four times, they was four men in the street, dead or dyin'. The kid was snake quick and on the mark. He disappeared shortly after that." The old man pointed toward the dust trail of the buggy. "That there, boys, is the Reno Kid!"

22

"The *Reno Kid!*" Golden hissed, as his front chair legs hit the boardwalk.

"He's right!" Gandy, a member of Cat Jennings's gang almost shouted the words. "I was there! I seen it! That there is shore nuff the Reno Kid. He's all growed up and put on some weight, but that's him!"

"Damn right!" the wino said. "I said it was, din I. I was thar, too."

"That's why he don't never pack no gun," another said. "Who'd have thought it?"

"He's mine," Golden said.

"We'll both take him," Gandy insisted. "Man lak 'at you cain't take no chances with."

"But he ain't packin' no iron!" another said. "Hit'd be murder, pure and simple."

Golden said a cuss word and leaned back in his chair.

"Here they come!" Gandy looked up the street. "To hell with it. I'll force his hand and call him out. Make him git a six-gun."

"I'll keep you covered in case he's packin' a hideout gun," Golden told him.

Both men stood up, Gandy stepping out into the wide street, directly in the path of the buggy.

Parnell whoaed the horse and sat glaring at the gunslick.

Gandy glared back.

"Will you please remove your unwashed and odious presence from the middle of the street, you ignorant lout!" Parnell ordered.

"Whut the hale did you say to me, Reno?"

Parnell blinked and looked at Rita, who was looking at him. "I'm afraid you have me confused with someone else," Parnell said. "Now kindly step out of the way so we may proceed on our journey."

"Git outta that thar buggy, Reno! I'm a gonna kill you."

"He thinks you're the Reno Kid." Rita gripped Parnell's arm.

"Who, or what, is the Reno Kid?"

"A legendary gunfighter from the Nevada Territory. He'd be about your age now. No one has seen him in fifteen years."

"What the hale-far is y'all whisperin' about?" Gandy hollered. "What'd the matter, Reno, you done turned yeller?"

"I beg your pardon!" Parnell returned the shout. "Begone with you before I give you a proper hiding with a buggy whip, you fool!"

No one seemed to notice the tall, lean, darkly tanned stranger standing in the shadows of the awning in front of the Pussycat. He was wearing a gun, but then, so did nearly every man. He stood watching the goings-on with a faint twinkle of amusement in his dark eyes.

If it got out of hand, he would interfere, but not before.

"Y'all heard it!" Gandy shouted. "He called me a fool! Them's fightin' words, Reno. Now get out of that there buggy."

"I most certainly will not, you . . . you . . . hooligan!"

"I think I'll just snatch your woman outta there and lift her petticoats. Maybe that'll narrow that yeller stripe a-runnin' down your back."

Before he even thought about the consequences, Parnell

stepped from the buggy to the street. His coat was covering his pistol. "I demand you apologize to Miss Rita for that remark, you brute!"

"I ain't a-gonna do no sich of a thing, Reno."

"My name is not Reno and oh, yes, you will!"

"Your name shore as hell is Reno and I will not!"

Gandy could not see most of Parnell for the horse. Parnell brushed back his coat and put his hand on the butt of his gun, removing the leather thong from the hammer and stepping forward, drawing as he walked.

Gandy saw the arm movement and grabbed iron. Parnell stubbed his toe on a rock in the street and fell forward, pulling the trigger. The hammer dropped, the slug striking Gandy right between the eyes and knocking him down, dead before he hit the dirt.

Shocked at what he'd done, Parnell turned, the muzzle pointing toward Golden just as Golden jerked his gun out of leather.

Parnell instinctively cocked and fired, the bullet slamming into Golden's stomach and doubling him over. By this time, Rita had jerked a Winchester out of the boot and eared the hammer back.

"That's it, Reno!" Eddie Hart hollered. "We don't want no more trouble."

Parnell looked at the dead and dying men. He felt sick at his stomach; fought back the nausea as he climbed back into the buggy, first holstering his pistol. He picked up the reins and clucked the mare forward, moving smartly up the street.

"I feel quite ill," Parnell admitted.

"You're so brave!" Rita threw her arms around his neck and gave him a wet kiss in his ear.

Parnell almost lost the rig.

"I seen some fancy shootin' in my days, boys," Pooch Matthews said. "But I ain't never seen nothing like that. Damn, but that Reno is fast."

"Like lightnin'," another said. "Smoke's been holding an ace in the hole all this time."

The stranger walked back into the Pussycat and up to the bar. "You got rooms for rent upstairs?"

"Sure do. Bath's out back. That was some shootin', wasn't it?"

"Yes," the stranger chuckled. "I will admit I have never seen anything like it. I'll take a room; might be here several days."

"Fix you right up. Even give you a clean towel. Them sheets ain't been slept in but once or twice. Maybe three times. Clean sheets'll cost you a quarter."

The stranger laid a quarter down on the bar. "Clean ones, please."

"We ain't got no registry book. But I'm nosy. You ain't from around here, are you."

"No."

"If you gonna hire on with Dooley, the room is gonna cost you fifty dollars a night."

"I never heard of anyone called Dooley. I'm just tired of riding and would like to rest for a few days."

"Good. Fifty cents a night, then. The schoolteacher is really the Reno Kid. Dadgum! How about that? Where are you from, mister?"

"Oh, over Nevada way."

"Dammit, Parnell!" Smoke grabbed the reins behind the driving bit. "I told you not to go into town wearin' that gun."

"He's the Reno Kid!" Rita shouted, and everybody within hearing range turned and came running. "I just watched him beat two gunnies to the draw and kill them both. Right in front of the Hangout."

Smoke looked at Parnell, shock in his eyes. "You *hit* something? With a pistol?"

"I stubbed my toe. The gun went off. I am not the Reno Kid."

"He ain't the Reno Kid!" Charlie said. "I been knowin' Reno for twenty years."

Parnell turned to Rita. "You see. I told you repeatedly that I am not the Reno Kid."

"Oh, I know *that*, honey. But I sure got everybody's attention, didn't I?" She hopped from the buggy and raced over to Sandi to tell her story.

"Reno changed his name about fifteen years ago and went to ranchin' up near the Idaho border." Charlie cleared it up. "But he shore left a string of bodies while he was gunslingin'."

Smoke turned back to Parnell. "You really got them both?"

"One was hit between the eyes. I'm sure he's dead. The lout called Golden took a round in the stomach. If he isn't dead, he'll certainly be incapacitated for a very long time."

"What the hell is in-capassiated?" Hardrock muttered.

"Beats me," Pistol said. "Sounds plumb awful, though."

Parnell climbed down from the buggy and Corgill led the rig to the barn. Smoke faced the man. "All right, Parnell. You're tagged now. There'll be a hundred guns looking for you . . ."

"That is perfectly ridiculous!" Parnell cut in. "I am not the Reno Kid!"

"That don't make no difference," Silver Jim told him. "This time tomorrow the story will be spread fifty miles that the Reno Kid has surfaced and is back on the prowl. By this time next week it'll be all over the territory and they'll be no tellin' how many two-bit punks and would-be gunhawks comin' in to make their rep. By killin' you. Welcome to the club, Schoolteacher," he added bitterly.

Charlie patted Parnell on the back. "You go git out of them town duds, Parnell. The four of us is gonna take you under our wing and teach you how to handle that there Colt."

Parnell stood with his mouth open, unable to speak.

"But Parnell don't sound like no gunfighter's name to me," Silver Jim said. "Where was you born, Parnell?"

"In Iowa. On the Wolf River."

"That's it!" Charlie exclaimed. "You ain't the Reno Kid, so from now on, your handle is Wolf."

"Wolf!" Parnell stared at the man. "Have you taken leave of your senses?"

"Nope. Wolf, it is. The Wolf is on the prowl. I like it."

"This is madness!" Parnell yelled.

"Go on now, Wolf," Hardrock told him. "Git you some jeans and boots. Strap on and tie down that hog leg. We'll set up a target range."

"See you in a few minutes, Wolf." Pistol grinned at him.

"This is absurd!" Parnell muttered. He started up the steps, tripped, and fell face down on the porch. He picked himself up with as much dignity as possible and entered the house.

Charlie shook his head. "We got our work cut out for us, boys."

Golden died that night, cursing the man he believed to be the Reno Kid as he slipped across that dark river. Twenty-four hours later, a dozen men were riding for Gibson, their burning ambition to be the one man who faced the Reno Kid and brought him down. Another twenty-four later, two dozen more punks and tinhorns would be on their way, until those looking to make a reputation by killing the Reno Kid would grow to a hundred. And the news had spread that Smoke Jensen was really in Gibson—nobody had believed it up to now; indeed, many people believed that Smoke Jensen really did not exist, he was such an elusive figure.

Telegraph wires began humming and a dozen big newspapers sent reporters into Montana to cover the story. Within a week, Gibson had a brand-spanking-new hotel and had been added to the stagecoach route.

The stranger from Nevada decided to stay, watching all the fuss with amusement in his eyes, spending most of his time sitting in a chair under the awning in front of the Pussy-cat.

Dooley had pulled in his men, cussing at all the notoriety

and knowing this was no time to enlarge the range war. The hate within the man continued to fester, ready to erupt at any moment, spewing blood and violence all over the area.

Judge Ford was at some sort of conference, out of the state, and would be back in about a month.

"Another good idea shot down," Cord said, disgusted at the news.

Four more saloons had been thrown up in Gibson, along with several more stores, including a gunshop, a dress shop—for a lot of ladies of the evening were coming in—an apothecary shop, and another general store.

A lot had happened in a week.

Thanks to the Reno Kid aka Parnell.

"We found out what was wrong with Wolf not bein' able to shoot worth a damn," Charlie told Smoke.

Smoke closed his eyes for a few seconds and shook his head. "Wolf," he muttered. "What a name. What was wrong with him, Charlie?"

"He's scared of guns! Pistols 'specially."

"Good God! Charlie, there's about a hundred people in Gibson—new people—with one thought in mind: to kill the Reno Kid, real name Parnell, now called Wolf. He's a schoolteacher, Charlie. Not a gunfighter. The poor man is a walking target."

Hardrock grinned. "But we come up with something, Smoke. Lookee here." He held up the ugliest and most awesome-looking rig Smoke had ever seen.

"What in God's name . . . !"

The old gunfighters had taken two double-barreled shotguns and sawed the barrels down to about ten inches long. They had then fashioned a pistol-type butt for the terrible weapons.

"Those things would break a man's arm!" Smoke said, eyeballing the rigs.

"Not Wolf's arm. For a schoolteacher, he's powerful

strong. And he's just as fast with these here things as he is with a pistol," Silver Jim said with a nearly toothless grin.

"That's all the booming I been hearing."

"Right! Man, Wolf is plumb awesome with these here things," Pistol said. "We got 'um loaded up with rusty nails and ball-bearin's and raggedly little rocks and the like. We done loaded up near'bouts a case of shells for him. He's ready to go huntin' him a rep."

"Pistol, Parn . . . Wolf doesn't want a rep," Smoke said.

Charlie grinned. "You ain't seen much of him for a week, Smoke. You gonna be ass-tonished at the change. Come on."

Smoke was more than astonished. He didn't even recognize the man. Parnell had grown a mustache, and that had completely changed his appearance. He was dressed all in black, from his hat down to his polished boots. He looked very capable and very tough.

"I gotta see him draw and cock and fire these hand cannons," Smoke said.

"With pleasure, Cousin." Parnell strapped on the weapons.

"You watch this," Charlie said, as Cord and several others gathered around.

Pistol and Silver Jim rolled several full water barrels out and backed away.

"They's a-facin' you, Wolf!" Charlie said, excitement in his voice. "Watch 'um now. Watch they eyes. That'll give 'em away ever time."

Parnell tensed, his hands hovering over the butts of the terrible weapons.

"They's about ready to make their play!" Hardrock called out. "You got to take out the man on your left first, he's the bad one."

"Now!" Silver Jim yelled.

Parnell's right hand dipped and his left hand came across to support the sawed-off shotgun. One barrel exploded in a roar of gunsmoke, the second barrel was shattered as Parnell let loose the second charge. As fast as anything Smoke had ever seen—considering the cumbersome weapons he was using—Parnell dropped the first sawed-off to the ground and drew the left hand shotgun. The third barrel was reduced to splinters.

"I'm impressed," Smoke said.

"I'm proud of you, Brother!" Fae said.

"I love you!" Rita yelled.

Hardrock looked close at Parnell and shook his head. "Furst time I ever seen a wolf blush!"

23

"Feel like trying out the new general store?" Cord asked Smoke.

"I thought you'd never ask. I forgot to pick up some tobacco last time in."

"Ah . . . Parnell wants to go along. I refuse to call him Wolf. I just can't!"

Smoke laughed. "I can't either. Sure, if he wants to come along. I notice he's been in the saddle for the last week. He's turned out to be a pretty good rider."

"Man is full of surprises. And speaking of surprises, I'm told that we're all in for a surprise when we see what's happening, or has happened, to Gibson."

"Yeah. I hear there's even a paper."

"*The Gibson Express.* I want to pick up a copy."

"How about your boys?"

"I ordered them to stay close to their ma. They'll obey me."

"I'll put on a clean shirt and meet you out front."

Cord, Smoke, Parnell, Lujan, Beans, Del, Charlie, and Ring rode into Gibson. A wagon rattled along behind them to carry the supplies back, Cal at the reins. At the edge of town, they reined up and stared in disbelief. The once tiny and sleepy little town was now a full three blocks long and several blocks deep on either side. Many of the new stores were no more than knocked-together sideboards with canvas tops, but it was still a very impressive sight.

"This spells trouble, gentlemen," Lujan said.

"Yeah," Charlie agreed, standing up in his stirrups for a moment. "You bet your boots it does."

"I fail to see how the advancement of civilization, albeit at first glance quite primitive in nature, could be called trouble," Parnell stated.

"That town ain't filled with nothin' but trash," Charlie told him. "Hurdy-gurdy girls, tin-horn hustlers and pimps, two-bit gunslingers, slick-fingered gamblers, and the like. It's dyin' while it seems to be growin'. As soon as this war is settled, one way or the other, ninety-nine percent of them down yonder will pull up stakes and haul their ashes. Town will be right back where it started from."

"How about the one percent that will stay?" Parnell questioned.

"Good point," Charlie agreed. "Wolf, you stay on top of things down yonder in that town. They's gonna be a bunch of people eyeballin' ever move you make. And you gonna get called out. Bet on it."

"I am aware of that," the schoolteacher turned gunfighter said. "I am ready to confront whatever comes my way."

"Me and you, Parnell," Beans said, "will have us a cool beer in one of them new saloons. Check things out."

Parnell glanced at him. "I detest the taste of beer. However, I might have a sarsaparilla."

The Moab Kid returned the glance. "You go sashayin' up in a saloon in the middle of a bunch of hardcases and order sodee pop, Parnell, you better be ready for trouble, 'cause it's shore gonna be comin' at you."

"I am aware of that, too."

"Let's go," Smoke said.

The men rode slowly toward the now-crowded street of the West's newest boom town. The news of their arrival spread as quickly as a prairie fire across dry grass. In less than a minute, the wide street had emptied. No one wanted to be caught in the middle of a gunfight, and that was something that everybody knew might be, probably was, only a careless word away.

As the men rode past the Pussycat, Charlie cut his flint-hard eyes to a stranger sitting on the boardwalk, his chair tilted back. Charlie smiled faintly.

Gonna get real interestin' around here, Charlie thought.

Ring reined up in front of Hans and dismounted. "I shall be visiting Hilda," he told them. "I will come immediately if there is trouble."

Cord, Del, and Cal pulled up in front of the new general store. "Which one of those new joints are you boys going to try?" Cord asked.

"How about Harriet's House?" Parnell asked. "That sounds quite congenial."

"Oh, I'm sure it will be," Beans said. "Harriet always runs a stable out back."

"Well, then, that will be a convenient place for our horses."

"A stable of wimmin, Parnell," Beams told him. "For hire."

"You mean . . . I . . . ladies who sell their . . . ?"

"Right, Parnell."

Smoke dismounted and almost bumped into a small man wearing a derby hat and a checkered vest. The man's head struck Smoke about chest-high.

"Horace Mulroony's the name, sir. Owner and editor of *The Gibson Express*. And you would be Smoke Jensen?"

"That's right."

Horace stuck out his hand and Smoke took it, quickly noticing that the hand was hard and calloused. He cut his eyes just for a flash and saw that the stocky man's hands were thick with calluses around the knuckles. A Cornish boxer sprang into Smoke's mind. Not very tall, but built like a boxcar. Something silently told him that Horace would be hard to handle.

"And your friends, Mister Jensen?"

Smoke introduced the man all around, pointing them out. "Charlie Starr, Lujan, The Moab Kid, Parnell Jensen."

"The man they're calling the Reno Kid."

"I am not the Reno Kid."

"Name's Wolf," Charlie said shortly. He didn't like newspaper people; never wanted any truck with them. They never got anything right and was always meddlin' in other folks' business.

"I see," Horace scribbled in his notebook. "That is quite an unusual affair strapped around your waist, Wolf."

"I would hardly call two sawed-off shotguns an affair, Mister Mulroony. But since this is no time to be discussing proper English usage, I will let your misunderstanding of grammer be excused—for now."

Mulroony laughed with high Irish humor. "You sound like a schoolteacher, Wolf."

"I am."

"Ummm. Are you gentlemen going to have a taste in Miss Harriet's saloon?"

"We was plannin' on it," Charlie said. "The sooner the better. All this palaverin' is makin' me thirsty."

"Do you mind if I join you?"

"Could we stop you?" Charlie asked.

"Of course not!" Horace grinned. "After you, Mister Starr." He waved at a man toting a bulky box camera and the man came at a trot. Horace grinned at the gunfighters. "One never knows when a picture might be available. I like to record events for posterity."

Charlie grunted and pushed past the smaller man, but not before he saw the stranger leave his chair in front of the Pussycat and walk across the street, toward the saloon they were entering.

Charlie had a hunch the stranger was thinking about joining the game. He knew from experience that the man was a sucker for the underdog.

The saloon was filled with hardcases, both real and imagined. Smoke's wise and knowing eyes immediately picked out the real gunslingers from the tinhorn punks looking for a reputation.

Smoke knew a few of the hard cases in the room. Several from Dad Estes's gang were sitting at a table. A few that had left Cord's spread were there. A couple of Cat Jennings's bunch were present. They didn't worry Smoke as much as the young tinhorns who were sitting around the saloon, their guns all pearl-handled and fancy-engraved and tied down low.

The known and experienced gunhandlers had stiffened when their eyes touched the awesome rig belted around Parnell's waist. Nobody in their right mind wanted to tangle with a sawed-off shotgun, since a buckshot load at close range would literally tear a man in two. Even if a man could get lead into the shotgun toter first, the odds were, unless the bullet struck him in the brain or the heart, that he could still pull a trigger.

"Beer," Smoke said.

"Tequila," Lujan ordered.

Beans and Charlie opted for whiskey.

Horace ordered beer.

Parnell, true to his word, looked the barkeep in the eyes and ordered sarsaparilla.

Several young punks seated at a nearby table started laughing and making fun of Parnell.

Parnell ignored them.

The barkeep served up the orders.

"What's the matter with you, slick?" a young man laughed the question. "Cain't you handle no real man's drink?"

Parnell took a sip of his sarsaparilla and smiled, setting the bottle down on the bar. He turned and looked the young man in the eyes. "Does your mother know where you are, junior?"

The punk's eyes narrowed and he opened his mouth to retort just as the batwings swung open and the stranger entered.

There is an aura about really bad men, and in the West a bad man was not necessarily an outlaw. He was just a bad man to fool with. The stranger walked between the punk and Parnell, his hands hanging loosely at his side. He wore one gun, a classic Peacemaker .45, seven-and-a-half-inch barrel. It was tied down. The man looked to be in his mid-to-late thirties, deeply tanned and very sure of himself. He glanced at Parnell's drink and a very slight smile creased his lips.

Walking to Charlie's side, he motioned to the barkeep. "A sarsaparilla please."

Another loudmouth sitting with the punk started giggling. "Another sissy, Johnny. You reckon they gonna kiss each other."

"I wouldn't be surprised."

The barkeep served up the stranger's drink and backed away, to the far end of the bar. When they had entered, the bar had been full. Now only the seven of them remained at the long bar.

The stranger lifted his bottle. "A toast to your good health," he said to Charlie.

Charlie lifted his shot glass and clinked it against the bottle. "To your health," he replied. If the man wanted to reveal his real identity that was up to him. Charlie would hold the secret.

"Hey, old man!" Johnny hollered. "You with them wore-out jeans on."

Charlie sipped his whiskey and then turned to face the mouthy punk. "You talkin' to me, boy?"

"I ain't no boy!"

"No," Charlie said slowly, drawling out the word. "I reckon you ain't. Strappin' on them guns makes you a man. A loudmouth who ain't dry behind the ears yet. And if you keep flappin' them lips at me, you ain't never gonna be dry behind your dirty ears."

Johnny stood up, his face flushed red. "Just who the hell do you think you are, old man?"

"Charlie Starr."

The words were softly offered, but they had all the impact of a hard slap across Johnny's face.

Johnny's mouth dropped open. He closed it and swallowed hard a couple of times. Beads of sweat formed on his forehead.

Charlie spoke, his words cracking like tiny whips. "Sit down, shut your goddamned mouth, or make your play, punk!"

The experienced gunhandlers had noticed first off that the men at the bar had entered with the leather thongs off their hammers.

"You cain't talk to me lak 'at!" Johnny found his voice. But it was trembly and high-pitched.

"I just did, boy."

Johnny abruptly sat down. He tried to pick up his beer mug but his hand was shaking so badly he spilled some of it on the tabletop.

Charlie turned his back to the mouthy punk and picked up his shot glass in his left hand.

But there wasn't a man or woman in the bar who thought it was over. The punk would settle down, gulp a few more drinks to boost his nerve, and would have to try Charlie, or leave town with his tail tucked between his legs.

"Been a long time, Charlie," the stranger said.

"Near'bouts ten years, I reckon. You just passin' through?"

"I was. I decided to stay."

"What name you goin' by nowadays?"

"Same name that got hung on me seventeen-eighteen years ago."

Being a reporter—Charlie would call it being a snoop, among other things—Horace leaned around and asked, "And what name is that, sir?"

The stranger turned around, facing the crowd of punks and tinhorns, loudmouths and barflys, hurdy-gurdy girls, gamblers, and gunfighters, who were all straining to listen. He let his eyes drift around the room. "I never did like a lop-sided fight, Charlie. You recall that, I suppose." It was not posed in question form.

"I allow as to how I do. I 'member the time me and you stood up to a whole room filled to the rafters with trash and cleaned it out." He chuckled. "That there was a right good fight." Charlie held up his shot glass in salute and the stranger clinked his sarsaparilla bottle to the glass.

"I got my other gun in my kit over to the roomin' house. I reckon I best go on over and get it and strap it on. Looks like we got some house-cleanin' to do."

"I couldn't agree more."

Smoke was smiling, nursing his beer. He'd already figured out who the stranger was.

One of Cat Jennings's men lifted his leg and broke wind. "That's what I think about you, stranger."

"How rude!" Parnell said.

"Sissy-pants," the man who had made the coarse social comment stood up. "I think I'll just kill you. 'Cause I don't believe you're the Reno Kid."

"Of course, he isn't," the stranger said. "I am!"

24

That news broke the spirit of a couple of men who had already been toying with the idea of rattling their hocks. They stood up and walked toward the door. Charlie Starr and them old gray-headed he-cougars with him was bad enough. Add the Moab Kid and Lujan to that mixture and you was stirrin' nitro too fast with a flat stick. Smoke Jensen was the fastest gun in the West. Now here comes the Reno Kid, and there goes anybody with a lick of sense.

The batwings squeaked and two gunnies were gone.

The gunhand facing Parnell didn't back down. Without taking his eyes from Parnell, he said, "Did anybody pull your chain, Reno?"

"Nope," Reno answered easily.

"You gonna fight Sissy-pants' battles for him?"

"Nope."

"You ready to die, Sissy-pants?"

"Oh, I think not." Parnell had turned, facing the man, his right hand hovering near the butt of the holstered sawed-off. "But I do have a question?"

"Ax it!"

"What is your name?"

"Readon. What's it to you?"

"I just wondered what to have carved on the marker over your grave."

"Draw, damn your eyes!" the man shouted, and grabbed for his six-gun.

Parnell was calm and quick. Up came the awesome weapon, the right side hammer eared back. Across went his left hand in a practiced move, gripping the short barrels. The range was no more than twelve feet and the booming was enormous in the beery, smoky room. The ball-bearings and rusty nails and ragged rocks hit the gunhand in the belly and lifted him off his boots while the charge was tearing him apart. He landed on a table several feet away from where he had been standing, smearing the tabletop with crimson and collapsing the table. He had never even cleared leather.

The hurdy-gurdy girls began squalling like hogs caught in barbed wire and ran from the room, their short dresstails flapping as they ran.

Parnell, seeing that no one was going to immediately take up the fight, but sensing that was only seconds away, broke open the shotgun pistol and tossed aside the empty, loading it up full. He snapped it shut and eared back both hammers.

The gunhand Smoke had first seen at that little store down on the Boulder stood up. "Me and Readon had become pals, Jensen," Dunlap said. "You a friend of that shotgun-toter, so that makes you my enemy. I think I'll just kill you."

He grabbed for his guns.

Smoke shot Dunlap in the chest just as his hands gripped the butts of his guns. Dunlap looked puzzled for a moment, coughed up blood, and sat down in the chair he should never have gotten out of. He slowly put his head on the tabletop and sighed as that now-familiar ghost rider came galloping up, took a look around, and grinned in a macabre fashion. He decided to stick around. Things were quite lively in this little town.

The ghost rider put a bony hand on another's shoulder as

half the men in the barroom grabbed for iron and Lujan shot one between the eyes.

Mulroony jumped behind the bar and landed on top of the barkeep who was already on the floor. He'd been a bartender in too many western towns not to know where the safest place was.

Parnell's sawed-off shotgun-pistol roared again, the charge knocking two gunnies to the floor. Johnny picked that time to make his move. Just as he was reaching for his guns, Parnell stepped the short distance as he was reversing the weapon. Using it like a club, he hit Johnny in the mouth. Teeth flew in several directions and Johnny was out cold. Parnell dropped to the floor and once more loaded up.

The Reno Kid was crouched by the bar, coolly and carefully picking his shots.

Charlie had dropped two before a bullet took him in the shoulder and slammed him against the bar. He did a fast border-roll with his six-gun and kept on banging. When his gun was empty, Lujan grabbed the older man and literally slung him over the bar, out of the line of fire.

The Moab Kid took a round in the leg and the leg buckled under him, dropping him to the floor, his face twisted in pain.

But it was Parnell who was dishing out the most death and destruction. Firing and loading as fast as he could, the schoolteacher did the most to clear out the room and end the fighting.

The gunnies and tinhorns gave it up, one by one dropping their still-smoking six-guns and raising their hands in the air. Cord, Del, Ring, and Cal stepped through the batwings, pistols drawn and cocked, Ring with his double-barrel express gun.

"Get Doc Adair," Smoke said, his voice husky from the thick gunsmoke in the saloon.

Cal was gone at a bow-legged trot to fetch the doctor.

Lujan helped Charlie to a chair. The front of the old gunslinger's shirt was soaked with blood.

"Did I get the old bassard?" a gunhawk moaned the question from the floor. He had taken half a dozen rounds in the chest and stomach and death was standing over him, ready to take him where the fires were hot and the company not the best.

"You got lead in me," Charlie admitted. "But I'm a long ways from accompanyin' you."

"If not today, then some other time. So I'll see you in hell, Starr." The gunny grinned the words, his mouth bloody. He started to add something but the words would not form on his tongue. His eyes rolled back in his head and he mounted up behind the ghost rider.

Smoke had reloaded. He stood by the bar, his hands full of Colts, his eyes watching the gunnies who had chosen to give up the fight.

Johnny moaned on the floor and rolled over on his stomach one hand holding his busted mouth. The other hand went to his right hand gun. But it was gone.

"Are you looking for these?" Parnell asked, holding out the punk's guns in his left hand. His right hand was full of twelve gauge sawed-off blaster.

Johnny mumbled something.

"You're diction is atrocious," Parnell told him. He looked at Smoke and smiled. "My, Cousin, but for a few moments, it was quite exhilarating."

Smoke grinned and shook his head. "Yeah, it was, Parnell. I'll stand shoulder-to-shoulder with you anytime, Cousin."

Mulroony had crawled from behind the bar and waved his photographer in. The man set up his bulky equipment and sprinkled the powder in the flashpan. "Smile, everyone!" he hollered, then popped his shot, adding more smoke to the already eye-smarting air.

Beans had cut his jeans open to inspect the wound, and it was a bad one. "Leg's busted," he said tightly. "Looks like I'm out of it."

The flashpan popped again, the lenses taking in the bloody

sprawl of bodies and the line of gunhawks standing against a wall, their hands in the air, their weapons piled on a table.

While Doc Adair tended to Charlie and Beans, Smoke faced the surrendered gunhandlers. His eyes were as cold as chips of ice and his words flint-hard.

"You're out of it. Get on your horses and ride. If I see any of you in this area again, I'll kill you! No questions asked. I'll just shoot you. And no, you don't pack your truck, you don't get your guns, you don't draw your pay—you ride! Now! Move!"

They needed no further instructions. They all knew there would be another time, another place, another showdown time. They rushed the batwings and rattled their hocks, leaving in a cloud of dust.

"You tore up my place!" a woman squalled, stepping out of a back room.

"Howdy, Harriet," Beans called. "Right nice to see you again."

"You!" she hollered. "I might have known it'd be you, Moab." Her eyes flicked to the Reno Kid. "You back gun-handlin', Reno?"

"I reckon."

She looked at Smoke. Took in his rugged good looks and heavy musculature. "Remember me, big boy?"

"I remember you, Harriet. You were one of the smart ones who left Fontana early."

"Did you kill Tilden Franklin?"

"I sure did."

"Man ever deserved killin', that one did. You gonna run me out of Gibson?"

"I didn't run you out of Fontana, Harriet."

"For a fact. See you around, baby." She turned and pushed through a door.

"He can't sit a saddle," Adair said, standing up from working on Beans's leg. "And I'd rather he didn't for a few days." The doctor pointed to Charlie.

"I'll put some hay in the wagon," Cal said, and left the saloon.

The undertaker and his helper, both of them trying very hard to keep from smiling, entered the saloon and walked among the dead and dying, pausing at each body to go through the pockets.

"Does I get my guns back?" Johnny pushed the words through mashed lips and broken teeth.

Parnell looked at Smoke. Smoke nodded his head. "Give them to the punk. He'd just find some more. One of us is gonna have to kill him sooner or later."

The flashpan belched once again.

"What a story this will make!" Horace chortled, rocking back and forth on his feet. "I shall dispatch it immediately to New York City."

"Do try to be grammatically correct," Parnell reminded him.

Horace gave him a smile. A very thin smile.

Sandi hollered and bawled and carried on something fierce when she saw Beans in the back of the wagon but then brightened up considerably when she realized he'd be laid up for several weeks and she could nurse him.

Reno had checked out of his room and rode back to the Circle Double C with the men. He had strapped on his other Peacemaker and was in the fight to the finish.

Charlie bitched about having to be bedded down in the main house so the ladies could take proper care of his wound. Hardrock told him to shet his mouth and think about what a relief it would be to the others not to have to look at his ugly face for a spell.

"It works both ways," Charlie popped back, smiling as the ladies fussed over him.

Parnell had taken a slight bullet burn on his left arm. But the way Rita acted a person would have thought he'd been riddled. She insisted on spoon-feeding him some hot soup she fixed—just for him.

"What did we accomplish?" Cord asked Smoke.

"Damn little," he admitted. "Seems like every time we run off or kill a gunhawk, there's ten to step up taking his place."

Cord added some more numbers in his tally book and shook his head at the growing number of dead and wounded. "Why did the Reno Kid toss in with us, Smoke? Charlie says he's married, with several children."

"So am I," Smoke reminded the man.

Something good did come out of the gunfight inside Harriet's saloon: many of the hangers-on decided to pull out; the fight was getting too hot for many of the tin-horn and would-be gunfighters. They'd go back to their daddy's farms and be content to milk the cows and gather the eggs, their guns hanging on a peg.

But it left the true hardcases, many of them on no one's payroll. Like buzzards, they were waiting to see the outcome and perhaps pick up a few crumbs of the pie.

Johnny and his punk sidekick, Bret, were still in town, swaggering around, hanging on the fringes of the known gunslingers, talking rough and tough and lapping up the strong beer and rotgut and snake-head whiskey served at most of the newer saloons.

Crime had increased in Gibson, with foot-padders and petty thieves plying their trade on the unsuspecting men and women who had to venture out after dark. And the hardcases were getting surly and hard to handle, craving action.

There were several minor run-ins among the gunhawks provoked by recklessness and restlessness and booze and the urge to kill and destroy. The leaders of the gangs had to step in and calm the situation, reminding the outlaws that their fight was not with each other, but with the Double Circle C.

"Then gawddammit!" Lodi snarled. "Let's *make war* on them!"

The Hangout, jammed full of hired guns, shook with the roars of approval.

Dad Estes did his best to shout his boys down while Jason Bright and Cat Jennings and Lanny Ball tried to calm their people.

They were only half successful.

The leaders looked at each other and shrugged their shoulders. Dad jerked his head toward the boardwalk and the men stomped outside, to stand in the night.

"We got to use them or lose them," Dad summed it up. "My boys ain't gonna stand around here much longer twiddlin' their thumbs."

The others agreed with Dad.

"So you got some sort of a plan, Dad?"

"We hit them, tonight."

"What does Dooley have to say about that?" Jason asked.

"I ain't discussed it with him."

The others smiled, Dad continuing, "Look here, we could turn this into a right nice town, and if we was all big land owners, why, we'd also own the sheriff and deputies and the like."

"We got to kill Dooley and them first," he was reminded by Cat Jennings.

Dad shifted his chewing tobacco to the other side of his mouth. He took out an ornate pocket watch and clicked it open. "Well, boys, I got some people doin' that little thing in about an hour."

25

Dooley came awake, keeping his eyes closed. The slight creaking of the hall door had brought him awake. He had drank himself to sleep, sitting in the big chair just inside the living room. The first time he'd ever done that. Now wide awake, he sat very still in the darkness and opened his eyes.

"I tole you to oil that door!" His oldest boy, Sonny, hissed the words.

"Shet your mouth," Bud whispered. "The old fool was prob'ly so drunked up when he went to bed a shotgun blast wouldn't wake him up."

Conrad giggled. "A shotgun blast is what we're goin' give him!"

Cold insane fury washed over the father as he froze still in his chair. If he'd had a gun in his hand, he'd have killed all three of them right this minute. But his gun belt was hanging on the peg in the hall.

Sonny shushed his brothers. "Stay here and keep watch, Conrad. Me and Bud will do the deed."

"I don't wanna keep no watch! I wanna see it when the buckshot hits him. And what the hell is I gonna be watchin' for anyways? There ain't nobody here but us. The others is all back in town.

"Do what I tell you to do."

Dooley carefully drew his feet up under the chair, hiding them from view should any of his traitorous offspring look into the living room. The sorry sons of bitches.

The dark humor and irony of that thought almost caused him to chuckle.

The stillness of the house was shattered by twin shotgun blasts.

Then he remembered he hadn't made up his bed from the past night; the pillows and covers must have fooled the boys into thinking their dad was lying in bed.

Boots ran up the hall. "Got the old nut-brain!" Sonny shouted. "The ranch is ourn. Let's go join the other boys and finish the deed."

The front door slammed shut.

What deed? Dooley thought.

The thunder of hooves hammered past the house. Dooley moved to the window and watched his bastard sons gallop out of sight.

That damn Cord put them up to this! Dooley's fevered brain quickly reached that conclusion. He jerked on his boots and ran into the hall, pausing to yank his gun belt from the peg and belt it around his waist. He ran to the kitchen and filled a gunnybag with cans of food, a side of bacon, some hardtack. He took a big canteen and filled that at the kitchen pump. Then he ran to the study and quickly opened his safe, stuffing a money belt full of cash money he'd just received from the army cattle buyer. He belted the money bag around his middle. In his bedroom, he rolled up some clothes in a blanket and slipped out the back of the house, stopping only once, to fill his pockets with .44 rounds and pick up a small coffee pot and skillet.

Dooley saddled a horse and stuffed the saddlebags full of supplies. He hung the canteen and bag on the saddle horn and took off into the timber of the Little Belt Mountains.

When his boys come back, they'd find that what they'd shot was only a bed, and they'd come lookin' to kill their pa.

"Come on, you miserable whelps," Dooley muttered, talking to his horse. His best horse. His favorite horse. Dooley could sleep in the saddle and his horse would never falter. The horse also knew where Dooley was going as soon as Dooley guided the way toward the old Indian trail that wound in a circuitous route to the base of Old Baldy, the highest peak in the Little Belts, which ran for some forty miles from southeast of Great Falls to the Musselshell. Dooley and his horse had come here often, just to think—to let the hate fester over the past few years.

"Goddamn you, Cord," Dooley muttered. "You heped take my woman from me and now you done turned my sons agin me. I'm a-gonna kill ever' one of you. Ever' stinkin' one of you!"

"Here they come!" The shout from Smoke was only seconds before the mass of riders entered the Circle Double C ranch complex. But it was enough to roust everybody out of bed.

Smoke's shout was followed by a war whoop from Hardrock that echoed across the draws and hollows and grazing land of the ranch.

"Hep me close to that winder." Charlie told Parnell. "I'll take it from there. I can shoot jist as good with my left hand as I can with my right."

Across the hall, Beans told Sandi, "Get some help and shove my bed to that window and hand me my rifle. Then you and Rita get on the floor."

The girls positioned the bed and reached for their own rifles.

"Cain't you wimmin take orders?" Beans asked over the thunder of hooves.

"We stand by our men," Sandi told him. "Now shut up and shoot!"

"Yes, dear," Beans said, just as a bullet from an outlaw's gun knocked a pane of glass out of the window.

Before Beans could sight the rider in, Parnell's sawed-off blaster roared, the charge lifting the man out of the saddle and hurling him to the ground, his chest and throat a bloody mess.

"Give 'em hell, baby!" Rita shouted her approval.

"You curb that vulgar tongue, woman!" Parnell glared at her.

"Yes, dear," Rita muttered.

From the bunkhouse, Ring was deadly with a rifle, knocking two out of the saddle before a round misfired and jammed the action. Ring turned just as a man was crawling in through a rear window. Reversing the Winchester, Ring used the rifle like a club and smashed the outlaw on the forehead with the butt. The sound of a skull cracking was evident even over the hard lash of gunfire. Ring grabbed up the man's Colts and moved to a window. He wasn't very good with a pistol, but he succeeded in filling the night with a lot of hot lead and made the evening very uncomfortable for a number of outlaws.

Smoke and the Reno Kid had grabbed up rifles and bandoleers of ammunition and raced to the barn and corral, knowing that if the outlaws succeeded in stampeding their horses they were doomed. Reno climbed into the loft, with Jake and Corgill. Fitz, Willie, and Ol' Cook stayed below, while Smoke and Gage remained outside, behind watering troughs by the corral.

The outlaw, Hartley, who was wanted for murder down in the Oklahoma Nations, tried to rope the corral gates and bring them down. Smoke leveled his pistol and the hammer fell on an empty chamber. Running to the man, Smoke jerked him off his horse and smashed the man in the face with a balled right fist, then a left to the man's jaw. He jerked Hartley's pistol from leather and rapped the outlaw on the headbone with it. Hartley lay still in the dirt.

Smoke stuck both of Hartley's pistols behind his belt, reloaded his own .44's, and climbed onto Hartley's horse, a big dun. He would see how the outlaws liked the fight taken to them.

Smoke charged right into the middle of the confusing dust-filled fray. He saw the young punk gunslick Twain and shot him out of the saddle, one of Twain's boots caught in the stirrup. Twain's horse bolted, dragging the wounded and screaming young punk across the yard. His screaming stopped when his head impacted against a tree stump.

Smoke stayed low in the saddle, offering as little target as possible for the outlaws' guns. He slammed the horse's shoulder into an outlaw's leg. The gunny screamed in pain from his bruised leg and then began screaming in earnest as the horse lost its balance and fell on him, breaking the outlaw's other leg. The horse scrambled to its feet, the steel-shod hooves ripping and tearing flesh and breaking the outlaw's bones.

Cat Jennings rammed his big gelding into Smoke's horse and knocked Smoke to the ground. Rolling away from the hooves of the panicked horse, Smoke jumped behind a startled outlaw, stuck a pistol into the man's side, and pulled the trigger. Shoving the wounded man out of the saddle, Smoke slipped into the saddle, grabbed up the reins, and put his spurs to the animal's sides, turning the horse, trying to get a shot at Cat.

But the man was as elusive and quick as his name implied, fading into the milling confusion and churning dust. Smoke leveled his pistol at Ben Sabler and missed him clean as the man wheeled his horse. The bullet slammed into another outlaw. The outlaw was hard-hit, but managed to stay in the saddle and gallop out of the fight.

"Back! Back!" Lanny Ball screamed, his voice faint in the booming and spark-filled night. "Fall back and surround the place."

Smoke tried to angle for a shot at Lanny and failed. Jumping off his horse, Smoke rolled behind a tree in the front yard of the main house, and with a .44 in each hand, emptied guns into the backs of the fast-retreating outlaws. He saw several jerk in their saddles as hot lead tore into flesh and one man fell, the back of his head bloody.

Smoke ran to the house. Jumping on the front porch, he saw the body of Willie, draped over the porch railing. On the other side of the porch, Holman was sprawled, a bloody hole in his forehead.

"Damn!" Smoke cursed, just as Cord pushed open the screen door and stepped out.

Cord's face was grim as he looked at the body of Willie. "Been with me a long time," the rancher said. "He was a good hand. Loyal to the end."

"Man can't ask for a better epitaph," Smoke said. "Cord, you take the barn and I'll run to the bunkhouse. Tell the men to fortify their positions and fill up every canteen and bucket they can find." He cut his eyes as Liz and Alice came onto the porch. "You ladies start cooking. The men are going to need food and lots of it. We might be pinned down here for days."

Cord said, "I'll have some boys gather up all the guns and ammo from the dead. Pass them around." He stepped off the porch and trotted into the night.

"Larry!" Smoke called, and the hand turned. "Get the horses out of the corral and into the barn. Find as much scrap lumber as you can and fortify their stalls against stray lead.

The cowboy nodded and ran toward the corral, hollering for Dan to join him.

Smoke and Parnell carried the bodies of Holman and Willie away from the house, placing them under a tree; the shade would help as the sun came up. The men covered them with blankets and secured the edges with rocks.

Snipers from out in the darkness began sending random rounds into the house and the outbuildings, forcing everyone to seek shelter and stay low.

"This is going to be very unpleasant," Parnell said, lying on the ground until the sniping let up and he could get back to the house.

"Wait until the sun comes up and the temperature starts rising," Smoke told him. "Our only hope is that cloud buildup." He looked upward. "If it starts raining, I plan on heading into the timber and doing some head-hunting. The rain will cover any sound."

"Do you think prayer would help?" Parnell said, only half joking.

"It sure wouldn't hurt."

There were seven dead outlaws, and all knew at least that many more had been wounded; some of them were hard-hit and would not live.

But among their own, Corgill and Pat had been wounded. Their wounds were painful, but not serious. They could still use a gun, but with difficulty.

Smoke and Cord got together just after first light and talked it out, tallying it up. They were badly outnumbered, facing perhaps a hundred or more experienced gunhandlers, and the defenders' position was not the best.

They had plenty of food and water and ammunition, but all knew if the outlaws decided to lie back and snipe, eventually the bullets would seek them out one by one. The house was the safest place, the lower floor being built mostly of stone. The bunkhouse was also built of stone. The wounded had been moved from the upstairs to the lower floor. Beans, with his leg in a cast, could cover one window. Charlie Starr, the old war-hoss, had scoffed off his wound and dressed, his right arm in a sling, but with both guns strapped around his lean waist.

"I've hurt myself worser than this by fallin' out of bed," he groused.

Parnell had gathered up a half dozen shotguns and loaded them up full, placing them near his position. The women had loaded up rifles and belted pistols around their waists.

Silver Jim almost had an apoplectic seizure when he ran from the bunkhouse to the main house and put his eyes on the women, all of them dressed in men's britches, stompin' around in boots, six-guns strapped around their waists. He opened his mouth and closed it a half dozen times before he could manage to speak. Shielding his eyes from the sight of women all dressed up like men, with their charms all poked out ever' whichaway, he turned his beet-red face to Cord and found his voice.

"Cain't you do somethin' about that! It's plumb indecent!"

"I tried. My wife told me that if we had to make a run for it, it would be easier sittin' a saddle dressed like this."

"Astride!" Silver Jim was mortified.

"I reckon," Cord said glumly.

"Lord have mercy! Things keep on goin' like this, wimmin'll be gettin' the vote 'for it's over."

"Probably," Parnell said, one good eye on Rita. There was something to be said about jeans, but he kept that thought to himself.

"Wimmin a-voting?" Silver Jim breathed.

"Certainly. Why shouldn't they? They've been voting down in Wyoming for years."

The old gunfighter walked away, muttering. He met Charlie in the hall. "What's the matter, that bed get too much for you?"

" 'Bout to worry me to death. Layin' in there under the covers with nothing on but a nightgown and wimmin comin' and goin' without no warning. More than a body can stand."

"Where are you fixin' on shootin' from?"

"I best stay here with these folks. Come the night they'll be creepin' in on us."

"Gonna rain in about an hour. My bones is talkin' to me."

"Then Smoke is gonna be goin' headhuntin'. Preacher taught him well. He'll take out a bunch."

"You reckon some of us ought to go with him?"

"Nope. You know Smoke, he likes to lone-wolf it."

"He's been diggin' in his war bag and he's all dressed up

in buckskin, right down to his moccasins. He was sittin' on a bunk, sharpenin' his knife when I left."

Charlie's grin was hard. "Them gunhandlers is gonna pay in blood this afternoon. Bet on that, old hoss."

"Who's gonna pay in blood?" Cord asked, walking up to the men.

"Them mavericks out yonder. Smoke's fixin' to go lookin' for scalps come the rain."

"Sounds dangerous to me." The rancher shook his head.

Silver Jim laughed. "Oh, it will be." He jerked his thumb toward the hills. "For them out there."

26

The sky darkened and lightning began dancing around the high mountains of the Little Belt, thunder rolling ominously. Then the sky opened and began dumping torrents of rain. With his rifle slung over his shoulder with a strap, hanging barrel down, and his buckskin shirt covering his six-guns and a long-bladed Bowie knife sheathed, Smoke slipped out into the rain on moccasin-clad feet. He kept low to the ground, utilizing every bit of natural cover he came to. He moved swiftly but carefully and made the timber and brush without drawing a shot.

Once in the brush, he paused, studying every area in his field of vision before moving out. He had shifted his long-bladed knife to just behind his right hand .44.

He froze still as a mighty oak at the sound of voices. Clad in buckskins, with the timber dark and gloomy as twilight, Smoke would be hard to spot unless he was right on top of a man.

And he just about was!

"I shore wants me a crack at that Sandi McCorkle," the voice came to him very clear, despite the driving rain and gusts of wind.

"We'll use all them pretty gals 'fore we kill them," a second voice was added. "You see anything movin' down yonder?"

"Naw. They all shet up in the buildings."

"I be back, Tabor. I got to . . ." His words were drowned out by a clap of thunder. ". . . Must have been somethang I et."

Slowly Smoke sank down behind a bush as a red-and-white checkered shirt stood and began moving toward him. The pair must be Tabor and Park. Two thoroughly tough men. When Park passed the bush, Smoke rose up like a brown fog. His Bowie in his right hand. He separated Park's head from his shoulders with one hard slash, catching the headless body before it could come crashing to the ground and alert Tabor.

Easing the body to the wet earth, Smoke picked up the head and placed it in a gunnybag he'd tucked behind his belt.

Then he went looking for Tabor.

Circling around to come in behind the Oklahoma outlaw, Smoke laid his bloody-bottomed sack down on a rock and Injuned up to Tabor, coming in slowly and making no sound.

Tabor never knew what happened. The big-bladed and heavy knife flashed in the stormy light and another head plopped to the earth. That went in the sack with Park's head.

Smoke moved on through the rain and spots of fog that clung low to the ground, swirling around his moccasined feet, as silent as his footsteps.

Someone very close to him began firing—not at Smoke, for at the sound of the hammer being eared back, Smoke had bellied on the gound—but at the house. More guns were added to the barrage and Smoke added his .44 to the man-made thunder, his bullet striking a gunman in the head.

"Hey!" a man shouted, his voice just audible over the roar of rifles. "Pete's hit!" He stood up, an angry look on his face, sure that someone on his side was getting careless.

Smoke shot him between the eyes and the man fell back with a thud that only Smoke could feel as he lay on the ground.

Smoke worked his way back into the timber, climbing up the hill as he moved. Behind a thick stand of timber, he paused for a break and squatted down, the bloody sack beside him. He hadn't made up his mind what to do with the heads, but an idea was formed.

He ate a biscuit and cupped his hands for a drink of rainwater. He did not have one ounce of remorse or regret for what he was doing. He knew only too well that to fight the lawless, one must get down and wallow in the muck and the crud and the filth with them, using the same tactics, or worse, that they would use against an innocent. To win a battle, one must understand the enemy.

Rested, Smoke moved out, staying above the positions of the outlaws. He circled wide, wanting to hit them at widely separated spots, wanting them to know they had not been alone and had been attacked by someone who had walked among them with the stealth of a ghost.

A hard burst of gunfire came from the house, the bullets hitting the rocks and the rain-soaked earth several hundred feet below Smoke's position. As the outlaws returned the fire, Smoke leveled his Winchester and counted more coup, his fire covered by the outlaw's own noise. The lone outlaw—Smoke did not know his name and did not recall ever seeing him before—slumped forward, his rifle sliding from lifeless hands, a bloody hole in the man's back.

Smoke slipped down to the man's position and left the bloody bag of heads by the dead man's side. He added his ammunition to that he'd gathered from the others and moved on.

He had planned on sticking the heads up on poles but decided this way would be just as effective.

He continued his circling, which would eventually bring him out on the north end of the ranch complex. He caught just a glimpse of the Hanks boys. Bellying down, he started working his way to their position, freezing log-still as two gunslicks, wearing canvas ponchos, stepped out of the timber and headed in his direction. They were so sure of themselves they were not expecting any trouble and were not checking their surroundings. Smoke could catch only a few of the words that passed between them.

". . . Never thought them boys would do it . . ."

". . . Didn't like my old man, but I don't think I'd have had the . . . kill him with a shotgun."

". . . Be gettin' ripe layin' up in that bed . . . Sonny pulled the trigger, I reckon."

". . . All three of um's crazy as a bessy-bug."

The outlaws moved out of earshot and Smoke lay for a moment, putting some sense into what he'd heard. The Hanks boys had killed their father with a shotgun, probably as he lay sleeping in bed.

Smoke broke off his head-hunting and began making his way back to the ranch. If the news was true, and he had no reason to doubt it, for the Hanks boys were as goofy as their father, that meant that part of the outlaws' plans had been accomplished. And everyone at the Circle Double C had to die for the outlaws' planned takeover to succeed.

Smoke moved quickly, always staying in the brush and timber. As he was approaching the ranch complex, he heard a horrified shout from the hills and knew that the bag of heads had been found . . . either that or the headless bodies of the outlaws.

Smoke began moving cautiously, for at this point he was open to fire from either side. Closer to the house, he began a meadowlark's call. Charlie waited for a moment and then returned the call. When a human gives a birdcall, a practiced ear can pick up the subtle difference, no matter how good the caller is.

Smoke ran the last few hundred feet, zigging and zagging to offer a hard target. But if the outlaws saw him, they did not fire; probably they were too busy searching the ridges for the unknown headhunter. On the back porch, Liz and Alice had towels for him, a change of clothes—Cord's long underwear and jeans and shirt—and a mug of coffee, for Smoke was soaked and cold.

Smoke broke the news to a horrified audience.

Liz shook her head but shed no tears for her husband or sons. And neither did Rita.

"Killed their own father!" Cord was visibly shaken by the news. "Good God!"

Parnell was the first to put the upcoming horror into words. "Then we—all of us—have to die if their plans are to succeed."

The women looked at each other. They knew that for them, it would not be a quick bullet. They would be used, and used badly, until the outlaws tired of them. Only then would death bring relief.

"Reno comin' at a run," Charlie said, looking out the window. "He's been out eyeballin' the situation close to home."

The gunfighter was as soaked as Smoke had been. The women shooed him into a room and handed him towels and dry clothing. When he emerged, they had coffee waiting for him.

He took a gulp of the strong hot coffee. "They blocked off the road leading south and have men waiting in the passes. They have so many men it was no problem to seal us off. Any bust-out is gonna be difficult, if not downright impossible."

"And walking out will be tough with the wounded," Smoke added. "But if we stay here, they'll eventually overrun us by their number. Or they'll burn the buildings down around us. Beans is gonna have to be carried out of here. Pat and Corgill can walk out with him. I'm going to suggest that the women leave with them." He looked at Parnell. "Parnell, you and Gage, Del and Bernie will spell each other with the litter. Me and Reno will make the litter right now. You people pack some food and blankets; make a light backpack and get ready to move out at dark. Let's do it."

All knew that Smoke had casually but deliberately chosen the men to accompany the women. Then he irritated the hell out of Charlie Starr by suggesting that he accompany the foot party.

"I'll be damned if I will!" the old gunfighter flared up.

"Charlie . . . ," Smoke put a hand on his friend's shoulder. "They need you. They need your experience in guiding them and they need your gun."

"Well . . ." Charlie calmed down. "If you put it that way. All right. But I hate like hell to miss out on this here fight."

"Damned ol' rooster with a busted wing." Hardrock told him. "You look after them folks, now, you hear me, you old coot?"

"I've told them to head for the old Fletcher gold mine in the Big Belt," Cord said. "It's been abandoned for years and we cache supplies there. From there, they can angle back East and make it into Gibson. But it's gonna be a long hard haul for them all."

"You just get me in a saddle!" Beans groused. "I ain't never seen the day I couldn't sit on a hurricane deck."

"Oh, hush up!" Lujan told him. "Just lay back and enjoy the trip. Amigo, you injure that leg again, and you'll be a cripple for the rest of your life. It's better this way and you know it."

Beans did some fancy cussing, but finally agreed to shut up about it and accept his fate.

Smoke pulled Cord to one side. "How do you feel about leaving your ranch to those jackals out there on the ridges?"

"I don't like it. But I think it's gonna happen. See if my plan agrees with yours: We give them walkin' out a full twenty-four hours. Then we saddle up, put sacks on the horses' hooves, and lead them out a'ways. Then we all hit one spot just as hard as we can."

"That's it. We'll get the foot party moving just after dark and pray that this rain doesn't let up. They're going to be wet and cold and miserable, but I think they've got more of a chance out there than staying here."

Cord nodded his big head. "I'll pass the word to the hands. You sure you don't want a diversion?"

"No. That would be a sure tipoff that we're up to something. Anyway, I think they'll hit us at full dark. That'll be enough."

The afternoon wore on with only a few shots being exchanged from each side. Those in the house knew that the outlaws would be cold, soaking wet, miserable, and their patience would be growing thin with each sodden hour that passed.

And those in the ranch compound also knew, some more than others, that after finding the sack of bloody heads and several more of their kind shot to death, most of the outlaws would be wanting revenge in the worst sort of way, for they would know it had been Smoke stalking them silently on the ridges.

Smoke looked out onto the gray dripping afternoon. Twenty-four hours. They had to hold out for twenty-four hours.

Reno seemed to read his thoughts. "We'll hold, Smoke. Some of them might breech the house, but it'll be a death trap for them. One thing in our favor, they damn sure can't burn the place down . . . at least not this night."

"From the outside," Smoke stuck an amendment to that. "A couple of torches tossed inside, though . . ."

Cord heard it. "I've got some lumber out in the shed. Rock, Troy, you boys fetch the lumber while we get some nails and hammers. We'll board up windows we're not shooting from. On both levels of the house." He began ripping down curtains and drapes to lessen the fire hazard.

As the sounds of the muffled hammering began drifting to the outlaws on the ridges, the gunfire picked up, forcing the men to work more carefully, without exposing themselves. Those inside the house didn't have to worry about breaking a window with all the hammering, all the windows were already shot out.

Those windows not being used as shooters' positions boarded up, Smoke went to find Fae.

He put his arm around her shoulders and kissed her cheek. "I'm headin' back outside, Fae. I like to be outside when the action goes down." He looked at the other women. "You ladies watch your step this night. We'll see you all in a couple of days."

He shook hands with the men who were leaving that night. "You boys enjoy your stroll. As soon as it gets full dark, take off. And good luck."

He walked back into the living room, leaving Cord to say his goodbyes to wife and daughter.

"I'm going to pull Ring and Hardrock, Silver Jim, and Pistol in the house with you and Cord and the boys," he told Reno. "The rest of us will be in the bunkhouse and the barn." He looked outside. "Be dark shortly. I'm heading out yonder. The others will be showing up one at a time about five minutes apart. Good luck tonight."

"Luck to you, Smoke."

There was nothing left to say. The two famed gunhandlers looked at each other, nodded their heads, and Smoke slipped out onto the stone and wood porch. He knew the chances of his being seen from several hundred yards away were practically nonexistent, but he stayed low from force of habit.

Smoke darted off the porch and to a tree in the yard, then over the fence and a foot race to the corral. Then, as he got set for the run to the bunkhouse, a cold voice spoke from behind him.

"I'll be known as the man who kilt Smoke Jensen. Die, you meddlin' bastard!"

27

Smoke threw himself to one side just as the pistol roared. He could feel the heat of the bullet as it passed his arm. He twisted his body in the air and hit the muddy ground with a .44 in his hand, the muzzle spitting fire and smoke and lead.

Hartley took the first slug in his chest and Smoke fired again, the force of his landing lifting his gun hand, the second slug striking the gunhawk in the throat. Hartley, with a knot plainly visible on his rain-slicked head, the hair matted down, leaned up against a corral rail and lifted his six-gun, savage all the way to the grave.

A .44-.40 roared from the bunkhouse and Spring's aim was true. Hartley's head ballooned from the impact of the slug and he pitched forward, into a horse trough.

Riflemen from the ridges and the hills opened up, not really sure what they were shooting at, but filling the air with lead. Smoke lay where he was, as safe there as anywhere in the open expanse between house and bunkhouse. When the fire from the outlaws slacked up, Smoke scrambled to the bunkhouse and dove headfirst into the building, rolling to his feet.

"Thanks, Spring," he told the old hand. "Hartley must have laid out there in the corral all covered up with hay since I conked him on the noggin last night."

"Hell, he was dead on his feet when I shot him," the old hand said. "I just like some in'shorence in cases like that."

He poured Smoke a cup of coffee and returned to his post by a window.

Smoke drank the strong hot brew and laid out the plans. One by one, the old gunfighters began leaving the bunkhouse, heading for the house. Ring was the last to stand in the door. He smiled at Smoke.

"You always bring this much action with you when you journey, Smoke?"

"It sure seems like it, Ring," Smoke said with a laugh.

The big man returned the laugh and then slipped out into the rapidly darkening day, the rain still coming down in silver sheets.

"I got to thinkin' a while back," Spring said. "After Ring asked me how it was nobody come to our aid. Smoke, they's sometimes two, three weeks go by don't none of us go to town. Ain't nobody comin' out here."

"And even if they did come out, what could they do? Nothing," he answered his own question. "Except get themselves killed. It'd take a full company of Army troops to rout those outlaws."

There had been no fire from the ridges, so the men had safely made the house. Darkness had pushed aside the day. Those walking out would be leaving shortly, and they had a good chance of making it, for the move would not be one those on the ridges would be expecting. To try to bust out on horseback, yes. But not by walking out. Not in this weather.

When the wet darkness had covered the land for almost an hour, Smoke turned to Spring. He could just see him in the gloom of the bunkhouse.

"I don't think they'll try us on horseback this night, Spring. They'll be coming in on foot."

"You right," Donny whispered from the far end of the bunkhouse. "And here they come. You want me to drop him now or let them come closer?"

"Let them come on. This rain makes for deceptive shooting."

A torch was lighted, its flash a jumping flame in the windswept darkness. The torch bobbed as the carrier ran toward the house. From the house, a rifle crashed. The torch stopped and fell to the soaked earth, slowly going out as its carrier died.

All around the compound, muzzle flashes pocked the gloom, and the dampness kept the gunsmoke low to the ground as an arid fog.

A kerosene bomb slammed against the side of the bunkhouse, the whiskey bottle containing the liquid smashing. The flames were slow to spread and those that did were quickly put out by the driving rain. Spring's pistol roared and spat sparks. Outside, a man screamed as the slug ripped through flesh and shattered bone. He lay on the wet ground and moaned for a moment, then fell silent.

Smoke saw a moving shadow out of the corner of his eye and lifted his pistol. The shadow blended in with the night and Smoke lost it. But it was definitely moving toward the bunkhouse. It was difficult, if not impossible, to hear any small sounds due to the hard-falling rain and the crash of gunfire. Smoke left the window and moved to the door of the bunkhouse, standing some six feet away from the door. Spring and Donny and two other hands kept their eyes to the front, occasionally firing at a dark running shape within their perimeter.

The bunkhouse door had no inner bar; most people didn't even lock their doors when they left for town or went on a trip. If somebody used the house to get out of the weather or to fix something to eat, they were expected to leave it as they found it.

The door smashed open and the doorway filled with men. Smoke's .44's roared and bucked in his hands. Screaming was added to the already confusing cacophony of battle. More men rushed into the bunkhouse, leaping over the bodies sprawled in the doorway. Smoke was rushed and knocked to the floor. He lost his left hand gun but jammed the muzzle of his right hand gun into the belly of a man and pulled the trigger. A boot caught him on the side of the head, momentarily addling him.

Smoke heaved the badly wounded man away and rolled to the far wall. Men were all over him swinging fists and gun barrels. Using his own now-empty pistol as a club, he smashed a face, the side of a head. Jerking the pistol from a man's holster, Smoke began firing into the mass of wet attackers. A bullet burned his side; another slammed into the wooden leg of a bunk, driving splinters into Smoke's face.

Jerking his Bowie from its sheath, Smoke began slashing out, feeling the warm flow of blood splatter his arm and face as the big blade drew howls of pain from his attackers.

He slipped to one side and listened to the cursing of the outlaws still able to function. Lifting the outlaw's pistol, Smoke emptied it into the dark shapes. The bunkhouse became silent after the battle.

"You hit, Smoke?" Spring called.

"Just a scratch. Donny?"

The young cowboy did not reply.

"I'll check," Fitz spoke softly. He walked to the cowboy's position and knelt down. "He rolled twelve," Fitz's voice came out of the darkness.

"Damn!" Smoke said.

Another attack from the outlaws had been beaten back, but Donny was dead and Cal had been wounded. Smoke's wounds were minor but painful. No one in the house had been hurt.

They had bought those walking out some time and distance. By this time, if they had not been discovered, they were clear. Clear, but facing a long, cold, wet, and slow march into the Big Belts. The house, the barn, and the bunkhouse were riddled with bullet holes. They had lost two horses, having to destroy them after they'd been hit by stray bullets. And no cowboy likes to shoot a horse.

The rain slacked and the clouds drifted away, exposing the moon and its light. With that, the outlaws slipped away into the shadows and made their way back to the ridges overlooking the ranch.

The moonlight cast its light upon the bodies of outlaws sprawled in death on the grounds. Some of those with wounds not serious tried to crawl away. Cord and Smoke and the others showed them no mercy, shooting them if they could get them in gunsights.

After the intitial attack had been beaten back, the outlaws fired from the ridges for several hours, finally giving it up and settling down for some rest.

The moonlight was both a blessing and a curse, for it would make their busting out a lot more difficult.

Smoke ran to the house to confer with Cord.

"I figure just after sunset," the rancher said. "After the moon comes up, it'll be impossible."

"All right. We'll head in the opposite direction of those walking out. We'll start out like we're trying to bust through the roadblock, then cut east toward the timber. That sound all right to you?"

"Suits me."

Dooley had changed his mind about heading farther into the mountains, turning around when he was about halfway to Old Baldy. He rode slowly back toward Gibson.

At dawn of the second day of the attack on the Circle Double C, he was standing in front of the newly opened stage offices, waiting for the station agent. He plopped down his money belt.

"Stash that in your big safe and gimme a receipt for it," he told the agent.

That taken care of, Dooley walked over to the new hotel and checked in. He slept for several hours, then carefully bathed in the tub behind the barber shop, shaved, and dressed in clean clothes. He was completely free of the effects of alcohol and intended to remain that way. Nuts, but sober.

He walked over to Hans and enjoyed a huge breakfast, the first good meal he'd eaten in days. Hans and Olga and Hilda eyeballed the man suspiciously.

"Vere is everybody?" Hans broke the silence.

"I ain't got no idea," Dooley told him, slurping on a mug of coffee. "I ain't been to the ranch in two-three days." Really, he had no idea how long he'd been gone. Two days or a week. Time meant nothing to him anymore. He had only a few thoughts burning in his brain: to kill Cord McCorkle and then turn his guns on his traitor sons and watch them die in the muddy street. And if he didn't soak up too much lead doing that, and he could find her, he wanted to shoot his wife.

That was the sum total of all that was in Dooley Hanks's brain. He paid for his meal and took a mug of coffee with him, sitting in a chair on the boardwalk in front of the cafe. He would wait.

He sat in his chair, watching the town wake up and the people start moving around. He drank coffee and rolled cigarettes, smoking them slowly, his eyes missing nothing.

He watched as two very muddy and tired-looking riders rode slowly up the street, coming in from the north. Dooley set his coffee mug on the boards and stood up, staying in the morning shadows, only a dark blur to those still in the sunlight. He slipped the thongs from the hammers of his guns. The two riders reined up and dismounted, looping the reins around the hitchrail and starting up the steps to Hans. They stopped and stared in disbelief at the man.

Hector and Rod, two punk gunslicks Dooley had hired, stood with their mouths open.

"You 'pposed to be *dead!*" Hector finally managed to gasp.

"Well, I ain't," Dooley told them. "And I want some answers from you."

"We ain't got no quarrel with you," Rod told him. "All we want is some hot coffee and food."

"You'll get hot lead, boy," Dooley warned him. "Where the hell is my no'count sons?"

"I . . ." Hector opened his mouth. A warning glance from Rod closed it.

"You'd better talk to me, pup!" Dooley barked. " 'Fore I box your ears with lead."

Hector laughed at the man. "You ain't seen the day you could match my draw, old man." Hector was all of nineteen. He would not live to see another day.

Dooley drew and fired. He was no fast gunslinger, but he was quick and very, very accurate. The slug struck Hector in the heart and the young man died standing up. He fell on his face in the mud.

Dooley turned his gun toward Rod, the hammer jacked back. "My boys, punk. Where is they?"

"They teamed up with Jason and Lanny and Cat Jennings," he admitted. "I don't know where they is," he lied.

Dooley bought it. He sat down in the chair, his gun still in his hand. He would wait. They would show up. Then he'd kill them. He'd kill them all.

Rod backed up and led his horse across the street, to a little tent-covered cafe. Horace Mulroony had stood on the boardwalk across the street and witnessed the shooting. He motioned for his cameraman to bring the equipment. They had another body to record for posterity.

"Mister Hanks," he said, strolling up. "I would like to talk to you."

"Git away from me!" Dooley snarled, spittle leaking out of one corner of his mouth.

Horace got.

28

In the middle of the afternoon, in order to keep suspicion down, Smoke risked a run to the barn and began saddling all the horses himself. He laid four gunnybags or pieces of ripped-up blankets in front of each stall, to be used to muffle the horses' hooves when they first pulled out. Smoke went over each saddle, either taping down or removing anything that might jingle or rattle.

That done, he climbed up into the warm loft to speak to the men. Lujan was reclining on some hay. He opened his eyes and smiled at Smoke.

"At full dark, amigo?"

"At full dark. If you know any prayers, you best be saying them."

The gunfighter grinned. "Oh, I have!"

The other men in the loft laughed softly, but in their eyes, Smoke could see that they, too, had been calling—in their own way—for some heavenly guidance.

He climbed back down and decided to stay in the barn until nightfall. No point in drawing unnecessary gunfire from the ridges. He lay down on a pile of hay and closed his eyes. Might as well rest, too. It was going to be a long night.

* * *

Gage and Del had led the party safely past the gunmen on the ridges. An hour later they were deep in the timber and feeling better. It was tough going, carrying Beans on the stretcher, but by switching up bearers every fifteen minutes, they made good time.

Dawn found them miles from the Circle Double C. But instead of following Cord's orders, Del had changed directions and was heading toward Gibson. He had not done it autocratically, but had called for a vote during a rest period. The vote had been unanimous: head for town.

By midafternoon they were only a few miles from town, a very tired and foot-sore group.

Late in the afternoon, they came staggering up the main street of Gibson. People rushed out of stores and saloons and houses to stand and stare at the muddy group.

"Them wimmin's wearin' men's britches!" a man called from a saloon. "Lord have mercy. Would you look at that."

Gage quickly explained what had taken place and why they were here, Dooley listening carefully.

Rod stood on the boardwalk and stared at the group, his eyes bugged out. Parnell felt the eyes on him and turned, his hot gaze locking with Rod's disbelieving eyes. Parnell slipped the thongs from his blasters and walked toward the young man.

"I ain't skirred of you!" Rod shouted.

"Good," Parnell said, still walking. "A man should face death with no fear."

"Huh! It ain't me that's gonna die."

"Then make your play," Parnell said, and with that he became a western man.

Rod's hands grabbed for iron.

Parnell's blaster roared, and Rod was very nearly cut in two by the heavy charge. It turned him around and tossed him through the window and into the cafe, landing him on a table completely ruining the appetite of those having an early supper.

Beans had been keeping a good eye on Dooley; a good eye and his gun. Crazy as Dooley might be, he wasn't about to do anything with Beans holding a bead on him.

Dooley stood up slowly and held out his hand as he walked up to Gage. With a look of amazement on his face, Gage took the offered hand.

"You got a good woman, Gage. I hope you treat her better than I did." He turned to Liz and handed her the receipt from the stage agent. "Money from the sale of the cattle is over yonder in the safe. I'm thinkin' straight now, Liz. But I don't know how long it's gonna last. So I'll keep this short. Them boys of ourn took after me. They're crazy. And they got to be stopped. I sired them, so it's on my shoulders to stop them." Then, unexpectedly, and totally out of character for him, he took off his hat and kissed Liz on the cheek.

"Thank you for some good years, Liz." He turned around, walked to his horse, and swung into the saddle, pointing the nose of the horse toward the Circle Double C.

"Well, I'll just be damned!" Gage said. "I'd have bet ever' dollar I owned—which ain't that many—that he was gonna start shootin.' "

Liz handed him the receipt. "Here, darling. You'll be handling the money matters from now on. You might as well become accustomed to it."

"Yes, dear," the grizzled foreman said meekly. Then he squared his shoulders. "All right, boys, we got unfinished business to take care of. Let's find some cayuses and get to it."

Their aches and pains and sore feet forgotten, the men checked their guns and turned toward the hitchrails, lined with horses. "We're takin' these," Del said. "Anybody got any objections, state 'em now."

No one had any objections.

Hans rode up on a huge horse at least twenty hands high. He had belted on a pistol and carried a rifle in one big paw. I ride vit you," he rumbled. "Friends of mine dey are, too."

Horace came rattling up in a buggy, a rifle in the boot and a holstered pistol on the seat beside him. "I'm with you, boys."

More than a dozen other townspeople came riding up and driving up in buggies and buckboards, all of them heavily armed.

"We're with you!" one called. "We're tired of this. So let's ride and clean it out."

"Let's go, boys!" Parnell yelled.

"Oohhh!" Rita cooed. "He's so manly!"

"Don't swoon, child," her mother warned. "The street's too muddy."

Del leaned out of the saddle and kissed Fae right on the mouth, right in front of God and everybody.

Parnell thought that was a good idea and did the same with Rita.

The hurdy-gurdy girls, hanging out of windows and lining the boardwalks, all applauded.

Olga and Hilda giggled.

Gage leaned over and gave Liz a good long smack while the onlookers cheered.

Then they were gone in a pounding of hooves, slinging mud all over anyone standing close.

Dooley rode slowly back to his ranch. He looked at the buckshot-blasted bed and shook his head. Then he fixed a pot of coffee and poured a cup, taking it out to sit on the front porch. He had a hunch his boys would be returning to the ranch for the money they thought was still in the safe.

He would be waiting for them.

"I don't like it," Jason told Lanny, with Cat standing close. "Something's wrong down there. I feel it."

"I got the same feeling," Cat spoke. "But I got it last night while we was hittin' them. It just seemed like to me they was holdin' back."

Lanny snapped his fingers. "That's it! Them women and probably a few of the men walked out durin' the rain. Damn them! This ain't good, boys."

Cat looked uneasily toward the road.

Jason caught the glance. "Relax, Cat. There ain't that many people in town who gives a damn what happens out here. Then he smiled. "The town," he said simply.

Lanny stood up from his squat. "We've throwed a short loop out here, boys. Our plans is busted. But the town is standin' wide open for the takin'."

But Cat, older and more experienced in the outlaw trade, was dubious. "There ain't nobody ever treed no western town, Lanny. We done lost twenty-five or so men by the gun. Them crazy Hanks boys left nearabouts an hour ago."

"Nobody ever tried it with seventy-five-eighty men afore, neither. Not that I know of. 'Sides, all we've lost is the punks and tin-horns and hangers-on."

"He's got a point," Jason said.

"Let's ride!"

Dooley Hanks sat on his front porch, drinking coffee. When he saw his sons ride up, he stood up and slipped the thongs from the hammers of his guns. The madness had once more taken possession of his sick mind, leaving him with but one thought: to kill these traitor sons of his.

He drained his coffee mug and set the mug on the porch railing. He was ready.

The boys rode up to the hitchrail and dismounted. They were muddy and unshaven and stank like bears after rolling in rotten meat.

"If you boys come for the money, you're out of luck," Dooley called. "I give it to your momma. Seen her in town hour or so back."

The boys had recovered from their initial shock at seeing their father alive. They pushed through the fence gate and stood in the yard, facing their father on the porch. The boys spread out, about five feet apart.

"You a damn liar, you crazy old coot!" Sonny called. "She's over to Cord's place. Trapped with the rest of them."

"Sorry, boys." Dooley's voice was calm. "But some of 'em busted out and walked into town, carrying the Moab Kid on a stretcher. Now they's got some townspeople behind 'em and is headin' back to Cord's place. Your little game is all shot to hell."

Sonny, Bud, and Conrad exchanged glances. Seems like everything that had happened the last several days had turned sour.

"Aw, hell, Daddy!" Bud said, forcing a grin. "We knowed you wasn't in that there bed. We was just a-funnin' with you, that's all. It was just a joke that we made up between us."

"Yeah, Daddy," Sonny said. "What's the matter, cain't you take a joke no more?"

"Lyin' scum!" Dooley's words were hard, verbally tossed at his sons. "And you knowed who raped your sister, too, didn't you?"

The boys stood in the yard, sullen looks on their dirty and unshaved faces.

"Didn't you?" the father screamed the question at them. "Damn you, answer me!"

"So what if we did?" Sonny asked. "It don't make no difference now, do it?"

A deadly calm had taken Dooley. "No, it doesn't, Sonny. It's all over."

"Whut you mean, Daddy?" Conrad asked. "Whut you fixin' to do?"

"Something that I'm not very proud of," the father said. "But it's something that I have to do."

Bud was the first to put it together. "You can't take us Daddy. You pretty good with a gun, but you slow. So don't do nothing stupid."

"The most stupid thing I ever done was not takin' a horse-whip to you boys' butts about five times a day, commencin' when you was just pups. It's all my fault, but it's done got out of hand. It's too late. Better this than a hangman's noose."

"I think you done slipped your cinches agin, Pa," his old-est told him. "You best go lay down; git you a bottle of hooch and ponder on this some. 'Cause if you drag iron with us, you shore gonna die this day."

Dooley shot him. He gave no warning. He had faced men before, and knew what had to be done, so he did it. His slug struck Sonny in the stomach, doubling him over and drop-ping him to the muddy yard.

Bud grabbed iron and shot his father, the bullet twisting Dooley, almost knocking him off his boots. Dooley dragged his left hand gun and got off a shot, hitting his middle son in the leg and slamming the young man back against the picket fence, tearing down a section of it. The horses at the hitchrail panicked, breaking loose and running from the ugly scene of battle.

Conrad got lead in his father before the man turned his guns loose on his youngest boy. Conrad felt a double hammer-blow slam into his belly, the lead twisting and ripping. He began screaming and cursing the man who had fathered him. Raising his gun, the boy shot his father in the belly.

But still Dooley would not go down.

Blood streaming from his chest and face, the crazed man took another round from his second son. Dooley raised his pistol and shot the young man between the eyes.

As the light began to dim in Dooley's eyes, he stumbled from the porch and fell to the muddy earth. He picked up one of Sonny's guns just as the gut-shot boy eared back the hammer on his Colt and shot his father in the belly. Dooley jammed the pistol into the young man's chest and emptied it.

Dooley fell back, the sounds of the pale rider's horse coming closer.

"Daddy!" Conrad called, his words very dim. "Help me, Daddy. It hurts so bad!"

The ghost rider galloped up just in time to see Dooley stretch his arm out and close his fingers around Conrad's hand. "We'll ride out together, boy."

The pale rider tossed his shroud.

29

"They're pullin' out!" Lujan yelled from the loft.

Smoke was up and running for his horse as the men streamed out of the bunkhouse, all heading for the barn.

"Why?" Reno asked.

"That damn crazy Del led 'em into town!" Cord said, grinning. "We got help on the way. Bet on it."

In the saddle, Smoke said, "That means the town is gonna get hit. That's the only thing I can figure out of this move."

"Let's go, boys!" Cord yelled the orders. "They'll hit that town like an army."

The men waited for a few minutes, to be sure the outlaws had really pulled out, then mounted up and headed for town. They met the rescue party halfway between the ranch and Gibson.

Smoke quickly explained and the men tore out for Gibson.

"There she is, boys," Lanny pointed toward the fast-growing town. "We hit them hard, fast, grab the money, and get gone."

"I gotta have me a woman," one of Cat Jennings's men said. "I can't stand it no more."

"Mills," Cat said disgustedly. "You best start thinkin' with your brain instead of that other part. You can always find you a woman."

"A woman," Mills said, his eyes bright with his inner cruelty.

"Let's go." Jason spurred his horse.

Some seventy strong, the outlaws hit the town at a full gallop, firing at anything that came into sight. They rampaged through on the first pass, leaving several dead in the muddy main street and that many more wounded, crawling for cover.

At the end of the street, the men broke up into gangs and began looting the stores and terrorizing the citizens. Mills blundered into Hans's cafe and eyeballed Hilda.

"You a fat pig, but you'll do," he told the woman, walking toward her.

Hilda threw a full pot of boiling coffee into the man's face.

Screaming his pain and almost blind, Mills stumbled around the cafe, crashing into tables and chairs, both hands covering his scalded face.

Olga ran from the upstairs, carrying two shotguns. She tossed one to Hilda and eared back the hammers of her own, leveling the double-barrel twelve gauge at Mills. She gave him both barrels of buckshot. The outlaw was slung out the window and died on the boardwalk.

Mills's buddy and cohort in evil, Barton, ran into the cafe, both pistols drawn. He ran right into an almost solid wall of buckshot. The charges blew him out of one boot and sent him sailing out of the cafe, off the boardwalk, and into a hitchrail. Barton did a backflip and landed dead in the mud.

Hilda and Olga picked up his dropped pistols and reloaded their shotguns, waiting for another turkey to come gobbling in.

Harriet and her hurdy-gurdy girls had armed themselves and already had accounted for half a dozen outlaws, the bodies littering the floor of the saloon and the boardwalk out front a clear warning to others not to mess with these short-skirted and painted ladies.

The smithy, a veteran of The War Between The States and several Indian campaigns, stood in his shop with a Spencer .52 and emptied several saddles before the outlaws decided there was nothing of value in a blacksmith shop anyway.

Some of Dad Estes's men had charged the general store and laid a pistol up side Walt Hillery's head, knocking the man unconscious. They then grabbed his sour-faced wife, Leah, dragging her to the storeroom and having their way with her.

Leah's screaming brought Liz and Alice and Fae on the run, the women armed with pistols and rifles. Sandi and Rita were at the doctor's office with the wounded men.

Fae leveled her .45 at a man with his britches down around his boots and shot him in the head just as Alice and Liz began pulling the trigger and levering the action, clearing the storeroom of nasties.

Liz tossed a blanket over the still-squalling and kicking and pig-snorting Leah and gave her a look of disgust. "They must have been hard up," she told the shopkeeper.

Leah stopped hollering long enough to spit at the woman. She stopped spitting when Liz balled her right hand into a fist and started toward her.

"You wouldn't dare!" Leah hissed.

"Maybe you'd like to bet a broken jaw on it?" Liz challenged.

Leah pulled the blanket over her head, leaving her bony feet sticking out the other end.

The agent at the stagecoach line had worked his way up the ladder: starting first as a hostler, then a driver, then as a guard on big money shipments from the gold fields. He didn't think this stop would be in operation long, but damned if a bunch of outlaws were going to strip his safe.

When some of No-Count George Victor's bunch shot the lock off the door, the agent was waiting behind the counter, with several loaded rifles and shotguns and pistols. With him was his hostler and two passengers waiting for the stage, all heavily armed.

The first two outlaws to step through the door were shot dead, dying on their feet, riddled with bullet holes. Another tried to ride his horse through the big window. The animal, already frightened by all the wild shooting, resisted and bolted running up the boardwalk. The outlaw, just able to hang on, caught his head on the side of an awning and left the saddle, missing most of his jaw.

Beans was sitting next to an open window of the doctor's office, a rifle in his very capable hands. He emptied half a dozen saddles.

And Charlie Starr was calmly walking up the boardwalk, a long-barreled Colt in his hand. He was looking for Cat Jennings. One of Cat's men, a disgustingly evil fellow who went by the name of Wheeler, saw Charlie and leveled his pistol at him.

Charlie drilled him between the eyes with one well-placed shot and kept on walking.

A bullet slammed into Charlie's side and turned him around. He grinned through the pain. Doc Adair had seen the lump, pushing out of Charlie's side and their eyes had met in the office.

"Cancer," Charlie had told him.

Charlie lifted his Peacemaker and another outlaw went on that one-way journey toward the day he would make his peace with his Maker.

"Cat!" Charlie called, and the outlaw wheeled his horse around.

Charlie shot him out of the saddle.

Cat came up with his hands full of Colts, the hate shining in his eyes.

Charlie took two more rounds, both of them in the belly, but the old gunfighter stayed on his feet and took his time, carefully placing his shots. Cat soaked up the lead and kept on shooting.

Charlie border-rolled his second gun just as he was going to his knees in the muddy street. He could hear the thunder of hooves and something else, too: singing. It sounded like a mighty choir was singing him Home.

Charlie lifted his Peacemaker and shot Cat Jennings twice in the head. Propped up on one elbow, the old gunfighter had enough strength to make sure Cat was dead, then slumped to the floor.

Hardrock and Silver Jim and Pistol LeRoux had seen Charlie go down, and they screamed their rage as they jumped off their horse, their hands full of guns.

Silver Jim stalked up the boardwalk, holding his matched set of Remington .44's, looking for No-Count George Victor. Hardrock was by his side, his hands gripping the butts of his guns, his eyes searching for Three-Fingers Kerman and his buddy, Fulton. Pistol had gone looking for Peck and Nappy.

The Sabler Brothers, Ben, Carl, and Delmar were waiting at the edge of town, waiting for Lujan.

Diego, Pablo, and a gunfighter called Hazzard were waiting to try Smoke.

Twenty or more gunslicks had already hauled their ashes out of town. They had realized what the townspeople already knew: nobody hogties and trees a western town.

The Larado Kid had teamed up with several more punks, including Johnny and his buddy, Bret, and the backshooter, Danny Rouge. They had turned tail and galloped out of town. There would be another day. There always was. Besides Johnny had him a plan. He wanted to kill Smoke Jensen. And he knew this fight was just about over. Smoke would be heading home. And a lot could happen between Montana and Colorado.

"No-Count!" Silver Jim yelled, his voice carrying over the din of battle, the screaming of the wounded, and the sounds of panicked horses.

No-Count whirled around, his hands full of pistols. Silver Jim drew and fired as smoothly as he had forty years back, when he had cut the flap off a soldier's holster and tied it down.

Both the old gunfighter's slugs struck true and No-Count squatted down in the muddy alley, dropped his pistols, and fell over face first in the mud.

Hardrock felt a numbing blow striking him in the shoulder, staggering him. He turned, falling back up against a building front, his right-hand gun coming up, his thumb and trigger finger working as partners, rolling thunder from the muzzle.

Three-Finger Kerman went down, the front of his shirt stained with blood. Fulton fired at Hardrock and missed. Hardrock grinned at the outlaw and didn't miss.

Pistol Le Roux rounded a corner and came face-to-face with Peck and Nappy. Pistol's guns spat fire and death before the two so-called badmen could react. Pistol looked down at the dead and damned.

"Pikers!" he snorted, then turned and walked into one of the new saloons, called the Pink Puma, and drew himself a cool one from the deserted bar. He could sense the fight was over. He had already seen Dad Estes and his gang hightail it out of town.

Damn! but he hated that about Charlie. Him and Charlie had been buddies for nigh on . . . Hell, he couldn't remember how many years.

He drew himself another beer, sat down, and propped his boots up. It could be, he mused, he was getting just too old for this type of nonsense.

Naw! he concluded. He looked up as Hardrock came staggering in, trailed by Silver Jim.

"What the hell happened to you, you old buzzard?" he asked Hardrock.

"Caught one, you jackass!" Hardrock snapped. "What's it look like—I been pickin' petunias?"

"Wal, sit down." He shoved out a chair. "I'll fetch you a beer and then try to find the doctor. If I don't, you'll probably whine and moan the rest of the day." He took his knife and cut away Hardrock's shirt. "Bullet went clear through."

He got Hardrock a beer and picked up a bottle of whiskey. "This is gonna hurt you a lot more than it is me," he warned.

Hardrock glared at him.

Pistol poured some whiskey on the wounds, entrance and exit, and took a reasonably clean bar towel that Silver Jim handed him and made a bandage.

"You'll keep. Drink your beer."

"Make your play, gentlemen," Lujan told the Sabler Brothers.

Parnell stood by Lujan's side, smiling faintly.

The sounds of battle had all but ceased.

The Sablers grabbed for iron.

Lujan's guns roared just a split second before Parnell's blasters boomed, sending out their lethal charges. In the distance, a bugle sounded. Someone shouted, "The Army's here!"

Ben, Carl, and Delmar Sabler lay on the muddy bloody ground. Ben and Carl had taken slugs from Lujan. Delmar had taken a double dose from Parnell's blasters. He was almost torn in half.

Lojan holstered his guns and held out his hand. "My friend, you can stand shoulder-to-shoulder with me anytime you like. You are truly a man!"

Parnell blushed.

"Thank you, Lujan." He shook the hand.

"Come on, amigo. Let's go have us a . . . sarsaparilla."

30

The commander of the Army contingent, a Captain Morrison, met with Cord, Smoke, and a few others in what was left of the Hangout, while the undertaker and his helper roamed among the carnage.

"A lot of bad ones got away," Smoke told the young captain. Smoke's shirt was stiff from sweat and dirt and blood. "I expect I'll meet up with some of them on the trail home."

"Are you really Smoke Jensen?" The captain was clearly in awe.

"Yes."

Horace's photographer popped another shot.

The captain sighed. "Well, gentlemen. This is not an Army matter. I will take a report, certainly, and have it sent to the sheriff. But I imagine it will end there. I'm new to the West; just finished an assignment in Washington. But during my short time here, I have found that western justice is usually very short and very final."

"I don't understand part of what you just said." Cord leaned forward. "You mean you weren't sent in here?"

"No. We were traveling up to Fort Benton and heard the gunfire. We just rode over to see what was going on."

Smoke and Cord both started laughing. They were still laughing as they walked out of the saloon.

"The strain of battle." Captain Morrison spoke the words in all seriousness. "It certainly does strange things to men."

A grizzled old top sergeant who had been in the Army since before Morrison was born shifted his chew of tobacco to the other side of his mouth and said, "Right, sir."

Smoke went to the tubs behind the barber shop and took a long hot bath. He was exhausted. He dressed in clean clothes purchased at the new general store and walked over to Hans's for some hot food. The bodies of the outlaws were still being dragged off the street.

Hans placed a huge platter of food before the man and poured him a cup of coffee. Smoke dug in. Cord entered the cafe and sat down at the table with Smoke. He waved away the offer of food and ordered coffee.

"We have a problem about what to do with the wounded, Smoke."

"I don't have any problem at all with it. Treat their wounds and when they're well, try them."

"We don't have a jail to hold them."

"Build one to hold them or hang them or turn them loose."

"Captain Morrison is leaving a squad here to see that we don't hang them."

"Sounds like a real nice fellow to me. Very much law and order."

"You're being sarcastic, Smoke."

"I'm being tired, is what I am. Sorry to be so short with you. Is it OK to have Charlie buried out at the ranch?"

"You know it is," the rancher replied, his words softly spoken. "I wouldn't have it any other way."

"Any reward money goes to Hardrock and Silver Jim and Pistol."

"I've already set that in motion." He smiled. "You really think they're going to open a home for retired gunfighters?"

"It wouldn't surprise me at all."

"I tell you what: I'd hate to have them for enemies."

The men sat and watched as wagons pulled up to the four new saloons and began loading up equipment from Big Louie's, the Pink Puma, The JimJam, and Harriet's House.

"I'll be glad to see things get back to normal," Cord said.

"It won't be long. I been seeing that fellow who opened up the new general store makin' trips to Walt and Leah's place. Looks like he's tryin' to buy them out."

Cord's smile was not of the pleasant type. "Liz and Alice paid Walt and Leah a visit. They convinced Walt that it would be the best thing if they'd sell out and get gone. Parnell is buyin' their house. Him and Rita will live there after they're married."

"Beans?"

"I told him he was my new foreman. He's gonna file on some sections that border my spread."

Smoke finally smiled. "Looks like it's going to be a happy ending after all."

"A whole lot of weddin's comin' up next week. You are goin' to stay for them, aren't you?"

"Oh, yeah. I couldn't miss those." He looked up at Hans, smiling at them from behind the counter. "Hilda and Ring gonna get hitched up, Hans?"

The man bobbed his big head. *"Ja.* Ever'boody vill be married at vonce."

Smoke looked out at the muddy, churned-up street. All the bodies had been toted off.

"I reserved all the rooms above the saloon," Cord said. "The hands are back at the ranch, cleaning it up and repairing the damage. Bartender has your room key."

Smoke stood up, dropped some money on the table, and put on his hat. "I think I'll go sleep for about fifteen hours."

Bob and Spring and Pat and some hands from the D-H and the Circle Double C began rebuilding Fae's burned-down house and barn. Smoke, Hardrock, Silver Jim, and Pistol began driving the cattle back onto Box-T Range.

The legendary gunfighter, Charlie Starr, was buried in a quiet ceremony in the plot on the ridge above the ranch house at the Circle Double C. His guns were buried with him. He had always said he wanted to be buried with his boots on. And he was, a brand-new pair of boots.

Dooley Hanks and his sons were buried in the family plot on the D-H.

Horace Mulroony said he would stay around long enough to photograph the multiple weddings and then was going to open a paper up in Gibson.

"How about you, Lujan?" Smoke asked the gunfighter.

"Oh, I think that when you pull out I might ride down south with you. I have talked it over with Silver Jim and the others. They're coming along as well." He lit a long slender cigar and looked at Smoke. "You know, amigo, that this little war is far from over."

"I think they'll wait until we're out of Montana Territory to hit us."

"Those are my thoughts as well."

"We'll hang around until Hardrock's shoulder heals up. Then we'll ride."

Lujan smiled. "The first of the reward money has arrived. The old men said I would take a thousand dollars of it or we'd drag iron. I took the money. It will last a long time. I am a simple man and my needs are few."

"I'd hate to have to drag iron against those old boys," Smoke conceded. "They damn sure don't come any saltier."

Lujan laughed. "They have all bought new black suits and boots and white dusters. They present quite a sight."

Parnell packed away his double-barreled blasters. But his reputation would never quite leave him. He would teach school for another forty years. And he would never have any problems with unruly students.

Walt and Leah Hillery pulled out early one morning in a buckboard. They offered no goodbyes to anyone, and no one lifted a hand in farewell. It was said they were going back East. They just weren't cut out to make it in the West.

Several of the wounded outlaws died; the rest were chained and shackled and loaded into wagons. They were taken to the nearest jail—about a hundred miles away—escorted by the squad of Army troops.

The brief boomtown of Gibson settled back into a quiet routine.

Young Bob drew his time and drifted, as Smoke had predicted he would. The hard-eyed young man would earn quite a name for himself in the coming years.

Then came the wedding day, and the day could not have been any more perfect. Mild temperatures and not a cloud in the sky.

Del and Fae, Parnell and Rita, Liz and Gage, Ring and Hilda, and Beans and Sandi got all hitched up proper, with lots of fumbling around for rings and embarrassed kisses and a big hoo-rah right after the weddings.

Beans took time out after the cake-cuttin' to speak to Smoke.

"When you pullin' out, partner?"

"In the morning. I'm missin' my wife and kids. I want to get back to the Sugarloaf and the High Lonesome. Reno is pullin' out today; headin' back to Nevada."

"Them ol' boys is gonna be comin' at you, you know that, don't you?"

"Oh, yes. Might as well get it over with, way I look at it. No point in steppin' around the issue."

"You watch your backtrail, partner."

Smoke stuck out his hand and Beans took it. "We'll meet again," Smoke told him.

"I'm countin' on it."

As was the western way, there were no elaborate or pro-longed goodbyes. The men simply packed up and mounted up before dawn and pointed the noses of their horses south, quietly riding down the main street of Gibson, Montana Territory, without looking back.

"Feels good to be movin'," Pistol said. "I git the feelin' of being all cooped up if I stay too long in one place."

"Not to mention the fact that your face was beginnin' to frighten little children," Hardrock needled him. "All the greenbacks you got now you ought to git you a bag special-made and wear it over your head."

Smoke laughed and put Dagger into a trot. It did feel good to be on the trail again.

They followed the Smith down to the Sixteenmile and then followed an old Indian trail down to the Shields—the trail would eventually become a major highway.

The men rode easily, but always keeping a good eye out for trouble. None of them expected it until they were out of the territory, but it never hurt to be ready.

They began angling more east than south, crossing the Sweetgrass, taking their time, enjoying some of the most beautiful scenery to be found. They would stop early to make camp, living off the land, hunting or fishing for their meals, for the most part avoiding any towns. They ran out of coffee and sugar and bacon just north of the Wyoming line and stopped in a little town to resupply.

The man behind the counter of the general store gave Smoke and the others a good eyeballing as they walked into the store. The men noticed the clerk seemed awfully nervous.

"Fellers got the twitchies," Hardrock whispered to Silver Jim.

"I noticed. I'll take me a stroll down to the livery; check out the horses there."

"I'll go with you," Hardrock said. "Might be walkin' into something interestin'."

"You Smoke Jensen, ain't you?" the clerk asked.

"Yes."

"You know some hard-lookin' gents name of Eddie Hart and Pooch Matthews? They travelin' with several other gents just as hard-lookin'."

"I know them."

"They here. Crost the street in the saloon. My boy—who earns some pennies down to the stable—heared them talkin'. They gonna kill you."

"They're going to try." Smoke gave the man his order and then took a handkerchief and wiped the dust from his guns. Hardrock stepped back into the store.

"Half a dozen of them ol' boys in town, Smoke."

"I know. They're over at the saloon."

As the words were leaving his mouth, the town marshal stepped in.

"Jackson Bodine!" Hardrock grinned at the man. "I ain't seen you in a coon's age."

"Hello, Hardrock." The marshal stuck out his hand and Hardrock gripped it.

"When'd you take up lawin'?"

"When I got too old to do much of anything else." He looked at Smoke. "I don't want trouble in my town, Mister-whoever-you-are."

"This here's Smoke Jensen, Jackson," Hardrock said.

The marshal exhaled slowly. "I guess a man don't always get his wishes," he said reluctantly.

"I don't want trouble in your town or anybody else's town, marshal. But I'm afraid this is something those men over in the saloon won't let me sidestep." Briefly, he explained what had taken place over the past weeks.

The marshal nodded his head. "Give me ten minutes before you call them out, Smoke. That'll give me time to clear the street and have the kids back at home."

"You can have as much time as you need, Marshal."

The marshal smiled. "I never really knew for sure whether you were real or just a made-up person. They's a play about you, you know that?"

"No, I didn't. Is it a good one?"

The marshal laughed. "I ain't seen it. Folks that have gone to the big city tell me they got you somewheres between Robin Hood and Bloody Bill Anderson."

Smoke chuckled. "You know Marshal, they just may be right."

Jackson Bodine left the store to warn the townspeople to stay off the streets.

"He's a good man," Hardrock said. "Come out here 'bout oh, '42 or '43, I reckon. Preacher knows him. 'Course, Preacher knows just about everybody out here, I reckon."

Silver Jim stepped inside. "I could have sworn we dropped Royce back yonder at the ranch," he said. "But he's over yonder, 'live and well and just as ugly as ever."

"Anybody else?" Lujan asked.

"Lodi, Hazzard, Nolan . . ." His eyes touched Lujan's unblinking stare. "And Diego and Gomez. Three or four more I know but can't put no names to."

The Chihuahua gunfighter grunted. "Well, gentlemen, shall we cross the street and order us a drink?"

"I am a mite thirsty," Hardrock said. "Boredom does that to me," he added with a smile.

31

The men walked across the dusty street, all of them knowing the gunfighters in the saloon were waiting for them, watching them as they crossed the street.

Smoke was the first to push open the batwings and step inside, moving to one side so the others could follow quickly and let their eyes adjust to the dimmer light.

The first thing Smoke noticed was that Diego and Gomez were widely separated, one standing clear across the room from the other. It was a trick they used often, catching a man in a crossfire.

Smoke moved to the bar, his spurs jingling softly with each step. He walked to the far end of the bar while Lujan stopped at the end of the bar closest to the batwings. The move did not escape the eyes of Diego and Gomez. Both men smiled knowingly.

Only Smoke, Lujan, and Hardrock were at the bar. Pistol and Silver Jim positioned themselves around the room, and that move made several of the outlaws very nervous.

Smoke decided to take a chance and make a try for peace. "The war is over, boys. This doesn't have to be. You're professionals. Dooley is dead. You're off his payroll. There is no profit in dying for pride."

A very tough gunfighter that Pistol knew only as Bent sighed and pushed his chair back. "Makes sense to me. I don't fight for the fun of it." He walked out the batwings and across the boardwalk, heading for the livery.

"One never knows about a man," Diego spoke softly. "I was certain he had more courage than that."

"I always knowed he was yeller," Hazzard snorted.

"Maybe he's just smart," Smoke said.

Diego ignored that and stared at Lujan. "The noble Lujan," he said scornfully. "Protector of women and little children." He spat on the floor.

"At least, Diego," Lujan said, "I have that much of a reputation for decency. Can you say as much?"

"Who would want to?" the gunfighter countered. "Decency does not line my pockets with gold coins."

There was no point in talking about conscience to the man—he didn't have one.

Lujan flicked his dark eyes to Smoke. No point in delaying upcoming events, the quick glance seemed to say.

Smoke shot the Mexican gunfighter. He gave no warning; just drew, cocked, and fired, all in a heartbeat. Lujan was a split second behind him, his slug taking Gomez in the belly.

Hardrock took out Pooch Matthews just as Smoke was pouring lead into Eddie Hart and Silver Jim and Pistol had turned their guns on the others.

Royce was down, hanging onto a table. Dave and Hazzard were backed up against a wall, the front of their shirts turning crimson. Blaine and Nolan were out of it, their hands empty and over their heads, total shock etched on their tanned faces.

Diego raised his pistol, the sound of the cocking loud in the room.

"Don't do it, Diego," Smoke warned him.

The gunfighter cursed Smoke, in English and in Spanish,

telling him where he could go and in what part of his anatomy he could shove the suggestion.

Smoke shot him between the eyes just as Lujan was putting the finishing touches to Gomez.

The batwings pushed open and Jackson Bodine walked in, carrying a sawed-off double barrel express gun.

"There might be reward money for them two," Hardrock said, pointing to Blaine and Nolan. "You might send a telly-graph to Fort Benton."

Hazzard finally lost the strength to hang onto the table and he fell to the floor. Dave hung on, looking at Smoke through eyes that were beginning to lose their light.

"We was snake-bit all through this here job," he said, coughing up blood. "Didn't nothin' turn out right." The table tipped over under his weight and he fell to the floor. He lay amid the cigar and cigarette butts, cursing Smoke as life left him. Profanity was the last words out of his mouth.

"Anyone else gunnin' for you boys?" the marshall asked.

"Several more," Smoke told him.

"I sure would appreciate it if y'all would take it on down the road. This is the first shootin' we've had here in three years."

Hardrock laughed at the expression on the marshal's face. "I swear, Jackson. I do believe you're gettin' crotchety in your old age."

"And would like to get older," the marshal replied.

Hardrock slapped his friend on the back. "Come on, Jackson, I'll buy you a drink."

The men rode on south, crossing the Tongue, and rode into the little town of Sheridan, Wyoming. There, they took their first hot soapy bath since leaving Gibson, got a shave and a trim, and enjoyed a cafe-cooked meal and several pots of strong coffee.

The sight of five of the most famous gunslingers in all the West made the marshal a tad nervous. He and some of the locals, armed with shotguns, entered the cafe where Smoke and his friends were eating, positioning themselves around the room.

"I swanny," Silver Jim said. "I do believe the town folks is a mite edgy today." He eyeballed the marshal. "Ain't it a bit early for duck-huntin'?"

"Very funny," a man said. "We heard about the shootin' up North. There ain't gonna be no repeat of that around here."

"I shore hope not," Hardrock told him. "Violence offends me turrible. Messes up my di-gestive workin's. Cain't sleep for days. I'm just an old man a-spendin' his twilight years a-roamin' the countryside, takin' in all the beauty of nature. Stoppin' to smell the flowers and gander at the birds."

"Folks call me Peaceful," Silver Jim said, forking in a mouthful of potatoes and gravy. "I sometimes think I missed my callin'. I should have been a poet, like that there Long-britches."

"Longfellow," Smoke corrected.

"Yeah, him, too."

"I think you're all full of horse hocky," the marshall told them. "No trouble in this town, boys. Eat your meal and kindly leave."

"Makes a man feel plumb unwanted," Pistol said.

They made camp for the night a few miles south of town. Staying east of the Bighorns, they pulled out at dawn. They rode for two days without seeing another person.

Over a supper of beans and bacon, Smoke asked, "Where do you boys pick up the rest of your reward money?"

"Cheyenne," Silver Jim replied.

"You best start anglin' off east down here at the Platte."

"That's what we was thinkin'," Pistol told him. "But I just don't think it's over, Smoke."

"You can't spend the rest of your life watching my back-trail." He looked across the fire at Lujan. "How about you, Lujan?"

"I'll head southwest at the Platte." He smiled grimly. "My services are needed down on the Utah line."

Smoke nodded. "Are you boys really going to start up a place for old gunfighters and mountain men?"

"Yep," Hardrock said. "But we gonna keep quiet about it. Let the old fellers live out their days in peace and quiet. Soon as we get it set up, we'll let you know. We gonna try to get Preacher to come and live thar. You think he would?"

"Maybe, you never know about that old coot. He's near-abouts the last mountain man." '

"No," Silver Jim drawled the word. "The last mountain man will be ridin' the High Lonesome long after Preacher is gone."

"What do you mean?"

"You, boy. You be the last mountain man."

The men parted ways at the Platte. They resupplied at the trading post, had a last drink together, and rode away; Lujan to ply his deadly trade down on the Utah line; Silver Jim and Pistol Le Roux and Hardrock to get the bulk of their reward money and find a spot to build a home for old gunfighters. Smoke headed due south.

"We're goin' home, boy," he spoke to Dagger, and the horse's ears came up. "It'll be good to see Sally and the babies."

Smoke left the trail and took off into the wild, a habit he had picked up from Ol' Preacher. He felt in his guts that he was riding into trouble, so he would make himself as hard to find as possible for those wanting to kill him.

He followed the Platte down, keeping east of the Rattle-snake Hills, then crossing the Platte and making his way south, with Bear Mountain to his east. He stayed on the west side of the Shirley Mountains and rode into a small town on the Medicine Bow River late one afternoon.

He was clean-shaven now, having shaved off his mustache before leaving Gibson, although he did have a stubble of beard on his face, something he planned to rectify as soon as he could get a hot bath and find a barber.

He was trail-worn and dusty, and Dagger was just as tired

as he was. "Get you rubbed down and find you a big bucket of corn, boy," Smoke promised the horse. "And me and you will get us a good night's sleep."

Dagger whinnied softly and bobbed his head up and down, as if to say, "I damn well hope so!"

Smoke stabled Dagger, telling the boy to rub him down good and give him all the corn he could eat. "And watch my gear," he said, handing the boy a silver dollar.

"Yes, *sir!*"

Slapping the dust from his clothes, Smoke stopped in the town's only saloon for a drink to cut the dry from his throat.

He was an imposing figure even in faded jeans and worn shirt. Wide-shouldered and lean-hipped, with his arms bulging with muscle, and cold, emotionless eyes. The men in the saloon gave him a careful onceover, their eyes lingering on the guns around his waist, the left gun butt-forward. Don't see many men carrying guns thataway, and it marked him immediately.

Gunfighter.

"Beer," Smoke told the barkeep and began peeling a hard-boiled egg.

Beer in front of him, Smoke drank half of the mug and wiped his mouth with the back of his hand and then ate the egg.

"Passin' through?" the barkeep asked.

"Yeah. Lookin' for a hot bath and a shave and a bed."

"Got a few rooms upstairs. Cost you . . ."

"He won't be needin' no bath," the cold voice came from the batwings. "Just a pine box."

Smoke cut his eyes. Jason Bright stepped into the room, which had grown as silent as the grave.

Smoke was tired of killing. Tired of it all. He wanted no trouble with Jason Bright. But damned if he could see a way out of it.

"Jason, I'll tell you the same thing I told Diego, just before I killed him."

Chairs were pushed back and men got out of the line of

fire. Diego dead? Lord have mercy! Who was this big stranger anyways?

"Speak your piece, Jensen," Jason said.

Smoke Jensen! Lordy, Lordy!

"The war is over," Smoke spoke softly but firmly. "Nobody's paying you now. There are warrants all over the place for you. Ride out, man."

"You queered the deal for me, Smoke. Me and a lot of others. They scattered all around, from here to Colorado, just waitin' for a shot at you. But I think I'll just save them the trouble."

"Don't do it, Jason. Ride on out."

The batwings were suddenly pushed inward, striking Jason in the back and throwing him off balance. Smoke lunged forward and for the second time in about a month, Jason Bright was about to get the stuffing kicked out of him.

Smoke hit the gunfighter in the mouth and floored him, as the man who had pushed open the batwings took one look inside and hauled his freight back to the house. He didn't need a drink noways.

Smoke jerked Jason's guns from leather and tossed them into a man's lap, almost scaring the citizen to death.

"I'm tired of it, Jason." Smoke told the man, standing over him like an oak tree. "Tired of the killing, tired of it all."

Jason came up with the same knife he once tried to use on Cord. Smoke kicked it out of his hand and decked the man with a hard right fist. He jerked Jason up and slammed him against the bar. Then Smoke proceeded to hammer at the man's midsection with a battering ram combination of lefts and rights. Smoke both felt and heard ribs break under the hammering. Jason's eyes rolled back in his head and Smoke let him fall to the floor.

"You ought to go on and kill him, Smoke," a man called from the crowd. "He ain't never gonna forget this. Someday he'll come after you."

"I know," Smoke panted the words. "But I'm tired of the killing. I don't want to kill anybody else. Ever!"

"We'll haul him over to the doc's office for you, Smoke," a man volunteered. "He ain't gonna be ridin' for a long time to come. Not with all them busted ribs. And I heard 'em pop and crack."

"I'm obliged to you." He looked at the bartender. "The tub around back."

"Yes, sir. I'll get a boy busy with the hot water right away."

"Keep anybody else off me, will you?"

Several men stood up. "Let us get our rifles, Mister Jensen. You can bathe in peace."

"I appreciate it." He looked down at Jason. "You should have kept ridin', Jason. You can't say I didn't give you a chance."

32

Dagger was ready to go when Smoke saddled up the next morning. Not yet light in the east. He wanted to get gone, get on the trail home. He would stop down the road a ways and fix him some bacon to go with the bread he'd bought the night before. But he would have liked some coffee. He looked toward the town's only cafe. Still dark. Smoke shrugged and pointed Dagger's nose south. He had his small coffeepot and plenty of coffee. No trouble to fix coffee when he fixed the bacon.

About an hour after dawn, he stopped by a creek and made his fire. He fixed his bacon and coffee and sopped out the pan with the bread, then poured a cup of coffee and rolled a cigarette.

The creek made happy little sounds as it bubbled on, and the shade was cool. Smoke was reluctant to leave, but knew he'd better put some miles behind Dagger's tail.

Jason's words returned to him: "They scattered all around, from here to Colorado, just waitin' for a shot at you."

He thought back: Had there been a telegraph wire at that little town? He didn't think so. And where would the nearest wire office be? One over at Laramie, for sure. But by the time he could ride over there and wire Sally to be on the lookout, he could be almost home.

He really wasn't that worried. The Sugarloaf was very isolated, and unless a man knew the trails well, they'd never come in from the back range. If any strangers tried the road, the neighbors would be instantly alerted.

Smoke made sure his fire was out, packed up his kit, and climbed into the saddle. He'd make the northernmost edge of the Medicine Bow Range by nightfall. And he'd stay in the timber into Colorado, doing his best to avoid contact with any of the outlaws. Ol' Preacher had burned those trails into his head as a boy. He could travel them in his sleep.

Nightfall found him on the ridges of the Medicine Bow Range. It had been slow going, for he followed no well-traveled trails, staying with the trails in his mind.

He made his camp, ate his supper, and put out his fire, not wanting the fire's glow to attract any unwanted gunslicks during the night. Smoke rolled up in his blankets, a ground sheet under him and his saddle for a pillow.

He was up before dawn and built a hat-size fire for his bacon and coffee. For some reason that he could not fathom, he had a case of the jumps this morning. Looking over at Dagger, he could see that the big horse was also uneasy, occasionally walling his eyes and laying his ears back.

Smoke ate his breakfast and drank his coffee, dousing the fire. He filled his canteens from a nearby crick and let Dagger drink. Smoke checked his guns, wiping them free of dust and then loaded up the chamber under the hammer, usually kept empty. He checked his Winchester. Full.

Then, on impulse, he dug out a bandoleer from the saddlebags and filled all the loops, then added a handful of cartridges to his jacket pocket.

He would be riding into wild and beautiful country this day and the next, with some of the mountains shooting up past twelve thousand feet. It was also no country to be caught up high in a thunderstorm, with lightning dancing all around you. That made a fellow feel very small and vulnerable.

And it could also cook you like a fried egg.

The farther he rode into the dark timber, the more edgy he became. Twice he stopped and dismounted, checking all around him on foot. He could find nothing to get alarmed about, but all his senses were working hard.

Had he made a mistake by taking to the timber? The outlaws knew—indeed, half the reading population of the States knew—that Smoke had been raised in the mountains by Preacher, and he felt more at home in the mountains.

He pressed on, slowly.

He came to a blow-down, a savage-appearing area of about thirty or forty acres—maybe more than that—that had suffered a ravaging storm, probably a twister touch-down. It was a dark and ominous-looking place, with the trees torn and ripped from the earth, piled on top of each other and standing on end and lying every which-a-way possible.

He had dismounted upon sighting the area, and the thought came to him that maybe he'd better picket Dagger and just wait here for a day, maybe two or three if it came to that. He did not understand the thought, but his hunches had saved his life before.

He found a natural corral, maybe fifty by fifty feet, with three sides protected by piled-up trees, the front easily blocked by brush.

He led Dagger into the area and stripped the saddle from him.

There was plenty of grass inside the nature-provided corral, so he covered the entrance with brush and limbs and left Dagger rolling; soon he would be grazing. There were pools where rainwater had collected, and that would be enough for several days.

Taking a canteen and his rifle, Smoke walked several hundred yards from where he left his gear, reconnoitering the area.

Then he heard a horse snort, another one doing the same. Faint voices came to him.

"Lost his damn trail back yonder."

Smoke knew the voice: Lanny Ball.

"We'll find it," Lodi said. "Then we'll torture him 'fore we kill him. I done had some of that money spent back yonder till he come along and queered it for us."

Smoke edged closer, until he could see the men as they passed close by. Cat Jennings's gang were in the group.

"Hell, I'm tarred," a man complained. "And our horses are all done in. We gonna kill them if we keep on. And we got a lot of rough country ahead of us."

"Let's take a rest," Lodi said. "We can loaf the rest of the day and pick up the trail tomorrow."

"Damn good idee," an outlaw named Sutton said. "I could do with me some food and coffee."

"All right," Lanny agreed. "I'm beat myself."

Smoke kept his position, thinking about this new pickle he'd gotten himself into.

It was only a matter of time—maybe minutes or even seconds—before Dagger caught the scent of other horses and let his presence be known. Then whatever element of surprise Smoke had working for him would be gone.

There were few options left for him. He could backtrack and saddle up, hoping Dagger didn't give his position away, and try to ride out. But he knew in his heart that was grabbing at straws.

His other option was to fight.

But he was body and soul sick of fighting. If he could ride out peacefully and go home and hang up his guns and never strap them on again he would be content. God, but that would be wonderful.

The next statement from the mouth of a outlaw drifted to him, and Smoke knew this fight had to be ended right here and now.

"They tell me that Jensen's wife is a real looker. When we kill him, let's ride on down to Colorado. I'd like to have me a taste of Sally Jensen. I like it when they fight." Then he said some other things he'd like to do to Sally. The filth rolled in a steady stream from his mouth, burning deep into Smoke's brain. Finally he stood up, the verbal disgust fouling the pure clean mountain air.

Smoke lifted his Winchester and shot the man in the belly.

Smoke shifted position immediately, darting swiftly away. He was dressed in earth colors, and had left his hat back at the corral. He knew he would be nearly impossible to spot. And after hearing the agreeing and ugly laughter of the outlaws at the gut-shot man's filthy, disgustingly perverted suggestions, Smoke was white-hot angry and on the warpath.

He knelt behind a thick fallen log, all grown around with brush, and waited, his Winchester at the ready, hammer eared back.

Movement to his right caught his eyes. He fired and a wild shriek of pain cut the air. "My elbow's ruint!" a man wailed.

Smoke fired again into the same spot. The man with the ruined elbow stood up in shock and pain as the second bullet slammed into him. He fell forward onto his face.

As the lead started flying around him, thudding into the fallen logs and still-standing trees, Smoke crawled away, working his way around the outlaw's position, steadily climbing uphill.

He swung wide around them, moving through the wilderness just as Ol' Preacher had taught him, silently flitting from cover to cover, seething mad clear through; but his brain was clear and cold and thinking dark primal thoughts that would have made a grizzly back up and give him room.

In the West, a man just didn't bother a good woman—or even a bad woman for that matter. Or even say aloud the things the now-dead outlaw had mouthed. Molest a woman, and most western men would track that man for days and either shoot him or hang him on the spot.

Smoke caught a glimpse of color that did not fit into this terrain. He paused, oak-tree still, and waited. The man's impatience got the better of whatever judgment he possessed and he started to shift positions.

Smoke lifted his rifle and drilled the outlaw, the bullet entering his right side and blowing out the left side.

Smoke thought the man's name was Sweeney; one of Cat Jennings's crud.

Lead splattered bark from a tree and Smoke felt the sting of it. He dropped to one knee and fired just under the puff of gunsmoke drifting up from the outlaw's position, working the lever just as fast as he could, filling the cool air with lead.

A crashing body followed the spray of bullets.

"He ain't but one man!" a harsh voice shouted. "Come on let's rush him."

"You rush him, Woody" was the reply. "If you so all-fired anxious to get kilt."

"I'm gonna kill you, Jensen!" Woody hollered. "Then drag your stinkin' carcass till they ain't nothing left for even the varmits to eat."

Smoke remained still, listening to the braggart make his claims.

"I'll take him," a high thin voice was added to the brags.

Danny Rouge.

The only thing that moved was Smoke's eyes. He knew he couldn't let Danny live, couldn't let Danny get him in gunsights, for the punk's aim was deadly true.

There, Smoke's eyes settled on a spot. That's where the voice came from. But was the back-shooter still there? Smoke doubted it. Danny was too good to speak and then remain in the same spot. But which direction did he take?

There was only one direction that was logical, at least to Smoke's mind. Up the rise.

Smoke sank to the cool moist earth that lay under the pile of storm-torn and tossed logs. As silent as a stalking snake he inched his way under a huge pile of logs and paused, waiting.

"Well, dammit, boy!" Woody's voice cut the stillness, broken only by someone's hard moaning, probably the gut-shot outlaw. "What are you waitin' on, Christmas?"

But Danny was too good at his sneaky work to give away his location with a reply.

Smoke lay still, waiting.

Someone stepped on a dry branch and it popped. Smoke's eyes found the source and he could have easily killed the man. He chose to wait. He had the patience of an Indian and knew that his cat-and-mouse game was working on the nerves of the outlaws.

"To hell with you people!" a man spoke. "I'm gone. Jensen ain't no human person."

"You git back here, Carlson!" Lanny shouted.

Carlson told Lanny, in very blunt and profane language, where to go and how to get there.

That would be very painful, Smoke thought, allowing himself a thin smile.

He heard the sound of horses' hooves. The sound gradually faded.

Rifle fire slammed the air. A man cursed painfully. "Dammit, Dalton, you done me in."

A rifle clattered onto wood and fell to the earth with a dull thud. The outlaw mistakenly shot by one of his own men fell heavily to the earth. He died cursing Dalton.

Still Smoke did not move.

"Smoke? Smoke Jensen? It's me, Jonas. I'm gone, man. Pullin' out. Just let me get to my hoss and you'll never see me agin."

"Jonas, you yeller rabbit!" Lanny yelled. "Git back here."

But the fight had gone out of Jonas. He found his tired horse and mounted up. He was gone, thinking that Smoke Jensen was a devil, worser than any damn Apache that ever lived.

Smoke sensed more than heard movement behind him. But he knew that he could not be spotted under the pile of tangled logs, and he had carefully entered, not disturbing the brush that grew around and over the narrow entrance.

For a long minute the man, Danny, Smoke felt sure, did not move. Then to Smoke's surprise, boots appeared just inches from his eyes. Danny had moved, and done so with the stealth of a ghost.

He was good, Smoke conceded. Very good. Maybe too good for his own good.

Very carefully, Smoke lifted the muzzle of his rifle, lining it up about three feet above the boots. The muzzle followed the boots as they moved silently around the pile of logs, then stopped.

Smoke caught a glimpse of a belt buckle, lifted the muzzle an inch above it, and pulled the trigger.

Danny Rouge screamed as the bullet tore into his innards. Smoke fired again, for insurance, and Danny was down, kicking and squalling and crying.

"I'm the bes'," he hollered in his high, thin voice. "I'm the bes' they is."

Wild shooting drowned out whatever else Danny was saying. But none of the bullets came anywhere near to Smoke's location. None of the outlaws even dreamed that Smoke had shot the back-shooter from almost point-blank range.

Danny turned his head and his eyes met those of Smoke, just a couple of yards away, under the pile of logs.

"Damn you!" Danny whispered, his lips wet with blood. "Damn you to hell!" He closed his eyes and shivered as death took him.

Smoke waited until the back-shooter had died, then took a thick pole and shoved the body downhill. It must have landed near, or perhaps on, an outlaw, for the man yelped in fright.

"Lanny, let's get out of here," a man called. "He ain't gonna get Jensen. The man's a devil."

"He's one man, dammit!" Lanny yelled. "Just one man, that's all."

"Then you take him, Lanny." The outlaw's voice had a note of finality in it. " 'Cause I'm gone."

Lanny cursed the man.

"Jensen, I'm hauling my freight," Hayes called. "I hope I don't never seen you no more. Not that I've seen you this day," he added wearily.

Another horse's hooves were added to those already riding down the trail, away from this devil some called the last mountain man.

Smoke remained in his position as Lanny, Woody, and a few more wasted a lot of ammunition, knocking holes in trees and burning the air.

Smoke calmly chewed on a piece of jerky and waited.

33

Smoke had carefully noted the positions of those left. Five of them. He had heard their names called out. Woody, Dalton, Lodi, Sutton, and Lanny Ball.

The outlaws had tried to bait Smoke, cursing him, voicing what they were going to do to his wife and kids. Filthy things, inhuman things. Smoke lay under the jumble of logs and kept his thoughts to himself. If he had even whispered them, the white-hot fury might have set the logs blazing.

After more than two hours, Sutton called, "I think he's gone, Lanny. I think he suckered us and pulled out and set up a new position."

"I think he's right, Lanny," Woody yelled. "You know his temper, all them things we been sayin' about his wife would have brought him out like a bear."

Sutton abruptly stood up for a few seconds, then dropped to the ground. Lodi did the same, followed by the rest of them, and cautiously, tentatively, the outlaws stood up and began walking toward each other. Lanny was the last one to stand up.

He began cursing the rotten luck, the country, the gods of fate, and most of all, he cussed Smoke Jensen.

Smoke emptied his rifle into Lodi, Sutton, Dalton, and Woody, knocking them spinning and screaming to the littered earth.

Lanny hit the ground.

Smoke had dragged Danny's fancy rifle to him with a stick. Dropping his empty Winchester, Smoke ended any life that might have been left in the quartet of scum, then backed out of his hiding place and stretched his cramped muscles, protected by the huge pile of logs.

Smoke carefully checked his Colts, wiping them free of dirt with a bandana. "All right, Lanny!" he called. "You made your brags back in Gibson. Let's end this madness right here and now. Let's see if you've got the guts to face a man. You sure have been real brave telling me what you planned to do with my wife."

"You know I wouldn't do that to no good woman, Jensen. That was just to make you mad."

"You succeeded, Lanny."

"Let's call it off, Smoke. I'll ride away and you won't see me no more."

"All right, Lanny. You just do that little thing."

"You mean it?"

"I'm tired of this killing, Lanny. Mount up and get gone."

"You'll back-shoot me, Jensen!" There was real fear in the outlaw's voice.

"No, Lanny. I'll leave that to punks like you."

Lanny cursed him.

"I'm steppin' out, Lanny." This was to be no fast draw encounter. Smoke knew Lanny was going to try to kill him any way he could. Smoke's hands were full of Colts, the hammers eared back.

At the edge of the piled-up logs, Smoke started running. Lanny fired, missed, and fired again, the bullet burning Smoke's side. He turned and began pulling and cocking, a thunderous roar in the savage blow-down.

Lanny took half a dozen rounds in his upper torso, the force of the striking slugs driving him back against a huge old stump. He tried to lift his guns. He could not. His strength was gone. Smoke walked over to him, reloading as he walked.

"You ain't human," Lanny coughed up the words. "You a devil."

"You got any kin you want me to write?"

"You go to hell!"

Smoke turned his back to the man and walked away.

"You ain't gonna leave me to die alone, is you?" Lanny called feebly.

Smoke stopped. With a sigh, he turned around and walked back to the outlaw's side. Lanny looked up as the light in his eyes began to dim. Smoke rolled a cigarette, lit it, and stuck it between Lanny's lips.

"Thanks."

Smoke waited. The cigarette fell out of Lanny's lips. Smoke picked it up and ground it out under the heel of his boot.

"Least I can go out knowin' it wasn't no two-bit tinhorn who done me in," were Lanny's last words.

Smoke returned to the natural corral and saddled up. He wanted no more of this blown-down place of death. And from Dagger's actions, the big horse didn't either. Smoke rode out of the Medicine Bow Range and took the easy way south. He crossed the Laramie River and made camp on the shores of Lake Hattie.

He crossed over into Colorado the next morning and felt he was in home territory, even though he had many, many hard miles yet to go.

He followed the Laramie down into the Medicine Bow Mountains, riding easy, but still with the smell of sudden and violent death seeming to cling to him. He wanted no more of it. As he rode he toyed with the idea of selling out and pulling out.

He rejected that almost as quickly as the thought sprang into his brain.

The Sugarloaf belonged to Smoke and Sally Jensen. Fast gun he might be, but he wasn't going to let his unwanted reputation drive him away. If there were punks and crud in the world who felt they just had to try him . . . well, that was their problem. He had never sought the name of Gunfighter; but damned if he was going to back down, either.

The West was changing rapidly. Oh, there would be a few more wild and woolly years, but probably no more than a decade before law and order settled in. Law and order was changing everything and everybody west of the Mississippi. Jesse James was dead, killed in 1882. Clell Miller had been dead for years. Clay Allison had died a very ignoble death back in '77. Sam Bass was gone. Curley Bill Brocius had been killed by Wyatt Earp in Tombstone in '82. John Wesley Hardin was in a Texas prison. Rowdy Joe Lowe had met his end in Denver, killed in a gunfight over his wife. Mysterious Dave Mather had vanished about a year back and no one knew where he was.

Smoke doubted Dave would ever resurface. Probably changed his name and was living respectable.

Smoke rode the old trails, alive with the ghosts of mountain men who had come and gone years back, blazing the very trails he now rode. He thought of all the gunfighters and outlaws that were gone.

Charlie Storms was dead—and not too many folks mourned his passing. Charlie had been sitting at the table in Deadwood back in '76 when Cross-Eyed Jack McCall walked up behind Wild Bill and blew his brains out. Charlie tried to brace Luke Short in Tombstone back in '81. He rolled twelve.

I've known them all, Smoke mused. The good and the bad and that curious combination of both.

Dallas Stoudenmire finally saw the elephant back in '82.

Ben Thompson had been killed just the year back, Smoke recalled, down in San Antonio. Killed while watching a play.

The list was a long one, and getting longer.

And me? Smoke reflected. How many men have gone down under my guns?

He really didn't know. But he knew the count was awesomely high. He knew that he was rated as the number-one gunfighter in all the West; knew that he had killed a hundred men—or more. Probably more.

He shook those thoughts out of his head. There was no point in dwelling on them, and no point in trying to even think that he could live without his guns. There was no telling how many tin-horn punks and would-be gunslicks would be coming after him after the news of Gibson hit the campfires and the saloons of the West.

He stopped at a small four-store town and bought himself a couple of sacks of tobacco and rolling papers. He cut himself a wedge of cheese and got him a pickle from the barrel and a sackful of crackers. He went outside to sit on the porch of the store to have his late-afternoon snack.

"That there's Smoke Jensen." The words came to him from inside the store.

"No!"

"Yeah. He's killed a thousand men. Young, ain't he?"

"A thousand men?"

"Yeah. 'Course, that ain't countin' Indians."

Small children came to stand by the edge of the store to stare at him through wide eyes. Smoke knew how a freak in a carnival must feel. But he couldn't blame the kids. He'd been written about so much in the penny dreadfuls and other books of the time that the kids didn't know what to think of him.

Or the adults, either, for that matter.

Damn! but he was tired. Tired both physically and mentally.

Once he got back to Sally and the Sugarloaf, he didn't think he'd ever leave her side until she got a broom and ran him off.

He offered a cracker to a shy little girl and she slowly took it. "Jeanne!" her mother squalled from a house across the dusty street. "You get away from him!"

Jeanne smiled at Smoke, grabbed the cracker and took off.

Smoke looked up at the sounds of horses walking toward him. He sighed heavily. The two-bit punk who called himself Larado and that pair of no-goods, Johnny and Brett, were heading his way.

He slipped the thongs off his hammers and called over his shoulder, "Shopkeep! Get these kids out of here—right now!"

Within half a minute, the street was deserted.

Smoke stood up as the trio dismounted and began walking toward him.

"Back off, boys!" Smoke called. "This doesn't have to be."

Larado snorted. "What's the matter, Jensen? You done turned yeller on us?"

"Don't be a fool!" Smoke's words were hard. "I'm tryin' to make you see that there is no point to this."

"The point is, Mister Big-Shot," Johnny said, and Smoke could smell the whiskey from all of them even at this distance, "we gonna kill you."

Smoke shook his head. "No, you're not, boys. If you drag iron, you're dead. All of you." He started walking toward them.

Bret's eyes widened in fear. Johnny and Larado wore looks of indecision on their young faces.

"Well!" Smoke snapped, closing the distance. "At this range we're all going to die, you know that don't you boys?"

They knew it, and it literally scared the pee out of Bret.

Smoke slapped Larado with a hard open palm, knocking the young man's hat off and bloodying his mouth. He backhanded Johnny with the same hand and drove his left fist into Bret's stomach.

Reaching out, he tore the gunbelt from Larado and hit the young man in the face with it, breaking his nose and knocking him to the ground.

Smoke tossed the gunbelt and pistols into a watering trough. He looked down at the young men, lying on the ground.

"It's not as easy as the books make it out to be, is it,

boys?" Smoke asked them. He expected no reply and got none.

Smoke reached down and jerked guns from leather, tossing them into the same trough.

"You can keep your rifles. Keep them and ride out. Go on back home and learn you a trade. Go to school, make something out of yourselves. But don't ever brace me again. For if you do, I'll kill you without hesitation. I'm giving you a chance. Take it."

The young men slowly picked themselves up off the ground and mounted up. They rode out without looking back.

"Mighty fine thing you done there, Mister Smoke," a man said. "Mighty fine. You could have killed them all."

Smoke looked at the citizen. "I'm tired of killing. I know that I'll have to kill again, but I'm not looking forward to it."

"The wife is fixin' a pot roast for supper. We'd be proud to have you sit at our table. She's a good cook, my old woman is. And the kids would just be beside themselves if you was to come on over. Don't a home-cooked meal sound good to you?"

A smile slowly creased Smoke's lips. "It sure does."

Smoke did not leave the Sugarloaf for a week. He got reacquainted with Sally every time she bumped into him . . . and she bumped into him a lot.

He rolled on the floor with the babies and acted a fool with them, making faces at them, letting them ride his back like a horse, and in general, settling back into the routine of being a husband, father, and rancher.

On the morning that he decided to ride into town, Sally's voice stopped him in the door.

"Aren't you forgetting something, Smoke."

He turned. She was holding his guns in her hands.

He stared at her.

"I know, honey," she said. "I've known for a long time that you're tired of the killing."

"It just seems like a man ought to be able to ride into town without strapping on a gun."

"I don't know whether that day will ever come, honey. As long as you are Smoke Jensen, the last mountain man, there will be people riding to try you. And you know that." She came to him and pressed against him. "And speaking very selfishly, I kind of like to have you around."

Smoke smiled and took the gunbelt, hooking it on a peg.

She looked up at him, questions in her eyes.

He whispered in her ear.

She laughed and bumped into him again.

THE FIRST
MOUNTAIN MAN:
CHEYENNE CHALLENGE

BOOK ONE

1

Nothing much moves in the High Lonesome when Old Man Winter holds the land in his frigid grasp. The mountain man known simply as Preacher—though to many, the name held far more meaning than its simplicity implied—settled in at the cabin of an old friend, in a steep-walled valley that shielded it from the violent blasts of Canadian northers. He hunted for meat, smoked and jerked it, gathered other provisions, and watched the sky for signs of snow.

When the white powder lay hip-high, he had enough wood split and stacked to last the winter. By the time it grew to belly-high on a seventeen-hand horse, he had every small crack chinked, the chimney brushed clean, and a neat little corral set up with a four-sided shelter backed against one stern granite wall. Heavy yield in that winter of 1840–41 soon brought the snow level to roof-ridge height. Preacher had a tunnel out to the livestock, and kept the corral clear by some energetic, body-warming shoveling. Through it all, his cuts, scrapes, and bullet wounds healed.

All together, Preacher reckoned, when the buds began to swell on the willows, the cabin had been snug enough, nearly warm enough, and he had been almost amply fed. Lean and fit, although a little gaunt from his limited diet, Preacher began to itch to move along. He figured it was getting on toward late March and his only complaint came from a rhumaticky knee that resulted from too many hours in cold streams tending his traps in days gone by. Time to stretch like a cream-filled tomcat on the hearth and look for new places. The sun felt warm on Preacher's back as he breathed in the heady, leathery aroma of freshly saddle-soaped tack.

Looking up from tightening the last rope that secured the load on his pack saddle, he took in another chest-swelling breath tinged with the tang of pine resin and needles. Suddenly, his ebullient mood collapsed as he sensed the presence of another person. Preacher hadn't seen a single human since last October, when he went to the trading post at Trout Creek Pass for supplies. And he for certain didn't recall inviting anyone to drop in for a visit.

Thunder, his spotted-rump Appaloosa stud, had become aware of the intrusion, Preacher saw, as he cut his eyes to the suddenly tense animal. Thunder had gone wall-eyed, his ears pointed toward the front of the cabin beyond the corral. No doubt in his mind now, Preacher stepped away from the pack-horse and walked past the brush-and-pole shelter. With what quiet he could muster, he mucked his way through the March mud toward the stout log dwelling. His right hand rested on the butt of one awesome four-barrel pistol.

Behind Preacher, the horses snuffled and whickered, having caught human scent and that of at least one of their own kind. Preacher tensed slightly. One did not survive more than twenty years in the wilds without being constantly alert. Preacher had come to the Shining Mountains as a wet-behind-the-ears lad of twelve or so and had so far kept his hair. He sure didn't hanker to lose any of it now.

So, Preacher had the big four-shooter halfway out from behind the broad, red sash at his waist when he rounded the cabin. He came face-to-face with a small, rat-faced individual who exhibited considerable surprise.

"Uh! You be the mountain man name of Preacher?" a fittingly squeaky rodent voice asked.

Right off, Preacher took in the long, narrow head, oversized nose, and small, deep-set black eyes. Buck teeth and slicked-back ebony hair completed the likeness to a weasel. In fact, though Preacher didn't know it, the man before him went by the handle "Weasel" Carter. Preacher saw, too, that his unexpected visitor exhibited all the nervousness of a tomcat in a room full of rocking chairs. It all served to set Preacher's internal alarms to clanging.

"I be," Preacher allowed as he cut his eyes for a careful glance around the treeline.

That glance revealed to him some furtive movement among the aspen saplings and underbrush. His alarm system instantly primed Preacher for whatever might happen next.

Weasel Carter forced a fleeting, sickly, lipless smile, removed his hat and mopped his brow with a grimy kerchief. A fraction of a second later, Preacher's keen eyesight picked out a thin spurt of smoke from the priming pan of a flintlock rifle, an instant before he whipped out his four-shot and blasted a ball into the gut of his Judas goat.

At the same time, Preacher lashed out with his free hand, closed on a big fistful of shirt, and yanked his betrayer in front of himself. He did it in time for misfortune to strike the man in the form of the bullet meant for Preacher. A second later, three men rushed out of the concealment of the trees and fired at Preacher.

One ball moaned past, close to Preacher's left ear. The other two delivered more punishment to the runty piece of sorry trash Preacher held before himself like a shield. By then, Preacher had his four barrel back in action. The hammer dropped on a brass cap and the big .54 caliber ball spat out in a cloud of smoke and flame.

It struck the nearest would-be assassin in the breast bone and tore out a fist-sized chunk of spine on the way out of his body. Preacher worked the complicated action, lining up another barrel, and fired again. Double-shotted, it had considerably more recoil, yet the charge went true and gut-shot a scruffy, bearded man whom Preacher reckoned deserved to be called "Dirt."

With his final load, Preacher blew away the left side of the head of the last killer trash. The flattened ball left a glittering brown eye dangling on a sallow, hollow cheek. Bleeding horribly, the thug managed to draw a pistol from his waistband and bang off a round in Preacher's direction.

Preacher dodged it as though it represented nothing more than a snowball. While he did, he switched for the other fully-charged four-barrel and let fly. "I didn't ask for this," he yelled at the miraculously upright man, whose skull had been shot away in a wide trough above his left ear.

This time the ball entered the empty eye socket and blinked out the lights for the verminous gun man. That barrel always had shot a little high and right, Preacher recalled as he surveyed his littered dooryard.

"But I ain't disinclined to jine the dance to someone else's tune," he muttered a moment before Dirt moaned pitifully. Preacher crossed to the fallen ambusher. "You ain't got long. Speak," he commanded roughly.

"Th-tha's a fact. You done got me through the liver."

"Good riddance to trash like you, I say," Preacher growled as he knelt beside the dying man.

"You—you gonna jist leave me out here? Ain't gonna give me no Christian burial?"

"Weren't no Christian thing you done, sendin' that weasel faced punk in to set me up, neither."

"Jeez, you really are Preacher."

"I be. Who sent you four after me?"

Dirt eyed Preacher a long moment. Then he swallowed hard. "Thirsty."

"You're gut-shot right enough. Shouldn't be givin' you nothin' liquidy." Then Preacher grunted, shrugged and came to his moccasins from one knee. "Seein' as you're dyin' anyhow, I don't find no harm in it. I'll be back . . . and I'll be wantin' the name of whoever it was sent you."

Preacher returned to Dirt's side after what the back-shooter thought to be an eternity. Preacher carried a small stoneware jug in one hand and a gourd ladle in the other. He eased down beside Dirt and put the ladle to the dying man's lips.

Dirt spluttered and tried to push it away. "That's not whiskey," he gasped out. "That—that's water."

"You got the right of it. The whiskey is for me, water for you. Last time, then I give you a whole world of more hurt. Who . . . sent . . . you?"

"Ez-Ezra Pease," Dirt gulped out, along with a bright crimson spew.

"Damn!" Preacher exploded. "I knewed that man were no good, first time I laid eyes on him. Ezra Pease," and Preacher pronounced the name to rhyme with *peas*. "Knew he was crooked, cheated the Injuns and whites alike, sold guns and whiskey to the Injuns. That finally riled me enough I beat the hell out of him and runned him out of the High Lonesome. He was tough, right enough, and I'd never have figgered him for a coward, that'd hire someone else to do his killing for him."

"Ain't no coward in Ez," Dirt retorted in a raspy whisper.

Preacher took a swig of whiskey. "That depends on whether you're on the receiving end or not. Where can I find him?"

Dirt forced a wan smile. "Ain't tellin' you that, Preacher."

Preacher shrugged, indifferently. "Then you'll take it to hell with you."

"I'll see you there," Dirt snarled, then he shivered violently and died.

"Maybe . . . maybe not," Preacher observed idly, took another swallow of whiskey and set the jug aside.

He roused himself and dragged the four corpses to a deep wash, rolled them down to the bottom and collapsed a wide section of dirt and rocks from the lip on top of them. That would at least keep the critters away from them. He gathered up their weapons and located their horses. These he freed from bridle and saddle and sent them off on their own.

"Time to get goin', Thunder," he announced when he returned to the corral.

Preacher swung into the saddle and caught up the lead rope to the pack animal, then gigged them into motion. Ezra Pease had returned, Preacher mused as the miles slowly rolled by in an endless stream of aspen, hemlock, and pines. It had all begun some ten years ago at Rendezvous. . . .

"New trader in camp," Jim Bridger confided to Preacher when he rode into the wide, gentle valley that housed Rendezvous for those in the fur trade that year. "I'll point him out. Like to see what you make of the cut of him."

Right then, Preacher suspected there might be something not quite right about the man. Bridger didn't often take to the judgments of other men, lessen he thought himself a mite too harsh in his own. Not that Jim Bridger was given to an overwhelming flow of the milk of human kindness. Most of his decisions were harsh. That's what kept him, or any man, alive out here in the Big Empty. All the same, Preacher ambled on into the growing gathering of white canvas tents, buffalo hide tipis, brush lean-tos, and other mobile dwellings of the hard, adventurous men who worked the mountains for the valuable furs that fed a hungry eastern market.

He came upon the new man only a quarter mile into the swarm of white men, Indians, and breeds. A big canvas awning had been stretched from the side of a small, mountain-type wagon. In its shade, behind the upright brass rods that held the outer edge, piles of boxes and crates, and stacks of barrels had been laid out to make what their owner hoped would be an attractive display. Several of the barrels bore the black, double-X mark that had already become a common symbol for the contents: whiskey.

Well and good, Preacher thought to himself. Wasn't a man-jack among them who didn't plan on some powerful likkerin' up while there. That's a lot of what Rendezvous was all about. For his own taste, though, Preacher opted to push on until he found the stout, pink-faced German fellow from Pennsylvania who dispensed the finest Manongahela rye this side of heaven.

A couple of hours later, his campsite staked out and shelter erected, somewhat mellowed by some of that smooth whiskey, Preacher had his warm attitude of contentment shattered by an uproar. It reached his ears from the direction of the new trader's layout he had passed on the way in. Always curious, and always eager to view or get involved in a good brawl, buckskin-clad streams of mountain men flowed past Preacher's haven.

Smacking his lips, Preacher put aside the jug of Manongahela rye, pushed upright to his moccasins and trotted off to witness the excitement. He elbowed his way between Slippery Jim and Broken Jaw Sloane to get a better view. The new trader, with the help of a pair of louts who turned out to be his swampers, was whipping up on a slender, youthful Nez Perce brave. The white man looked to be in his mid to late thirties, which put him a good ten to twelve years older than Preacher at that time. While the louts held down the teenaged Nez Perce, the factor smashed vicious, painful blows to the Indian's face.

"You were gonna steal that knife, gawdamnit, I saw you," he roared.

"No, no," the brave protested in his own language, which Preacher had just put in six long months of winter learning. "I give two hands sable skins. Poor pelts you say," he added in heavily accented English. "Two hands sable skins for one knife. That too much but I take."

His watery blue eyes narrowed, the trader sneered back at the bleeding Indian. He hit the boy twice more and growled. "You don't have any way to prove that, buck. So, give up that knife and get out of here before I finish you off."

"I got it right here, Ez," one thick-lipped lout blurted,

reaching under the securing thong of the Nez Perce's loincloth and pulling free a scabbarded Green River black iron butcher knife.

"Good. Toss it on the table over there." He bunched the youngster's hunting shirt in both fists and yanked the bruised and blood-smeared Indian upright. Ez spun him and gave the groggy youth a powerful boot to his posterior.

Propelled forward off balance, the Nez Perce rebounded off the shoulders of laughing mountain men. Some offered him a swig from a jug of liquor, others gave him friendly claps on the shoulders, or pitying looks. Two more rocky steps and he came up against the broad chest of Preacher.

"Blue Heron," Preacher said softly, recognizing the youth.

"White Wolf. That man cheats. He lies. He steals from us." It wasn't a self-pitying whine, or an excuse, it was said with the hot fire of anger burning brightly.

"You are sure?"

"I am sure," Blue Heron responded.

For a moment, Preacher looked beyond the shoulder of the young Indian and his eyes grew to slits. "It will be taken care of."

"White Wolf does not lie. I will be satisfied. Come visit us again. My sister misses you awfully." The last was delivered with as much as a mischievous expression as his bruised features could produce.

Preacher chose to ignore this reference to his amorous proclivities of the past winter. "Go with the wind, Blue Heron."

Despite his pain and discomfort, Blue Heron's eyes twinkled. "Find sleep in a warm lodge, White Wolf."

Their exchange had been observed by Ez, who came at Preacher in a rush. "What'd that thievin' Hole-in-Nose say to you?"

Preacher gave him a cool, appraising gaze. "Nothin' that's any of your business, feller."

"B'God it is my business."

"Nope. Not by half," Preacher assured him. Then, his eyes

the color of glare-ice, he added. "But I can make it a whole lot of mine."

Ez glowered as he studied the young man before him. Lean-hipped and rawhide tough, Ez could see this stranger had tremendous power in his upper body. He figured him to be smart, too, since he had learned that heathen savage's turkey-gobble lingo. Something about the casual way he wore those two .50 caliber pistols in his sash warned Ez that this stranger could be panther quick and deadly accurate with them. That, most of all, gave him pause. With a snort of impatience, Ez broke their locked gaze first.

He turned on one boot heel and stomped off. Slippery Jim and several others swarmed around Preacher in the next instant to welcome him and press invitations on him to visit firesides for a friendly round of "cussin', discussin', and drinkin'." Preacher said yes to all, though many knew full well he would not make it to their camp that night. Preacher spent the rest of the day asking questions about the new trader, Ez, and sharing jugs.

First off, he got a last name for the surly man. Pease. "He says it like them little green vegables," Beckworth informed Preacher. Coupled with what he had witnessed, Preacher soon developed an image of the man which far from pleased him. Yet, Ez Pease had done nothing directly to Preacher and he, like most of his fellow trappers, strongly believed in a man tending his own trapline.

As a result, Preacher decided to leave well enough alone. Yet, if the shadow of Pease ever fell across his path, Preacher would be more than happy to do something about it. The opportunity had come sooner than Preacher expected.

Three days went by in the usual boozy, raucous *bon homme* of Rendezvous. Preacher had all but forgotten the incident with his young Nez Perce friend. He had traded with the boy's father for Thunder. Now, horse trading was serious business to the Nez Perce. If a feller entered into the spirit of it, and they believed he had treated them fairly, although shrewdly, they respected that man for it. If he was generous with his sugar and coffee in the bargain, that man could have friends for life. Not forgetting, of course, that Injuns have notions. The day that recalled all of this to Preacher began normally enough.

Around noon, he and Big Foot Joe got into an eating contest. The man who could consume just one more than half of the small lumps of force meat, onions, and wild rice in a chain of pit-roasted intestine, in this case from an elk, was the winner. He split half of the gold, pelts, or other items bet on the outcome. Preacher's stout, youthful teeth gave him an advantage, which put him well on the way to the mid-point in the chain when an uproar rose from the southern end of the string of camps.

Preacher ignored them and munched on. More voices joined the clamor of support for opposing sides. They ended abruptly in a shout of alarm.

"Look out!" Followed by the flat report of a pistol shot.

Ah, hell. Just when I had this thing won, Preacher silently lamented. He had no doubt as to the source of the disturbance, or who had fired his weapon. He bit off the tasty rope and set out at a trot for the gathering crowd of men and haze of dust that rose in the still air of the valley.

Although independent, tough, and wild, several men gave way when they saw the hard expression on the face of Preacher as he approached the center of the dispute. A mountain man lay, writhing, on the ground, shot through the meaty place above one hip bone. Two others held onto the trader, Ezra Pease, who still waved a smoking pistol in one hand.

One old timer nodded a curt greeting to Preacher and brought the young mountain man up to date. "Liver Eatin' Davis caught that one sellin' a gun to an Injun."

"Ain't nobody's business who I sell to or what," Pease growled.

"It is in this neck o' the woods," a burly mountain man with a flaming beard snapped.

Considered quite young, especially by mountain man

standards, Preacher had already accumulated a considerable reputation. Enough so that when he stepped forward, the others fell silent to hear what he had to say about the situation. Preacher approached Pease and got right up close and personal in his face.

"Pease, you've out-lived your welcome at this Rendezvous. Hell, in all the Big Empty for that matter." Preacher paused and cut his eyes from face to face in the crowd. "I reckon these fellers will go along with me when I say we want you out of camp before nightfall."

A sneer broke out on the face of Pease. "Why, hell, you ain't even dry behind the ears as yet. Who are you to tell me that?"

"I'm the man who's an inch from slittin' yer gizzard, which is reason enough."

Pease cut his eyes to the men holding him. "Turn me loose. I'll show this whippersnapper where the bear crapped in the buckwheat."

Knowing grins passed between his captors. "Oh, we'd be mighty pleased if you did," Yellowstone Frank Parks, a close friend of Preacher's responded, releasing the arm he held.

Ezra Pease had only time to realize his challenge had been accepted when one of Preacher's big fists smashed into his thin, bloodless lips. Strands of his carroty mustache bit into split flesh and those lips turned right neigh bloody all at once. Preacher followed up with a looping left to the side of Pease's head. It staggered the corrupt trader and set his legs wobbly. Dimly he saw an opening and drove the muzzle of his empty pistol into Preacher's exposed belly.

Hard muscle absorbed most of the shock, yet the blow doubled Preacher over and part of the air in his lungs whooshed out. He raised both arms to block the attack he expected to come at his head. He had reckoned rightly. Still grasping the pistol, Pease slashed downward intent on breaking Preacher's wrist. The wooden forestock landed on a thick, wirey forearm instead. It would leave a nasty bruise, but at the time, Preacher hardly felt it.

Without pause, he raised a knee between the wide-spread legs of Pease and rammed it solidly into the cheat's left thigh. That brought Pease to his knees. He dropped the empty pistol and groped for another. Preacher kicked him in the face. Pease flopped over backward and Preacher was on him in a flash.

Instantly they began to roll over and grapple for an advantage. Pease gradually worked his arms down into position around Preacher's ribs. Slowly he raised one leg to get his knee into position to thrust violently upward on Preacher's stomach and snap downward with his arms. The result would be to break the back of the younger man. Preacher would have none of it, however.

He wooled his head around until the crown fitted under the chin of Pease. Then he set his moccasin toes and rammed upward. Pease's yellowed teeth clopped closed with a violent snap. A howl followed as stressed nerves signaled that the crooked trader had bitten through his tongue. Blood quickly followed in a gush and his grip slackened.

It proved enough for Preacher, who broke the bear hug and came up to batter the exposed face of Pease with a series of rights and lefts. Pease swung from the side and hard knuckles put a cut on Preacher's right cheek. A strong right rocked back the young mountain man's head. Preacher punched Pease's mushed mouth again and sprang to his moccasins. Pease slowly followed.

Dazed, yet undefeated, Pease tried to carry the fight to Preacher. A sizzling left and right met his charge. Preacher danced away and pounded Pease in the middle. Then he worked on the chest, at last he directed his violent onslaught to the sagging head of Pease. For the second time, Pease went to his knees. Preacher squared up facing him, measured the angle, and popped hard knuckles into Pease's forehead. The lights went out and Pease crumpled in the dirt, jerked spasmodically for a few seconds and went still. A faint snore blubbered through his smashed lips.

Preacher stumbled away to wash off the blood, slobber,

and dirt that clung to him, oblivious of the man he had defeated. Behind him, the other mountain men gathered up the stock in trade Pease had brought with him, loaded his wagons and provided an escort out of the valley.

And now Pease was back . . .

Preacher shook off the dark recollection as he topped the crest of a low saddle and found himself facing four hard, coppery faces, topped by black, braided hair, with eagle feathers slanted downward from the back, past the left ear. Preacher also noted that the four Indians held their bows casually, low over their saddle pads, and that arrows had already been nocked.

2

Preacher's hand automatically dropped to the smooth butt-grip of one four-barrel pistol at sight of the warriors. Then he recognized the older man in the middle. Talks To Clouds could be considered an old friend. Particularly since he had been the man Preacher traded with for Thunder. Now a fleeting smile curled the Nez Perce's full lips.

"Ghost Wolf. I am pleased to see you," Talks To Clouds broke the silence in his own tongue.

"And I, you. It has been a long time," Preacher acknowledged.

"Too long for friends who have shared meat and salt," the expert horse breeder responded.

Preacher studied the men with Talks To Clouds. They were not painted for war and appeared well enough at ease. "What brings you so far from your green valley?"

"We trade horses with the Cheyenne. My son remembers you. I heard of what you did. An old man is grateful."

Preacher grunted; that had been ten years ago. He had traded for Thunder only four years past. No accounting for the depth of an Injun's gratitude. "You are not an old man."

"I am if I must rely on others to protect my own." Talks To

Clouds paused, then gestured behind him. "Come, Young Joseph is watching our spotted ponies." He paused, chuckled. "Only he is not so young any more. He is a father. A boy named *In-Mut-Too-Yah-Lat-Lat** was born to him this past winter. Already, *he* is being called *Young* Joseph. We will eat, drink coffee, talk of the times since we last saw one another."

An agreeable nod preceded Preacher's answer. "It would be my pleasure."

The Nez Perce had located their camp over the next rise. The camp's appearance completely relaxed Preacher's innate caution. Women and children accompanied the group of half a dozen warriors and their sub-chief, Talks To Clouds. The youngsters swarmed out to surround Preacher when he was recognized. Laughing, he dismounted to bend and chuck the girls under their chubby chins, eliciting giggles all around.

Then he turned and hoisted the four boys to the back of Thunder and let them walk the Appaloosa stallion into the encampment. The boys had the big horse cooled out by gentle walking in just under a half hour. By then, the women had completed preparations and served up a meal of thick, rich venison stew, fry-bread, and cattail slips. Preacher made a generous offer of salt, coffee, and sugar that complimented the feast to the satisfaction of all.

When everything was in readiness, the men filled bowls and settled in to enjoy. Talk centered around the weather; the unusually early spring in particular. Forked Tail gestured to the east and made the sign for the Sioux.

"That is why we decide to go afar in our trading of horses. Talks To Clouds wants to reach the Dakota. They are said to be hungry for our spotted ponies. And not to eat them," he added with an expression of disgust.

"There was no snow left in the valley of Wil-Ah-Met by

---

*This is the Nez Perce name for Chief Joseph, who later led his people in resisting white encroachment of their reservation and on a desperate flight to reach Canada. He was captured by Nelson Miles.

the first of the Moon of Returning Buds," Talks To Clouds verified. "I see many warm buffalo robes for next winter if we can start early."

"Good idea," Preacher contributed. "How are things between here and your valley?"

Talks To Clouds and the others considered it. "Peaceful. Except for the Blackfeet. There is much green showing and it will be a fat spring. That should keep peace."

Always the Blackfeet, Preacher ruminated. He'd get into that after the eating was done. He asked of men among the Nez Perce he had known, of babies born and the talk slid away the time until their bowls had been emptied. As a man, those around the small fire in the lodge of Talks To Clouds wiped grease from their chins, rubbed full bellies, and belched loudly. At once the women and children fell to their eats. Once more, and more appropriately according to Indian etiquette, the man-talk turned to the world around them.

"Is there anything that would cause you to say the Blackfeet are more troublesome than usual?" Preacher cautiously prompted.

Talks To Clouds broke out a pipe, a habit obtained from the plains tribes, and tamped it full of kinnikinnick and wild tobacco. He lighted it with a coal and drew a long, satisfying puff before answering. "Yes, White Wolf. They are already making for war. They have many guns, provided by white men in trade for pelts and horses. It is not a good thing."

Preacher nodded and Forked Tail reached for the pipe, took a drag, then put in, "The word on the wind is that the Northern Cheyenne are also fixing to make war medicine when spring opens up a little more."

That's odd, Preacher thought, and frowned. Although known as fierce fighters and highly territorial, most skirmishes with the Cheyenne in the past had been between small bands of warriors and some enemy tribe, to settle a score or to raid for horses. That, or in reaction to what must appear to be an avalanche of whites pressing westward.

Talks To Clouds spoke again. "The Cheyenne will be making war on the Blackfeet, that is certain. They must do so to protect the western villages. It is said they know of the white men arming the Blackfeet." He spat, to show his contempt for such an action.

"It looks bad, then?" Preacher pressed.

"Yes. We may spend the summer in trading with the Dakota and even the Omaha. Let the fighting wear itself out, and then we can go home with our robes."

"Will they come south?" Preacher asked.

Talks To Clouds considered this. "I think so. One or the other. Whoever gets the worst of their fight together."

Preacher sighed and cleared his throat. "I would be sorry to see that."

A fleeting smile lifted the corners of the mouth of Talks To Clouds. "So would I. Yet, we must accept what we get."

Preacher ruminated on all he had heard through the evening. When the night's chill reminded him, he broke out his bedroll and settled down for the night. When morning came, he would head on toward Trout Creek Pass.

Preacher left for the trading post before daylight. Talks To Clouds stood silently in the open door flap of his lodge and waved a dimly seen salute to his friend. Preacher rode with the warmth of that friendship. He also rode with the awareness of the return of Ezra Pease. Constantly on the lookout for any more low-grade trash who might be working for Pease, he kept well below the ridge lines and frequently circled on his backtrail.

Ezra Pease removed the floppy felt hat from his head and ran a hand over the balding dome with its fringe of carroty hair. His fractured smile was hidden from the men with him, though they caught his high spirits from the tone of his voice.

"There it is, fellers. Just like them wanderin' Injuns told us. Black Hand's village. I reckon they've had time to hear about the Blackfeet. Should be glad to see us."

"We break out the whiskey first, huh, boss?" a not-too-bright thug named Bartholamue Haskel gulped out between chuckles. "Likker up them bucks right good, huh—huh—huh?"

"Awh, hell, Haz," Ezra complained, embarrassed by the low state of the henchmen he had been able to attract.

In truth, Ezra had to admit, times had not been good for him. His fortunes had plummeted, rather than soaring as he always envisioned. After his ignominious expulsion from these mountains some ten years past, Pease had wandered his way back to St. Louis. Down on his luck, he had been forced to lower himself to the basic of scams; for half a year he rolled drunks for whatever they had on their bodies.

He had nearly been caught by the law several times. And he had been caught once by a riverboat man who appeared a whole lot more drunk than he turned out to be. The brawny riverboater thoroughly and soundly beat the living hell out of Pease. He'd done a job to rival that handed out by Preacher. Ezra Pease lay in a bed for three weeks recovering, and thought of both those shaming incidents.

When he could once again face his fellow man on the streets of St. Louis, he visited a dockside swill house that he had frequented when first in town. There he bought whiskey and many beers for furtive men who inveterately glanced nervously over their shoulders at the doorway. They drank his whiskey and chased it with the beer and nodded in silent agreement.

After three days of this, Ezra Pease and his gathering of bullyboys set out one night to find a certain loudmouthed rafter. They located him, all right. What resulted was that Ezra again got the tom-turkey crap stomped out of himself. He wound up in the hospital this time. When he regained consciousness, he learned the identity of his assailant. Mike Fink.

By damn, that was worser than Preacher, Pease reasoned. Because Preacher was near to a thousand miles away and no immediate threat. Ezra Pease would learn the error of his judgment when he finally worked up nerve enough to return to the High Lonesome.

Meanwhile, he had to recover from his broken bones, mashed face, one chewed ear, and an eye that no longer saw clearly. Mike Fink had missed by only a fraction of an inch from gouging the orb from its socket. While he mended, Pease went about rebuilding his minute criminal empire. He left the infirmary with seven men solidly behind him. They drifted into Illinois and tried stagecoach robberies.

Three of them died in the process and the survivors did five to nine years in prison. Ezra Pease proved to be a model prisoner and was released after only four years and seven months for good behavior. He thanked the warden with almost fawning gratitude and immediately set out to organize a new, better, and definitely stronger gang.

At last, it seemed, his fortunes had taken a turn for the better. Ezra Pease met Titus Vickers inside prison, and when the opportunity presented itself, Pease broke Vickers free from the chain gang on which he labored in a granite quarry in southeastern Illinois. Together they attracted a dozen hard men, who knew how to fight with tooth, nail, knife, and gun.

Some scattered successes drew more of those disinclined to exert any honest effort or sweat to earn a living. Before long, he had thirty heavily armed, morally bankrupt representatives of the worst dregs of border trash, scoff-laws, back-shooters, rapists, and sadists ever assembled in one place at one time. It offered a splendid promise for the future.

They spilled over into Missouri. Pickings were slim there. All the while, Ezra Pease had his dreams disturbed by a slowly awakening vision. There was vast wealth just waiting for the picking out beyond the prairie. Even though the fur trade had all but dried up, an enormous fortune waited only for an enterprising man to seize it. When the image became full formed, Ezra and Titus conferred with a shadowy group from New York, and announced to their men that they would outfit an expedition to the far off Shining Mountains.

Buffalo robes and hides were beginning to bring high

prices back East. Those could be traded for, if one had the right things to offer the Indians. And Ezra knew what they wanted: guns, powder and shot, and whiskey. Better still, he knew that gold just waited out there. He had seen plenty evidence of it during his short, disastrous year as a trader. Mining it would be easy.

More people moved west every year. They left St. Louis and Independence by the hundreds from March to June. Before long it would be in the thousands. Some of them never made it. Those not killed by accident, disease, or Indians sometimes went mad from the emptiness, or got lost, and wandered off to simply disappear. They could be found by someone intent and with the time to look for them. And they would make excellent slaves to produce that precious yellow metal.

Another snicker from Bartholamue Haskel jerked Ezra Pease out of his reverie. He blinked and refocused his eyes on the thin smoke trails rising from cook fires before the Cheyenne red-topped lodges.

"We'll go on down now, and get all we can get," he declared.

Black Hand knew of the white men long before they came into view on the downslope toward the camp. He had known of them for three days. That would have surprised Ezra Pease. He had not seen any sign of Indians since leaving the last Blackfoot village where they had traded munitions for high quality, beadwork buckskins, bearskin robes and other items. He had not spent enough time among the trappers and ridge runners of the High Lonesome to be familiar with the statement that had become almost their credo.

"Just because you don't see any Injuns, don't mean they ain't there."

Often, those who lived in ignorance of that didn't live long. But the day would prove beneficent to Ezra Pease and his worthless followers, if barely. Black Hand had heard of the rifles, powder, shot, and bar lead these men brought with them. He badly wanted them, along with bullet molds and replacement ramrods for the older weapons in the Cheyenne camp. So, he made ready to welcome the white men.

To do that, he paid them the infrequent compliment of meeting them at the edge of the village, instead of waiting in his lodge until they made their presence known. Behind him ranged a dozen warriors, one for each of the whites, weapons to hand but not held at the ready. A ring of women, children, and camp dogs formed behind them. Cheyenne ponies neighed greetings to their iron-shod brothers from the meadow to the left. The one who looked to be the whites' leader reined up in front of Black Hand and made the universal sign for peace.

"I am called Pease," he announced.

Better he spoke the language of the people, Black Hand thought as he answered in fair English. "I am Black Hand."

"Good," Pease responded, then went on to diminish their welcome. "I'm glad someone around here speaks a sensible language. We've come to trade."

"What do you have to trade with us?"

Grinning, Pease turned in the saddle and gestured to one of the heavily laden packhorses. "Well, now, I was just fixin' to show you. I think your bucks are gonna like what we have."

"Come in among our lodges then. We will eat, smoke, then make trade." A slight frown furrowed the high, smooth brow of Black Hand. He wanted the rifles this man brought, but he didn't like the insulting way the one called Pease spoke.

"Mighty generous of you, Chief, but we ain't got the time. Need to be pushin' on. We'll just break out our goods right here."

"Too close to the ponies," Black Hand protested.

Meanin' you know we've got rifles, you old fox, Pease thought as he gave in with a shrug and led the way behind the chief to the center of the village. All considered, the white men received a warm welcome. Black Hand did give in to their time concerns by offering the bare minimum of food, a quantity any decent Cheyenne would consider insultingly small. While the women brought it, Pease directed his henchmen to unload the whiskey and open one crate of rifles.

Black Hand's eyes narrowed when he recognized the XX marking on the barrels taken from the gray horse. For all he wanted the rifles, he had no use of the spirit-stealing water. Even so, convention required him to wait, with mounting anger, until Pease had finished rambling on about the excellence of the rifles he had brought.

"You may stay and trade, but the headache water must go," Black Hand stated with a noticeable lack of diplomacy.

Pease took on an expression as though he had just been struck. "Well, now, I don't see any reason for that. 'Never trust a man who won't take a drink,' my poppa always said. Won't do no harm. C'mon, Chief, I'll fill you the first cup."

"Take it out of my village," Black Hand demanded hotly.

Angry mutters rose among the warriors surrounding the white men, and Pease noted that they apparently shared their chief's dislike of liquor. There appeared to be nearly twenty-five of them, all armed. Although only a few had pistols or old trade muskets, Pease knew that a good man could get off six arrows in the time it took to recharge a rifle or pistol. At this range it would be slaughter.

He also considered their usual practice of getting the savages drunk and then trading for inferior rifles and even smooth-bores instead of the fine weapons displayed beforehand. They got more valuable trade items that way, too. Pease noticed the reaction of his men. They were spoiling to do something rash. If they wanted to come out of this with their hair, he had to act fast.

"Uh—sure. Anything you say, Chief. You boys put that whiskey back on the packsaddle, hear?"

Two hours went by haggling over the rifles. Shrewd barterers, the Cheyenne gave precious little of value and wound up with the good weapons to boot. All in all, Ezra Pease considered they had gotten the better of the deal in that they got out of the camp with scalps in place.

From the top of the ridge, he looked back on the village. "We're coming back to this place," he declared ominously.

3

Three of the scruffiest, louse-infested louts Preacher had ever seen in the Big Empty hunkered down around a hastily constructed ring of stones at the bottom of the slope. They warmed their hands over the coals that roasted hunks of fresh-killed venison and slopped down coffee from steaming tin cups. He took that in with his first glance. Then his eyes narrowed and his lips turned down as he viewed the rest of the scene.

A trio of men lay sprawled in death, two of them clearly back-shot. A fourth, whom Preacher recognized at once, lay with his back against an aspen sapling, several turns of rope binding him in place. He had also been shot, although in the leg. John Luscomb, Preacher named the captive as he studied the grayed face behind a brush of beard.

That would make the others Quail Egg Walker, Trent Luddy, and 'Possum Smith. The four had been partnered up for a number of years, trying to make up for low prices with volume. They had also scouted for a couple of the pestiferous wagon trains making the westward push, shot meat for the soldier boys, and done other odd jobs available to men who preferred to live the solitary, free life of the High Lonesome. Well, they had been done dirt, for certain sure.

One of the many things no mountain man could abide was treachery. The ruined campsite showed no indication of a prolonged struggle. No doubt, Preacher read the signs, the three piles of buzzard puke had come on friendly, gotten in among Luscomb and the others and done their foul deed. It seemed to Preacher that a little lesson in right and wrong was in need.

With that in mind, he withdrew from the screening line of pines and walked Thunder down in the clear. At about a hundred yards, he howdied the camp and asked to ride in. Their bellies full of pilfered supplies and fresh meat, the three killers tended to be friendly. And, after all, it was only one man. They could easily jump him, rob him, and kill him once his suspicions cooled down.

Preacher approached with caution and dismounted still some distance from the scuzzy trash. He cut his eyes around the clearing. "Looks like you had some ruckus."

"That we did, friend," said a gap-toothed brute with a brow so low it left no room to hang a hat on his forehead. "This bunch of driftin' trash came up on us and tried to give us what for. We tooken care of them, didn' we, boys?"

"Sure enough. That's what we did, all right," a sawed-off, shallow faced punk with dirty yellow hair joined in.

"Don't reckon anyone will miss them," Preacher drawled.

"No. Not likely. It's gettin' so a man don't know who to trust out here anymore."

Preacher fought to keep the disgust from showing on his face. "I'd say that's mighty keen figgerin'." He'd heard enough of their lies. So he cut his eyes to Luscomb. "What do you figger ought to be done now, John?"

"Kill 'em all, Preacher." John Luscomb gave the obvious answer.

"Preacher!" the acne-ravaged punk squealed.

"Ohmygod!" gulped the smooth liar.

"Mother Mary, help me!" an Irish-looking dirtbag wailed.

In all their reactions, every one of them forgot to draw iron. Preacher's big, right-hand pistol spoke with final authority. The first barrel, double-shotted, discharged its burden into the chest and gut of the gap-toothed braggard. He promptly sat down, spraddle legged, and lost his supper. Preacher ignored him to turn another barrel into position.

He banged off another twin load at about the same time as the remaining pair concluded that they had a fight on their hands. The black-haired son of Erin actually got to one of a trio of pistols shoved behind his wide, leather belt. He had it out and the hammer back when Preacher's second shot took him through the throat and his open, cursing mouth.

His legs jerked reflexively and he flopped over on his back as the rear of his skull exploded in the late afternoon air. By then, Preacher had worked the complicated trigger mechanism to put the next barrel in line.

"It flat irritates me," he lectured the dough-faced fugitive from someone's secondary school, "when I come across four men I count as friends, one shot up an' the others murdered in cold blood by buzzard punks like you three."

"I didn' have anythin' to do with it," the juvenile trash whined as he wet his trousers.

"You don't lie any better than these other horses' patoots. Now, you gonna use one of those pistols you're totin' or do you want to settle it another way?"

Such an option had not occurred to the trashy brat. "Like what?"

Preacher's lips quirked rapidly up and down. "There's always knives. Or how about war hawks? I'm sure John here would lend you his."

The young punk blanched even whiter. "I won't do nothin' like this ever again I swear it," he pleaded.

"Oh, I know you won't. 'Cause you'd best face it, you murderin' scum. One way or the other, you're gonna die this very day."

"But I don't want to die! I'm—I'm too young to die."

"You're old enough to pack those shooters, you're old enough to die with one of them in your hand. Now, pull iron, or I'll just up and kill you with my bare hands," Preacher growled ferociously.

Quaking with fear, desperation decided the boy's actions. He clamped palsied fingers around the butt-stock of a Hopkins .64 caliber, single-barrel pistol, and yanked it free from his waistband. As he raised it to eye-level, he was surprised to see the black hole of the awesome four-barrel pistol in Preacher's hand centered steadily on his forehead. Flame spurted from the muzzle and became the last thing that piece of human vermin ever saw.

Preacher watched him twitch awhile, then walked over to the aspen. He bent low and cut John Luscomb free. A second length bound the mountain man's hands behind him. Preacher sliced through it and Luscomb remained in place, flexed his wrists, rubbed them to revive circulation and beamed a wide smile up at his rescuer.

"You done good, Preacher."

"I'm only sorry I didn't happen along sooner. Might have saved your partners." He knelt beside Luscomb and cut away the buckskin trouser leg to reveal the wound.

"We all got our time to be called," John Luscomb responded philosophically.

Preacher nodded agreement. "Though it don't seem fittin' to be at the hands of maggoty trash like these. I got some Who-Shot-John. Take a few knocks and hang on."

"I'll wait 'till it's over," a white-lipped John Luscomb said. Preacher nodded, then probed the through-and-through hole with a peeled willow stick. Luscomb gasped, gritted his teeth and nearly passed out. When Preacher finished his exploration, he rocked back on moccasin heels.

"It went plum through."

"Good. Didn't hit no bleeder either, or I'd be a goner by now. We gonna bury them?" Luscomb asked.

"Hell no. Let the buzzards claim their own. Where you headin', John?"

"With this bullet through my leg, I reckon I'll mosey up toward the trading post."

"I'm for Trout Crick Pass myself," Preacher advised him, as he bandaged Luscomb's wound. "Don't reckon you'll fork a horse too well. I'll rig a travois an' come mornin' we can go on in together."

"Mighty nice of you, Preacher. I'll be obliged."

"Naw, you won't." He offered the whiskey jug. "Not after givin' me such a prime opportunity to rid the earth of some of its filth. Can you do for some eats and coffee while I cut saplin's and tend my horseflesh?"

"Sure enough. If they didn't eat it all."

"I can see to that, if needs be," Preacher added as he headed to picket out and unsaddle Thunder and the pack-horse. First, though, he saw to reloading his pistol. Never could tell what else might happen by.

Ezra Pease sat on a folding camp stool and glowered into the embers of the fire in front of his gray canvas tent. The more he thought of the loss of high quality rifles and plenty of powder, lead, and molds to those stinking savages, the madder he got. Forced to knuckle under to a man whose people had not even managed to invent the wheel rubbed him in a sore spot. He had been smarting over it for several days.

Morale had fallen among the men as a result. He knew that, though would have been hard-pressed to articulate it that way. The men he sent for supplies had not been in camp as yet to hear of the humiliation. Perhaps when they returned their enthusiasm would fire up the others. Pease came to his boots and crossed to a small trestle table where he poured half a cup of good Tennessee sour mash from a barrel of his private stock. None of that snake-head rotgut he provided for the Indians for as refined a taste as his. After the second sip, sudden inspiration illuminated him.

"Vic," he summoned his second in command. "Come here."

When the lean, hard six-footer arrived, worry lines furrowed his brow. It gave his gaunt face more of a human aspect, rather than the likeness of a skull, its usual appearance. "It's bound to be another three, four days before Ham and the boys get back from the pass. I want to round up everyone in camp at first light tomorrow. We're going back to teach those savages a lesson."

"You think that's wise, Ez?" Titus Vickers asked.

"I think it's necessary, which counts for more. You've seen how the men go around all hang-dog. Give them a little blood to let and they'll snap right out of it."

Preacher's keen hearing, enhanced by years of having little or nothing to dull it, picked up the clamor long before they scaled the long, muddy slope to the clearing at the summit of Trout Creek Pass. He screwed his features into an expression of distaste, halted Thunder and went back to check on John Luscomb. Hands on hips, Preacher tilted his head in the direction of the clearing ahead.

"Can ya hear that carryin' on?"

"Don't, I reckon. Sounds like a passel more of them brain-numb pilgrims."

"Perzactly," Preachers napped with a sharp snort. "Now what in tarnation could have brought them clear up here? Ain't no clear trail to the Oregon Trail this-a-way."

"No accountin' for pilgrims' whims, Preacher. Say, you got a bit more of that Who Flung Chuck? My leg's givin' me a mite of a twinge."

A gross understatement. Mountain men were known for many things, a high pain threshold one of the more notable. Any lesser man than John Luscomb would have been a scream-ing wretch long before this. Preacher dug into the smaller of two parfleche envelopes on the right side of the packsaddle and pulled out his rapidly dwindling supply of whiskey.

"Swill down your fill, John. We'll be resupplyin' right soon."

"How much longer?"

"Quarter hour, tops," Preacher estimated.

"That long? From the beller that's rollin' down on us, I'd have judged we be no more than a long rifle shot from the place."

"Waugh! When I think of all them East Coast idjits swarmin' out here, ruinin' our clean, purty-smellin' country, I just—just want to bawl." Preacher did a double-take, blinked, and nodded. "I do. I done said it an' I mean it, too. Makes a feller plu-perfect sick to see it all happenin'."

"Won't argue with you," Luscomb said by way of agreement. "First thing you know, they'll be puttin' them iron rails out here with those steam cars runnin' on 'em."

Preacher wore a rueful expression. "Pilgrim type told me about them near a year ago. Didn't believe him at the time. Then I flung myself back East way for a spell and seen them with my own eyes. Still don't know if I believe in them. Somethin' that'd go that fast would plain suck the air out of a body."

"Seems likely." Luscomb took another long pull, smacked sallow lips. "Might as well be on our way." He offered the jug. "Best you take a little to keep off the chill."

Preacher accepted the ceramic jug and put it to his lips. His Adam's apple rose once, sank, then rose again, and went still. "A *little* is all there was, John." He peered closely at the container. "You know, I think this thing's got a hole in it."

Glassy-eyed, John slurred his words. "Sure does. Right up there at the top . . . for whiss I'm e-ternal grateful." Gently, he slumped into a boozy daze.

Preacher got the horses moving again and his scowl deepened with each hoof fall as he gradually made out the antlike crawl of humanity between buildings and white-capped wagon boxes. "Damn," he muttered over and over. "Damn pilgrims."

"Stars and garters!" the big, burly man in the doorway to the trading post bellowed when he recognized the rider approaching. "It's Preacher. How'd you winter out in that place?"

"Just fine, Walt," Preacher answered.

Then Walt Hayward saw the bundle on the travois. "Who you got here?"

"John Luscomb. He ran afoul of some cowardly trash."

Hayward bustled to the travois. His belly swelled out as far as his barrel chest, but consisted of a slab of solid muscle. He frowned as he looked down on the wounded man.

"We'll have to get you in a good bed for a while," he commiserated.

Luscomb roused enough to respond. "I'd rather it were a lean-to, if you don't mind, Walt."

"Good. He can reckanize folks he's seen before."

"Well, hell, Walt, he's shot in the leg, not in the head," Preacher drawled.

The bearlike Hayward chose to ignore the sarcasm. He tugged on his shaggy, salt-and-pepper beard. "I'll get Lone Deer to fix up one of those little cabins we built last fall. Now, c'mon, Preacher, I've got something important to talk to you about."

"I'd favor a drink of your good rye, first, Walt. I'm right on the edge of bein' parched."

"Fair enough," the trader allowed and led the way inside.

After the first tin cup of whiskey went down Preacher's throat with the speed of one of those steam cars, Walt poured another and launched into his appeal. "What we've got here is somewhat of a problem. I'm sure you saw the pilgrims out there. They wintered at Bent's an' now they're up here all full of piss and vinegar. Well, they're real pilgrims, if you catch my drift? It's a flock of missionaries on their way, so they say, to bring the Word to the heathen Injuns."

"Why, that's a damn-fool notion if ever I heard one," Preacher erupted.

"Sure it is. At least if they are left on their own. What they need is someone with experience to see them through to wherever they want to settle."

Preacher quickly took in the meaning behind Walt's bright blue eyes. "No sir! Not this chile. I've had all I want of gospel-shouters and Bible-thumpers. You of all people ought to know that, Walt."

"Oh, I know you've had your encounters with the—ah— type. But . . ."

"But nothin'," Preacher all but shouted. "The thought of any of these pilgrims an' tenderfeet westernin' plain sours my stomach. You got yourself the wrong boy this time, Walt. I plum ain't gonna do it."

In the awed silence that followed Preacher's outburst, a snotty, sneering voice rose from the direction of the bar. "My, my, I always knew you was yellow clear through, Preacher. A lazy, shiftless no-account Injun lover who hates every white man on God's green earth." The speaker turned from his hunch-shouldered stance at the plank bar.

Preacher recognized him at once. That nerve-rasping voice, like sawteeth on a nail, pegged him as Bull Ransom, a failed trapper who hung around in the High Lonesome doing odd jobs from time to time, stealing what he wanted the rest. Preacher's eyes narrowed.

"Where I come from, we never stack bullshit that high, Ransom," Preacher said in a deceptively mild voice.

Bull Ransom went livid. "You callin' me bullshit, Preacher?"

Preacher cut his eyes around the nearly empty saloon portion of the trading post. "Seein' as how there's nobody else here but me an' Walt . . . yeah, I say you're nothin' but a great big over-sized pile of shit."

Raging inwardly, Ransom nearly choked on his hot words. "I'll stopper that smart-aleck mouth of yourn. I'll fix you good." Bull changed his tone, became taunting and oily. "I can take you, you know that, Preacher? I can shoot you where you sit before you can touch a gun. I could slice your lilly-livered throat with my Greenriver. Or I might turn your face into ground dog meat with my bare hands."

Preacher shook his head and sighed sadly. "Either you're stupid enough to believe that, or you're the worst, bald-faced liar I ever met, Bull."

That tipped the scales for Bull Ransom. With a roar, he came at Preacher, who rose to his moccasins with the fluid grace of a panther. Preacher didn't wait. He met Ransom halfway. At least the big, balled fist at the end of a rapidly snapped right arm met Bull there with full force. White knuckle marks stood out on the florid skin of Bull's forehead. He grunted and his eyes crossed. Then Preacher began to seriously whip up on Ransom.

Swift, powerful one-two combinations hammered the rib cage of Bull Ransom. Each blow threatened to break ribs. The fat on Ransom's belly jiggled and his jowls wobbled from the tremendous force. Preacher remained squared off with him, which proved to be a mistake the moment Bull recovered from the shock of the sudden, ferocious attack. Grunting with the effort, Bull brought a knee up into Preacher's crotch.

Bent double from the flare of pain, Preacher left himself wide open. Bull moved in and seized the advantage. His fat, though whang-leather tough hands pummeled Preacher's head. A scarlet haze settled over Preacher's vision. Bull had stepped in so close Preacher had no target for his own punishing fists. Then he recalled an old trick he learned from a Pawnee. Having been on the receiving end might account for his undiminished dislike for the Pawnee, he thought giddily before he flexed his knees and rammed the top of his head into the point of Bull's chin.

Teeth clicked together as Bull's jaw snapped shut. Instantly, Preacher sprang backward and went to work on the face of his adversary. Callused knuckles bit and tore into fleshy lips. The upper one split and Bull bellowed his burning rage. Before he could recover, Preacher finished the job of mashing Bull's mouth into a crimson smear. Then he took on Bull's nose. He landed a solid right, then a left and another right. Preacher heard cartilage pop like the hinge-gate stopper of a bottle of beer.

Bull Ransom back-pedaled from the violence of Preacher's assault. Desperately he made a swipe at the bar. His fingers closed around the neck of a blown glass whiskey bottle, with which he took a swing at Preacher's head. Preacher ducked as the container whistled past. Then he planted a ringing left on Bull's right ear.

Nearly dropping the bottle, Ransom readjusted his grip, broke the bottle against the raw plank of the bar top and lunged at Preacher's face. "Enough's enough, goddamnit," Preacher did his thinking out loud.

Then he side-stepped and let the jagged glass whiz past. In a flash, he snatched the wrist and upper arm of Bull Ransom and swung down hard. At the same time he shot his right leg upward, the top of his thigh forming a hard crossbar. Both bones of Ransom's forearm snapped with a loud, sickening sound. The bottle fell from instantly numbed fingers. Howling, Ransom went to his knees. Preacher gauged his enemy and delivered a sturdy kick to Ransom's ruined face. When he turned back to Walt Hayward, the trader noted that Preacher wasn't even breathing hard.

"He certain sure had that comin', Preacher. Let me get another bottle and we'll wet our whistles some more." Walt started across the floor to the bar when he noticed weak, furtive movement from the fallen Ransom. Almost before it could register, Walt watched the battered trash come to his feet, a long, sharp Greenriver knife in his left hand.

"Preacher, look out," Walt shouted. "He's got a knife!"

4

It happened so fast that afterward the hastily gathered witnesses had difficulty recalling if they had, indeed, seen the lithe, lanky mountain man draw and fire. The sharp report of the pistol in Preacher's hand did make its impression clearly. The force slammed painfully into their ears, causing squawks of alarm. This remarkable display of speed and accuracy came as a result of Preacher's strict adherence to the basics of staying alive on the frontier.

Not long after possessing himself of these remarkable firearms and making custom holsters for them, Preacher had experimented with means of getting them into action the easiest and quickest way.

Unknown to him, and to history, Preacher had invented the style that was to become known in later years as the fast draw. It saved his life again this day. His bullets arrested Bull Ransom's lunge in mid-stride. The back-stabber rocked back on boot heels from the impact of the double-shotted load that pierced his sloppy-fat belly. Slowly, a forest giant yielding to the lumberjack's saw, Bull Ransom toppled backward to strike the unfinished planks of the floor with a resounding, drumlike thud.

"I'm dyin', Preacher," Bull said weakly.

"I reckon you are, Bull. You want to make yer peace with God?"

Black-hearted hate distorted Bull's last words. "Damn Him and damn you, too, Preacher." Then his boot heels made a brief, rapid tattoo on the floorboards, he uttered a gurgling rattle and left to meet the Supreme Judge.

"I'd say it's you should be most worried about bein' damned," Preacher observed. A certifiably feminine shriek sounded from beside the inner doorway immediately after.

Preacher cut his eyes that direction and saw three women, over-dressed in the current Eastern style. They had entered during the ruckus caused by his fight with the dead Bull Ransom. One, her gray hair protruding from the fringe of a bonnet, had a hand to her mouth, her face pale and waxen. She appeared about ready to swoon. With her other hand, she clung to the arm of another lady about her own age. The third had uttered the scream. She was much younger, Preacher took in at a glance, and really quite pretty. At least until she screwed her smooth-complexioned face into a mask of moral outrage and advanced on Preacher, small fists flailing the air.

"You barbarian! You savage brute! Why, you—you murdered that poor man for no earthly reason."

Preacher caught both flailing arms by the wrists, in one hand, and stilled her furious assault. He gazed down into deep, cobalt eyes, like hidden mountain pools. "I consider him tryin' to knife me in the back more'n enough reason."

She rounded on Walt Hayward then. "Where's the law around here? This cold-blooded killer must be arrested."

Walt produced a smile that parted the hair around his mouth. "If by that you mean an honest, God-fearin' man who rights wrongs, I'd have to say it's Preacher, Miss Cora."

"'Preacher?' You mean you have a minister nearby, Mr. Hayward?"

"Nope. Preacher's been called a lot of things, but a minister ain't one of them. He's—ah—he's the one's got you caught up by the hand."

A startled squeak emanated from the throat of Cora Ames. Her eyes got an even darker blue and went wide and round. "Oh, Lord have mercy! Spare us from the madness of this wilderness," she prattled.

"The best way for Him to have done that is to have seen that you stayed where you belong," Preacher offered his opinion.

That proved too much for Cora. Not that she backed down. Rather, she stamped her tiny foot, clad in a black, high-button shoe, and jerked free of Preacher's relaxed grasp. "I'm not finished with you. You must be judged for the awful thing you did."

"Oh, I figger as how that's all taken care of. I asked the Man Above to weigh the soul of the departed Bull Ransom and decide where's best to put it. And not to look too harshly on my havin' to send him off so unexpected like. Thing is I can't abide a snake who'd stab a man in the back."

Cora realized what was going on and spoke her mind. "You're making fun of me, aren't you?"

"I wouldn't say that, miss. You're much too pretty to be made fun of."

"Uh—Preacher," Walt began tentatively. "I reckon as how you'll have to act as guide now. Seein' as how you've just done for these mission folks' wagonmaster, that is."

Shock registered on the face of Cora Agnes. "No! Absolutely not! Why, the very idea of allowing this—this—this monster in the company of gentle souls and God-loving people like our family of missionaries is out of the question."

Grinning, Preacher agreed. "Oh, you've got the right of it, miss. Couldn't have said it better myself."

Walt gave Preacher a, "You've got to get me out of this" look. "Really, it's the best solution. There's no one who knows these parts better than Preacher, Miss Cora."

"Bu—bu—but he—he just killed a man right before our eyes."

"And considering conditions out here, is likely to do so again if the situation calls for it," Walt advised her.

"I would not permit it," Cora announced bravely. "I would stand between this wretched beast and his intended victim and defy him to shoot me first."

That, said with such a tone of serious intent, brought a laugh from Preacher. "That's all fuss and feathers, miss, if you don't mind me sayin' so. There's wild Injuns, renegade whites, border trash, and all sorts out there. Bunches of them deserve killin'. They'd not be kind to you and, when they'd had their way, they'd like to kill you for good measure."

Icily, Cora defied his advice. "I don't believe you."

"Suit yourself. But it don't cut no jerky strips, 'cause I ain't gonna take you folks anywhere."

Suddenly realizing her plight, Cora changed her stand. "Oh, but you must. We simply have to reach our mission site in time to build lodgings and a meeting house. We have to plant crops and care for our livestock. And . . . that—that lout didn't impress me with his ability to carry out his duties. We need someone reliable."

The more this fiery damsel spluttered, the more beguiled Preacher became. She had plenty else to say and at great length. Eyes twinkling, Preacher bantered right back. Her passion at their goal made her even more attractive in Preacher's eyes. At last, he relented enough to ask the key question.

"Jist where abouts are you headed, miss?"

"We are going to bring the Word of God to the heathen Cheyenne up north of here," a portly man, done up all in black, complete with dickie and Roman collar, announced as he pushed through the Hudson's Bay blanket that served as a divider between the saloon and the trading sides.

Knowing what he did from Talks To Clouds made it imperative for Preacher to see that these folks understood. "No. No, you're not," he told them, all humor erased from his voice. "There's war talk flyin' around the Cheyenne lodges. From what I hear, they're fixin' to take the war trail against their old enemies, the Blackfeet. That means someone's gonna get their hair lifted." Preacher paused a moment and then went on earnestly. "I'd be the worst sort of some of those names the young lady called me if I was to take you into that. And, besides, I ain't eager to get my scalp picked off by any Injun, Cheyenne or Blackfoot."

"We have no fear, sir," the minister blithely told Preacher. "We have the protection of God, who sent us to the Cheyenne."

Preacher pulled a droll face. "Now, isn't that right comfortin'? Must let a feller lay down to sleep with an easy mind. Pardon my bein' so pushy, but I ain't never met a man on such close personal terms with the Almighty before this. Might I have your name?"

The minister drew up his short, portly figure and spoke with the ringing tones of the pulpit. "I am the Reverend Thornton Bookworthy, sir. It is my privilege to serve the United Mission Conference to the heathen."

Bookworthy? Preacher nearly stumbled over the name. "Well, Reverend Bookworthy, the 'heathen' are fixin' to make war this whole summer. All the signs say that's so, an' my ol' friend Talks To Clouds says so, an' he's one mighty savvy Nez Perce, so I expect he's right. So, there's no way you're goin' up in Cheyenne country this year an' settle down. Unless to settle on the ground and let your bones bleach in the sun. If you're smart, you'll take that as the last word on the subject."

"You astound me, sir! Surely a man of such prowess with fist and gun can have no fear of any mere ignorant savages," Reverend Bookworthy blustered.

"Now, there's where you missed the point entire, Reverend. From personal experience, I allow as how those 'ignorant savages,' as you put it, are ever' bit as smart as you or me. They don't want your God, ain't got no need for Him. They got their own. Hear me good, Mister Minister, they ain't heathens, an' they might do savage things by our lights, but they's kind to their youngins, provide for their old folks, love their wives, and are loyal to their friends. They are only different. They have their own ways, but if you ask me, so long as they're livin' by their own lights, they're doin' the exact things our God wants of us to do."

During what to Preacher constituted a windy speech, Cora listened with a growing expression of understanding and enchantment. With his conclusion, she inserted her now gentle voice between the two men. Her tone alerted Preacher to the fact that she sought to try some modestly Christian forms of feminine wiles on him.

"That was most eloquent, er—ah . . ."

"Preacher, miss."

"Cora Ames, Mr. Preacher. Quite stirring indeed."

"Just, Preacher."

"Ah—Preacher. It gives remarkable insight into the sav— er—Indians to those of us who are woefully ignorant of their ways. But, our dilemma remains the same. Even were we to want to go back where we came from—"

"A capital idea," Preacher broke in to say.

"If we were, we could not get there without a guide. We would, in fact, be stranded here, at this remote place, forced to spend another dreary winter."

"I thought you wintered at Bent's Fort?" Preacher asked, astonished.

"They did. Came in week ago, more's a pity, Preacher," Walt Hayward contributed. "Lost their guide on the way up from Bent's Fort. Hired Bull Ransom first thing he showed up after the thaw, in mid-March."

Preacher eyed the Reverend Bookworthy. "You could have hired any one of the wooly-backs hereabouts and done better for it."

"They were in a hurry," Walt advised Preacher with a wink. "I told them it was a mistake."

Preacher muttered softly to himself for a while, then pulled the weather-beaten hat from his head. "I reckon I could take you as far as down to Bent's Fort. From there you can find an escort back East. But, there ain't no way anyone will take you north into Cheyenne country. By now the word's out all through the Big Empty about the Blackfeet and the Red Top Lodges mixin' it up come summer."

"I must protest," Reverend Bookworthy gobbled in agitation. "We've been directed by God to carry salvation to the savages. Nothing can turn us from our course."

"God didn't direct you to get these lovely ladies killed, did He?" Preacher snapped back. "Listen close, Mr. Reverend Bookworthy, you'd be smart to take what you've been offered and be grateful for it. I've got no time for more of your insistin', an' I jist might change my mind if you keep that jabber up."

Running Bear, Stone Drum, Wind Rider, and Falling Horse stood in the midst of the charred lodge poles and ashes that had been the village of Black Hand. They found the body of their fellow chief, along with four warriors, where they had fallen. Behind their corpses lay a mound of dead women and children, whom they had been protecting. The ruins of the village, in its once beautiful, peaceful valley sweltered under the stench of so much death.

"It was white men, I'm certain of it," Running Bear stated flatly. "Who else would waste the food and burn the lodges?"

Falling Horse nodded thoughtfully. "I agree."

"It might have been the *Absaroka*. Those Crow dogs have rubbed up against the whites so long that they even think like them. We must gather a large war party and send it against our old enemy."

"And have the Blackfeet at our backs?" objected Wind Rider.

"What do you know about it, Breaks Wind?" Stone Drum asked in jest, using the irreverent form of his fellow chief's name.

"I know that the Blackfeet have been buying guns from some white men, that they have many of the latest kind. I know, too, that these white traders had visited Black Hand's village."

"Too much talk about whites." Falling Horse grunted. "I say we take the war trail against all whites, run them out. They have no reason to be here. They kill the game and leave most to waste, or run it off. They foul the ground with their waste, muddy the water, and cut deep gashes in the breast of Earth Mother. It is for us to stop their coming."

"You would stop the flow of the Great Water to the east?" Wind Rider countered. "The whites number like the drops of that mighty river. These are different days. We must learn to be tolerant of our enemies, the Crow and the whites."

All three of his companions looked at him as though he had confessed some unspeakable vice. Running Bear spoke first. "That is not for us to decide. We must take this to the grand council and gain agreement of a plan that will work."

Nodding their approval of this idea, Stone Drum and Falling Horse walked with Running Bear to their ponies. Wind Rider hesitated a moment, then followed.

Arapaho Basin had long been a gathering place for the Indians who roamed the fringes of the Rocky Mountains. The hot sulfur springs that bubbled up from the depths of the earth were considered good for the bones of the old. The current occupants of the basin had little consideration for that. Ezra Pease had established his base camp there because of the shelter provided by the high peaks that surrounded the lush valley.

He was taking his ease outside his tent and sipping on his fifth cup of coffee, laced with rum, when two of his disreputable gang rode into camp. They barely dismounted from their lathered horses when the older of the two blurted out his bad news.

"Weasel Carter an' those you sent with him to do in Preacher? He done kilt them all."

Ezra Pease came to his boots in a jerky motion. "What! I

sent Weasel because not even Preacher could figure out that he was a danger, until it was too late."

"Well, Preacher sure must have learned mighty fast," the shaggy-haired brute with a waxen scar from his left ear to the corner of his mouth opined.

"Damnit! Our whole operation hinges on getting rid of him. Preacher is all too friendly with most of the Indians, and he's known by every white man in this country. If he gets word of what we're up to, he can make the world a mighty mean place for us."

"What should we do about it?" the knife-cut thug asked bluntly.

"Get the job done right," Pease snapped. "Get Bart Haskel, Two Thumbs Buehler and about ten more over here right now."

When the reluctant volunteers assembled, they wasted no time making it clear they were none too happy about the reason for their summons. Ezra Pease eyed them coldly, then reminded himself that these were the best he had, better than most in the past. Too bad most of them came out of the prairie lands of Missouri and Illinois. He'd be glad to trade the lot for half a dozen wild and wooly mountain men. Nevertheless, they were loyal to him to the man.

He could at least count on them not to shirk in their duty and eventually succeed or die in the process. Pease preferred not to think of dying. Every day Preacher remained alive increased the risk for him and his bully-boys. He took a deep breath and launched his effort to spell finis to Preacher.

"I can see by the looks on your faces that you know what happened to Weasel and the men with him. I never said Preacher was going to be easy to stop. He's smart, mean, and knows these mountains better than any man living. He'll be wary now, and a whole lot harder to run to ground. That's why I'm sending a dozen of you. Preacher is a legend, out here as well as in those silly penny dreadfuls you may have seen back East.

"It's going to be your job to track him down and finish

him. But . . ." Pease let the word hang. "I don't simply want him dead. I want him dragged around from place to place so folks know for certain sure that he's a goner. With him out of the way, our path is clear to fortune and power. Provision yourselves and ride out within the hour. The sooner you go, the sooner Preacher dies."

5

Preacher slouched in the saddle of his spotted horse, Thunder, at the crest of the notch that led south out of Trout Creek Pass. He had replaced his battered, floppy hat with a crisp new one, though he had to allow as how it didn't shade his face the way the old one had. It made him look a little less disreputable, Cora Ames thought as her wagon rolled by the immobile mountain man.

"You all keep rollin'," Preacher advised to the drivers. "I'll catch up and scout ahead in awhile."

Complaints still came from the missionaries about being turned back, yet Preacher noted that most of the women accepted it with relief evident in the less pinched expressions they wore. Not all of them, he reminded himself as he gazed on the ash-blonde hair that escaped in wisps around the bonnet on the head of Cora Ames. Drat it, it somehow didn't seem right to him that someone who looked so pretty should be wrapped up in saving the souls of folks who didn't want 'em saved. She belonged in a nice, white, clapboard farmhouse, like the ones he'd seen back East, with a gaggle of kids running around her knees and clinging to her skirt.

Could she have made up her mind to the spinster's life so

young? There were plenty of married couples among the twenty wagons in the missionary train. Youngsters, too, blast the luck. Preacher firmly believed that brat-kids had no business out in the Big Empty, leastwise not those too young to take care of themselves. Grownups had their hands full keeping themselves alive and their possessions intact. They had no time to give to doing for a batch of babies and infants.

Yet, they persisted in coming, more each year, damn their stars. He recalled the year he took a train of tenderfeet clear to the Big Water in Oregon country. Three women had birthed on the trail. Only one of the infants survived the trip. Fools. Preacher dismissed his gloomy contemplation to mentally review for the hundredth time the trail south and eastward to Bent's Fort. It would be rough, but these pilgrims had been over it once. Maybe they had learned something.

At least, the fort was out on the flats and these folks would have easy going from there. They could take the Santa Fe Trail as far as Independence, for that matter, and then on down to St. Louis. They'd just have to look out for the Southern Cheyenne, the Kiowa, Pawnee, Kaw, and the Osage. No mean feat, but with the right men to guide them, it could be done, was done day in and day out for that matter. There was some talk of building some military forts along the Trail, but Preacher doubted he'd live to see the day.

He pushed that out of his mind and gigged Thunder into a lazy trot. In a short time he caught up with the wagon that carried Cora Ames. She greeted him with more cordiality than he might have expected. Enough to encourage him to rein in to the slow walk of the mules pulling the lumbering vehicle. Preacher might prefer only his own company in the High Lonesome, but the lure of a pretty young woman could be resisted by just a few.

"I suppose you know we're terribly curious, Mr.—er—Preacher," the good looker offered without preamble.

"Curious about what?" Preacher asked, genuinely unaware.

"About you, of course. Surely you have a Christian name, unless, like some of those scallywags at the trading post tried to get us to believe, you were mothered by a she-wolf."

Preacher couldn't figure out if she was teasing him or not. "Yes, Miss Cora. I do. Name's Arthur." He said it so softly she barely heard it.

"That's a perfectly lovely name, Arthur."

Pink touched Preacher's cheeks. "Maybe that's why I don't cotton much to usin' it."

"I would think your mother would be disappointed you did not," Cora tossed at him without being censorious. "Where were you born, Arthur?"

Preacher winced. "Please, jist Preacher." Then he went on to answer her. "On a farm in Ohio. Long enough ago that it was the frontier at the time. The Sauk and Fox were still there in great number."

"Do you have living kin? Brothers or sisters?"

"I do," Preacher answered curtly. "If you don't mind, it's downright uncomfortable talkin' so much about myself. Don't think me bold, but what about you? What sort of life has brought you out into all this emptiness?"

Cora gave a moment's thought before answering. "My family are all Green Mountain folks from Vermont. I am the fifth of seven children my mother bore. In addition to dairy cattle and harvesting maple syrup, my father was a circuit-riding preacher." She let go a brief trill of laughter. "No pun intended."

Preacher shared her amusement. "Then your family all grew up God-fearin' and full of rectitude?"

A fleeting frown darkened Cora's forehead. "Not . . . all of them. But, that's another story. I don't mean to offend, but I've noticed that you don't talk like an *uncouth,* unlettered dolt all the time. You seem to pick and choose."

Preacher shot her a quick grin. "You're not the first to make that observation. I had acquired some six years of book learnin' before I made tracks for the Shinin' Mountains.

After that it was mostly self-taught, but I did learn some proper grammar. Some of the men I associated with helped me on that."

"How was that? No, please, I really am interested," Cora urged.

"A number of years back, I don't remember exactly when, some of us who could read and write and do our sums took to sharing our knowledge amongst ourselves an' those who could not read for themselves. I even learned some Shakespeare, and about the heroes of long ago, Horatio and Odyssius, Julius Caesar."

Cora Ames clapped her hands in delight. "I'm so glad you called him by his proper name. Ever since those terrible translations of the *Illiad* and the *Odyssey,* people have taken to calling him Ulysses."

Preacher nodded his thanks for her compliment. "You're a learned woman, then?"

"My, yes. More, I'm sure, than a lot of people think I should be. Most girls back East still finish school with the eighth form. Then it's off to a home and children, or to one of the sweatshops to labor until death."

"Don't reckon a sprightly filly—er—pardon, a spirited lady like yourself would be content with either of those," Preacher stumbled out.

"A few go on to the young ladies' seminary—that's where I matriculated." She paused, frowned, then made a surprising revelation. "I'd not turn down a husband, family, and a stout home." Then Cora confided with vigor, "As for the other alternative, it is, as they say, 'a man's world.' They have all the positions on the top of the heap. For a woman who undertakes to support herself or her family, the workplace offers little more than it does for slaves down in the South. Drudgery and dehumanization are the watchword of the few factories and sewing shops, or even teaching positions open to women in the East."

"But you chose missionary work," Preacher brought her back to speed. "What influenced that decision?"

Cora flushed and diverted her cobalt gaze from Preacher's slate eyes. "As you said, there are some things I am 'downright uncomfortable' talking about."

"Sorry I brought it up. Well, I'd best get along up the string and see what's ahead. We'll be makin' camp in about two hours."

"So early?" Cora responded. "There are still hours of daylight."

"First day on the trail. There'll be need to fix what broke and shake down the way the wagons are loaded. That all takes time. Good day to you, Miss Cora."

Preacher rode off along the line of wagons. Behind him he left Cora Ames with a vague sense of being unfulfilled.

Cook fires had been lighted and the pilgrims settled in. Three wagons needed to replace wheels with loose iron tires. Preacher had to admit that was one fancy Eastern idea that had a practical use out here. Shod wheels made sense. The rough trails, mostly only enlarged animal tracks, punished wheeled vehicles mercilessly. The recent advent of iron-tired wheels had its downside as well. It made it easier for these pestiferous greenhorns to travel far beyond any hope of help from civilization when they got in trouble.

"Will you take supper with us, Preacher?" Lidia Pettibone asked sweetly from where she bent over a tripod that held a bubbling pot of stew.

Preacher drew a deep breath of the rich aroma and identified fresh venison. "Don't mind if I do. I want to make a round of camp first, if that's not makin' it too late for you folks."

"Not at all. It will be a while, at least."

Her husband, Asa, had the strangest occupation Preacher had ever heard of. He was an organist. The freight wagon that accompanied their living quarters held a large bellows-pumped pipe organ, complete with brass tubes to produce the majestic, imperial sounds of that instrument.

"Good dang thing they ain't headed clear to Or-e-gon," Preacher muttered aloud to himself. "The tribes twixt here an' there would be supplied with arrow and lance points for the next century." Brass, he knew, was mighty precious to the Indians.

For a people who had never learned to smelt metals, or forge them, or even invented the wheel, they were right adaptable. They appreciated the value of forged or cast metal almost at once. Which meant they were right smart. Which made them damned dangerous. All of a sudden Preacher came upon an impression that was so far-reaching and pre-scient that it all but staggered him. Given enough time, like the white man had with this new science, and the Indians could easily push folks whose families came from Europe back into the sea.

"Good evening—ah—Brother Preacher," the Reverend Thornton Bookworthy rumbled as he passed by where Preacher stood staring into space over the concept of industrialized Indians.

"Evenin', Reverend Bookworthy." Suddenly he had a burning desire to share his revelation with someone. "I just had me a startlin' thought."

Although he looked pained, Reverend Bookworthy re-sponded with enthusiasm. "I'd be delighted to hear it."

"It just come to me, thinkin' about Pettibone's pipe organ. What if, when our ancestors came here, the Injuns had been smelting and forming metal objects for as many hundreds of years as the white man had?"

"But, they're ignorant savages," Bookworthy protested with typical white blindness.

"Yeah. Only what I said was, 'what if?' You may not be-lieve it, but what I said at the trading post is true. They're smart, they're crafty, they's absolutely fearless, and they know bet-ter than to line up and march off to shoot at each other and stab away at one another with bayonets in the heat of the day. I tell you, Reverend, it's downright frightening to consider."

Bookworthy still wasn't sold. "You've been out here,

among them, for longer than any of us. I suppose you could be right. If so, let us be thankful it wasn't that way."

Preacher grunted and went on his rounds, inspecting the fringes of the camp. He didn't expect any hostiles to swarm down on them, not so close to the trading post in Trout Creek Pass. Nor had he seen any sign throughout the day of any drifting bands of white trash. Yet, an uneasiness gnawed at him.

Maybe it was his stomach, Preacher considered a half hour later when he returned to the Pettibone wagons. The aromas rising from the cook fire made him growly as a grizzly on the first day after hibernation. His mouth watered when his nose made out the distinct scent of apple pie. Guiding these folks would have a few advantages after all, he decided.

Over a week's time, Preacher learned a lot more about the gospel-shouters. Enough, indeed, to make him uncomfortable. Some, he knew, had joined this crazy expedition as a last-chance opportunity. They considered themselves to be losers, talked and acted like it, too. They wouldn't last a year out here.

Some would go around the bend, wander off, and get killed by any number of roving predators, human as well as animal. That would be their problem, he supposed. Others, like the Bookworthys, had the wild fire of the zealot in their eyes. They could be trouble. Good thing they were all going back. If they got there, he reminded himself.

Since early that morning, which Preacher reckoned put them a short three days travel from Bent's Fort, he had been seeing signs of others out there. Indians, and a lot of them, with no indication of women or children along. Of course, they could be a hunting party. Not likely, Preacher reasoned. Accordingly, he rode back to the lead wagon and spoke with one of the several drivers hired by those unable to handle their own teams.

"When we make camp for the night, Buck, I want you to

circle the wagons. Make it nice and tight. After the teams are unhitched, make it box to box. No spaces between. And leave the animals inside the circle."

Having grown wise on the way out, the burly driver frowned at this. "You expectin' trouble?"

"Might be. There appears to be Injuns out there. I've seen signs. That means they know we're here."

"I'll see to it, Preacher," Buck Dempsey agreed.

Preacher studied the stout, dark-complexioned Buck Dempsey. He gauged a steadiness in the hickory nut eyes and smooth brow, the set of a square chin. Yeah, he'd do to lead the other drivers. "I see you've got a good Hawken along. Were I you, I'd see to it being loaded and at hand from now on. I'm gonna drift along the line and tell the others."

Preacher's efforts met with somewhat less than enthusiastic results. Reverend Bookworthy was quite vocal in his objections. "We will do no such thing. I am a man of God, and these are the children of God. Besides, we'll only be inviting trouble," he pontificated. "If the savages see us all bristling with arms and in a defensive position, it will alienate them."

"Reverend, they don't need us to alienate them. If it's some what's got it in for whites, they'll already be as sore as a boil on your behind. What's going to happen is that if they see us all ready to take them on, if they're not already cooked up for war, they will decide to ride on and leave us in peace."

"That doesn't make sense," Bookworthy protested. "A belligerent posture invokes a belligerent response."

"It might be so back where you come from. But, Injuns think different from us. If they believe their medicine is strong, that the light is just right, and specially if we're afeared of them, they'll attack. On the other hand, if they ain't too sure about their medicine, or that we are able to knock too many of them off their ponies, they won't. Injuns ain't stupid. Numbers are real important to them. Gotta have men to protect the village, to hunt meat for everyone. Get too many killed off in battle and everybody suffers. Some might starve, or the village get wiped out by an enemy tribe."

"Why, that's preposterous, Preacher. I've been informed by knowledgeable men at Harvard and other colleges that the Indians are peaceful among themselves, at least until the white man came. Only the white man represents a threat to their way of life."

Preacher wanted to laugh in the fool's face, he held it back, though. "An' that's just so much heifer dust, Reverend, if you'll pardon my language. Their lives are as precarious as I've said, but war's a part of their way of life, they're used to it. Over thousands of years they have become expert survivors. Now I'd advise you to make some arrangements to be armed through the next day or so, like I'm tellin' everyone else."

Preacher found the attitudes divided along the lines of the nature of those he advised. The hired drivers, there were six, all loaded up and spent the nooning hour twisting cartridges out of paper, powder, and shot. The soul-savers were uniformly horrified by the prospect of violence, except, surprisingly, Cora Ames.

"My father sent along his fine Purdy English rifle and a pair of horse pistols. He may be a man of the cloth, but he's practical, too. We have our share of highwaymen in Vermont."

"Ummmm—yes," Preacher muttered through his dismay. He also revised his estimate of Cora upward by several notches.

Later, once camp had been established, Cora came to where Preacher peered beyond the circled wagons. "We were fortunate in not having trouble with the Indians on the way out. Maybe it would have been better if we had. Reverend Bookworthy is expending great effort to talk our people into having nothing to do with guns. He wants us all to stay close to the fire . . . and to build it up even more."

Preacher turned to her. "That danged fool. He'd make perfect targets out of all of you."

"He pointed out that night has fallen and we've not been attacked. And everyone knows that Indians don't attack in the dark."

Preacher made a rude sound. "What 'everyone knows' ain't necessarily true. Injuns will attack at night. Like I tried to make him understand, if the Injuns think their medicine is good and their numbers big enough, they'll attack day or night. Now, I'd better go do something about gettin' that fire down to coals, so's we can see them when they come."

"You're . . . that sure?" Cora asked uncertainly.

"I feel it in my bones. I can smell 'em out there. I reckon they'll pick a time closer to the middle of the night. When they do, you'd best be ready to bang away with that rifle and the pistols you brung."

Preacher excused himself and went to get something done about the fire, which he insisted be put out entirely. He got a windy objection from Reverend Bookworthy and several missionaries, which he addressed by simply shouting them down. Cora looked on and shook her head in dismay. With that accomplished, Preacher retrieved his two rifles and checked the loads in them and a brace of pistols from saddle-boxes Thunder carried.

Then he went around the circled wagons until he found a place where, if he were an Indian, he would figure as a prime one to launch an attack against. There he settled in to wait. It turned out not to be as long as he had expected.

A mixed band of Kiowa and Pawnee hit about ten o'clock, in the dark of the moon. Preacher first saw blacker shapes flitting from one bit of sparse cover to another. It didn't take long to figure out that it wasn't a pack of coyotes or wolves. One of them reared up abruptly and drew taut a bowstring.

Preacher let one of the big .70 caliber horse pistols bang away. A brief, shrill cry of pain answered and the bowman disappeared from sight. Another quickly took his place. Preacher put a fat .70 caliber ball in the Kiowa's breast bone, showering both lungs with bone and lead fragments. The hostiles were in too close for rifle work, so Preacher ignored them to get one of his four-barreled blitzers into action.

By then, the drivers, led by Buck Dempsey, had opened up on the invading Indians. Preacher took his eyes off the assault to cut a quick look around the compound. He turned back in time to all but stuff the muzzle of his four-barrel in the screaming mouth of a Pawnee warrior. The double-shotted load took off the entire back of the hostile's head.

Showered by brain tissue, a youthful brave behind him gagged and mopped at his eyes. That reflex bought him a quick trip to the Happy Hunting Ground. Preacher had barely turned the next barrel into line when the young Pawnee rushed at him. He gut-shot the teenage brave and quickly cranked the last load into position.

"Pour it on, boys!" he shouted encouragement as he took a quick, inaccurate shot at a Kiowa who had leaped onto the tailgate of the wagon belonging to Cora Ames.

Preacher's ball cut a thin line across the bare back of the warrior, who disappeared into the wagon's interior. A pistol barked and flame lighted the canvas cover from inside. Preacher had moved within reach of Cora's wagon when the warrior appeared again, a look of disbelief that a woman had mortally wounded him clear on his face.

"Good shootin', missy," Preacher called to Cora. He would have liked to do more, but right then he had his hands full of two Pawnee braves. One bore down on him with a lance, the other brandished a tomahawk. Preacher promptly drew his second fearsome pistol and plunked a double load into the lancer's chest and belly.

The Pawnee went rubber-legged and wobbled off toward the side. Preacher turned back toward the one with the war hawk. Lightning quick, the man had closed in on Preacher so fast it prevented revolving the barrels of his four-shot. He used it to parry the overhand blow instead.

While he did, he drew his own tomahawk and planted it deep in the base of the Pawnee's neck. Numbed by massive shock and sudden, profuse blood loss, the man sagged against Preacher, who wrenched his hawk free and stepped back. From behind him he heard a shrill scream and cut his eyes over his shoulder in time to see Cora Ames disappear over the outer side of her wagon, in the arms of a howling Kiowa.

"One of them Kiowa got Miss Cora," Preacher shouted. "Buck, Luke, come over here and hold 'em off. I'm goin' after her."

6

Preacher leaped to the top of a wagon wheel and vaulted the driver's seat. He swung his legs over and dropped free. His moccasined feet came down on the back of a Pawnee who sought to crawl under the vehicle and enter the defensive circle. With a stout flex of his knees, Preacher put an end to that plan. The audible crack of the hostile's spine was music to Preacher's ears. He bounded across the ground in the faces of the astonished Indians.

Only vaguely could he make out his goal. Two darker blobs in the faint, frosty starlight wavered unsteadily. Cora Ames fought her captor with tenacity. Preacher closed gradually. He managed to draw his second four-barrel pistol and held it ready. A sharp howl came from the mouth of the Kiowa who carried Cora upright with an arm around her waist. Improving night vision gave Preacher a sight he would marvel over for years to come.

Cora had not worn her bonnet in her bedroll and her ash-blonde hair, done in thick sausage curls, star-frosted, flailed about as she violently shook her head. Then he realized the reason for the scream of anguish and her actions. Cora had the Kiowa's right ear in her teeth and was worrying it like a terrier with a rat.

Good girl, Preacher thought as he drew close enough to think about firing a shot. Not a good idea, he rejected, recalling he had double-shotted this one, too. He shoved the gun back into its holster and brought out his tomahawk instead. He had come close enough to hear the hostile grunting and grinding his teeth in pain. His breath came in harsh, short gasps. Incredibly, Cora was growling like the terrier to which Preacher had compared her.

Then he was where he wanted to be. Preacher raised his arm and brought the hawk down swiftly on the crown of the Kiowa's head. It buried its flange blade to the haft in the Indian's skull. With a final grunt the warrior let go of Cora and sank to the ground. Without breaking stride, Preacher yanked his war hawk free, caught up Cora, and reversed course. They started back at once.

"My Lord, what did you do?" Cora gasped.

"I got you away from that Kiowa brave," Preacher said simply.

Speechless, Cora stared in shock at Preacher. His face was grimed with powder residue and spattered with Kiowa blood. He looked every bit as savage as the hostiles who had attacked them. Then she amended that when she realized where she had been only moments before. No, Preacher didn't look like a savage . . . he was absolutely gorgeous. Preacher's stride faltered to a stop.

He had been keeping unconscious track of the battle's progress and now noted a sudden increase in the volume of fire. Either the pilgrims had taken up arms or at least realized the sense of reloading for those who were fighting back.

"I can walk perfectly well, Preacher," Cora advised him.

"Uh—sure—sure." He released her and they started off again. Preacher had his charged pistol in hand, the hammer back on the ready barrel. The sound of moccasined feet crashing through the grass ahead came to his ears. In a second two figures in fringed buckskin shirts came rushing at them. Preacher spotted a low sage bush and gave Cora a light shove toward it.

"Get down," he commanded.

"What . . ."

"Just do it." He crouched low in accord with his words.

The two Pawnees rushed on past them without even a glance. Behind them came five more. Gradually the firing slackened from the circled wagons. To left and right, hostiles fled past where Preacher and Cora huddled. They all seemed intent on but one thing. They wanted to get as far away from that deadly fusillade as they could.

In what seemed no time at all, Preacher and Cora found themselves alone in the meadow where the wagons had stopped. Cautiously, Preacher raised upright. Without moonlight to help, he found himself unable to verify that the hostiles had all departed. Slowly he turned a full circle. Faintly in the distance he heard the rumble of departing hooves. Holding back a smile, Preacher bent and helped Cora to her feet, which he noted by starlight to be narrow, pale white, and nicely formed.

"If you're determined to get cactus spines and sand burrs in those dainty feet of yours, it's all right with me. But I do think I should carry you in from here."

"Oh! Oh, dear!" she blurted in realization. "I never thought of that."

Preacher reholstered his pistol and extended his arms invitingly. Cora settled herself with an arm around Preacher's neck. Preacher strode across the uneven ground as though completely unincumbered. To her consternation, Cora released a contented sigh.

"I hope you know this does not constitute a proposal of marriage, Miss Cora," Preacher said quietly.

Cora tittered in delight. "The thought hadn't entered my mind. But it is a pleasant way to travel."

When Preacher could make out the shapes of the caravan,

he paused and called out loudly. "Hello, the wagons. It's Preacher. I'm comin' in with Miss Cora. Don't nobody get trigger happy."

"Come on in, Preacher," Buck Dempsey called back. "I got all the guns grounded."

Preacher started off again, only to detour around the body of a Pawnee. He would be gone before morning, Preacher knew. With that he dismissed the dead Indian . . . a little too soon.

The Pawnee, who had been shot through the arm, had been playing possum. Preacher had taken only three steps beyond him when he came up off the ground, a wicked knife in the hand of his good arm. Cora looked over Preacher's shoulder in time to see him lunge.

"Preacher!" she hissed in his ear. "Indian," she added. In the next instant she found herself roughly dumped on the ground, Preacher turned around and standing over her, one of those terrible-looking pistols already in his hand. The sound of its detonation pained her ears. In the flame from the barrel, she saw two dark spots appear on the chest of the Pawnee. Then it went dark again.

She heard the body fall and gasped. Then Preacher said something that struck her as remarkably odd. "Never could abide the Pawnee. Maybe it's because they're sneaky."

Back inside the ring of wagons, Cora Ames gratefully wrapped herself in a wooly house robe, offered by Patience Bookworthy, and shuddered. The females among the missionaries made over her and showered her with questions about her ordeal. When she had quieted them, Cora shivered again and faced their avid, curious faces with a wide-eyed expression.

"It was terrible. He—he just jumped in while I was reloading, grabbed me and dragged me off. My skin was crawling. I—I feel sullied and shamed forever."

Preacher snorted and turned away. He thought of telling her about some of the women he'd come upon, victims of hostile action; brutally raped, tortured, their heads bashed in.

Then he decided not to. There were other things to take care of first.

"I want every gun in camp loaded, double-shotted. We'll take turns keeping watch. No fires at all. We have to be able to see without being seen."

"Surely you don't think they will come back," Reverend Bookworthy blustered.

"As certain as Old Nick, I'd say. Somethin' just scared them off. Injuns are notionable, don't you know?"

"But, we soundly defeated those savages," the reverend persisted.

"Nope. Nothin' of the sort." He cut his eyes to the jubilant faces of the unaware missionaries. They may have just won a battle, but they hadn't won the war. Exasperation colored his words. "I don't think it's possible for you lint-brained Eastern folk to learn anything out here. Them hostiles have just gone off to whup up some better medicine. They'll sneak back for their dead and any wounded they missed, then pound the drums and dance until they drop. Come mornin', they'll be back."

At dawn, the hostiles came again. This time they charged on horseback, howling their fierce war cries and brandishing lances. Some reined in and nocked cumbersome-looking arrows to their bowstrings. Preacher took it in and quickly issued his commands.

"Get them water barrels ready. We're gonna get fire arrows." Several women squeaked in fright. "Water'll put 'em out. Have some kettles ready for throwin' it on where they hit. We're backed against this ledge, so they can't circle us. You drivers spread out anyway."

That made sense, Buck Dempsey reasoned. The savages would hit more than one place at the same time. He settled in under a wagon and patted the barrels of his two rifles and a shotgun provided by one of the missionaries. Strange fellow, he called it a "fowling piece." Buck sure hoped the nipples didn't foul when he needed to use it. Preacher stopped by where Buck lay and patted the man on one shoulder.

"That Hawken's got good range. See if you can knock that big, handsome brute out of the saddle." By then the warriors had spread out, ready to close on the wagons and swarm over them.

Buck took aim and fired at the same time the first volley of fire arrows took flight. "Here they come," Preacher shouted. The ball from Buck's .54 Hawken smacked flesh in the shoulder of the muscular Pawnee that Preacher had indicated and the brave dropped his lance, though he remained in place. Preacher moved off to his own position.

He crouched in the space between the dashboard and seat of the wagon behind Cora's. From there he had a good view of the attacking force. Too bad that shot of Buck's went high and left, he mused. That buck had the look of a leader. Might have been able to end it without any damage done. He took aim with one of his rifles and let it bang away.

One of the warriors who had shot the fire arrows uttered a brief scream and pitched backward out of the saddle, shot through the chest. Preacher immediately set that rifle aside and took up the other. This was the finely made, French sporting rifle he had taken off one of those fancy-pants, titled dudes who had chased him and the boy Eddy across most of Indian Territory and into the mountains of the High Lonesome.

Weren't many of them went home, except in boxes, Preacher recalled. He'd not liked the feel of being a wanted man, with a bounty on his head. Preacher sincerely hoped that the last of those flyers had been disposed of. For now, though, he had other things to worry about.

Beyond the Kiowa and Pawnee renegades rushing the wagons, he had seen the colorful feathers of a war bonnet. Might be the real leader, and this Frenchy rifle had the legs to reach him. Preacher rested the forestock of the long-barreled weapon on the side of the wagon and took aim.

Right then the defenders opened up. Six rifles spoke almost as one, with a seventh a moment later from nearby.

That would be Cora Ames. The very real danger of the hostiles had sure changed her outlook on turning the other cheek. Or maybe she figured she'd turned all the cheeks she had and it was time for a little "eye for an eye." Preacher fined down his sight picture and squeezed off a round.

After a short pause, feathers flew from the war bonnet and the head beneath disappeared as its owner sought communion with the earth. He wouldn't be giving orders for a while, Preacher thought with satisfaction. No time to reload. He pulled free one of his pistols as he sensed a hand move past him and take the Hawken. Preacher cut his eyes in a backward glance to see Mrs. Pettibone.

"My husband has a shotgun. He has joined the defenders. I'll load for you," she said, as pleasantly as welcoming worshipers to their little New England church.

"You folks have got some sand, I'll say that," Preacher returned in high praise.

Less than fifty feet separated the laagered wagons from the hostiles when Preacher returned his gaze to the front. At once he cocked and fired. The double-shotted load cleaned a Kiowa off his pony and sent him sprawling in the grass. A quick turn, hammer back, another pair of .50 caliber balls on their way. A howling Pawnee leaped from his horse to the side of the wagon Preacher occupied. He took the third barrel point-blank in the face.

Sizzling lead and hot gases blew off the back of his head. Preacher cranked the barrel again. Another shower of fire arrows made weird sounds overhead. One punched into the rump of a draft mule, which promptly went mad with pain and fright. It broke away from the picket line and crow-hopped toward a wagon side.

Mrs. Landry appeared at its side to soak its rump with a kettle full of water. Her husband, Art, caught up the animal, snatched the barb from its haunch and worked to calm the beast. "They also serve who stand and wait," Preacher said to himself.

Then he unloaded the last barrel into the chest of a lance-wielder who loomed large in his vision. Quickly reholstering the pistol, Preacher reached out in time to take the Hawken from Mrs. Pettibone. "Obliged," he muttered as he shouldered the rifle and took quick aim.

Another hostile died and Preacher traded for his other big pistol. If this kept up much longer, he'd be down to his brace of horse pistols. Fully a dozen hostiles lay writhing on the ground, or still in death. So far the drivers had kept the pace with the assault. Preacher picked a target and let fly. Shot through the throat, the Kiowa hastily departed the earth for the Happy Hunting Ground. Motion from beyond the swarm of Indians around the wagons caught Preacher's attention. Their war chief must have gotten over his scare.

Preacher gathered up the cartridge box for the French rifle and then blasted another hostile off his horse with a ball that shattered the hapless Indian's collarbone and lodged in his shoulder blade. Preacher turned away.

"Miz Pettibone, I'd be obliged if you'd load this one for me right away," he asked, handing her the long-range weapon.

When he had the French rifle back in hand, Preacher stood and took careful aim at the war leader. When the chest of the Pawnee centered in the sights, Preacher squeezed off with care and rode the mild recoil as the weapon discharged. At that range, it took the bullet a hair over two seconds to reach the target, the sound of the shot a second longer.

Preacher couldn't see the surprised look on the war chief's face when the heavy lead ball smacked into his chest and burst his heart. He did see the buckskin-clad Indian rise in the stirrups and then fling forward along the neck of his mount. At once a loud wailing came from those near to the dead leader. That proved too much for the warriors assaulting the wagon train.

With yips and howls, they pulled off out of rifle range and sat their ponies wondering aloud what could be done. Preacher seized the moment to try a little medicine of his own. He remained standing in the wagon in full view, raised his rifle over his head and let go a loud whoop.

"I am White Wolf! Man Who Kills Silently! White Ghost to the Arapaho, who fear me," he shouted in Pawnee. "You have lost one of every three. Your war chief is dead. This fight is over. Go now, or you will all meet Corpse Eater before the day ends."

The older and wiser among the hostiles now knew only too well who they faced. Badly shaken, they cut worried eyes to the fallen war chief and back to Preacher. A few words were exchanged, then they turned their ponies and withdrew. Many rode with lances reversed, points to the ground, to signify the battle had truly ended.

"Well, we got out of it that time," Preacher announced into the stunned silence that followed. "Next point of call, Bent's Fort."

Ezra Pease stood spread-legged over the man he had just punched in the mouth and knocked to the ground. "What are you skulking around, spying on us for?" he demanded again.

"I weren't spyin', mister. I heared you was lookin' for some men with a gun."

"And you are, I suppose," Pease sneered. Anger tended to banish his carefully cultured, rough-hewed, frontier persona. His excellent Eastern upbringing and education seeped out readily. "If you're such an excellent specimen, how in hell do you explain why my men were able to sneak up on you so easily?"

"I was—I . . . I don't know," the lean, rugged man admitted.

"Where do you call home?" Pease snapped.

"Mis-Missouri. Really, mister, I ain't got any bone to pick with you. If you feel I'm not fit for your outfit, jist let me up and I'll go on my way."

Pease looked pleased with himself. "Well, now, we can't do that, can we? You've been watching our camp for the past two days, made a count of how many I have riding for me without a doubt. You have an idea of how many firearms we possess. And, most likely, seen us trading guns and whiskey to the Indians who have dropped in. What's to keep you from dropping off at the closest settlement and passing all that on to whatever passes there for the law?"

The man looked blank. "Why, I'd never do that. Didn' I just say I wanted to get in on it with you?"

"There's no room for amateurs in this organization," Pease stated bluntly. "I suppose we could take you in, but that would be too much like running a charity ward." So saying, Pease drew one of the fancily engraved, double-barrel pistols from his waistband and eared back the hammer.

Instantly the drifter's face washed white. His lower lip trembled and he raised a hand in pleading. "Say now, mister, I don't even know your name. I'd sure not spread word on you, if you were to let me go, mister, *please!*"

Ezra Pease shot him in the chest. The man jerked and raised on one elbow. Eyes wide and showing a lot of white, he again tried to plead for his life. Only a gush of blood came from his mouth. Pease cocked the second hammer and fired again. This time the ball entered the center of the drifter's forehead and pulped a mass of brain tissue.

He jerked and twitched for a while, then lay still. "Drag that trash out of camp," Pease commanded. "Vic, when are you expecting those men who went after Preacher to report back?"

Titus Vickers contemplated a second. "Most any time now, Ez."

"They had better, and soon. I want that black-hearted jackal dead, dead, dead."

7

Cora Ames stood on a low knoll overlooking Bent's Fort with one of Preacher's big hands in both of hers. "I shall never forget the experiences we shared, Preacher. Before now, I never considered myself capable of taking a human life. Not that I'm proud of myself for having done so."

"You did what you had to, missy. And I'm sure these folks with you are grateful . . . if only they could get it past their gospel-spoutin' ways an' admit it. Asa Pettibone turned out to be a mighty cool shot, too. Though I doubt any of you will need those skills back home."

Cora sighed. "I really wish we didn't have to leave here, Preacher. It's so lovely, so clean and sweet-smelling. I'll miss it, awfully. Why, when we were up in the mountains north of here, it felt as though I could reach out and touch the hand of God."

"You're not the first to think that, Missy. I said those very words myself for the first time back when I was thirteen. Or was it the year I turned fourteen? No matter." Preacher flushed slightly, made the more evident by his meticulous shaving which had left only a full, brushy mustache. "I'll admit, the Big Empty will seem a little more empty with you gone. But, you'll be safe where you're headed. Maybe, some day when the Shinin' Mountains fills up with people—God forbid—it'll be all right for you to journey here again."

He saw the pained expression on her lovely face and hastened to stammer an explanation. "No—not that I mean to ask God to forbid you return. It's . . . jist all those people fillin' up space out here that rubs wrong."

"I understand, Preacher. Well, I had better be getting back to the wagons."

"I'll be leavin' shortly, so I reckon this is goodbye, Miss Cora Ames."

"Not 'goodbye,' Preacher. Just farewell . . . Arthur." She turned on one neat heel and walked back to her wagon, gathered with the others outside the front wall of the fort.

Preacher crossed to Thunder and his packhorse. He had resupplied upon their arrival the previous afternoon. Nothing held him back now. He felt good about that. He would head north. Curiosity about the Cheyenne directed that decision. What could be stirring them up so much? No one at Bent's trading post had an idea. Well, at least he'd seen the last of the Bible-thumpers.

Or so he thought.

With a violent cast of one arm, Ezra Pease hurled the tin cup of coffee at a thick old oak. He showered those near him with the hot, brown liquid. "Goddamn that man! How could he do that? Not a one of them got away?" he asked of the messenger sent from the dozen he had dispatched to bring an end to Preacher.

"No, sir. All five were done for when we came upon them. It had to be Preacher. There was sign of only one horse and rider and a pack animal."

"Five good men lost and we have to send someone else for supplies. Is Preacher headed this way?"

"More or less. Vickers wanted you to get the word so I

rode back while they followed the trail. Looks to me like he's cuttin' due north toward Trout Crick Pass."

"They'll get him then." He turned to those around him. "Time's running short. We'll break camp and get on the trail. We need to move further north into Cheyenne country."

"Do you think that wise? I mean, considering the slaughter at Black Hand's village, they might be laying for us," Two Thumbs Buehler prompted.

Pease dismissed it contemptuously. "Those savages have the minds of children. By now they've forgotten all about that. Besides, the only thing they understand is force. Any who might still remember will have learned their lesson and be on their good behavior. After all, they'll want the rifles we have so they can make war on the Blackfeet."

Activity grew to a bustle then, and Pease took the final cupful from the coffee pot. He laced that with a spoon of sugar and a dollop of whiskey from a silver flask he carried in his full-cut Eastern coat. Privately he considered the impact of that fit of temper over Black Hand's village on the men who had employed him to create a war between the Blackfeet and Cheyenne. What attitude might they take over it?

They shouldn't get too upset. After all, it all went to the ends they desired. The gold was there, waiting, he knew that. And slavery was totally legal everywhere in the country. All that had been outlawed was a man importing fresh slaves from Africa. And Pease held personally that those woolybuggers would not do well at mining and sluicing gold anyway. Didn't do well in mountains and cold country either. A man could lose his whole investment that way.

The only investment in obtaining their slaves would be in a little powder and ball. Let all these starry-eyed idiots strike out in droves from the East. He'd soon have them broken and cowed and bending their backs to dig the yellow metal out of the ground. And he, Ezra Pease would be rich, rich, rich!

* * *

A week's journey to the east of Bent's Fort, on the old portion of the Santa Fe Trail, which had long been known as "the hard way," just west of Indian Territory, two wagons had stopped for the night. Silas Phipps, the owner, was being royally catered to by a scruffy band of eight children, aged eight to fifteen.

They were not kin, rather they were orphans, gathered by Phipps from Eastern cities teeming with castaways. The boys had built a fire ring, kindled a fire, and got it burning well, two hours before sundown. The oldest girl, Ruth, worked with Helen and Gertha to make corn bread, heat a pot of beans from the previous morning, and cut slices from a slab of bacon that had long ago gone green around the edges. They would be needing fresh supplies soon, but Ruth dreaded bringing that up to Phipps.

When the coffee had boiled long enough, Ruth took a cup to Phipps, who sat in a large, thronelike chair under the spreading branches of a solitary cottonwood. He grunted acknowledgment of it and smacked his lips over the first taste.

"Tastes peaked," he grumbled.

"We—we're running low on coffee beans," Ruth responded in a quavery voice.

"There's supposed to be some place up ahead where we can get supplies."

"Yes. Bent's Fort. Will we—will we be staying there?" Ruth asked eagerly.

"Nope. We're gonna go amongst them New Mexicans," Phipps expanded. "Santa Fe, that's the place. Nothin' but miles and miles of miles and miles around there. We can settle in an' no one will ever know we're there."

Ruth's eyes narrowed. "That's what you want, isn't it? For us to disappear off the face of the earth." Her bold confrontation shocked her.

Phipps squinted his close-set, mean, black eyes and taunted her. "Seems like a good idea, now you mention it. Git along now and tend to supper."

Back at the fire, Ruth cut her eyes to Helen. With a nod of her head, Ruth indicated that they should get off to somewhere that offered a bit of privacy. They rounded the wagons and walked a way onto the prairie. Certain they were out of earshot, Ruth still talked in a low, whispery voice.

"He says we're going to New Mexico and just . . . disappear."

"Oh, Ruth, that's awful. What will happen to us? How can we keep on like . . . this?" Tears sprang to Helen's eyes.

"I noticed earlier that you'd been cryin', Helen."

"It's nothin', Ruthie. I—I just felt bad. It's so empty out here."

"I know, believe me, I do. But, I want you to answer me honestly now. Has Silas been pesterin' you, too, now?"

Helen lowered long lashes over her blue eyes and gave a shake of her head, which disturbed the long, auburn sausage curls. "Not—not before this. He—he's asked me to come to the rear wagon after the younger ones have been put down for the night. I—I'm afraid. I've heard . . . things, and imagined what he must be doing with you."

"It's not your fault, and it's not mine. We can't help what he does and we can't get away."

"I feel so awful, Ruthie. The way he looks at me and licks those fat, ugly lips of his makes me seem so *dirty.*"

"It's not you who's dirty. He's the only filth around here." Ruth planned to say more to comfort Helen, but an only too familiar roar of furious impatience interrupted her.

"Where'n hell are you lazy girls? Git back to your work."

Summoned thusly into the presence of Silas Phipps, the girls stood next to Peter, their faces alight with trepidation. Phipps studied them a while, then pushed out his fleshy lower lip in purple imitation of a small boy's pout.

"I got something to tell you," Phipps began, his voice a raspy taunt. "I been thinkin' on it, an' there's too much law in that Mezkin country around Santa Fe. I've decided we will continue west to Bent's Fort and then figure out where to go next while we're there."

Ruth, Helen, and the twelve-year-old Peter, shared stricken expressions. Only minutes ago he had been talking of settling around Santa Fe. Now Phipps had come up with another vague idea of their destination. It flooded them with despair. They knew that if they were ever to get away from this foul, evil old man it would have to be somewhere with people around. But all realized that the law never gave a damn about orphans. They would most likely be shoved into some cold, grimy institution, like the ones they had escaped so recently, and forgotten. They would have to come upon folks who cared a lot for children. And Ruth had read in a book at the orphanage where she had last been held that the Mexicans thought the world of their children and treated all children kindly.

Ruth thought fast for a defense of the original destination. "Oh, but you made Santa Fe sound so wonderful, so grand an adventure."

"You can forget all about it now. We're goin' somewhere else. Now, git back to your cookin' before you feel my switch. An' you, little miss," he directed to Helen. "Don't forget our little talk a while back. I'll be lookin' for you."

Three of them. Preacher studied the faint sign left by the men ahead of him on the trail and made note of the distinctive marks that separated the trio. They had left no more tracks than he did.

"Mountain men for sure," he said aloud. "Wonder if I know them?"

An hour later he came upon the three, stopped to give their horses a blow. A wide, white smile split Preacher's face. He knew them for sure. That big, house of a man in the bearskin vest could be no one but Beartooth. The slender, hawk-nosed feller to his right had to be Nighthawk. Which made the last the dapper Frenchman, Dupre. Preacher skirted the trail and circled behind his old friends.

He dismounted and made a cautious approach. They would jump right out of their britches when he walked in among them, he reckoned. When he reached a spot some ten yards from the trio, Nighthawk spoke up loudly.

"Did anyone ever tell you that you made too much noise, Preacher?"

Laughing, Preacher stepped out from among the aspen. "Ain't lost your hearin' yet, I see, Nighthawk. How long have you knowed I was behind you and that it was me?"

"Better part of half an hour, Preacher," Beartooth boomed. He gave Preacher a mighty hug and all three danced around a while, slapping one another on the back.

"Still ugly as always," Dupre gleefully insulted Preacher. "When are you going to learn that clothes make the man?"

Preacher studied Dupre's store-bought coat, shirt, vest, and trousers and waggled his head in dismay. "You look like that Prince Albert, I swear, Dupre. Don't you think you are a mite overdressed for where you are?"

Dupre sniffed. For all his fine attire, his full mane of black hair was incongruously hidden under a fox-skin cap. "We are wearing our finest because we are on our way to visit Beartooth's in-laws."

Preacher removed his still stiffly new felt hat and scratched his head. "Last I heard, you was hitched up with a Cheyenne gal, Beartooth. That still right?"

"Right as rain, Preacher. She's a good cook," he added with a slap to his hard slab belly.

Preacher cocked an eyebrow. "Might not be the best time to visit with the Cheyenne," he suggested.

"We heard about the Cheyenne bein' stirred up," Nighthawk responded, his flawless English belying his Delaware origins.

"Yep," Beartooth contributed. "Figgered it would be better I went an' took a look, so's my wife wouldn't wear me to a nub with her curiosity. So I latched onto my old friends and partners and brung them along. Where you bound, Preacher?"

"Same place."

"You are welcome to ride with us, *mon ami*," Dupre offered.

"Obliged. Four sets of eyes are better than one," Preacher accepted.

That decided, the four men mounted up and took the trail northward. Late afternoon found them about halfway to Trout Crick Pass. Nighthawk located a small meadow for their night camp. The three rugged mountain men deferred to Preacher's skill with bean pot and skillet and all enjoyed a good meal, cooked over a hat-sized fire laid under a thick pine to disburse the smoke. Preacher finished the last of the coffee and came to his moccasins.

"I'm gonna turn in. No telling what tomorrow will bring," he announced as he headed for his bedroll.

Kid Ralston had almost ridden up on the four men camped in the meadow shortly before nightfall. Kid had been fortunate in that he had remained inside the tree line and quickly bent to cover the muzzle of his horse. He dismounted and studied the quartet through what remained of daylight. From the description they had been given, the tall, lean, broad-shouldered one had to be Preacher. But who were the others? They sure knew how to handle themselves, though.

Their fire had been put out before twilight settled on the grassy clearing. Preacher had rolled up first, his muscular form a mound under his blankets. Wisely, Kid Ralston waited until the others turned in before walking his mount out of the area. Once far enough away that the sound of hoofbeats would not carry to the unsuspecting men, he swung into the saddle and made tracks through the night to the rendezvous point given by Two Thumbs Buehler. Kid gave a shiver. That hand with two thumbs on it always got to him. Someone had told him once that those sort of oddities came from brother and sister getting married. Or even first cousins. Could that be? he wondered at the time.

Now the novel idea returned to fire his imagination. Suppose he and his cousin, Hilly, had done somethin' really bad when they had been fussin' around out behind the barn that day. Not that the Kid looked like anyone capable of something bad. He stood only an inch over five feet, and that in his boots. A remarkably slow developer, he had the bone structure and features of a twelve-year-old, although six years older. His blue eyes, cottony hair, and cherub's mouth artfully hid a hot, vicious temper and sadistic personality. He fantasized about that steamy afternoon with Hilly all the way to the meeting place.

Five of the dozen men sent to get Preacher waited at the isolated bald knob that stood out in the middle of a wide valley. Kid Ralston withheld his big news, choosing not to share it with them out of profound dislike. They, along with others in the gang, tormented him mercilessly about his small stature. Two of them, in fact, had hung the handle "Kid" around his neck. He overrode his discomfort over the two thumbs to ride apart from the others to meet Buehler when he arrived.

"I found him, Two Thumbs. I know where Preacher is. It's jist like we heard, he done went south of Trout Crick Pass. He's got three other fellers with him."

"You done good, Kid," Buehler praised and reached out to pat the youthful trash on one shoulder with the two-thumbed hand.

Kid Ransom nearly lost the supper he hadn't gotten to eat. He gritted his teeth and endured. "They're about four miles from here, to the south."

Two Thumbs grinned. "We'll move in on 'em durin' the night, hit them at dawn."

Preacher roused out first. A peach-blush band of soft light lay along the eastern horizon. With nothing to hurry him along the way, Preacher saw nothing to be gained by rising in total darkness and do everything by feel. He stretched and stood like a stork to shake some small pebbles from one moccasin, then stretched again and headed for the fire ring.

He blew some kindling to flame from the buried coals of the previous night, added some wrist-sized sticks and warmed himself out of the lingering March chill. Then he set the coffee pot to boil. He had just bent over his kitchen parfleche to retrieve coffee beans when a ball moaned over his bowed back and smacked into the trunk of the pine. Preacher dropped as though he had been shot.

But not before he freed one of his fearsome pistols from its cured-and-stiffened hide holster. His companions, wise in the ways of attacks by Indians and whites alike remained outwardly motionless. After a long, tense minute, voices came faintly to Preacher's ears.

"I done it! I done kilt ol' Preacher."

"I wouldn't be too eager to go down and take his hair, Kid," came sage advice.

"Why not?" Kid Ralston asked.

"You figger those other fellers up an' died of fright?" Two Thumbs Buehler taunted.

"Huh! I never thought about that. They ain't moved. You reckon they're layin' for us?" Blushing furiously at his *faux pas* the Kid reloaded hastily.

"I figger you did a fool thing in not waitin' until we all opened up. You've put us betwixt a rock an' a hard spot. Nothin' for it, though. We'd best get it on."

So saying, Two Thumbs and the other ten opened up on the reclining figures. Only the blankets of Beartooth, Nighthawk, and Dupre took the punishment. The moment smoke spurted from the muzzles of the assassins' weapons, the trio rolled violently to the side away from their attackers. Their answering fire roared across the meadow.

The volley was followed by a charge. As the bushwhacking trash came into sight, rifle balls tore into their irregular rank. Two men went down, one with a shrill cry and a shattered knee cap. Eager to claim a trophy from his victim, Kid Ralston charged ahead of the line. He had his knife out, ready to take Preacher's hair, when the wiley mountain man came up with a roar and let fly with the deadly four-barrel pistol in his right hand.

Hot lead stopped the Kid in mid-stride. The first ball of the double load clipped the lobe from his left ear. The second punched through a rib and tore a path from front to rear of his left lung. Kid's vision got all blurry and he dropped his skinning knife. It didn't matter at all to him that Preacher had apparently risen from the dead to take retribution.

Kid Ralston only knew that his chest burned with the fires of hell and he had gotten awfully weak. He thought of his Ma, of Pa and the hickory switch he'd used to try to make Kid walk the straight and narrow. How he wished now that it had taken effect. He thought of his brothers, all three younger than his eighteen years, yet every one bigger, taller, and stronger. He didn't think of his cousin Hilly. Or anything else for that matter, as his lung filled with blood and he passed into unconsciousness that would swiftly lead to death.

Preacher ignored the dying youth. He immediately turned his attention to the motley band of unwashed whites who streamed out of the trees toward them. "Don't cotton to your invite, you pond scum," Preacher hollered at them. "But I sure favor to join the dance."

With that he shot another of the dregs of the criminal brotherhood. To his right he saw Dupre dump a fat, red-faced specimen of depravity in a shower of buckshot with which he had charged a .70 caliber Flobert horse pistol. Beyond him, Nighthawk ducked a blow from a rifle butt and buried his knife in the belly of a similar dirtbag. Beartooth discharged a pistol in each hand and brought down a pair of vipers who had carelessly gotten too close together.

We work well as a team, Preacher thought, although we haven't been together for several years. He dodged to one side to avoid a shot from the thinning ranks of killer trash and ended the man's life with the last load.

"Sacre bleu!" Dupre cursed in French. "You have ruined my jacket and this shirt."

Preacher cut his eyes to Dupre, to see where a ball along his ribs had released a torrent of blood. While he studied his friend, Preacher exchanged his pistols.

"Dormez vous avec le Diable," Dupre spat in his assailant's face a moment before he shot him with another Flobert .70 caliber. The shot pellets wiped away all of the man's face above his lower jaw.

"What d'you call him, Dupre?" Preacher asked. Only four of the louse-infested thugs remained on their feet. Preacher took aim at one.

"I told him to go sleep with the devil."

"I reckon he will, partner." Preacher shot his target in the small notch between the collarbones. His head snapped to an odd angle when the .50 caliber ball shattered a vertebra. The field of battle fell suddenly silent.

"Say, fellers, I think we finished them all," Preacher called out.

Right then, to make a liar of Preacher, Two Thumbs forced himself up on his elbows and winged a shot at the mountain man that missed. Preacher put a round in the center of the balding spot on the top of Two Thumbs' head.

"We have now," Beartooth said through a powder-grimed grin.

After they inspected the dead, Preacher stood beside the last man he had killed, a deep frown on his forehead. "This one I'd know anywhere. He ran with Ezra Pease back ten years ago, when I drove Pease outta these mountains. He sent a lot of men to do a job on us. What's he done? Bring an army out here? If so, maybe we'd best split up. I've got a feeling there's a heap of trouble up ahead."

8

Reverend Thornton Bookworthy gazed at the tall ramparts that grew with each hour on the trail. They had been on the road for three days, but not headed east. Bookworthy removed his wide-brimmed, black hat and mopped at his sweaty brow with a snowy kerchief. Then he slapped his meaty palm on the leather cover of the Bible that rested on his black-clothed thigh.

"Yes, Patience, my dear. We have God's work to do, and no buckskin-bedecked near-savage is going to prevent us."

"What if that Preacher man was right about the Cheyenne going to war?" Prudence a bit more sharply than her usual submissive tone.

"Not even the Cheyenne can stop us, for I am certain they are thirsting for the Word. We're doing the right thing, mark my words, Prudence."

"Yes, dear." Prudence kept her composure although her mind swarmed with images of the painted, screaming faces of the Kiowa and Pawnee who had attacked them so recently. The mules in front of her shifted their rumps and complained with grunts as they labored up the incline.

Since leaving Bent's Fort, the grade had increased steadily.

Now, with the foothills of the Rockies towering over them, their progress had decreased by three miles each day. They would be in those mountains tomorrow, Prudence reminded herself. And within two weeks, they would reach the land where the Cheyenne lived. Her husband's singing put her gloomy thoughts to flight.

"Bringing in the sheaves . . . bringing in the sheaves, we shall come . . . Yes, my dear, that's the first song we shall teach the benighted heathen. Don't you see the symbolism of it. We will be the harvesters of their souls."

Prudence winced and wanted to groan like the mules. A tiny echo of her own question haunted the back of her mind. What if Preacher was right?

A tall column of smoke rose from behind the nearest ridge. Preacher and his companions reined in to study it a moment. Preacher raised an arm and pointed a long finger at the wide base of the dark cloud.

"That's comin' from more than one thing burnin'. Now, as best as I can tell there ain't any cabins up there, unless they be built in the last two weeks. And that ain't no fire in the woods."

Nighthawk nodded agreement. "That's elementary. The animals would be acting strange if it was a conflagration in the forest," he stated the obvious.

Preacher caught him with a cocked eyebrow, mischief glinting in his blue-gray orbs. "Do I have to remind you how gawdawful those fancy words sound comin' outta the mouth of an Injun?" he teased.

Nighthawk gave him a straight face. "Heap good idea, white-eyes. Many smokes mean many fires."

"Awh, git off that, 'Hawk," Beartooth grumbled. "You sound worser playin' dumb Injun than you do playin' edicated Injun."

"The question remains, what is burning?" Nighthawk returned to his usual cultured tones.

"I've got me an idea, an' I don't think any of us is gonna like it," Preacher announced.

He gigged Thunder in the direction of the fires. The others quickly joined him. They rode through saddle notch between two peaks and looked down on the tragedy below. It proved to be exactly what Preacher expected. A small wagon train of some twenty vehicles had been raided, the people slaughtered, their possessions rifled, and valuables stolen. Preacher grunted and walked Thunder forward. His Hawken out and ready, rested across the saddle horn.

"Right like I expected. More damn-fool pilgrims. We'll have to find some way to cover 'em up. Pease and his vermin can wait."

Dismounted, the mountain men took turns standing guard, two-and-two, while the other pair gathered bodies. Slowly something became clear. The men had been killed outright, the women and older girls raped and then killed, some of the boys under about the age of ten had been misused also and then killed. All of the adults had been scalped.

"There's a few arrows over here, Preacher," Beartooth announced. "Got red markin's on 'em."

Preacher didn't like that at all. He had been on friendly terms with the Cheyenne for a number of years. "I saw them. Given that all the horses were shod, I'd call it a clumsy attempt at puttin' blame on the Cheyenne. Did you notice something else? Like most of their kind, these poor fools brought along enough youngin's to fill a good-sized school. Only the balance is off.

"We got boys up to the age of—oh, maybe ten or so, an' older boys, about sixteen an' up. None others." Preacher paused to fix his thoughts into words. "Now, Injuns is known to take right small kids to replace some of their own lost to sickness or stolen by enemy tribes. It's rare for them to take off only boy kids from eleven to fifteen. Which says again that it must have been whites. And I've a good idea who is behind it."

"That Pease feller you mentioned?" Dupre asked.

"None other. Only thing I can't work out is why. What would a gang of no-accounts like that want with boys of that age?"

"Maybe for the same things these little nippers got done to 'em," Beartooth suggested.

"I doubt that. They'd have had their way an' left 'em dead, too," Preacher responded, brow wrinkled in concentration. "But I reckon we're gonna find out right soon. All we gotta do is run them down. Now, let's get these folks buried."

Beartooth kicked his mount in the ribs and trotted up beside Preacher. "We've got company over in there." He pointed with his chin to a thicket of chokecherry bushes.

They had cut signs that some of the folks from the doomed train had managed to slip away. Following the faint trail westward had brought them here. Preacher nodded his understanding to Beartooth.

"I wanted to ride on past them a ways. Give them a chance to relax a little. Wouldn't do to ride into a ball o' hot lead, now would it?"

"Sure nuff," the older mountain man agreed.

Preacher pointed ahead. "We'll cut back and approach on foot from where they don't expect us."

While they rode off, Preacher made light conversation to add a further cloak of innocence to their passing by. "What you reckon to do, Beartooth, once you find out the Cheyenne's intentions?"

"I figger to find me a place that's still got plenty deer an' elk and settle in with my woman. We've got a good start these past three years with two youngin's, an' I hanker for more. Trappin's all but done for. Ain't seen a bone-i-fied buyer out this way in two years."

Preacher grunted. "I sold my traps last year. Ain't like the good days. Rendezvous was wild and hairy, but it shore were fun. Now, a man alone, goin' to Trout Crick or Bent's to sell his pelts—an' dang few of them any more. Jist ain't the same."

They had ridden out of sight of the hiding survivors and Preacher signaled a halt. The four mountain men dismounted, tied their horses off to aspen saplings and slid silently into the woods. Years of this life had conditioned them all to move as quietly as possible. As a result, they reached their objective without giving any sign of their presence.

Even so, Preacher and his companions hunkered down low and studied the motley collection of women and a few youngsters for a long five minutes before making their presence known. The count came to eleven grown women, five girls a tad under marrying age, and seven boys, five of which were in their early teens. Preacher ghosted upright and stepped to the protection of a large pine behind the pilgrims.

"Howdy, folks. We're friendly, so don't go puttin' any holes in us," he called out. Two teenaged boys started and spun to train rifle muzzles in the direction from which he had spoken. "Now, now, jist lower them things, boys. If we had it in mind to do you harm, you'd been done for already. They's four of us. We need to come down amongst you an' figger out how to get you safely out of here."

"Oh, praise the Lord!" one female cried out, her face lifted to the sky. "We're delivered."

"I'm not so sure, Miz Kenny," one lad, still in the cracking voice stage, questioned the situation. "We'd better take some time on this."

"What you'd best do is lower them rifles an' let us come out before someone gets bad hurt," Preacher insisted. "'Sides, much as I like 'em, I don't cotton to huggin' a tree all day."

That broke the ice with some of the women. "Yes, boys, do put down those awful things," one matronly voice demanded. "This gentleman is right. If they meant us harm, they could have gotten to it a long time ago."

"Uh—well—all right," the adenoidal youth relented. "Chris, put your rifle down. I'm going to."

"Me, too, Bobby?" a voice asked from the far side of the cluster of women.

"Yeah, Nick," Bobby Gresham, the obvious leader, if such label could be applied to a boy not more than fifteen, answered.

The dowager quickly revised her appellation of gentleman when first Preacher, then Beartooth, Dupre, and Nighthawk drifted out of the trees and came down among them. Preacher looked around and then addressed himself to Bobby.

"You picked a good place. Only thing is you left too much sign."

Bobby looked chagrined. "I never thought of that. Are those men coming after us?"

"The ones who hit your train, boy?" Preacher asked.

"Yeah. Er—I'm Bobby Gresham. Are they after us?" Bobby asked again, uncertainty in his eyes.

Preacher reassured him. "Not that we saw any sign of them. Pulled off to the north from the looks of it." He cut his eyes to the dowager and removed his hat like one would in polite society. "My name's Preacher, ma'am."

"Y-you're a minister?" she asked with inevitable doubt.

"No, ma'am. I'm on speakin' terms with the Almighty, but I ain't one of his servants. I—all of us—used to trap beaver before the demand dried up. These mountains," Preacher made a sweeping gesture to encompass their surroundings, "is sort of our home stompin' grounds."

"I'm Flora Sanders, this is Mrs. Grace Kenny, and this is Mrs. Falicity Jones. You've met Bobby, the other boys are Chris and Nick Walker."

"Did . . . anyone else . . . get away?" Nick, the youngest, asked with trepidation.

Preacher pulled an uncomfortable expression. Telling folks, and young ones in particular, that near everyone they held dear had died was a hard task. "I'm afraid not, son. You folk must be the only ones got away."

"Th-then I'm a widow—we all are," Falicity Jones cried in a tiny voice.

Preacher cut his eyes to Falicity for his first good look. What he saw was a devastatingly beautiful, young woman. Robust and busty, and quite obviously pregnant. She spoke on, stammering now. "My—my ba-baby wi-will be born an—an orphan!"

Preacher knew a great deal about a lot of things. He didn't know much about women. Particularly women in such a state. All he could do was answer, haltingly, "I—I'm afraid so, Mrs. Jones."

Wise in the mood shifts of her gender, Mrs. Sanders stepped into the breech. "I'm sorry to say we are all widows now, Falicity. But life does go on. What are we to do about that, Mr.—ah—Preacher?"

"There's a couple of wagon boxes didn't get burned clear down. And I reckon we can find enough stock to pull them. Gather what you brought with you and we'll start back to where you was ambushed." He paused and thought on it. "After that, it's closer to go on to Trout Crick Pass than back to Bent's. What is a puzzlement to me is what you folks were doin' wanderin' up into this country in the first place?"

"We were told it was a short-cut to the Immigrant Trail," Flora Sanders told him.

"It's that, right enough, but not for tenderfeet and wagons. You headed to Oregon?"

"Well, sort of. We were told back East that prime land abounded in the Snake River country."

"Oh, it's fine land," Preacher told her dryly. "Only thing is it's swarmin' with Nez Perce, Bannock, and Shoshoni. And they all feel mighty touchy about people settlin' in there."

"Then we were lied to?" Mrs. Sanders asked indignantly.

"Not exactly. There is fine country thereabouts. Let's say whoever told you about it and left out the Injuns sort of misrepresented the facts."

"Then what shall we do?" three of the women chorused.

"You can rest up at the trading post in Trout Crick Pass, and resupply. Then I'd advise you get a good guide, turn back and head for Bent's Fort."

"But we have no desire to turn back," Flora Sanders blurted.

"Suit yourselves," Preacher said pleasantly. "But don't expect us to burden ourselves with your protection any further than Trout Crick Pass."

Relief at their rescue turned to a smattering of grumpiness after this pronouncement. Ignoring it, the four mountain men helped gather the refugees, and herd them off toward the damaged wagons. Half an hour along the trail, Preacher spoke up to Falicity Jones.

"Miz Jones, you happen to get a look at the ones who attacked your wagons?"

"Oh, yes. I'll never forget their faces."

Preacher squinted and cocked his head to one side. "Were they Injuns?"

"No!" Falicity barked with certainty. "They were all white men. The lowest, crawling, filthy trash on the face of the earth. I shudder to think about . . . what happened to those who didn't get away."

"You wouldn't want to know, ma'am. We'll make camp just short of the place they hit you. Those big boys, my friends an' I will go rig up some wagons. Tomorrow we start for Trout Crick Pass."

Their journey so far had toughened these women and the teenaged boys who had volunteered to protect them. Preacher noted that with satisfaction as the two creaky wagons, assembled from salvaged parts of several, groaned along the narrow trail toward the trading post. At this rate, Preacher figured about five days to reach there. Several of the women had minor injuries, and a child had a cut on one foot. That slowed them considerably.

At least, Preacher thought, they were under way. The older two boys drove the wagons, while those children who could, walked. Nick had appealed with big, dark blue eyes until Preacher, embarrassed in front of his friends, let the lad ride behind him on Thunder. He would, Nick promised, trade off with the other boys at driving. The peace of their sojourn lasted two days.

Quentin "Squint" Flowers pulled the sodden poultice from the bullet wound in his left bicep and replaced it with a fresh one. Buster Chase helped him bind the bandanna around the injured appendage and stiffened and came to his boots.

"Hush, y'all," he harshly whispered to the others of the human vermin who had attacked the wagon train for Ezra Pease. "I hear somethin'."

"Sounds like wagons rollin'," Frank Clower opined.

"Couldn't be none of them folks got up from the dead," Rubber Nose Jaspar declared flatly.

"I wished we'd stayed with the rest," Squint Flowers offered mournfully.

Frank Clower, the nominal leader eyed him coldly. Squint's small pox scarred face rivaled the surface of the moon, Frank considered. Those eyes so close together and always scrunched near shut so's not to be able to tell the color. He made about the ugliest thing a man could look at and not run away. "It was you who whined about them brat boys always sobbin' an' takin' on. Wanted to get away from the li'l snot-noses, you said. Well, you're away now an' there's someone comin' our way. Rubber Nose, you an' Buster go take a look."

Within ten minutes the two devil's disciples returned with disturbing news. "They's some of them wimmin, must have got away when we hit the train, they's comin' on in two brokedown wagons. Got four tough-looking fellers with them. Also some kids."

Frank pulled a face. "Well, we sure's hell can't leave no livin' witnesses, now can we?"

"I say we set up a little ambush and finish them off," Buster Chase suggested. "They ain't much, jist some soft-in-the-head leftovers from the trappin' days, an' there's seven of us."

Frank considered that a while. Seven, with two of them wounded, their mounts tired and the wagons they had along with booty in them to slow them down. "What we ought to do is let them get on by us, then hit them in the rear. Complete surprise and we can take out those trappers, the rest'll be easy."

That decided upon, the human offal melted into the trees and Frank sent Squint Flowers back to obliterate the obvious sign of their presence. It wouldn't pass muster if anyone took time to study the ground, but folks like these, on the move, would miss the traces. It seemed to take no time for the first outrider to round a bend in the trail and come into view.

He looked tough, right enough, Frank Clower considered. Especially those pistols in the boxy-looking holsters slung around his hips. No nevermind, though. This would be easy. He hunkered down, like the rest of his men, and held his mount's nose. Slowly, then, the two-wagon cavalcade rolled past.

Frank gave them time to cover some three hundred yards and round another bend in the track, then motioned his corrupted followers out of concealment. They mounted quickly and left the wagons of loot behind. At a gallop, weapons at the ready, they streaked for the curve ahead. Tubby Slocum took the lead as they rounded the bend.

He let out a whoop when he saw the wagons, then a strangled cry as he ran into a powerful blast from the Hawken rifle in the hands of Beartooth. The burly mountain man lowered his rifle and got another of the riff-raff with the pistol that quickly filled his hand.

9

"Looks like the surprise is on you, buzzard breath," Bear-tooth shouted gleefully as he turned aside to avoid an answering volley from men slowed by astonishment.

Two more rifles cracked and Buster Chase flew from his saddle. One boot hung up in the stirrup and Buster flopped and sprayed the underbrush with his blood as the charging animal ran, unchecked, toward the wagons they had coveted so recently. Nighthawk watched him bound past and chose a pistol to replace his expended trap-door Olin-Hayes. Time later to slide in a paper cartridge and fit a cap in place.

Preacher gave Nighthawk a cheerful wave as he drew one of his deadly four-shooters and galloped back from the head of the column. The lean mountain man, with the smooth forehead and bright blue eyes, cackled as he drew near.

"Hee-hee, looks like it worked perfect. Damned amateurs, can't do anything right," Preacher chortled.

He filled his sights with the shocked face of Rubber Nose Jasper and shot away the pliable appendage that had earned Jasper his sobriquet. Jasper howled and clapped a hand over the blood-spouting stump. It brought him no mercy, though, as Preacher put another ball through Jasper's brisket.

Preacher bent forward to work the trigger mechanism and revolve the barrels again when a ball cracked through the space his head had occupied a moment before. That was down-right unfriendly, he judged it. Such goin's on would have to be brung to an end, and damn fast.

Preacher let his gaze rove over the remaining thugs and spotted the likely shooter. His big pistol banged out and the scowl of anger at missing changed to an expression of horror as Preacher's ball set off a bright flash in the brain pan of the lowly rubbish that illuminated his on-rushing afterlife.

Squint Flowers made an error in judgment. He continued his fatally determined charge against the men around the wagon instead of diving for cover among the boulders strewn along the road. He ran right into a pair of speeding balls fired by Dupre and Preacher. Flowers rose above his saddle and hung suspended a moment, before plopping into the churned-up turf to kick and jerk until death stilled his jammed reflexes.

Seeing this, Frank Clower managed to slow his horse and turn about. With balls chasing him, and Hashknife close at his side, he beat a hasty retreat. Preacher went to his second pistol and downed another lump of Pease slime. Through the fury of battle, Preacher faintly sensed a reduction in the volume of fire. A cross-eyed lout in a paisley shirt slid from his mount, caught himself at the last minute, and staggered toward the shelter of a boulder.

He didn't make it. Preacher fired a double-shotted load that put the first ball across the outer surface of the hard case's thigh and the second through its meaty portion. He went down in a graceless sprawl. Preacher gigged Thunder and approached the wounded man.

Two of the vermin who had taken shelter opened up in desperation then, intent on fixing Preacher's wagon once and for all. They both shot wide of the target and received a vengeful response from Dupre and Nighthawk. Lead balls

howled off the convex faces of the granite lumps and showered each killer scum with fragments.

One of them, blinded by rock chips and slivers of lead,
stumbled out into the open, one hand pawing at his blood-
streaming eyes, the other holding a pistol, which he discharged wildly. Not all that wild, Preacher discovered when
he felt the wind of the ball's passage by his cheek. Once
more he gave thanks to the All Wise Above for guiding him
to pause long enough to let little Nick jump from Thunder's
rump onto the seat of the lead wagon before answering the
call of the attack. That ball would have finished the little lad
right smartly.

A pang of sorrowful remembrance of young Eddie*, so
like the saucy image of Nick, came to Preacher as he let go
the final load in his pistol and split the breast bone of the
trashy thug. Dupre's rifle banged loudly close at hand and
the last skulker in the rocks gave up his hold on life.

"*C'est fini,*" Dupre declared.

"Yeah, it's done, all right," Preacher agreed. "Let's check
out the bodies."

They found one man still with breath in him. "Buster
Chase," he gasped out his name. "You boys done kilt me good.
H-how'd you know we was back there?"

"A blind ten-year-old could tell where you left the trail
and tried to cover it up," Preacher said with sincere contempt.

"Who be you men?" Chase spoke in a whisper.

"I'm called Preacher. This here's Beartooth, Dupre, and
Nighthawk."

Chase's lips curled into a sneer. "Back-shooters all, I've
been told. Damn you into hell, Preacher, and all your kind."
He went on cursing the mountain men while pink froth gathered around the hole in his chest and a huge bubble formed.
With a rapidly fading voice he hurled his last brag.

*See *The First Mountain Man:* Published by Pinnacle Books.

"There's thirty more just like us up ahead, Preacher. You an' your lice-infested friends won't find them so easy to take." With that said, he shivered, convulsed mightily, and went still.

"Don't bury that one," Nighthawk demanded. "He said I had lice."

"He's one to talk," Beartooth put in. "Look, there's a big gray one crawlin' out of his hair right now."

"Unpardonable manners," Dupre agreed. "I've never had a louse on me in my life."

Preacher peered at him studiously. Dupre's impeccable clothes bore not a wrinkle nor a smudge from their violent encounter. "You know somethin', Dupre? I believe you. Let's gather up what all we can. Those boys can put the guns to good use."

Cora Ames wore a worried frown as she approached the rotund figure of the Reverend Thornton Bookworthy. They had stopped for the nooning in a small swale only miles short of the ramparts of the Rocky Mountains.

"We should have come upon Bent's Fort before nightfall three days ago," she stated flatly. Then worry colored her words. "We've strayed from the trail somewhere along the line. We—we could be anywhere."

In fact, they had taken a trail much used by Indians in the area, that swung roughly northwest off the old Santa Fe Trail. With the decline in the fur trade, Bent's Fort also suffered a loss of activity. Few journeyed there from the east and the main trail had fallen into disrepair. The many horses' hooves and travois of the natives marked a clearer, rutted path for such novices as Bookworthy and his hired drivers. Totally convinced of his ability, the reverend could not accept criticism from a mere woman.

"I assure you, Sister Ames, that we are on the right path." Truth to tell, Thornton Bookworthy would have been hard pressed to point out which way was west at sunset.

"Beggin' yer pardon, Reverend, but I'm sure the lady is right," Buck Dempsey offered. "We're way north of Bent's Fort. Way I figger it, we'll come upon the trail to Trout Creek Pass by sometime tomorrow mornin'."

Reverend Bookworthy brightened. "Why, splendid! That puts us ahead of schedule. Let's push on, perhaps we'll find it yet today."

"I—ah—don't think so," Buck stated softly, looking beyond the portly minister.

"Why not?" Bookworthy demanded.

"We've got company."

Reverend Bookworthy turned abruptly to face three Arapaho women, with twice that number of small children at their feet, and a lithe, smooth-limbed youth of perhaps sixteen years. Bookworthy's jaw dropped and he felt faint. The oldest boy made the sign for peace and spoke in lilting-accented English.

"We are friendly. Not . . . make you harm."

"Why, you speak English," Bookworthy blurted in his surprise. "Are you Christian? Do you know Jesus?"

"I am called Little Raven. I not know that man. But I know . . . you lost. I know man who can help you."

"You do?" In his eagerness to find aid, Bookworthy dropped all pretense of being comfortable with their situation. "Who is that?"

"He is called White Wolf. You round eyes know him as Preacher."

Astonishment washed over Bookworthy's face. "He's nearby? How far? Come, my good boy, tell us."

A faint smile flickered on the young Arapaho's face. "You are going the right way. Preacher is two—three days ahead of you. He has three friends with him. They are with people in rolling lodges, like yours."

"That's simply marvelous," Bookworthy babbled, forgetting entirely that it was Preacher who had expelled them from these mountains. "We must make contact. He'll absolutely have to guide us now," he appealed to his fellow missionaries. "Buck," he called to the driver. "Take another teamster and push on ahead until you contact Preacher. Use my big Walker, Brutus, and make all speed. I shall drive your wagon."

"And I the other," Cora offered. Then, remembering what Preacher had told her about manners among the Indians, she turned to the youth. "Will you take food with us?"

Smiling broadly now, he told his companions of the invitation. The oldest of the three women said something in Arapaho, which he translated. "She asks do you have the sweet sand. She means sugar."

"Why, yes, of course," Cora responded with a light laugh. "We have plenty. Come, there's coffee and beans and corned beef."

Looking back on it later, Cora realized that a good time was had by all.

Peter looked around in wonder and awe. "These are the biggest mountains in the whole world," he declared after closing his sagging jaw. "Bigger than those in Pennsylvania or Missouri."

"It's the Rocky Mountains," Helen, the reader in the group of orphans informed him. "The fur trappers called them the 'Shining Mountains' or the 'High Lonesome.'"

"Are we goin' up there?" Peter asked of Silas Phipps, his thin arm extended, small finger pointing.

"Most likely," Phipps grunted. He regretted not resupplying on whiskey at Bent's Fort.

Things cost so dang much out here, he had soon discovered. It had taken all the rest of his cash money to get two wagon wheels repaired, buy food and some warm blankets. The latter were for him, of course, not the brats. They could make do with what they had.

Nightfall had them well enfolded in the ramparts of the Rockies. Silas Phipps sat in his usual, somewhat frumpy regal splendor in the large chair for which he had traded off a six-year-old boy to a childless couple in Missouri. Well and good. The kid had a constantly runny nose anyway. Ruth and Helen cooked supper, their regular chore. While they toiled over the fire pit, Helen shot nervous glances in the direction of Silas.

It made him smile, while he sipped sparingly at the whiskey jug. There was supposed to be a single other trading post up further north, at a place called Trout Creek Pass. Surely he could knock down something worth trading for, or the boys—who he had put to setting out snares—could trap some furry animals. The odor of cooking meat made his belly rumble.

Peter returned first from putting snares in the grass beside a stream. He had noted small footprints and calculated where the animal who had made them would be likely to walk. Proud of his accomplishment, he went to the fire to share his woodsman's wisdom with Ruth and Helen.

"I found an animal path. Put my snares along it by the creek," he informed the girls.

"What good will that do?" Helen asked, distracted, at least for the moment, from her contemplation of what awaited her later that night.

"It's been used more than once. I figger whatever made the prints will use it again: And . . . zap! One nice pelt for that ol' bassard to trade for booze."

"I wish he'd drown in the stuff," Ruth said hotly.

"Yes. And before tonight," Helen choked out.

"Again, honey?" Ruth asked with warm compassion.

Helen nodded jerkily and big, hot tears ran down her cheeks.

"You three shut up and tend to yer cookin'," Silas Phipps growled from his throne. "Ain't that grub about ready?"

"Yes, Mr. Phipps," Ruth replied, subdued. "Peter will bring you your plate." She gave Peter a "this will get even for Helen" look.

Ruth had no idea how terrible a form her attempt at revenge would take. Peter started apprehensively across the clearing to where Phipps slumped in his chair. He dreaded being around the filthy old man who held them captive. Why didn't they just run away? Peter had wondered that a hundred times. In his anxiety at not riling Silas Phipps, Peter missed seeing the wrist-thick bowed branch that had fallen from a big old cottonwood.

As a result, the boy tripped over it and went sprawling. The plate flew from his hand and the gravy-covered food took off from there. Some of it splattered on the boots of Silas Phipps. With a roar the thick-shouldered brute came to his feet and charged down on the terrified Peter.

"Goddamn you!" Phipps bellowed. "Can't any of you do anything right? I'll teach you to be so clumsy. Waste all that food, will you?"

He bent and yanked the petrified child upright. One big, hairy fist closed around the leather suspenders that held up Peter's trousers. Phipps pulled them off, then ripped the shirt from Peter's back. Peter lost it then and began to sob wretchedly. Long, dry, sharp wails came painfully from deep inside. Phipps dragged the boy into the light from the fire.

There he jerked down Peter's linsey-woolsey trousers and exposed the lad's bare behind. He snatched up a willow rod, thick as one of his muscular fingers, and yelled at the astonished orphans. "C'mere, all of you. You're gonna witness what happens for a show of defiance."

"I didn'—didn' defy you, sir," Peter pleaded.

Phipps shoved Peter roughly forward. "Bend over that wagon wheel."

Then he began to apply the willow switch. He started at Peter's shoulders, and worked downward. His arm rose and fell rhythmically. The wooden shaft made a wet, meaty smack with each blow. The more Phipps lashed the boy, the greater his fury grew. By the time he reached the small of Peter's back, each strike split the skin and blood ran in thin, red sheets.

Phipps had entered such a frenzy that he breathed in great, gusty bellows blasts when he reached Peter's buttocks. He spent the least time there, though, delivering only four sound, stinging stripes. Phipps desisted then, stood looking at the horrified expressions on the faces of the other children.

"Bring me some of that axle grease and some cotton waste," he commanded Ruth.

Through all his ministrations, Peter continued to whimper softly. When the clean-up had ended, the boy drew up his trousers, his face crimson with embarrassment and humiliation. Then he went to find another shirt.

His whole body throbbed with agony, stung and burned, an hour later, as Peter curled up near the fire pit, under a thin blanket. He bit his tongue to keep from making any outcry, and lay in icy fear as he listened to the whispered pleading, whimpers and cries of agony that Helen made from some distance beyond in the back of the second wagon. Mind awhirl in misery, Peter vowed that he would kill Phipps before anything like that happened again.

"He's a ring-tailed whoo-doo, ain't he?" Rupe Killian said proudly to the man who rode beside him.

"Who?" Delphus Plunkett asked.

Rupe rolled his eyes. "Who else? Mr. Pease, ya ninny. He's got more smarts than any man I know. Talks like a real gent'man, too."

"So's Hashknife, only he don't put on no airs," Delphus revealed his opinion of Ezra Pease.

Killian and Plunkett rode in a column of twos, along with the rest of Ezra Pease's gang of cutthroats, headed cross-country in the wide, fertile valley ringed by the Laramie and Medicine Bow Mountains. They had reached the heart of the Cheyenne country. Unlike many of the men, Rupert Killian did not experience any unease. Nearly 5,000 Indians called this land home. Most of those were warriors. The nearest help, in the form of white men in sufficient numbers, lay 800 miles to the west, nearly a thousand to the east. Yet, Rupe Killian had no fear.

Infused with his hero-worship of Ezra Pease, Rupe Killian waxed expansive on his favorite subject. "Take this little jaunt. Ol' Rough-house Pease gets word there's a big pow-wow goin' on about the Cheyenne makin' war with the Blackfeet. So what's he do? He saddles us all up and heads out. We're gonna ride right up to that confabulation an' offer to sell 'em guns to use against their enemy. Now, that's right smart thinkin', I tell you."

Delphus Plunkett cut his eyes around the flat terrain that surrounded their exposed position. "I ain't so sure of that. Those Injuns could find us out here quick as a wink."

"Why, hell, boy, we'd whup 'em easy. We's white men, ain't we?"

Delphus twisted his head to peer behind, just in case. "But there's a whole lot more of them than there is of us, Rupe."

"That don't matter none, nohow," Rupe dismissed with sublime contempt. "Besides we're comin' as friends. They'll welcome them guns, I tell you."

The sound of drumming hooves from ahead of the column reached Rupe's ears. He perked up and rose in the stirrups to look forward. One of the scouts sent forward by Pease came fogging down on the outlaw band on a foam-sheeted horse. He started shouting something while still out of earshot.

"My God, they're right behind me! Hunnerds of 'em!"

Ezra Pease and Titus Vickers spurred their mounts forward to meet the excited man. "Who are, my man?" Pease demanded.

"They be Cheyenne, Mr. Pease. Gobs of 'em. There's a village jist beyond this ridge. We showed up on the back slope an' they come boilin' out at us."

Shots cracked out before he could say more. Some

twenty, bare-headed warriors came into view on the crest of the ridge. They reined in and sat their ponies, took aim and fired another ragged volley. Rifle balls plowed dirt a hundred yards from the column of white men.

"What are we gonna do now?" Titus Vickers asked, his throat tight with fear.

10

Ezra Pease recovered rapidly. "Why, my good man, we're going to charge them."

Those around the well-dressed leader blinked in incomprehension. The number of Indians on the ridge continued to grow. Eyes widened as the count of the angry Cheyenne increased to overwhelming odds. Several of the hard-bitten thugs with Pease cut their eyes to Titus Vickers in appeal. He gave them a curt nod, though not a word had been spoken. Titus Vickers *knew*.

"Not likely, Mr. Pease," he responded with more formality than usual. "At least not by this chile. I think we'd best make a run for it while the gettin's good."

Pease studied the ranks above, war lances aflutter with feather decorations, bows and rifles ready. He sighed gustily and gave a reluctant nod. "Your calm evaluation of the situation may have saved our lives again, Vic. Under the prevailing conditions, I have no choice but to defer to your wisdom." He paused and then sucked in wind. "Let's get the hell out of here!" he bellowed.

None of the men needed encouragement. They reversed their mounts on the narrow trickle of a trail and put spurs to flanks. In an eye-blink, only a column of roiling dust remained where the invading white men had been. A smug smile bloomed on the face of Falling Horse. He pointed to the retreating backs of their enemy.

"We will follow them, punish them some. It will be for the honor of Black Hand, not our own."

At once, the Cheyenne warriors streamed down the slope from the saddle notch in the ridge. Hooting and whooping, they set up rapid pursuit. Those at the rear of Pease's disorganized column heard them even over the rumble of the hooves of their galloping horses. They cast apprehensive glances behind them.

When the swift Cheyenne ponies closed enough, those in the forefront loosed rounds from their rifles and trade muskets. Balls whined overhead and one took a chunk from the fat rump of Vern Beevis. His wail blended with the war cries of the Indians.

"You know, I think we've got ourselves in some deep cow plop," Rupe Killian shouted over the pounding hooves.

"I don't 'think' no such thing," Delphus returned the shout. "I damn well *know* it."

"How we gonna get outta this?" Rupe wanted to know.

"You acquainted with foldin' yer hands together an' lookin' up at the Almighty?"

"You mean *pray?*" Rupe asked, astounded.

Delphus answered soberly. "Seems the only thing might work."

Tension so thick she could almost taste it, Falicity Jones thought as she heard the call from the rear of the column. "Riders comin'!" Whatever did that mean? Would they be attacked again? She cut nervous eyes to the broad-shouldered figure of the man called Preacher.

"Dismount the wagons," he ordered. "Up in them rocks until we know who it is."

Quickly the refugees from the ill-fated wagon train halted

the patched-up wagons and scrambled into the tumble of boulders at the uphill side of the trail they followed. While they did, Falicity observed Preacher checking the caps on his multitude of weapons and sighed with relief.

What a competent man he was. Had she not been so recently widowed, she might look upon him as handsome and dashing. Silly goose! she chastened herself. Preacher worked by feel, she noticed, while his eyes remained set on their back-trail. With that accomplished, he trotted his horse to the rearmost wagon and lowered the long-barreled Hawkin rifle to his saddle bow. From a pocket sewn into the saddle skirt, Preacher withdrew a compact brass tube. He drew it out to form a spyglass and peered through the single lens.

White men, Preacher detected at once. Only two of them, so far, his thinking progressed. Might be more of Pease's trash and again, might not. Then he, too, left the trail, secured his horse and disappeared into the rocks.

A flight of arrows sailed their way overhead. Ezra Pease winced at the moaning sound and instinctively ducked his head. Three of the projectiles found sticking points in horse flesh. The animals turned frantic. They uttered nearly human squeals and groans. The men atop them flung about like stuffed rag bags. The Cheyenne fired their rifles in irregular order. Fortunately for Pease and his gang it was as equally hard for a Cheyenne to hit a moving target from a moving mount as for a white man.

In the lull to reload, following the discharge, the desperate white men put more distance between them and their pursuers. All form of order had disappeared. Their flight had become a matter of staying alive. Titus Vickers hung back, urging the men to get control of themselves. At last a few overcame their panic enough to offer some resistance. They reined in among some rocks and took careful aim.

Rifles cracked and two Cheyenne fell from their saddles.

Hastily the empty weapons got reloaded while a handful of others took up positions and opened up on the charging Indians. Vickers looked forward to see the scattered riders disappear around a bend he did not recall from their approach. He had to find out what had happened.

"Hold them off as long as you can, then pull back," Titus Vickers told Bart Haskel.

He spurred ahead to discover a terrible blunder. In their eagerness to evade their enemy, those in the lead had turned into a blind canyon. Sheer granite walls rose along a narrow stream, through which the unwitting men splashed, silver sheets of icy water spraying nose-high on their mounts. They could not be left behind, Vickers realized and held in place to direct those beyond to join the others. Their only chance remained with superior fire power.

When Bart Haskel and the last two thundered down the main trail, Titus Vickers waved his hat at them and drew them into the box canyon. "We didn' come this way," Bart observed.

"I know. Ride on to the others. I'll be right with you."

Vickers dismounted and led his mount away from the entrance to a place of safety. There he tied off the lathered roan and pulled a short-handled spade from his saddle gear. He rushed back to the mouth of the canyon and up a tallus-strewn slope to the base of a large boulder. Working cautiously at one side of the huge stone, he began to sling away shovel-loads of dirt. It didn't matter to him why the Cheyenne had held back. While he labored on, an idea came to him.

This was their home country and they probably knew it better than anyone. They would figure out that the gang had trapped itself. No need to hurry. Take time, reload. Bind up any slight wounds, and come on at their convenience. Meanwhile, he had plenty to do. The dirt and decomposed granite flew faster. Finally the boulder rocked precariously with each solid chunk of the spade.

Carefully, Vickers worked his way to the upper inside edge of the big rock and put his shoulder to it. Flexing his legs he pushed with all his strength. At first it seemed as though nothing would happen. Then, with a loud, grating groan, the ponderous rock canted out over the excavation Vickers had made. He bunched his legs and shoved again. The top of the boulder rocked past the center point and the whole mass let go. Loudly it crashed down into the notch that defined the mouth of the box canyon. That would slow the Indians one hell of a lot, Vickers thought with satisfaction as he walked back to his horse. In minutes he joined the milling stew of misfits and high country trash.

"I've got the entrance partly closed off," Vickers announced to a pale-faced Pease. "We can get out, single file, but the Injuns will have to come at us the same way. A few good shots can hold them off for long enough for them to lose interest."

"Good thinking, Vic. You hear that, men?" he challenged. "All it takes is a little cool thinking and some determination and we'll get out of this without any harm done. I want ten of you to go back with Vic and take up positions where you can keep the entrance under fire. Make every shot count. The rest of you settle down your mounts and someone, for God's sake, start a pot of coffee."

That last brought a grudging ripple of laughter from the thoroughly demoralized outlaws. By the time the dust settled and the horses had been wiped down and cooled out, a fire crackled in a stone pit, a coffee pot of chill stream water put in place and a tripod erected to hold a pot for beans. Noting this last, Pease nodded toward it with satisfaction.

"Good idea. We may be here awhile."

His prediction proved all too true. The coffee water had yet to boil before sporadic gunfire came from the mouth of the canyon. Light and irregular at first, the output quickly increased in volume. Many of the hard cases in camp wore worried frowns. A wounded man straggled back into camp.

"Them damn Cheyenne must know another way into this place. They're swarmin' all over us out there."

"We had all better get down there," Ezra Pease decided

aloud. "Check your powder and shot. If we hit them hard, they should pull back."

With twenty guns roaring in action, the gang fought the Cheyenne to a stand-still. Then, as the muzzle-loading rifles and pistols ran dry, the bows and arrows of the warriors made up the difference. Ezra Pease was shocked to discover that less than a dozen braves had penetrated into the box canyon. Their bows had devastating effect, wounding men more often than fatal shots. Half a dozen rifles cracked again, soon followed by more, and stalemate returned. Fatigue must be playing with him, Pease thought as visibility seemed to lower in a gray haze. A quick count showed his men to be less than fifteen still on their feet. More Cheyenne had slithered up through the rocks and fitted shafts to bowstrings. What he needed, Ezra Pease concluded, was a miracle.

A crash of gunfire set them to ducking before the warriors could release their arrows. Ezra Pease blinked rapidly. It had grown noticeably darker. A new sound intruded on the intermittent battle. A seething hiss grew in volume as it raced down the canyon. Suddenly visibility dropped to less than a hundred yards. Icy rain began to pelt Ezra Pease in the face. Titus Vickers appeared on his left.

"Rain, by God! That'll play hob with their bowstrings. I think we've got this-un won."

Wiping streams of chill droplets from his face, Ezra Pease made short reply. "Call it a draw and be damn grateful for that."

Another look through the spyglass revealed the riders to be Buck Dempsey and Kent Foster. They had been with those Bible-thumpers. What the hell were they doing up here? Preacher wondered to himself. Oh, no. That couldn't be. By the Almighty, ain't no way any proper guide could have been talked into something that stupid. No.

"Yes," Buck assured Preacher ten minutes later when they

reached the spot where he waited for them with growing unease. "They never engaged a guide. Took the wagons east out of sight of the fort, then cut back north. That Reverend Bookworthy's a determined man, even if he's a fool."

"I'll agree with all you've said. He's sure a fool. They must have taken that Injun trace to catch up so soon."

Relieved that the blame would not fall on him, Buck relaxed enough to produce an admiring smile. "Right you are. Me an' Kent, here, tried to talk them out of it. They weren't hearin' none of that. 'We've been sent from Gawd to minister to the heathen and nothing or no one is going to stop us,' ol' Bookworthy spouted when he ordered us to turn off. None of the other drivers is too happy about it, either. But the pay is good and the food even better. Them mission women sure know how to handle a skillet."

Preacher snorted through his nose. "I'll allow as how that's sure right. A feller could put on a few pounds right fast eatin' with them folks. Now, how far back would you say they were?"

Buck's brow furrowed. "Three days by horseback, but that don't mean much. They're plum lost and not on the right trail. Wagons won't make eight miles a day in this country. So I'd say five to eight days."

"Damnit!" Preacher slapped a thumb-thick aspen branch against his left thigh. "It's plumb ignorant. Any man'd know that. Well, me an' my friends ain't got time to lead them pilgrims outta here. You go on back for them, get 'em out of whatever pickle they got themselves into, 'cause they sure ain't up to doin' it on their own. I reckon the good Reverend Bookworthy knows as much about readin' trail sign as he does about real sinnin'. We'll wait for you here, then it's on to Trout Crick Pass. They'll just damn well have to spend the summer an' winter there."

Buck's eyes twinkled. "You know dang well they won't, Preacher. They'll just hire on some no-count guide like that Bull Ransom and head off into the wilds."

"An' get themselves kilt. Serves them right if they do,"

Preacher snapped as he turned away. "I've got these dang refugees to tend to. Might as well grain your horses out of their supplies an' rest 'em good. Then hit the road back after them idjit flatlanders."

By nightfall, Preacher almost had a mutiny on his hands. The refugees had grumbled among themselves about waiting at this spot for more lost souls to join the cavalcade. Their supplies were dangerously low, thanks to the raid on their wagon train. They wanted to push on to where they could make connections with the Immigrant Trail and join another train. Most of all, they felt put upon that these strangers were missionaries and thus considered by Preacher to be even more addle-pated than he thought his present charges to be. Finally, while magenta, gold, and purple painted the western sky, a delegation made up of Mrs. Kenny, Flora Sanders, and Falicity Jones came to where Preacher bent to put a cover over the cookfire.

Wise in the ways of handling their men, and aware of the covert admiring glances Preacher had been giving Falicity, the older women appointed her as spokeswoman. They approached with self-generated confidence. Preacher's stony expression quickly cooled some of that. "Preacher," Falicity began with firmness. "We have some say in what goes on. At least we should have," she hastily amended.

"Not in this, you don't," Preacher countered.

Falicity had still not been put in full retreat. "Back at the beginning, we elected for the train to be run as a democracy."

"Damn-fool word, you ask me. Means 'mob rule' in Greek," Preacher snapped.

Falicity's jaw sagged slightly. How could she reach this man? "What I'm saying is that we need to press on northward, to find a train to the west as soon as possible. We have nothing to return to. This delay might cost us any chance we have."

"Be a good thing if it did. Now, you take any of these men

here. Ain't a one couldn't guide you to the trail. Not Nighthawk, not Dupre, nor Beartooth. Especially since they're headed that way anyhow. Ain't a one of them will do it, though. None of them's crazy enough to. Miz Jones, you jist don't get it, do you? There ain't a one of you suited to be out here. This country is pretty civilized, compared to up north. Even so, we got to watch you like a mother hen does her chicks. Beyond the Medicine Bows, way up on the Platte, there plain ain't nobody to help you."

"We would have you—ah—gentlemen to protect us . . . if you'd agree to guide us that far," Falicity offered, less sure of herself.

"Nope. All's out there is high country meadows and mountains. And, of course, Injuns. Whole lots of Injuns, none of who take kindly to white folk invadin' their territory. What you propose, to sit out there an' wait for a wagon train to roll along, would only serve to get all our hair lifted."

"You're . . . serious about this, aren't you?" Falicity said wonderingly, reality at last dawning on her.

Preacher came to his moccasins, dusted off his hands as he spoke. "Dang straight I am. You ain't crossin' the Ohio River Valley, Miz Jones. Up there . . ." he pointed north, "there's the flats, the Platte, and Injuns."

"But, we're determined to live in the West." Falicity's tone had turned apologetic, pleading for understanding.

Now, Preacher had been thinking on that very thing for some time, since first encountering these displaced pilgrims. An idea had been toying with his brain for the past two days. Might be now was the time to trot it out and see if these female frontiersmen liked its shiny coat.

"Like I said, you can always summer at Trout Crick Pass. If you've all your minds set on livin' in God's Country, you could scout around, with someone local to guide you, locate a nice valley somewhere an' settle in. You could hire enough men from amongst the driftin' boys to build right smart cabins before the leaves turned. Anything more I can't guarantee. Hell, I can't even offer it. Plumb too dangerous."

Falicity's eyes came alight with bright new hope. She clapped her hands in enthusiasm and turned to the rest of the delegation. "You see? I told you Preacher would solve this dilemma for us. We're going to settle in the West after all."

"An' God he'p us all," Preacher grumbled as he turned away to wonder what new outrage would befall them next.

11

Scavengers had been at work on the hurried graves of the ambushed wagon train. When they arrived, after five hard days of travel, Reverend Thornton Bookworthy took one look at the gnawed limbs and eviscerated torsos and promptly lost his breakfast. The burned wagons presented a grim sight. Shaken to her core, Patience Bookworthy put a hand on her husband's arm.

"Why, we came through here not long ago. This . . . could have happened to us."

Himself badly unnerved, Reverend Bookworthy still relied on his main assurance. "We had God's protection, Patience. On the way up we had five capable, armed men to guide us. Coming—ah—coming back, we had that Preacher fellow to scout for us. This is an oddity, something rare if the accounts we saw back East are to be believed." He looked around, and back at the crude mass grave. "We should give these poor people proper Christian burial."

"We haven't time, Reverend," Buck Dempsey advised. "Preacher's waitin' for you all to catch up. An' I've a mind his patience runs on the thin side."

"Surely we can take the time to cover them up better," Bookworthy blustered. "It's the least we can do."

Some of Preacher's sass had rubbed off on Buck. "It's the most, you ask me. If we take our noonin' here, it might be all right."

Reverend Bookworthy made a face. "Our Deacons and the other brethren can be put to the task, naturally. Also myself, of course," Bookworthy hastened to add.

With that agreed, the wagons pulled on up the trail a short distance, to avoid the grisly scene and the women set about preparing a meal. Rocks, fallen branches, and dirt were used to enlarge and deepen the mound that served as a final resting place for the unknown adventurers. All of the missionaries kept the possibility of an attack on the surface of their thoughts as they went about the effort of entombing the less fortunate pioneers.

A warm sun soon put large, wet stains in the armpits of the white shirts worn by the Holy Joes. They labored until blisters and hot red spots covered the palms of their hands. The summons to the noon meal put their faces aglow with relief. After Reverend Bookworthy offered thanks for the food and called on God's blessing for their enterprise, they fell to.

For all its quantity, the food rapidly disappeared. Afterward, the good reverend made the hoped-for announcement. "We have completed the monument over our departed, unknown brothers and sisters. I think we can spare the time for a prayer and song over their earthly remains."

Buck Dempsey started to rise and object, but a stern look from Cora Ames, with whom he had become smitten of late, stilled him. He joined the others as they trooped back to the mass grave. Reverend Bookworthy stepped out in front of the semicircle of immigrants.

"Shall we all raise our voices in two verses of that comforting hymn, *Rock of Ages.*"

Asa Pettibone produced a mouth harp, and Tom Ashton

put bow to his fiddle. The women and other men among the mission group sang beautifully. When they had concluded, Bookworthy offered a long-winded prayer and they sang another hymn. As the last notes of that died away, Buck Dempsey stepped forward.

"Now, let's get the hell an' gone away from here before the renegade whites who did this decide to come back."

"How did you know it was white men who did this awful thing, Buck?" Cora asked.

"Preacher told me," Buck answered. Cora's expression of raw admiration cut him.

"Yes, he would know about such things," she replied in worshipful tones.

Ah, hell, there goes any chance I ever had, Buck thought miserably as the holy pioneers took their places in the column and he gave the command to move out.

He had been known only as Hashknife since he signed on with Ezra Pease back in St. Louis. Hashknife had a hard, cruel face, with a frozen expression of suppressed anger, small, glittery, close-set eyes and a beak of nose that had been broken several times. None of the second-rate hard cases would mess with Hashknife. They steered clear of him, even during the rare drinking bouts in the semi-civilized surroundings of Missouri and along the Santa Fe Trail. Even the few, quality frontiersman types among the forty man contingent walked softly around Hashknife. Ezra Pease did not miss this.

When the man came up the trail with a dozen hard-bitten drifters from the trading post at Trout Crick Pass, Pease summoned him to his tent. He waved a hand at the small keg of bourbon that rested on a folding stand, and nodded to a camp stool.

"Help yourself to the bourbon. Or, if you prefer, there's rum."

"Bourbon will do fine," Hashknife rumbled in that deep, Eastern-accented voice of his.

"Take a seat. I have a proposition I wish to discuss with you."

Hashknife downed half of the brass goblet of whiskey while Pease trimmed the end of a fine cigar. "What sort of proposition do you have in mind?"

Well-spoken bugger, Ezra Pease acknowledged silently. He mused on how to present his case before answering. "You seem to be a cut above most of the men who follow me, Hashknife. I'd put your frontier skills on a par with those of Titus Vickers. Your ability to handle those men you brought in speaks well for your initiative in recruiting them, and your leadership abilities." The blank look Pease received prompted him to inquire, "Am I speaking over your head?"

"Not at all, Mr. Pease. I was only surprised that you had taken note of me in the least."

"Quality shows, my good man," Pease answered flatteringly, to cover his misstep. "I'm in the process of making some changes in the organization. I feel we need more flexibility. You can do a lot for me in that direction. A lot for yourself, for that matter."

Hashknife looked interested, at least as much as his stone face would reveal. "Go on, you have me curious."

"As you know, each man receives a share in our enterprise, with a quarter share bonus for a successful completion. Titus Vickers receives ten times that. I want to split the group into two wings, to operate independently, but with the same common goal. I would like for you to command that second wing. With an equal share to Vic's."

Hashknife swallowed hard and nearly choked on the whiskey. "You amaze me, Mr. Pease."

"That's all? I 'amaze' you?"

"I'm grateful, of course. But, why me?"

"To put it crudely, Hashknife, like the men you'll be commanding, you've got the balls for the job." Ezra Pease cleared his throat on that one.

Savoring another swallow of the fine Tennessee sour mash, Hashknife considered the possibilities this opened to him. "It's an honor. One I appreciate more than I can say. Of how many men would I be in charge?"

"After that unfortunate run-in with the Cheyenne, but considering the twelve you've brought in, you would have twenty guns to direct. All will be of my choosing, though not all will be top quality. I have to spread around the inferior ones so that neither wing will be unduly weakened."

"I understand. When will this go into effect?" Hashknife asked.

"By tomorrow. I'll make the selections today."

Hashknife rose to his boots and extended his hand. "You have your man, Mr. Pease. You've got my word on it."

A twinkle blossomed in the eyes of Ezra Pease. "I suspect it's the word of a gentleman, in spite of that curious name you have," he stated flatly, taking the hand of Hashknife and giving his new lieutenant a conspiratorial wink.

Falling Horse was ready to give up the chase. He had brought his men far from their village, deep into the White Top mountains. They had punished the white men, though he would have liked to have done more. Falling Horse strongly suspected that these were the same men who had destroyed the village of Black Hand. If that turned out to be true, he would regret not taking the risk of hunting them down, even in this place where so many whites had settled. Although the white population of the Rocky Mountains at that time averaged around one per five hundred square miles, that constituted far too many for the Cheyenne, Arapaho, and Ute who had lived there for ages.

"It is wise to return to our village," old Red Hawk remarked to his nephew, Falling Horse.

"I am not so sure. I believe those to be the men who killed Black Hand."

Red Hawk nodded at the younger man. "I knew you would be thinking that. We are not strong enough to challenge them for now." The graying counselor produced a wisp of a smile. "Let them grow confident once more and come into our valleys and along our waters. Then is time enough to show them who is master of the high plains."

Falling Horse clasped his uncle on one shoulder. "My father told me that you were born wise beyond your years. Now I know it is so. Yes, Uncle, we shall return to our village . . . after one more day on this trail. There we can replenish our arrows, cast many balls for our rifles. And always the young boys will keep a watch for the return of the white men. They will not like what they find when they come."

All grumbling about the course northward, and the possible results of rejoining Preacher, ceased when the mission wagon train rolled into the camp set up by Preacher, Night-hawk, Beartooth, and Dupre. Brimming with compassion, sympathy, and understanding, Cora and the women descended on the refugee women with eyes spilling over.

"Oh, you poor, poor dears," Patience Bookworthy cooed to Mrs. Kenny. "Your menfolk are safe in the arms of Jesus. We prayed for them and sang three lovely hymns."

"Covered them up better, too," Buck Dempsey muttered behind her, which brought a hot scowl from the minister's wife.

"Covered? I don't understand," Mrs. Kenny began in confusion.

"Don't pay him any mind, my dear. We—ah—we understand the necessity for haste that drove you when you—ah—laid them to rest," Patience quickly injected. "We put more stones and earth on the grave is all."

"I think I see," Mrs. Kenny said vacantly.

Cora added a brightening bit of news. "We'll be traveling together now, so all will be safe. You can distribute what you saved among our wagons and get rid of those wretched vehicles."

"But we can't," Flora Sanders protested. "It—it's all we have of our past." She nodded to the jury-rigged wagons. "They've made it this far, they'll do for the rest of the way."

Accustomed to being the strongest woman in any group, Patience Bookworthy took careful note of Flora Sanders. Then she dismissed this show of obstinacy. Given time, she would be fully in charge, the stout, determined Patience assured herself. Preacher, who had been out hunting game for the hungry refugees, walked up then, a frown furrowed his brow.

"I can't say I'm glad to see you folks," came his first words. Then he addressed the Reverend Bookworthy. "Of all the tom-fool dangerous things for anyone to do, you've done the worst. Only thing for it is to take you all in to the tradin' post at Trout Crick Pass. Then us four," he indicated his companions, "are headed north to see how serious this Cheyenne trouble is gonna get."

"Good," Bookworthy boomed. "We shall accompany you. Our mission is to the Cheyenne."

Big fists on hips, eyes glacial gray, Preacher examined Reverend Bookworthy with a glance he might give to an insect on a pin. "We've been over this before, Reverend. 'Pears you've got a hearin' problem. So, I'll say it again. *Not this year.* Not any year if I have the say-so. Now, let's just let it rest. Trundle them wagons along best you can and do like these folks have decided."

Reverend Bookworthy's full lower lip formed a pink pout. He tried to copy Preacher's belligerent stance . . . and failed. "What, exactly, is that?"

"They are goin' to put up around the tradin' post, and scout for some nice little place where they'll be secure for next winter. After that, they're on their own. You'd be smart to join 'em, then all of you head back come next spring." Bookworthy started to voice more protest and Preacher raised a hand, palm out to halt him. "I'll not hear any more on the subject. It's plumb closed."

Preacher turned on one moccasin heel and took in the

cluster of wagons, the scampering children and grazing stock. "It's plain we ain't movin' anywhere today. Ever' one rest up, stock plenty of water and check yer wagons. We head out at first light tomorrow."

To Preacher's great surprise, the caravan made good time. Buck and Eric offered to drive the makeshift wagons of the refugees, and led the way, the pace set to the ability of their vehicles. Behind them stretched the missionary wagons. Preacher and Nighthawk ranged ahead, to keep constant watch. Not that they seriously expected to encounter any trouble. At least none that could not be handled by the weapons and fighting men at hand.

It came as a considerable turn, then, when Preacher's senses began to tingle with a faint edge of alarm. He had never been able to put a proper word to what he considered as his "notions," until a learned man Preacher had encountered on his first, and only, return visit to his father's house had put words to it. The gentleman visiting had labeled it as Preacher's "sixth sense."

Preacher preferred "notions," as in, "Injuns is notionable." What his notions told him now was that there were a whole lot of Indians around. It didn't surprise him that he and Nighthawk had not seen a single brave. Nor any sign left by unshod hooves. The air just . . . smelled different. The birds didn't sing as brightly as usual. A small, black-bellied cloud, high up in the azure sky passed over the sun and sent a tingle up Preacher's spine. All in all, he summed up, things had gotten out of kelter.

"You sense it too," Nighthawk remarked, his once handsome, Delaware face curving into smile lines.

"Yeah. But, I don't *know* it. If I didn't know better, I'd swear there was half a hundred Cheyenne around us. Only the southern Cheyenne stay mostly out on the flats, an' the northern ones don't often come south of the Big Horn Mountains."

Nighthawk sucked a deep breath into his barrel chest. "The air . . . tastes different from an hour back."

" 'Zactly," Preacher pounced on the observation. "An' listen to them birds. Slightly off key, wouldn't you say, Nighthawk?"

Nighthawk grunted and shifted his narrow-hipped rear in the saddle. Idly his right hand eased to the curved butt of a large .64 caliber horse pistol in a saddle holster in front of himself.

"Somethin' tells me we ought to mosey back to the pilgrims and make them ready for what might be comin'," Preacher speculated aloud. "Yet, we ought to scout it out complete so's we *know* what to expect."

"You can do that well enough on your own, old friend. While I can carry the news to our charges."

"Right enough, but somethin' else tells me that because there's two of us is why whoever is out there ain't takin' any pot-shots."

"You might have something there. Or, maybe they already know about the wagons and want us to get clear through them and long gone before they hit."

Instantly, a light glowed in Preacher's eyes. "I'll buy into that, 'Hawk. Sneaky things like that is usual amongst the Dog Soldiers. B'god, I swear I can smell me Cheyennes now."

In tense situations, Preacher had often noticed, Nighthawk tended to employ the best of his English vocabulary. "How do you propose we proceed?"

"I say we turn back and get the hell an' gone to them wagons. There'll be enough of those boneheads what won't have their guns loaded as it is."

Except for Beartooth—who had his familiar "itch" behind his eyeballs for the past hour—and Dupre—who could not recall the words to a well-known *voyajure* song for the same amount of time—it came as quite a shock to those in the column of wagons when shrill war whoops announced that they had come under attack by some forty-five Cheyenne warriors.

Led by Falling Horse, the Dog Soldiers took the forefront of the crescent sweep of braves who pounded down the slope ahead of the wagon train. They numbered only eleven, and rode in a straight line at the deepest part of the semi-circle, but made up for their number by the ferocity of their fighting skills. The Cheyennes first appeared well out of rifle range and made as swift a progress as the terrain would allow. Their surroundings also dictated that they had to use this tactic if they wanted to ride their horses. It didn't matter to Beartooth.

Rising in his stirrups, he bellowed, "Circle the wagons! Be quick about it. Git them guns ready."

Under a growing cloud of dust, a tight enclosure rapidly formed. The wagon box ahead served as shelter to the team from behind. The hired drivers had their weapons ready and close at hand. The pilgrims had to find and load theirs. Would they never learn? Beartooth wondered.

"Steady! Hold steady. No one fires until I say so. Watch them horns. They mean to close around us," Beartooth cautioned. "Take aim on them fellers first. Knock 'em outta their saddles an' we got a chance." He cut his eyes around the stockade. "You boys on this side, pick targets amongst them bucks in the center. Whang enough of them an' the whole pack will pull back to regroup."

"Who are they?" Bobby Gresham asked, clutching a .36 caliber Squirrel rifle in a competent manner. "Chiefs or something?"

"They be your worst nightmare, sonny. Them's Dog Soldiers unless I miss my guess," Beartooth told him. "Wonder where Preacher is?" he took time to puzzle aloud.

A few eager beavers among the warriors opened fire the moment they came into extreme range. It bothered Falling Horse that the gunfire failed to draw out a response. Someone had taught these white men well. Only a few heartbeats remained before they clashed with the wagons. Abruptly, the wagon sides facing Falling Horse and his Dog Soldiers erupted in a wall of white powder smoke.

A meaty smack and soft grunt came from the Dog Soldier on the right of Falling Horse and the young chief saw the man sag in his saddle, a bullet hole clear through the meaty part of his shoulder. Two more of the elite warrior society went down in sprays of blood. Falling Horse cut his eyes to the points of the crescent and saw more braves go down at each end. Without a spoken word, the cream of Cheyenne fighting men cut to left and right and raced to reinforce the edges of the formation.

Suddenly, from behind came the loud, flat reports of heavy caliber horse pistols discharging. Falling Horse nearly upset his pony as he wheeled it to see two buckskin-clad, wide-eyed creatures charging the Cheyenne from the rear.

12

"We got here too late," Preacher stated with chagrin.

"What are we going to do about that?" Nighthawk inquired.

"Simplest thing in the world, ol' hoss," Preacher appraised him. "We're gonna get down in among 'em and raise a little hell."

Nighthawk studied that over a while. "I can see that is the only way to get to the wagons. But is being there worth losing our hair over?"

"You've got too much anyway," Preacher bantered, his hand drawing a saddle gun and cocking it. "Well, like your friends the Dakota say, *hokka hey,* it's a good day to die."

He and Nighthawk charged as one. Their thundering hoofbeats could not be heard above the tumult of all those Cheyenne ponies. It allowed them to get right up behind the center of the crescent formation undetected. By then both men had their reins in their teeth, both hands filled with powerful, .64 caliber horse pistols. They fired point-blank into the backs of the nearest warriors and reholstered.

Preacher drew one of his awe-inspiring four-barrels and fired away at any bronze figure that caught his attention.

Working the complicated trigger mechanism to revolve the barrels with what speed he could accomplish, Preacher broke free of the double rank half a length ahead of Nighthawk, who had pulled a pair of .50 Hayes double-barrel pistols. Muzzles flashing fire, Nighthawk caught up to Preacher a moment after the Dog Soldiers broke away to either side.

"Nice of them to open the gate for us," Nighthawk shouted around the leather straps in his mouth.

"Now if those folks below will open the door, we'll be just fine," Preacher responded, eyes fixed on the circled wagons, while the Cheyenne wheeled away to regroup.

Slowly, one of the gathered smaller, lighter cousins of the Conestoga wagons began to roll backward. A warm glow filled Preacher's heart when he recognized it as Cora Ames's wagon. Bless her heart, that gal had all her gear in her possibles bag. He heeled Thunder that way and streaked for the small opening. Nighthawk matched him stride for stride, then reined sharply to let Preacher dash through the narrow opening first.

Cora's wagon had barely heeled into position again when the Cheyenne attacked for the second time. A torrent of arrows made a black cloud against the sky. Most thudded into the wooden sides of the wagons, a handful reached the inside to clatter on the hard ground. Now that he had time for it, Preacher studied the warrior he'd marked as the leader. Under the hastily applied paint, his face looked familiar.

"Naw, it couldn't be," Preacher opined aloud. "He's never stood against the whites before."

"Who is that?" Cora Ames took time away from aiming her rifle to ask.

"Falling Horse. I wintered in his camp a couple of times. He made it clear to me then that he held nothing against us whites, long as we didn't take up permanent space in their hunting grounds or such like."

"Do you really think you know the man leading these savages?" Cora pressed.

Preacher took another look. "That I do, Miss Cora. And I aim to do somethin' about it." Preacher levered himself up on the driver's stand of the wagon behind Cora's and waved his hat over his head. "Falling Horse!" he called out in Cheyenne. "It's me, White Wolf. I have shared your lodge before. I gave my protection to these people."

It worked so far, Preacher noted thankfully as the man he addressed raised his lance in the signal to halt. "Hold your fire, now," he cautioned the pilgrims. Then to Falling Horse, he challenged, "Is this how you honor an old guest?"

Tension did not whisk away at this impugning of the Cheyenne war chief's honor. Rather, Falling Horse rode forward alone, peering through the dust at the tall figure silhouetted on the wagon seat.

"Is that truly you, White Wolf?"

"In the flesh, Falling Horse."

"I see you now, White Wolf."

"I see you, too, Falling Horse. Sorta outta your usual range, ain't ya?"

"We seek some white men who wronged us."

"Well, this ain't them, Falling Horse." Thoughts of Ezra Pease and the sale of guns to the Blackfeet trickled across Preacher's mind. "These folks has got a message from their Great Spirit. They sure ain't sellin' whiskey and rifles to the Cheyenne, nor the Blackfeet for that matter."

Falling Horse lost his mask of impassivity. His eyes widened, eyebrows shoved up his high forehead, his mouth formed a black circle. "You know of them, then?"

"Sure do. We're takin' these folks to Trout Crick Pass an' then goin' on to look into what is carried on the wind about those bad men."

"It is said that Preacher never lies," Falling Horse responded. "We want to punish those men, but if you are hunting them I almost feel sorry for them."

"You'll put aside the war trail against these people and join us for coffee? We have lots of sugar."

Red and black streaks of war paint wriggled like snakes as Falling Horse split his face with a white smile. "Getting ready for war makes a man hungry, White Wolf."

Preacher laughed heartily and glanced over his shoulder at the anxious faces of the greenhorns inside the circle. Quickly he explained the gist of their exchange. Then, without waiting for a reply from the flatlanders, he turned back to Falling Horse.

"I think we can manage to fill your bellies. You lost a couple of ponies. I'd say six or more wounded. We have spare horses. They are yours to make right between us."

"You are generous, White Wolf. We accept," Falling Horse called back without consulting his followers either.

"It might take a while to fix for all of you, but these women are darn fine cooks. You'll see, they make a feller shine."

Weapons lowered, the Cheyenne warriors rode together and formed a double file. Much to the uneasy doubts of the missionaries, they walked their mounts like peaceful lambs to an opening that Preacher directed be made in the side of the ring of wagons. When half of the wagons had been drawn to the sides and the first Indians left their bows and rifles with their ponies, several of the women showed their relief with audible sighs.

"All rightie, folks," Preacher announced with arms raised over his head to command attention. "It's time to cook up the best feast you've ever whomped together. An' remember, these are our honored guests. Keepin' our hair depends on it."

Ezra Pease beamed his pleasure at the three men who had returned to report success. "That is exceptional news, gentlemen," he praised. "Rest yourselves and your horses and then you may have the honor of leading us to this paradise you have discovered."

"Wha'd he say?" one hard-faced, yellow-toothed ruffian asked his companions as they led their horses to the edge of a creek.

"I think he liked it, Blane," a hawk-nosed individual guessed correctly.

The third scout snickered. "Said we'd have the honor of leadin' 'em. You damn betcha. Ain't a one of them flatlanders he brung with him could find his butt with both hands in broad daylight. 'Course, that means we've got to ride right through Trout Crick Pass with all them like on pee-rade."

Blane studied on that while his horse took a long drink of the cold mountain water. "Say, couldn't us three jist mosey through there an' howdy any fellers we knew, then wait for the rest of them to come on?"

Hawk nose pointed to the sky, a smile bloomed on the face of the brightest of the trio. "They could go by the tradin' post a few at a time, attract less attention that way."

Blane nodded his head, his eyes vacuous. "That shines. I reckon they're lucky havin' three boys smart as us workin' for 'em."

Big slabs of teeth, like yellow tombstones, showed in a crooked grin on the second man's face. "Sure enough. An' I don't reckon any Cheyenne will be pokin' into that li'l valley, all tucked away amongst those high peaks. Uh-oh," he added a second later as the familiar, if irritating, sound of a triangle sounded the summons for a general conference. "Pease's dog-robber's bangin' that tinker bell again. Best go see what he wants."

When he saw the three scouts standing at the edge of the gathering, Ezra Pease made it short and sweet. "These three gentlemen have found us a likely place to establish camp and wait for the humor of the Indians to change. I have been assured we will be safe there, and more important, out of sight." The weight lifted from his shoulders, Pease allowed his thoughts to blossom on an old, sore subject.

"It will also allow us time to complete the destruction of Preacher and whoever is riding with him. That damned half-wild mountain man could ruin all of our plans. Make sure everything is secured, the wagon wheels well greased and the horses rested. We start out after the noon meal."

Later, at the head of the column that had turned northwest again for Trout Crick Pass, Ezra Pease had time to reflect on the plans to which he had referred. Indeed, it was paramount that they eliminate any threat, he admitted as he recalled his last conversation with the men who had brought him into this grand scheme . . .

"This must not fail," the stout, balding New York City banker stated vehemently. "We will hold you personally responsible, Ezra, for the success or failure of our enterprise. Reports our engineers have sent indicate a phenomenal quantity of high-grade ore and nuggets. I don't care what these Army engineers say—gold *is* out there. And not in small quantities either. All one need do is scratch the ground and gold appears. The land on which the finds are located is ours for the taking.

"Provided, of course, that you can bring about a situation that will force the Army to occupy the territory, drive the Indians out, or perhaps down into the Nations, and leave all that empty land for us to claim." The banker paused a moment. "The only fly in our ointment, according to all information at hand, is a tempestuous mountain man named Preacher. It is said he can keep peace between the Indians and whites, and even between the tribes."

Cheeks flared red with the remembered humiliation handed him by Preacher, Ezra Pease chose his words carefully. "Yes. Yet, he may no longer be there. The fur trade is moribund. Those shiftless men who prowled the mountains are scattered to the four winds. Or he may be dead, killed by Indians or some other half-animal like himself." Pease drew himself up in the big, leather chair. "But if Preacher is there, I have my own axe to grind with him. I'll bring him down and open the gateway to riches for us all."

"Umm, yes," the pinch-faced banker on Ezra's left offered acidly. "And using slave labor to do the mining, we will be on the way to cornering the gold market entirely."

Stunned, Ezra Pease fought to keep his expression unreadable. By an unguarded word, the frail, money-hungry little banker had revealed something to Ezra the likes of which he had never dreamed of before. And he stood in line to share in it. What a lovely proposition . . .

With a start, Ezra Pease brought his awareness back to the present. He had learned that Preacher was very much alive. And recently, with the help of his friends, had accounted for the demise of more than fifteen of the men Ezra had brought with him. That would end, Pease vowed, and soon.

With their guests—and former enemies—relaxed by many tin cups of coffee, laced with sugar to a syrupy consistency, the promised feast began an hour before nightfall. Through Preacher's interpretation, Falling Horse had offered some story dances for afterward by bonfire. Always the zealots, Reverend Thornton Bookworthy, along with the other male missionaries, spent the eating time trying to sell their God to the Cheyenne. It taxed the vocabularies of all four mountain men to explain the esoteric concepts of faith. Especially one with which they held little familiarity.

"Therefore, God is the Father of us all," Bookworthy summed up his recitation of the Creation. Bookworthy paused to allow this to be translated. To his great delight, Falling Horse nodded sagely, then spoke with what sounded like deep feeling. His first convert! Reverend Bookworthy rejoiced in this marvel . . . at least until the war chief's words were translated.

"I am puzzled by your words," Preacher took silent pleasure in interpreting, adding a few colorful turns of his own. "Falling Horse allows as how everyone, not touched in the head, knows about the One Above Us All, the Shaper of Men. That he formed man from clay is a true thing. We, he tells me, have always known that. Only now, why should we have to call Him by another name?"

Bookworthy's face went blank, then he drew a deep breath and launched into an explanation. "Because, of the revelation of the Savior. When man began to wallow in sin and degradation, He sent His only Son to redeem us. He did this through the power of the Holy Ghost. And here's the good news. We have come to lead you to His salvation."

"Oh, sure," Preacher offered the response. "White Buffalo Boy, who brought the bison and taught us to hunt in the time before the horse. He also taught us the rules of how to live with one another in peace."

All the while he had been translating, Preacher and his mountain man friends had been fighting the desire to roll on the ground and howl with laughter. Preacher watched the parson carefully while he recited this last bit of wisdom from Falling Horse. Reverend Thornton Bookworthy gaped, gasped, and snapped his jaw closed. His theology in full retreat, the good reverend spun on one boot heel and went off to sulk in the privacy of his wagon.

"Tomorrow is a Sunday, I have determined," he tossed over one shoulder as he walked off. "If you will excuse me, I have a sermon to prepare."

Beartooth ambled over and nudged an elbow into Preacher's ribs. "I think we've seen the last of that one for awhile."

"I reckon so." Then Preacher put a sly look on his face and cut his eyes to Falling Horse. "Why'd you choose them particular words to address to the sky chief?"

Falling Horse shrugged, eyes alight with mischief, a fleeting smile curled his full lips. "It seemed the right thing to say at the time. In my father's days, the Black Robes came to our people from the place you call Canada. They told of the same Almighty Father and his Son. Also they spoke of the good Mother."

"I know," Preacher said quietly, thinking of the French missionary priests who had come among the plains tribes.

"Their Blessed Mother could easily have been our Earth Mother. Or, so my father told me as a boy," Falling Horse went on. "We had no need then for new names for the creating spirits we had always revered. We don't now. Why is it that a man, and usually a white man, thinks his ways are always better?"

"That I can't answer you. Now, to this other thing. Why is it that you come so far south wearing war paint?"

"I have told you before, White Wolf. It is the white men who sell whiskey and guns to the Blackfeet and try to sell to us. Fifteen suns ago, they attacked the village of Black Hand. But, all of this you know. It is decided by the great council that they must be stopped."

"My friends and I are hunting the same men," Preacher told him. "Does the council have names for these white men?"

"The one who leads them, he is called Pease."

"By dang it!" Preacher flared. "I've known that no-account buzzard-poke was behind all this trouble in the north. You have my word on it, Falling Horse, if we come upon these men, we'll leave them wandering in darkness, unable to enter the Spirit World."

Another rare smile lighted the face of Falling Horse. "And if we find them first, the same will be true, my friend White Wolf."

Beartooth scratched in his full, ruddy brush of beard. "I hate to mention this, Preacher," he addressed to his companion where they sat their mounts in a deep pool of shade under an ancient fir tree. "But I think someone among them pilgrims we're babyin' along has got theyselfes some louses."

Preacher laid his head at an angle and cut his eyes to his friend. "What makes you say that?"

"Because I itch, that's what," Beartooth said hotly. "It feels like there's critters crawlin' around in my hair an' beard."

"Dust 'em with some sulphur."

Beartooth didn't think much of Preacher's suggestion. "What? An' smell of hell-fire an' brimstone for a month?"

"If you'd take a bath more'n oncest in three months, you wouldn't have to stink of sulphur."

"Don't get off on that now, Preacher. Least I don't smell as bad as Polecat Parker. You gotta admit that."

Preacher pursed his lips, canted his head left and right, cast a long gaze at the azure sky, and hummed a brief snatch of tune. "If you say so, Beartooth."

Beartooth's eyes went wide. "You sayin' I do stink as bad as Polecat?"

"Nooo," Preacher drawled. "Sometimes you got you a' aroma about you far worse than Polecat."

Spluttering, Beartooth flung his hat at Preacher, who ducked, laughed and set heels to Thunder's flanks. Beartooth was obliged to dismount to retrieve his floppy head cover, which made him late riding into the ambush laid among rocks at a narrow spot on the trail.

He saw Preacher, bellied down in the dirt, banging away with one of those awful four-barrel pistols. A ball moaned past Beartooth's head. He saw the puff of smoke and caught a hint of motion when the shooter drew back to reload. Hugging his Hawken to his cheek, Beartooth saw to it the man didn't need to charge his weapon.

Preacher's pistol made a flat crack almost upon the discharge of Beartooth's rifle and a scream came from the low scrub brush in the boulders. One of those new conical balls cracked past Beartooth's head and reminded him he made a good target sitting high in the saddle. He came down, cussing and squalling. He brought his second rifle with him.

It went into action at once as a buckskin-clad figure bolted from a spot made uncomfortably hot for him by Preacher. Beartooth put a ball through his left thigh and the would-be assassin went down with a shrill cry. His rifle clattered in the rocks as it slithered away from his grasp. Preacher emptied his first four-shot and went to the other as Beartooth pulled a .60 caliber pistol free and busted a cap. A healthy growl came from a dark puddle of shadow and Beartooth cut his eyes that way.

He focused in time to see Preacher stand upright and run toward the mysterious noise, firing his multi-barrel with all the speed possible. The growl turned to a scream of terror.

The brush thrashed and waved while the thud of pounding boot soles faded into the distance.

Preacher stopped firing and went to the rocks to gather weapons and powder. Beartooth joined him there. "You arrived in the nick o' time, friend," Preacher remarked dryly.

"Had to get my hat," Beartooth responded without any sign of contrition.

"If you'd been here, you'd likely taken a ball."

Beartooth squinted at his old sometimes partner. "You sayin' I done good comin' in behind like that?"

"Plum upset their plans, I'd say. Now, let's get these guns back to the folks on them wagons."

Remounted, Preacher scanned the scene of the ambush. "There's somethin' not quite right about this, Beartooth. I've got the feelin' we're missin' the most important part."

Beartooth sniffed the air and started to agree with Preacher when a slug cracked through the trees, releasing a shower of leaves, and smacked into the head of Beartooth's horse, killing it under him.

13

"That's what I didn't like about this set-up!" Preacher shouted to Beartooth as he finished reloading his second four-shooter.

Beartooth had rolled free of his dead horse, and used the animal for a barricade to protect him from the incoming balls of the rest of the frontier trash that came swarming down on them from among the jumble of boulders above. He looked around him and saw that Preacher had disappeared. Never mind. He leveled his reloaded Hawkin on a target and let her bang. "Looks like there's an ambush within an ambush," the older mountain man remarked as he poured powder down the barrel of the Hawken, added patch and ball and rammed home.

"Stars an' garters, my good man, however did you figure that out?" Preacher unleashed his tension in jocular sarcasm.

"No call to get pouty with me, Preacher," Beartooth bantered back.

Another thug attempted a dash from the cover of one boulder to another. He never made it as Preacher clipped his legs out from under him with a through-and-through shot from his own Hawken. The man yelped in pain and flopped on the ground. Thinly his voice came to the beleagured mountain men.

"He shot me through both legs, Quint. What do I do?"

"Good enough for you, ya sneaky polecat," Beartooth roared back.

Quint answered his wounded man. "Stay low. We'll get you out."

"But I'm in th' wide open," the wounded one protested.

"Not for long," Preacher muttered as he fined his sight picture and let go another ball. The ambushing scum died before Quint could offer more advice.

"Does seem we found the wrong place to be in," Beartooth quipped as he reloaded.

The downhill charge continued and the riff-raff swarmed into the meadow where Beartooth lay. They had a hundred yards of open ground to cross to reach the redoubtable mountain man. They got only a few feet into the clearing when Preacher opened up with his two rifles once more, then leaped into the open to charge their flank.

"They're gettin' in pistol range," Preacher advised as he abandoned his Hawken for a four-barrel terror. Two shaggy-haired louts reared up among the lupin and both went off to meet their maker in a twinkling as Preacher closed on their attackers and worked his complex shooter with a speed that surprised even him.

"How many more of them?" Beartooth asked as he sighted in on a burly ruffian in homespun who zig-zagged toward him.

"Been too busy to count," Preacher answered.

"I make it six," Beartooth advised as he triggered his .60 Hayes and grunted in satisfaction when the broken field runner tripped over his feet and went down with a hole in his chest.

"Before or after that one?" Preacher asked lightly.

"You're enjoyin' this, ain'tcha?"

"Ain't my favorite mess to be caught up in," Preacher allowed. "Still, there's somethin' to be said for it. It sure keeps the blood pumpin' through your veins right smartly."

Beartooth groped for another pistol. "We'd best put an end to this right sudden. There might be more of these rag bags out there."

Preacher changed his empty pistol for the second one. "I was thinkin' the same thing."

The one called Quint showed himself then, along with four others. "You ain't got a chance, Preacher We got you cold," he taunted.

A ball from his rifle put a plume of dust up inches from Preacher's face. "Now that's plumb unfriendly," Preacher growled. He sighted in and fired the first barrel.

Bark sprayed from the trunk of a big old silver-tipped fir and gouged half a dozen bloody cuts in Quint's face. He yelped and jerked back behind the tree for protection. Preacher took aim on another of the misbegotten brethren and watched dust puff off the jackal's leather vest as the .54 caliber ball smacked home.

His numbers cut down to three now, Quint decided that he had been sent on a fool's errand by Ezra Pease. Why, there was just two of them down there and they done killed off eleven men. Pease had been right about one thing, though. Preacher had been easy to find, right about where Pease and Vickers said he'd be. South of Trout Crick Pass, only moving slower than expected. They had laid out a good ambush.

If only young Lukins had not fired too soon. A lot of good it did, Quint decided. Time for him to get out of this. But how? he asked himself as another man went down, screaming, his neck ripped open on one side, and gushing blood. Keep the tree between him and those deadly shooters down there. That was the way.

"See him, Preacher?" Beartooth asked as he nodded toward the moving shadow of Quint.

"Shore enough. We'll give him a little time. He'll show in the open in a bit," Preacher answered calmly.

That prediction proved true some two minutes later as Quint gained more altitude up the slope of boulders. Preacher had readied himself with the fancy French sporting rifle and popped the cap when the whole of Quint's left shoulder filled his sights. The smaller caliber ball moved with incredible velocity and drilled through the shoulder blade of Quint, then collapsed his lung. Quint fell face-first through a spray of his own blood.

Both of the survivors had had enough. They fled in wild disorder, gaining ground in long bounds. To add to their panic, the sound of laughter followed them uphill from the men they had sought to kill. When they reached the safety of the beeline where their horses had been tied off, they silently thanked all they held sacred for being spared. From below, Preacher and Beartooth continued to hoot and guffaw in derision.

When their merriment subsided, Preacher spoke for them both. "It had to be Pease. Something's going to have to be done."

"Yep. An' iffin I know you, it ain't gonna be pleasant for our Mr. Pease."

Silas Phipps cocked his head and cupped a grimy hand around one ear. From far off, he faintly heard a booming sound, like thunder. There, it came again. Too fast and too many for lightning strikes, he guessed correctly. A sudden image came to him and he licked newly nervous lips. Once, long ago, a year or two before Silas had reached his teens, he had heard a sound like that. Gunfire!

Yes, it had to be. Long buried images resurrected themselves in his mind and he saw again, with the same horror as the first time, the gang of ruffians swarming down on the isolated cabin in the western part of Virginia that his parents called home. Located on a rocky slope in the Appalachian Mountains, the thin, sickly farmland claimed by the senior Phipps stood in the middle of a clearing hacked out of the tall, thick trees that surrounded it. Most of what it grew was rocks. The desperadoes were upon them before anyone knew it.

His father and two older brothers died in the first hail of gunfire. After that, the unshaven, unwashed hill bandits made sport of rounding up the younger children. They had their way with his Ma and the girls, down to seven-year-old Betsy.

He never forgot. He had been adopted by a kindly family in neighboring Pennsylvania, raised and educated through the secondary school. When he grew older, he hunted down some of those men and killed them, albeit they were shot in the back. That gave him moments of satisfaction, though he failed to find all of those responsible. Yet, his mind seemed filled with strange and terrible cravings. So, he had sought out some orphans, and street waifs, using his inheritance from his adoptive parents to put on a show as a philanthropist and gaining the trust of overburdened police, and operators of orphanages.

Through those first children, he had relived the childhood he had lost. He entered into games with all the enthusiasm they generated. He dressed them well and saw they received proper schooling. Later, a darker side emerged. He became cruel and harshly demanding of the youngsters. At last he could not contain the fiercely hot flares of outright lust that sent him into fits of agony. He gave in . . . and indulged.

None of which mattered in their present situation. The distant gunfire had engendered frightful memories to haunt him. Silas could not face yet another encounter with violent men. Peter, riding one of the saddle mounts beside the lead wagon stared at Phipps in surprise and puzzlement when he began to mutter to himself.

"I think we should turn off about here," Phipps mumbled darkly. "Maybe even go back."

Encouraged to boldness, despite his frequent bouts with the switch, Peter answered sharply. "Why? It's only thunder. I hear it too."

"That's not thunder, boy. It's something far more fearsome than a thunderstorm."

Beside him on the driver's seat, Ruth gave him a startled glance. Knowing that to get away from any source of whiskey would be their only hope, Ruth struggled with her thoughts to come up with some reason to keep going. A careful study of their surroundings gave her a direction.

Fearful of a stinging blow to her face with every word, she hesitantly stated her case. "We must go on, Mr. Phipps. There are no trails to follow otherwise. We would have to cut our way through this wilderness. At least we have to go on as far as that trading post we heard of."

Phipps swiveled his over-sized head and stared at her as though she was a stranger. He blinked and licked his dry lips again. Then he delved behind him for a half-full, stonewear jug of whiskey he had placed there that morning. He removed the stopper and put the mouth to his lips. His Adam's apple bobbed up and down three times before he set the container aside. Then he wiped whiskey off and courage back on his face. Ruth's blood turned icy in her veins as he produced a lewd grin, eyes twinkling, though badly bloodshot. He nodded to acknowledge her comments.

"You've got a good point there, missy, an' tonight I'll have to reward you for comin' up with it," Phipps stated as he patted Ruth's thigh through the thin cotton dress she wore. "Yep. We'll surely have to continue."

Neither Silas Phipps nor anyone else in the High Lonesome needed to worry about a spring thunderstorm. No, the signs Preacher noticed as the rag-tag wagon train set off again indicated something potentially far worse. It began as a gray haze on the horizon. The sky turned to slate, while the overcast extended downward until wisps brushed the mountain peaks. While the wagons creaked and groaned along the rutted trace that led to Trout Crick Pass, the front swept in with teasing slowness.

Within an hour visibility had been cut to below a mile. In the next half hour the temperature dropped into the uncomfortable range. Silvery plumes came from the nostrils of the mules that hauled the rickety wagons up the steep incline. The men and women of the train had clouds of white before their faces at all times. Preacher first noticed the dampness that formed on every metal object. He raised a hand to signal a halt and turned Thunder to face the on-coming pilgrims.

"We'd best make camp right now. Circle the wagons and send the youngsters out to fetch all the firewood they can find."

"Why should we do that, sir?" Reverend Bookworthy demanded. "It's barely mid-afternoon."

Preacher gave him a pained expression. "You greenhorns never learn, do you? When I say to do something, you do it an' be damn quick about it. That way you have a chance of stayin' alive. There's a snow comin', an' unless I'm addlepated, it could be a big one. Now, you folks what's got 'em, pitch yer tents on the lee side of the wagon boxes." The first wide-spaced flakes began to trickle down while Preacher spoke.

Reverend Bookworthy waved at them disdainfully. "What harm can a few light flurries like these do us?"

Preacher eyed him with stony gray disgust. "They can bury you nose deep in a couple of hours is what. Now, do as I say or me an' the boys is pullin' out to make camp where we have a chance of weatherin' the storm. We'll come back for yer bodies."

"My word, I think he means it," Bookworthy blurted, entirely flustered.

Buck Dempsey, in the lead wagon with Patience Bookworthy clucked to the team and began the circle. Visibility had been reduced to a couple of hundred yards. Heavier snowfall began to cut that even more. Preacher noted it and called out advice.

"Have a rope guide strung from the wagons to the edge of them trees. The youngin's will get lost without it."

The children had already become dark, indistinct figures

in the swirl of lacy flakes. They bounded about with youthful energy and began to form an antlike double file to and from the windfall that littered the beeline. When the wagons halted in place and the menfolk had unharnessed the draft animals, Preacher and his friends hastily constructed a corral from sapling poles carried under the vehicles for the purpose.

They erected it snug against the northwest wall of the cut they followed, a scant three paces from the wagons on that side. Twilight dimness descended on the encampment. Women set to making fires while shelters were rigged for the occupants of the train. Preacher stood with Dupre, eyeing the preparations.

"I reckon we got us a heller on the way," Preacher opined.

"I see it like you, *mon ami*. Mother Nature will have one last trick on her children *mais non?*"

"She al'ays does, Dupre. She al'ays does." Preacher sighed. "Thing is, can these tenderfeet survive it iffin it comes on real deep?"

"They are learning, Preacher. Most of them, at least. I cannot say the same for the good *Pere* Bookworthy."

Preacher chuckled softly. "Like most of his sort, his mind's made up, don't want nobody confusin' him with unpleasant facts."

"You are unusually harsh on this man of the cloth. Why is that?"

"You know as well as I, Dupre, Nature's got her own rules out here. She don't abide fools lightly. Truth is, I'm hard on him because I want him to survive. I want him to go back East an' tell the rest of that passel of fools to stay clear the hell an' gone away from here."

Dupre chuckled. "You are soft as a cream horn inside, Preacher. And transparent as isinglass."

Preacher put on an expression of mock resentment. "Am I now? Well, we'll just see about that." He bent and scooped up the first of the sticking snow and fashioned a ball of it, with which he pelted his old friend solidly in the center of

Dupre's chest. Dupre did likewise and soon the white stuff clung to the front of both men. Laughing uproariously, they grappled, fell over and rolled joyfully in the growing layer of snow.

Puzzled and shocked, Cora Ames and the other missionary women looked on at them as though they had lost their minds.

Yellow lantern light formed a fuzzy halo around the head of Martha Yates. Bundled up in the warmest clothing they could unpack in the short time at hand, she went frantically from wagon to wagon, calling out for her eleven-year-old son.

"Johnny are you in there? Johnny, you must come to our wagon right now. Johnny, are you there?"

"That's darn foolishness," Nighthawk grumbled from his warm nest in thick buffalo robes, piled high on pine boughs on the floor of his small, war-trail tipi.

A hat-sized fire flickered in its central ring of stones. Preacher and Dupre had crowded in with him and also looked out the raised flap of the doorway cover at the antics of the pilgrim woman. Beartooth stood first watch outside. It had not stopped snowing in four hours. Three feet of white fluff had piled up on the ground, insulating the sides of the skin lodge as effectively as thick cotton padding. Thankfully the wind had not whipped up with the usual force down the canyon walls.

That made for a slow, steady snowfall, rather than a howling blizzard. Yet the Eastern missionary had no business outside in this. Preacher said as much. "If she dropped that lantern, turned around a couple of times, and blinked, she'd be as lost as the damned souls in Perdition."

"I know it," Nighthawk agreed. "Maybe we should do something about it."

"You want to go out there? It must be nigh onto rock-crackin' cold outside," Preacher proposed.

"Uh-oh, where did that light go, *mes amis?*" Dupre asked uneasily.

"Where? Hell, I don't know," Preacher grumped.

Beartooth appeared at the door flap. "Did that fool woman climb into a wagon? She's done disappeared."

Grumbling, Preacher roused himself. He belted a thick buffalo capote around his middle, pulled on his rabbit-fur-lined moccasins and the sheepskin leggings, then covered his ears and face with wool scarves. His hat went on top of it all.

"Reckon I'd better go see. Beartooth, come along and show me where you saw her last."

"Dang-fool pilgrims. They gonna be the death of us yet," Beartooth predicted.

"Thing is not for them to be the death of theyselves," Preacher jibed back.

"Over here, you cantankerous galoot," Beartooth rumbled.

Beartooth led the way to a space between two wagons. Faint tracks showed in the disturbed snow. For all the darkness looming over them, Preacher and his old friend clearly marked the path between the high wooden walls. Preacher peered beyond. Then whipped back to Beartooth.

"How in hell did these wagons git separated?"

"I dunno. They's supposed to be tight closed. Someone made a bad mistake."

"That ain't the half of it." Far off, toward the treeline Preacher saw a faint splash of yellow ambling in a circle. "Nothin' for it, I've gotta go after her. See over there?"

Beartooth strained his eyes, blinked, gazed a long, quiet moment more, then shook his head. "I don't see nothin'."

Preacher stared into the distance. "Dang. She musta dropped it. I'm gonna have to find her and fast."

A harsh wind swept over them and blew the snowflakes

into whirling clouds that confused all direction. It brought a fierce chill to both mountain men. "You can't do that, Preacher. You'll get lost out there."

"No talkin' me out of it. Leastsomewise, we'll find that woman all friz up."

"More likely, we'll find *you* out there tomorrow, friz like a block of ice."

14

Preacher searched the ground near the tall, moaning fir trees with a sense of helplessness. He saw nothing. He had to work by feel in the billows of blowing snow. At last he admitted the worst possible case. The woman had wandered off among the trees. He returned to the wagons bent nearly double against the wind.

"That fool woman didn't drop her lantern. She took it off with her into that stand of fir," Preacher announced. Beartooth cursed hotly. "Yeah," Preacher agreed. "You could say that, and in spades, too. I'll have to get Thunder and go after her. Get me a lantern from one of the pilgrims, Beartooth."

"Sure enough. And a couple of extra buffalo robes."

Their activities awakened Cora Ames and the Reverend Bookworthy. Preacher explained that Mrs. Yates had misplaced her son, Johnny, and had blundered outside the wagons searching for him. "I'm goin' after her before she freezes solid."

"That woman never was wrapped too tightly," Reverend Bookworthy observed, coming as close as he ever had to using the mountain man vernacular.

Cora caught it and, despite the seriousness of the situation, responded amusedly. "Why, Reverend, I do think Preacher and his friends have had an influence on you."

Reverend Bookworthy garrumphed and huffed and stalked off to his wagon to take shelter from the increased storm. A small figure shuffled up, to reveal himself as a shame-faced Johnny Yates. Tears welled in the boy's eyes as he admitted his harmless prank that had suddenly turned dangerous.

"I—I'm sorry. I just wanted to get away from her for a while. I was gonna sleep in the little tent with Chris and Nick. They're so much more fun than the kids in the Missionary Alliance."

Preacher took the boy's thin, bony shoulder in one big, hard hand. "I know what you're gettin' at, boy. But you should have told your ma."

Johnny's eyes went wide and the tears spilled at last. "She wouldn'a let me. She says they ain't one of us, ain't been saved. That they're not washed in the Blood an' so not fit company. B-but, I like them."

"For now, then, you'd best go back with them. I'll find yer mother, son," Preacher advised.

Mounted on a protesting Thunder, Preacher left the circle of wagons to search for Martha Yates. Before he departed, he left a charge with his companions. "Find out who th' hell left that gap betwixt wagons."

Unlike the inexperienced woman, who had held the lantern high and blinded herself to her surroundings, Preacher kept the dim yellow glow down close to his mount's legs. The candle cast enough light for him to pick up the prints left in the snow by Mrs. Yates. Those, he noted, were rapidly filling with new fall and drift. Thunder snorted and threw long plumes of steam into the night.

Preacher rode on for half an hour. By careful note of the characteristics of rock formations and tree shapes, he came to the conclusion that the Yates woman wandered in a wide circle. He drew his big knife and put a blaze on a tree to check his assumption. Ten of Thunder's strides further on, he cut bark on another. He repeated it as he followed the tracks.

Sure enough, about an hour later, when he came to a spot where he felt certain he had passed before, he checked for any blaze marks, and found one. The tree was some sixty feet to his right, the yellow-white of the bared cambium layer a pale smear in the darkness. The befuddled woman had to be walking an inward spiral, Preacher decided. Should he cut across and intercept her?

A sudden increase in the force of the wind decided him against it. Stinging particles of snow, mixed with sleet, lashed at his exposed face. Himself confused for a moment, Preacher sat still on Thunder's broad back. After a hundred heartbeats, an imperceptible change in pressure occurred. Preacher didn't notice at first. Not until the snowflakes ceased to whirl and filtered straight down. Preacher was stiff with cold. His fingers and toes tingled and ached with the threat of frostbite. He longed to turn back, seek warmth and continue the search in the morning.

He couldn't do that. The face of that frightened little boy hovered before him. He couldn't let Johnny Yates down. But, more than that, his own honor goaded him on. He had given his word. Besides, the sky seemed to be lighter above. The black bellies of the larger snow clouds had moved on. Preacher blinked and then roused himself when his eyes picked out the tiny, pale pinpricks of starlight.

Preacher waited with legendary patience while the sky cleared. Slowly the banked and drifted snow took on an internal glow, frosty white, from the celestial rays, augmented by the fat presence of a three-quarter moon. Now the advantage had shifted to Preacher. He set out at a faster pace, for the moon's position told him it had to be around two in the morning. Thunder nodded and snorted his approval.

Time had grown short. No doubt the Yates woman would have done something foolish. Something else, Preacher corrected himself. The tracks he followed grew fresher, deeper.

After another hour, up ahead, Preacher made out the soft glow of a lantern, its candle nearly burned down. It began to sputter and flicker fitfully as he drew near. With a start, Preacher realized that the light was unmoving. Had she fallen?

A dozen strides brought Thunder up to the lantern. It rested on the top of the snow, which had mounded up against a low ridge with squiggles across its surface like waves in a sea. Preacher dismounted and went forward. No sign of the woman. He took another step . . . and sank out of sight below the snow. He rolled, arse over ears, to the bottom of a dry wash. Floundering in a suffocating miasma of powdery snow, Preacher knew at once what had happened. The early, heavy, wet snow had bent limber aspen branches over the wash and the later sleet had covered that so that it had frozen in place, forming a fragile platform. Later snowfall had covered this trap. First, Mrs. Yates had blundered into it, then he followed. He knew also that he had to save himself before he could look for the missing woman.

Preacher found himself on the rocky bottom of the draw. He moved his arms with great effort and began to work the compacted snow away from his face. He needed room to breathe. Ice crystals, from sleet that had fallen earlier, made his eyes sting. The desperate need for open spaces threatened to overwhelm Preacher as he forced the oppressive weight of snow away from his head.

He rested only a second when he had finished that, then started to free his torso. Preacher knew that he had to tunnel out before the flakes that had fallen in after him had time to compact. Then there was the woman. She might not have as much time left as he did. He would have to get to the top of this mess, find where Mrs. Yates had fallen through the crust, and then burrow back down to pull her free of the thick, white blanket.

Preacher began a swimming motion, thrusting upward. The compacted snow clung stubbornly to his legs. He thought a moment, began to scissor-kick, pointed the toes of his moccasins, and tried again. He moved. Hardly a foot yet it was progress. Another sweeping, pulling maneuver . . . another foot gained. Now he could shove against the snow below his feet.

He gained two feet the next time. On the fourth try, his fingers broke free into open air. One last effort and his head popped out. His brows, lashes and mustache wore a crust of frozen crystals. Sputtering, Preacher worked his way clear of his icy trap. For a long minute, he sat, spread-legged, bent over, heaving for breath. Slowly he became aware of a growing yellow glow to the east.

"Not possible," he dismissed aloud. He could not have been down there for what remained of the night.

Still the light grew. Preacher looked around him for some sign of where Mrs. Yates had fallen through the crust. He could see no dimple or disturbance of any sort. Only the now extinguished lantern on the edge of the drop-off. The grating crunch of a footfall on the crust came to his ears. He looked up, toward the dim light. His jaw sagged in disbelief.

"Whatever are you doing out here, Mr. Preacher?" Martha Yates asked as she approached, lantern held high overhead.

"Look—lookin' for you, ma'am. You wandered out of the corral," he stated the obvious dumbly.

"I'm looking for my boy. Johnny is lost out here."

"No, ma'am, he's not. He's safe an' sound inside the wagons. He wanted to bunk down with two of them refugee boys, Chris an' Nick."

Martha's lips pursed in disapproval in the dim lantern glow. "I do not approve. They are not . . . like us."

Preacher didn't see it that way. "They're no different than your Johnny. Jist boys."

Her lips compressed in a hard line of stubbornness. "That may be from your point of view. But then, you are not one of us either."

An' glad of it, Preacher thought, then nodded toward the dead lantern. "Your lamp, ma'am. I fell through the snow into that wash. Thought you might have also."

"No. I left that here to guide me back. I had brought a spare along. I thought the search might be a long one."

Preacher grunted acknowledgment of that and roused himself gingerly. He worked his way back toward solid ground. While he did, it came to him why she had not fallen into the wash. Her slight build wouldn't carry enough weight to cause her to break through the icy crust like he had. When he reached the place where Thunder waited, he turned back to Martha Yates.

"I've some spare buffalo robes. There's not much sense in us tryin' to get back to the wagons in what's left of the night. I came upon a sort of overhang back a ways. We can go there, I'll build a fire and we'll wait it out."

She agreed with a nod and they started off, Preacher leading Thunder by the reins. He found the shelter from the still-sharp north wind and set about locating dry branches. Preacher's fingers moved with practiced skill over tinder, flint, and steel. The first sparks were whirled away in the wind. On the third try, they landed in the wad of milkweed down and Preacher nursed them to life.

When a tiny flame bloomed, he edged the white strands under a tent of kindling, which caught rapidly. Martha Yates had been watching him intently in the dim light of her lantern. Now she clapped her hands delightedly.

"You have amazing abilities, Mr. Preacher. And you make them seem so easy."

"It is easy, once you get the hang of it. An' the name's Preacher, ain't no 'Mister' about it."

"Uh—yes, of course—ah—Preacher. Will we be safe here?"

"Safer than many places in the High Lonesome. Now, you just hunker down, put that buffalo robe over you, head and all, hair side in, and turn your back to the wind. Nothin' to it. Come mornin', we'll be back with the wagons right an' proper."

A scandalized expression darkened Martha Yates's face. "Won't people talk? I mean, our being out here alone, all night?"

"Ain't much night left," Preacher observed indifferently. "An' I can guarantee a good hard look from me'll discourage any of that sort of talk."

"Umm—yes, I can see that," Mrs. Yates said a moment before her head drooped and she fell into a deep, exhausted sleep.

Nighthawk saw them approaching first. He and Dupre had heard two, widely spaced gunshots near daybreak and judged that Preacher was taking advantage of his successful search to bring in a little fresh meat. Beartooth agreed.

"Reckon he found her right enough. Likely too far off to make it back durin' the night. Jist like Preacher to take the chance to bring in a couple of deer or such."

Preacher proved his friends right half an hour later when Nighthawk saw him and the woman emerge from the trees, walking ahead of Thunder, who had two young bull elk draped over his rump and saddle. That amount of meat would feed the lot of them through a couple of days.

"Plenty of good eating in those elk," Dupre remarked. "And sweet as the langouste the fisherfolk along the Gulf bring from the depths."

Beartooth removed his fox skin hat and scratched his head. "What's a langosto?"

"A saltwater dwelling shellfish," Dupre explained. "In the same general family with shrimp and crayfish, only much larger."

"Crawdaddies?" Beartooth squalled. "Lord, that's disgustin'. They's fishbait."

"Your English progeny call langostos lobsters, Beartooth," Nighthawk informed the huge mountain man. "And they are all the rage back East."

"Not to this chile, they ain't. Giant crawdads. Ugh!"

Nighthawk rolled his eyes. "So much for trying to enlighten the great unwashed."

Dupre joined the funning. "Right to the point, Nighthawk. This one is indeed the unwashed."

"There you go badgerin' me about my takin' baths. Well, I won't do it, won't, won't, won't."

"Won't what?" Preacher asked as he reached his companions.

"Take a bath," Beartooth replied in a wounded tone. "I'm not gonna do it. At leastwise, not until come blossom time in May an' I can cut myself outta these longhandle drawers."

Preacher treated Beartooth to a thousand-mile stare. "You amaze me, Beartooth. I was jist thinkin' that a nice, steamin' hot tub would feel right relaxin' after all this snow." Martha Yates had gone on past the mountain men to where her son stood with contrite expression, expecting at the least a stinging bottom for this escapade. That gave Preacher free rein to speak his mind.

"Fool woman took two lanterns out there with her. Left one of them on the edge of a dry wash that was filled up with drifted snow. Like to kilt myself searching for her on the bottom."

"How'd you get on the bottom?" Dupre asked shrewdly.

"You would have to ask. 'Cause I fell in, idjit." Then Preacher went on to describe his ordeal. He concluded with, "Then to add insult to injury, that fool woman comes walkin' up to me right as rain and nowhere near buried in snow."

Cora Ames wandered over from her wagon about that time, arms crossed over the thick, blanket-material coat she wore against the cold. "I thought it was spring out here?" she remarked, making a question of it.

Preacher touched thick fingers to the brim of his hat. "It is, Miss Cora. That'll probably be the last heller we see until, oh . . . late October."

"We'll be leaving soon, then?" Her eagerness was obvious.

Preacher studied on that for a while, as though for the first time. "Not for a while, Miss Cora. Not today, nor prob'ly tomorrow."

"And why not?" she asked with a tiny stamp of a shapely foot.

"There'll be some bodacious drifts in the narrow parts of the pass. Wouldn't do to hitch up to go only a mile or so and be stuck by the snow."

"But, isn't there something that can be done about it?" Cora's impatience grew more agitated.

"Yes, there is. We can sit tight right here and let 'er melt."

"We have our mission to the Cheyenne to fulfill," she countered.

"No, you don't. I've done told you an' told you. That's completely out. Too dangerous. And now we have these leftovers from that other train. You all have to be settled somewhere safe."

Cora gave Preacher a melting look of her own before she turned away with a predictable retort. "Oh, you men are all impossible."

Preacher's ears burned as his companions chuckled at his discomfort. "I can certain sure say the same thing about women folk," he grumbled. Then he put a big hand to his chin, worrying the bare skin where his beard had been, as he did when he sought to bring forth a great idea.

"'Hawk, Dupre, Beartooth, we gotta do something to take these folks minds off the delay. I think I have the answer."

"Do tell. What's that?" Nighthawk quipped.

"I'm gonna give them what they want . . . in a way, that is. I'm gonna call 'em all together and describe to them their paradise."

"Where you gonna find them that, Preacher?" Beartooth demanded.

Preacher got a sly look, and waggled a finger under Beartooth's nose. "You jist hide an' watch an' you'll hear all about it."

Twenty minutes later, all of the misguided pilgrims Preacher had taken under his wing gathered in the center of the circled wagons. They chattered among themselves, asking the reason for the summons. That ended abruptly when Preacher stepped up onto the top of a flour barrel and raised his arms above his head.

"Folks, I've been studyin' on something for the last few days, since we all joined up. I know of a perfect place, to the north and west of Trout Crick Pass. A lush valley, with plenty of grass for graze, trees to build cabins, a good water supply, even some flats that can be put to the plow," Preacher made a persimmon pucker at the flavor of that word, "to put in gardens an' even some grain. It's well sheltered for winters."

That sounded like what they'd been told about Oregon, so Flora Sanders burbled happily, "Why, that's exactly what we have been looking for."

Falicity Jones, Bobby Gresham, and the others from that train nodded agreement. Even some among the missionaries began to show interest. Then the pulpit voice of the Reverend Thornton Bookworthy boomed out.

"Where, exactly, is this place, my good sir?"

"I wintered there. It's far off the beaten path, where you'll be safe from Indians and anyone else wanderin' the High Lonesome. I told you I'd be leaving you off at the tradin' post. Well, if you accept this valley, I will agree to lead the way and my friends an' I will help you all get set up."

"What are you going to do after that, Preacher?" Cora Ames asked suspiciously.

"I'll be goin' after Ezra Pease, to make certain ever'one out in these mountains can have a safe time of it."

Spatters of conversation broke out over that. Asa Pettibone stepped forward. "What if we accept this offer, Preacher?"

Preacher clapped his hands and shot a wide-eyed gaze at the organist. "Why, exactly what I told you. Now, you folks talk it over amongst you an' I want your answer by the time the snows melt."

After the wondering pilgrims had wandered off, Dupre stepped close to Preacher. "I noticed that you neglected to mention that this splendid place of yours is also miles away from any large Indian camp, *mon ami.*"

Preacher pulled a droll expression. "Come to think of it, I might have left that out . . . accidental-like, so's to speak."

It took three days to clear the route through the mountains to Trout Crick Pass. When the wagons left, Preacher had his answer. They would "allow" him to lead them to his chosen refuge. Only Reverend Thornton Bookworthy showed an uncharitable reluctance, for a man of the cloth, to accept the refugees from the plundered wagon train, according to Preacher's lights.

15

Forty miles south of Preacher and his band of green-horns, it did not snow. Silas Phipps and his orphans made good time as a result. Unbeknownst to Silas or Preacher, only a day's travel separated them. When both parties stopped for their nooning, less than that divided them from a fateful encounter. It was then that Gertha, the ten-year-old, came to Helen and Ruth while they went about preparing the meal. The child told a frightful tale of abuse by Silas.

Ruth remained silently furious. Slowly she regained her composure enough to speak in a tight, angry tone. "This is too much. We have to make Phipps stop."

Peter had overheard part of the conversation and his high, smooth brow furrowed. "You're right. Someone is gonna get bad hurt."

Helen, the compassionate, studious one, brushed at a lock of auburn hair. "Your back, Peter. Isn't that hurt enough?"

The slender boy shrugged. "It's nothing, not along side what I mean. One of you . . . one of us, is gonna get hurt awful bad if someone doesn't stop him."

"You're right, Peter," Ruth said coldly. "Only what can we do?"

Peter thought on it a while. "We're bound to find someone who believes us. Some grownups *do* listen to kids."

Helen considered that. "That's true. Only what if they go and ask Phipps and believe him and don't do anything else?"

Gertha offered her solution. "We could tie him up some time when he is drunk. All of us could run away."

"To where?" Ruth asked. Gertha only shrugged.

They offered several more suggestions on how to achieve their goal. None of them seemed entirely satisfactory. In conclusion, Ruth pinched her brow in determination and her lips became a firm, straight line as she offered a final solution. "If nothing we can come up with works, then I'll . . . I'll take a butcher knife to him."

Ezra Pease and his gang of cutthroats set up business in the small valley in the core of the Mummy Range. For hardened criminals, more accustomed to town life, they did a fair job of building some roomy, brush-covered lean-tos and frame a cabin. By that time, men sent out under Hashknife to spread word of their enterprise had made contact and Indians from miles around came to trade for guns and whiskey.

Business grew brisk. Plumes of smoke from the outlaws' cookfires mingled with those of their visiting customers. A friendly atmosphere prevailed, though that did not prevent Pease from assigning men to keep a constant vigil over the Indians in the valley and those who left with new weapons.

"You can never be too careful," he reminded those he dispatched on these duties. "An Indian's mood can change in an instant. They're like children. I learned that much my first trip out here." Pease refrained from mentioning that it was his only trip into the High Lonesome.

Ezra Pease brightened considerably on the morning that the first Cheyenne rode into the valley. He had worried lest the savages' unfriendly greeting of them constituted a unified position. Apparently not, he decided as a feather-bedecked sub-chief and some fifteen warriors trotted their ponies down into the camp area and made a friendly sign.

"I am called Little Knife," the sub-chief announced in sing-song English. "Do you have coffee?"

"That we do, Chief," Titus Vickers responded, giving out a dazzling salesman's smile. "Y'all dismount and tether your ponies. We keep a pot hot and ready all the time."

Little Knife gestured with his chin to the tarpaulin-covered mounds. "We drink coffee, make talk, trade for guns."

Vickers did not like the sound of that "make talk." He worried it around his head a while, then elected to grab the wildcat by its tail. "What'd you have in mind to talk about, Chief?"

Curved lines deepened around the mouth of Little Knife, and frown furrows gullied his forehead. "It is said that you also trade for the burning water. Is this so?"

Even Titus Vickers could clearly hear the disapproval in the voice of Little Knife. "Oh, sure, Chief Little Knife, we keep a little around. To seal trades when we make them, just a token, you see?"

Little Knife, dismounted now, produced a scowl. "Running Fox took from here a small barrel of whiskey."

"Only a keg. A small keg," Vickers hastened to reassure the displeased chief. "That's seven and a half gallons."

Little Knife had no idea how much a gallon might be, but he knew one thing. "It is enough to make every man with Running Fox sick. They go crazy. Shoot at each other. Two men stab each other. It is not good." He drew himself up to his full six feet, Hudson's bay blanket wrapped tightly around his shoulders. "You will stop giving whiskey to my people. No more. Stop."

"Sorry. Can't do that, Chief Little Knife. It's part of the deal. You trade for guns, you trade for whiskey. Not one without the other."

Little Knife might not have heard him. He turned to order his men to search out the whiskey and destroy it. Titus Vickers had been on the frontier long enough to have learned the rudiments of the Cheyenne language. Vickers let his gut think for him. Swiftly he reached to the sash around his waist and drew a double-barrel pistol.

Vickers's first ball punched through the right forearm of Little Knife before it burst his heart. At once sidearms appeared in the hands of the gang members who surrounded the Cheyenne warriors. When the gunfire echoed away to silence, not an Indian lived.

His face ashen, Ezra Pease rushed up to the scene of slaughter. "You acted precipitously, my friend. And I fear that to be a mistake. We must dispose of the bodies and any sign they came in here."

They would find out later exactly how big a mistake it had been.

Preacher thought he had seen it all. Yet, what he saw through his spy-glass beat hell out of anything past or present. "What the Betsy-be-damned are Dakota warriors of the Raven Owners' Society doing this far south?" he asked himself in a whisper. "An' so deep in the high country?"

Settled down for a long spell, Preacher continued to observe the warriors, who rode along with the casual air of men well-pleased with themselves. When they drew nearer, he could make out more detail. All of them were armed with brand-spanking new rifles. Here and there, suspended from thongs around the necks of the owners, he saw untempered bullet molds. Several among the band passed a stoneware jug around.

Pease and his damned guns for sale. Preacher had seen enough. Carefully he edged his way back to where he had left Thunder to crop fresh spring grass. There, he confided his discontent to the patient animal. "Set out to do a good turn for someone, an' sure's there's heat in July, there's some ol' bull buffalo ready to dump a big patty on yer head. We got our work staked out right dandy for us, Thunder."

In the saddle, Preacher ruminated on what he could do.

First off, he had to make good and sure those pilgrims he an' the others were escorting stayed clear and hell far away from those proddy Dakota. Quietly he walked Thunder in the opposite direction from the Sioux braves. After a good two miles, to allow for the travel of sound, he put heels to Thunder's flanks and headed back for the wagon train at a fast trot.

Preacher would have gotten along well with ol' Bobby Burns regarding the best laid plans thing. At least that's what he thought when late in the afternoon there came a sudden *ki-yi* yell from behind the wagons on the trail and Dakota braves popped up among the surrounding trees.

"How'd they do it?" he asked of no one in particular. "I plumb left them behind."

"Must have had some braves following their back-trail," Dupre suggested.

"That or jist recovered from being passed out drunk, and cut my sign," Preacher grumbled as the wagons began to circle.

Arrows flew around them. Preacher cursed the foul luck that had delivered them into the hands of the Dakotas. For all the precautions he and his friends had taken, the hostiles had found the wagons and gave every appearance of hankering for a passer of scalps. More arrows showered on the wagons, then the Dakota opened up with their new rifles.

"Keep yer heads down, folks," Preacher called out urgently. "We're in for one whale of a fight."

Sits Tall let a broad, white smile split his coppery face as he gazed down on the approaching wagons. He had been wise to send men to observe their backtrail. They had seen sign left by a white man, not many, and those hard to find. A man who knew the mountains. Like the sort who had taken to leading more of their white brothers into where they did not belong. Perhaps this one did the same.

It would pay to find out, Sits Tall decided. He knew a way to quickly reach the main trail to the pass. He and his warriors could be in position to cut off the wagons, maybe even before the clever guide returned to them. His gamble had paid off. Although they had given too much for the rifles and ammunition five sleeps ago, now they had come upon enough whites in their rolling lodges to provide a quantity of loot that would get them even more of the precious firearms. The time to strike had come, he gauged, as the wagons drew closer.

Sits Tall raised his ceremonial lance over his head and turned his gaze from side to side, assured by the way his warriors made their weapons ready. When the last bow string had been drawn and the last rifle cocked, Sits Tall looked front again and swiftly slashed his lance downward. At once, his Raven Owners charged.

"Ki-yi! Ky-ky-ky-ky!" Broken Feather yipped beside his old friend Sits Tall.

"Huka-hey!" Sits Tall joined the growing volume of war cries.

This would be a very good day . . . and one where the whites would do the dying.

"Here they come," Ernie, one of the hired drivers, observed unnecessarily as the Dakota braves plunged down the hill toward them.

The wagons had no time to circle when the Dakotas hit them the first sweep. The Indians rode along the sides of the wagons, firing into them, albeit wildly. None of the pilgrims took a hit Preacher noticed as he urged greater speed from the team driven by Buck Dempsey. Gradually the circle closed. The Dakota pulled up in the meadow below them.

"They'll be comin' back," Preacher warned.

After a short palaver, the Sioux advanced in a line abreast

to barely inside rifle range. Preacher and his fellow mountain men easily picked out the leader; the one with the fancy lance. This one put moccasin heels into the ribs of his pony and walked it forward a few paces, another lean, handsome brave at his side. Beartooth, who spoke excellent Dakota, elected to open with an offer of peace.

"We are not in your land. We mean you no harm. Let us go in peace and we'll let you go in peace."

This seemed to anger Sits Tall. He barked out a harsh string of Dakota. "I am called Sits Tall. You are few, to our many. We will hurt you badly."

Beartooth stood his ground, arms across his chest. "Maybe so, maybe not, Sits Tall. I am called Beartooth. So far you ain't hurt any of us, not even women and children. If you try to harm us now, you'll find out how few we really are . . . to your regret."

Beartooth discovered he had gone too far when Sits Tall's expression changed to one of pure rage. His voice rang with his fury. *"Hu ihpeya wicayapo!"*

Preacher knew enough Dakota to understand the meaning of the obscene Dakota war challenge. He took Beartooth's place as he made a cleaned up translation to those around him. "He's callin' on his warriors for a total defeat of us."

"Why, that black-hearted bastard," Buck Dempsey growled.

Preacher had his own way of answering. *"Maka kin le* (I own the earth)! *Huka hey! Huka he!"* he added as he drew one of his four-barrel pistols.

"Huka he!" Preacher repeated.

It's a good day to die! echoed in Nighthawk's head. "Speak for yourself, white man," he tossed jokingly to Preacher.

The double load in Preacher's first barrel cleared Broken Feather from his saddle, shot through the heart and liver. Sits Tall whirled his pony and sought to gain ground. Without need to be told, the other Sioux made ready to charge.

They came the instant Sits Tall reached them and reversed his pony. This time they formed a deadly ring around the stalled wagons and opened up with accuracy little better than before.

"We're in for it now," Beartooth grumbled to Preacher. "Why in hell did you have to use that particular challenge?"

"Seemed like the thing to do. Look to your powder and shot, Beartooth, these fellers ain't givin' up easy."

"Hell no, they ain't givin' up easy," Beartooth said an hour later after two attacks had been repulsed. "What we need is a reg'lar goose downer. Wet up that powder and soften bow strings right smart."

"Hold that good thought, Beartooth," Dupre responded as he took careful aim on a charging Dakota.

With whirlwind swiftness, the warriors threw themselves at the wagons a third time. Around they circled, firing with little hope of hitting a target, so long as the flatlanders kept their heads down. Or so Preacher saw it. Sue Landry loaded for him and Cora Ames. In spite of the confusion created by the dust-billowing swirl of the hostiles, he had to take time to admire Cora's marksmanship.

So far she had hit two of the Dakota warriors, one seriously. When each shot went home she had muttered something under her breath, a prayer for her target, Preacher supposed. Then, when a third brave who had played possum to sneak up on the wagons reared up at close quarters and Cora blew off the top of his head, her words came louder.

"Take that, you heathen bastard."

Preacher couldn't help blurting through his laughter, "Why, Miss Cora."

Cheeks flamed scarlet, Cora Ames made a face. "Can't a girl have any privacy?"

She handed the rifle to Sue Landry, who said feelingly, "Atta girl, Cora."

Preacher fired again and spun a pudgy Dakota off his saddle pad. A hoot from Sits Tall and the warriors streamed away. Quickly as it had begun, the fighting ended. Slowly people peeped out of their wagons, or rose from firing positions under the boxes. A frightened mule had kicked forearm-sized billets of burning wood from the cookfire and Patience Book-worthy hurried to spill a bucket of water over two of them.

"Yer learnin', folks. Yer doin' jist fine," Preacher praised. "I think we've got 'em fit to a standstill." He studied the re-treating backs of the Dakotas. "Don't reckon they'll be back until some time in the night, maybe not until dawn."

"Why's that, Preacher?" Asa Landry asked.

"Like I done tole you a hunnard times, Mr. Landry. Injuns is notionable. They ran us down the line, an' then attacked three times in a row. Didn't get anythin' accomplished. That smacks of weak medicine to an Injun. They'll draw off to cook up some grub, dance and drum some and sing up some more good medicine. Speakin' of which, if you ladies don't mind? I think all that fightin's whipped up an appetite for everyone."

Shortly after the last of the Dakotas disappeared beyond the notches at the upper and lower end of the trail through the valley meadow, the faint, rhythmic, heartbeat thump of a drum invaded the consciousness of everyone in the train. Nighthawk began to tap a finger in time with it on the butt-stock of the rifle he cleaned. Preacher soon noticed that even Beartooth, who was rumored to have a touch of Cherokee or Chickasaw in him, began to rock his moccasined right toe with the tempo.

Funny how most white folk either heard them with dread, or didn't react in any manner to the drums. Yet, given the lest smidgen of Injun blood and the rhythm got to a feller right fast, Preacher mused. He saw to cleaning his own weapons, as he had advised the greenhorns to do, and thought on the meaning of this unprovoked attack by Indians far from their usual stomping grounds.

About the time a plate of thick stew came into Preacher's hands, he had the beginnings of a wild idea. One that in-volved a lot of risk, but one he saw as bearing a great deal more promise for their future. Provided he could carry it off without being killed.

16

Dupre thought Preacher's idea to be a crazy scheme. He minced no words in telling the mountain man so when he came upon Preacher as he worked on some gourds he had found in a narrow gulley. Preacher chuckled and patted his older friend on one shoulder.

"B'god, it's worked before, ain't it? Remember that time those Blackfeet had you an' me an' Lame Jack Riley cornered up in the Blue Smokes country? You an' Lame Jack slipped out an' done it whilst I kept the fire stoked up and talked to two bedrolls stuffed inside blankets. Skeert the livin' hell outta them Blackfeet. An' they knows the mountains. These Dakota don't. Likely to have 'em mussin' up their pretty beaded breech cloths iffin I do it right."

"I agree," Nighthawk put in his penny's worth. "They hadn't the opportunity to make an accurate count of how many we number. Come deep darkness, they'll not see one man slip away. If anyone can accomplish this, Preacher can."

Beartooth clinched it with his offer. "Sure you don't want anyone along for company?"

Preacher cut his eyes around the group and smiled broadly at Dupre. "There you are. It's settled. I'll be leavin' around ten o' the clock. The Dakota will be drummin' an' singin' up a storm about then. Any watchers they put out will be gettin' bored and droopy eyed. I'll catch the ones behind us first, that should start some confusion when they go rushin' in among their brothers. Then another dose ought to get the whole batch on the run."

True to his word, Preacher slipped unnoticed out of camp at ten that night. The Dakota had not the slightest idea what awaited them.

Preacher glided through the chest-high grass in a whisper of near silence. He had with him the gourds he had found near the circled wagons, left from last summer. He had spent a long, careful time preparing them in a special way. They would play a big part in his plan to break the spirit of the hostiles. The grade increased steadily as he advanced toward the beeline to the south of the meadow.

With all the skill he possessed, Preacher wormed his way through the stand of alder saplings and over the crest of the low hill. Once more he went over his plan. Ordinarily, his repertoire of animal and bird sounds would not fool any Indian over the age of ten or eleven. But, added to some special tricks he had prepared, he figured he might get these Dakota thinking something else was afoot besides a nasty mountain man. It all centered on those gourds.

Half of them had rags stuffed down hard around the fuse and cap stuck in them. The others did not. That way, he knew, some would go off with a big, loud bang, while the rest would produce a flash, a whumph, and a whole lot of smoke. Preacher made his way to where the watchers had set up a small camp. Only a handful of the braves had remained on this end of the trail. They had a fire and a small drum. Half their number must be keeping an eye on the wagons.

This would make it easy. He'd use the smoke bombs on these braves. Chuckling silently over the anticipated results, Preacher aimed for the rear of the Sioux camp. There he found the horses and made ready for his presentation. First, though, he had to find the pony guard.

Preacher located him after a patient fifteen minutes wait. A slender young man in his late teens, he squatted with his back against the bole of a large fir, head constantly turning, eyes alert to any hint of movement. Preacher watched longer, to determine any pattern. Slowly it emerged. The youth rose from his position after a quarter hour and moved to a rock, where he could cover the angle previously overlooked. This would be a tough one, Preacher decided.

It tasked all of Preacher's skills to sneak up on the competent, though youthful, warrior. In the last two minutes he held his breath as he closed the distance in a rush. His angle of attack put him atop the boulder against which the boy leaned. Preacher's moccasin made a small scraping sound as he slithered down the lichen-frosted stone face to land feet-first on the top of the Dakota's head.

A soft grunt came from the boy's mouth. Preacher continued on down, driving his knees into the exposed chest. Air rushed from a contorted mouth, the lad stiffened, convulsed, and went slack in unconsciousness. At once, Preacher set to work.

Bent low, he freed the ponies from their grazing tethers. Then, from a tinder box he extracted a live coal, touched it to the fuses in the gourds he held, then hurled them into the general area of the crude camp. At once he moved away from where he stood, burrowed into the underbrush, and made ready. When the first whumph came, he loosed a deep, soulful cough, followed by the hiss and roar of a cougar. The second projectile went off. Shouts of alarm rose from the resting warriors. Again, Preacher did his cougar act. The third bomb exploded. The ponies panicked. With a grunt of amusement, Preacher decided to throw in a little grizzly bear.

"Wahanksica!" a warrior shouted. *"Wahanksica!"*

With a single mind, the hostile Dakotas set off after their horses. Chuckling to himself, Preacher retraced his steps to where he had ground-reined Thunder. In a matter of minutes, he trotted toward the camp ahead, where the larger fire burned, the bigger drum throbbed, and more Dakota waited to be an audience for his next performance.

Preacher found his quarry easily enough. He screwed a ground anchor into the turf and tied off Thunder, then equipped himself with an armload of homemade bombs. As he had done before, he headed for where the ponies had been picketed. To his surprise, he found a boy of about fourteen guarding them. On his first war party, no doubt, Preacher reckoned. He set his deadly gourds aside and slipped up on the lad easily. With the butt of a pistol, he knocked the youth unconscious with a single blow to the head. He eased the body to the ground and went back for his explosives.

The Dakota sang a war song as Preacher laid out his bombs. These had longer fuses than the first set, and he lighted them as he went around the camp. He saved two to hurl in among the warriors. The drum stopped suddenly as Sits Tall rose from his cross-legged position on a blanket.

"Enough," he told his followers. "We must rest and be fresh to fight when the sun comes."

Not likely, Preacher thought to himself as he made his way back to the horses. A harsh panther cough and snarl set the ponies off in a restless trot. Wolf howls followed and then the first of the bombs went off. The Dakota's mounts stampeded. Around the fire, pandemonium erupted. The explosions shook the ground. Preacher turned back then, lighted the remaining pair of fuses and hurled the gourds into the camp.

They erupted seconds later and set off a wilder scramble. In the midst of it, he threw back his head and shouted his earlier challenge. "I own the earth!"

Preacher gave another panther cough and raced back to where he had left Thunder. A swift ride though the moonlit night brought him to the circle of wagons. Several of their out-facing sides still bristled with arrows. The folks would be able to get rid of them come morning, Preacher thought with satisfaction.

Early morning light showed evidence that the Dakota had given up any idea of an attack. No warriors lined the ridges, Preacher noted as he poured a second round of coffee into a tin cup. He cut his gray eyes left and right, seeking any hint of concealed braves in the tall meadow grass. He saw not the slightest presence.

"Well an' good," he rumbled as he sought the last of his Catlin clay pipes and a small pouch of tobacco.

Now was a good time for a smoke. Not even the powerful medicine of the Raven Owners' Society could prevail against the ghostly events of the night gone by, he reasoned with a touch of smugness. Best take advantage of it, before they got their nerves reined in and their wind up again. To that end, he turned to the late awakeners who crawled muzzily from their bedrolls.

"You'd all best make it a quick breakfast. Menfolk set to harnessin' the mules. Dupre, 'Hawk an' Beartooth will git you lined out on the trail. I'm goin' ahead to sniff the ground."

Cora Ames had a newfound friend in Falicity Jones. They came forward to where Preacher stood by the fire. "We heard the awfulest sounds last night," Cora began. "We thought the Indians must have gotten drunk and set fire to their ammunition when the explosions started."

Preacher gave her a small, secret smile. "Dakota don't take much to drink, leastwise not so far. I'd say they ran up against some medicine too big for them to handle."

Falicity caught the twinkle in Preacher's eyes. "You're not going to tell us, are you?"

"Nothin' to tell, Miz Jones."

"Are they going to attack?" Cora inquired.

"Nope. I reckon whatever spirits troubled them last night got 'em headed back toward their sacred Black Hills. We be makin' the tradin' post come mid-day tomorrow."

Preacher put a slab of fried fatback between the halves of two biscuits and wrapped them in a square of neatly worked buckskin. He stuffed that in a coat pocket and headed for Thunder. Saddled up, he rode out of the bustling camp. Flora Sanders called after him with words sweet to his ears.

"I'll have a dried apple pie waiting for you tonight, Preacher."

Immediately when he crossed the forward ridge, Preacher saw confirmation that he had read the mood of the Dakotas correctly. Or rather, he saw not a sign of any of them. Scuffed ground and wide-spaced moccasin prints indicated that the Indians had left, and in some considerable disarray. Preacher chortled softly. Must have taken them most of the night to round up their ponies. No doubt the rest of it packing up to get out of there. Be a lot of drooping eyes among them bucks on the trail today. He touched boot heels to Thunder and continued his scout.

Beartooth and Nighthawk remained behind to do what they could to wipe out any sign of their passage once the wagons left the narrow trace through the soaring mountains. While they worked, Beartooth spoke of past events.

"Preacher was smart to pick this side approach to the pass. Only thing, none of us could have expected them Dakota. If Pease has men lookin' for us, it'd be on the main trail."

"That's a mouthful for you, Beartooth," Nighthawk observed. "Although I suspect you are right. Bad fortune. We will be out of it before long, though."

"Yep. Only I don't reckon those wagons will make it as soon as Preacher expects. A couple of them look to be on the edge of breakin' down."

Nighthawk made a face. "All we need."

"So true. I was lookin' forward to findin' my woman's people and settlin' in for a summer of buffalo huntin'."

Nighthawk rubbed his lean, hard belly. "I can taste a plate full of roasted hump. Did you know that the forest bison were all but hunted out before the white man came? It was rare that any of our people ever tasted that sweet, rich meat."

"That's bein' deprived some, I'd say."

"You know it, friend."

With their task completed in early afternoon, Nighthawk and Beartooth came unexpectedly upon the wagons. They had halted due to a broken wheel on one of the vehicles salvaged from the raid by Pease and his men. Also, Asa Pettibone's wagon had a cracked connecting bar in the running gear.

"Might have known it," Beartooth sighed in resignation. "We'll be stuck here a day at best."

Four large, sacred drums throbbed in the central clearing of the Cheyenne village. A huge fire burned, although it was mid-day. Cooking went on at other, smaller fires among the concentric circles of lodges. Boys ran foot races in imitation of the more serious adult contests to come after the Grand Council concluded its business. Others played at mock hunting or war. The little girls helped their mothers by washing vegetables, cutting strips of meat into cubes for stew, and stirring bubbling cauldrons. A number of the older female population, those in their teens, looked on with admiring glances at the youthful warriors, excluded from the council hearing that had gone on for the past three days.

Everyone said it would end some time before the sun went to sleep in the west. No one knew for sure. Occasionally, angry voices raised from behind the brush walls of the ceremonial lodge, its top open to the sky. When the messenger, bowed with fatigue, wended his way among the lodges toward the entrance to the council lodge, most of the boys gave off their games to follow along. The camp crier preceded him. The lathered pony stopped outside the brush arbor and snorted. His rider stared stupidly, as though dazed and unaware of where he had reached. Two young civil chiefs came out to confront him.

Slowly he slipped from his mount and staggered forward. He had ridden hard for three days and nights without sleep. When he entered, his message roused new shouts of outrage and anger.

"Little Knife killed by whites!" Stone Drum blurted. "I say we know who they are. Where is this?"

Blinking, the messenger recited all he knew. "Some white men made a large camp in a valley on the slopes of the White Top Mountains that face the Medicine Bows. They are many in number. It is said they come to trade guns with our people. Little Knife heard they had whiskey. He went to make them spill it on the ground. A man I know, who died later, rode with Little Knife. He was much wounded and escaped the whites that way. He saw Little Knife fall."

Mutters ran among the gathered chiefs. Heads nodded, an agreement formed. Stone Drum spoke for the council. "We are agreed, brothers? We must hunt down these white men and fight them until all die." He looked around and noted three chiefs who had club lodges of Dog Soldiers in their camps. He nodded to them. "You will gather your best men, have criers sent out at once. Let the Dog Soldiers deal with these evil men."

"I will go also," Falling Horse announced from near the entrance.

Stone Drum turned, looked hard at Falling Horse. "Yes. You will take up the war pipe and lead them, Falling Horse. Let not a white man escape."

In a flurry of activity, nearly a hundred Cheyenne Dog Soldiers and others who wanted to avenge Little Knife, had gathered food, weapons, and equipment. The feast would be delayed, though the women showed not a sign of disappointment that all their hard work had gone for nothing. They knew that this day it would be they who ate until their bellies swelled like that of a woman with child.

* * *

Silas Phipps came upon a narrow, winding pathway that led off the sorry trace he had been following shortly after their nooning. He called for Peter to halt the front wagon and hold fast. Phipps, a poor excuse for a frontiersman, still had a good sense of direction. He studied the lay of the land and forced his whiskey-dulled mind into activity.

Best he could judge, this could be a shortcut to the pass and that trading post he had heard of. Maybe they should turn off into it? On the other hand, he ruminated, the trail he followed was supposed to be the main fork that led to Trout Crick Pass. Further careful scrutiny revealed what appeared to be recent wheel marks. Someone had taken this way. That decided him, almost more so than the crying need to replenish his whiskey supply.

"We gonna be taking this trail," he commanded his orphan entourage.

"Aren't we on the right one?" Ruth asked from beside Peter.

"Leave questions like that to your betters, missy," Phipps snapped. "I say we go on this one, then this is the trail we take."

Inadvertently, Silas Phipps put his two wagons behind Preacher and the larger train. The youngsters' spirits rose at the awesome beauty of the steep canyon walls. Thickly wooded at the lower levels, a silvery stream, alive with jumping trout beckoned. Peter dreamed idly of better days, long gone by, when he fished from the banks of the Taunton River in Massachusetts. On hot summer days, he and his friends would strip off their clothes and jump into a cool, deep pool formed by a bend in the river. Life had been good then, before his ma and pa had died in a boat wreck during a storm.

Even acidic Silas Phipps mellowed a bit, lulled out of his bad humor by the beauty of their surroundings. Gradually, though, the peacefulness awakened his darkest urges. At day's end, unbeknownst to him, they had come within a morning's journey behind Preacher's pilgrims. Phipps had the itch something powerful after he had eaten and given up his tin plate to be washed by the girls. His watery black eyes searched out the object of his desire and fixed on her. Grunting, he pushed himself to his boots and walked over to Gertha.

He draped an arm around her slender shoulder and spoke disarmingly. "I've sort of taken a fancy to you, Gertha. You know that?" Gertha did not reply, only looked up at Phipps with big, solemn, frightened eyes. "Oh, my, yes. We have those skins the boys trapped to sell at the trading post, and I'm going to buy you something pretty. How about that?" Again, Gertha did not reply. "Yes, well. I want to show you how much I've come to favor you, so I'll expect you at my wagon after the others have been settled down for the night. You won't disappoint me, will you?"

She could but shake her head and dread the night.

17

With the wagons overhauled, the last leg to the trading post went without event. At Preacher's insistence, they re-supplied and pushed on. That didn't happen without loud objections from the missionaries. Preacher and Nighthawk traveled ahead. Preacher wanted to get a close look at the valley where he had wintered, to make certain no one else had settled in.

No one had, only the early blossoms in the April warmth. Preacher and Nighthawk split up and went out to hunt for game. He wanted to give the gospel-shouters a headstart on laying in supplies. Plenty of smoked meat would be a sizable contribution. Well he did, for the wagons rolled in four days later.

Dupre, still nursing his shoulder wound, and Beartooth organized the missionary men and supervised while they felled trees to build cabins. Domestic tranquility settled over the valley. It made Preacher uncomfortable. He set off to hunt for more game.

* * *

Preacher leveled the sights of his Hawken on the big bull elk that stood spraddle-legged, its head lowered into the silvery spring to drink. That's it, he thought, right behind the left leg. A gentle squeeze. The big .54 caliber rifle slammed into Preacher's shoulder with a familiar impact. The elk stiffened, all four legs splayed now, then went down. The hooves dug into the ground beneath the dying animal while Preacher approached.

It shuddered its last and went still. A perfect heart shot. Hardly any blood had spilled onto the ground. Preacher's sharp knife opened the veins of the neck and he wiped the blade clean before resheathing it. Then he went for Thunder. It would take the powerful Appaloosa horse to raise the animal for skinning and field dressing.

With that task completed, Preacher buried the offal to keep away scavengers and washed his bloodied arms and hands in the stream. He brought his packhorse and loaded the quarters of elk, wrapped in sections of the hide. Weary from four days of hunting, Preacher decided to head for home, visiting each of his earlier caches along the way, to retrieve the meat waiting there. If Nighthawk had equal luck, he speculated, the pilgrims would not need to hunt again before fall. Plenty of time to build cabins, to shut themselves in from the spectacular summer nights.

"Fool folks," Preacher grunted to himself. "Winter's the time to be closed in, out of the cold. Anyone knows that."

Sundown would not be near for another three hours when Preacher rode down a slope into a tiny vale where a camp had been set up. His keen vision picked out five disreputable looking ruffians lounging around a low fire. Two of them looked up incuriously when Preacher had covered about half of the distance to them.

"Hello the camp," Preacher called to them.

"Howdy, yerself. You be friendly?"

"That I am. Mind if I ride in and set a spell?"

"C'mon. We got coffee."

"Good. An' I could sure use a sup of Who-Shot-John, if

you've got any," Preacher suggested, curious as to the nature of these strangers.

"Nope. Don't bring whiskey in where there's Injuns about. Makes 'em plumb crazy if they git their hands on it."

Tight lines around Preacher's eyes relaxed some. Didn't sound like they were tied up with Ezra Pease. He walked Thunder down close to the fire and dismounted. His sweat and blood-stiffened buckskins rustled as he walked to the fire.

Coffee in hand, Preacher cut his eyes from man to man, studying their features. None seemed tensed to spring. The one who had spoken first opened the conversation.

"Name's Clower. Ya been huntin' I see."

"Yup. Name's Arthur." For some reason, Preacher's inner caution warned him to use his given name. "Never too early to put away meat for winter."

"Then yer not jist passin' through?" Frank Clower prompted.

"Tired of roamin'," Preacher kept up the fiction. "Got me a little cabin tucked away a piece from here. I usually go far afield like this so's to keep the game close to home in case of need."

"Good idee, Art," Clower said with irritating familiarity. "You boys trappin'?"

Clower shook his head. "Nope. Jist driftin' through."

"Picked some pretty country for it," Preacher observed.

"Right you are."

Preacher finished his coffee, it tasted like sour mud, and cleaned the cup. Then he turned to walk to Thunder. "Nice jawin' with you gents," he said over his shoulder before he put his attention to tightening Thunder's cinch strap, which he had loosened when he dismounted.

That's the moment three of them chose to jump him. He caught the movement from the corner of his eye. Preacher swung in time to plant a hard fist flush in the mouth of a small, pinch-faced thug that dumped Preacher's attacker flat on the ground. He put an elbow in the gut of another. Raw whiskey fumes gushed out of a corded throat. Preacher popped him on the side of the head and he dropped like a log. He advanced on the last one. By then the third hard case had his knife out.

"Hey, stupid!" Preacher shouted in the man's suddenly astonished face.

"I ain't stupid," the riff-raff protested.

"Yes, you are," Preacher teased.

"Why?"

"You brought a knife . . . to a gunfight," Preacher concluded as he yanked one of his four-shooters and let bang with a double-shotted load.

Cut down like a thin sapling, the vermin fell away in time to reveal Clower and the last man groping for their guns. Preacher waited for the faster of the pair to clear his waistband. Then he sent the ugly sucker off to meet his maker.

Howling, Frank Clower dived off to one side, rolled and came up shooting. A ball whizzed past Preacher's right ear. Preacher replied. His ball also missed. By then one of the buzzards he had punched out roused enough to reach for his pistol. Preacher had stepped away from his animals in the opening round to save the lives of Thunder and the packhorse.

Still groggy, the filth bag fired hastily. It popped through the loose portion of Preacher's coat on the left side. Two holes. Damn, Preacher thought. He quickly educated the lout with a ball to the chest. Then he turned back to Clower in time to see the black hole of a . 60 caliber muzzle pointed directly at his face.

Triumphant, Clower pulled the trigger. The big Hayes misfired. Preacher's four-shooter didn't. One of the balls caught Clower at the base of his throat. The other broke a collarbone and punched through the shoulder blade behind. Clower gurgled as he went slack-kneed and sagged to the ground. His free hand twitched and clawed at his wounds. Then, his eyes glazing, he tried to focus on the big man standing over him.

"Y-you be Preacher, ain't ye?" Clower asked.

"I be."

"That Arthur thing had me fooled for a moment. Smart, thinkin' it up so quick."

"Didn't think it up. My ma did."

"No foolin'?" Clower said through a froth of pink foam.

"Nope."

"I'll be danged. I'm dyin', right Preacher?"

"You are."

"Bury me?"

"You work for Pease?"

"Yeah. Though I'm regrettin' it right about now."

"Then I won't bury you. Not fit for proper puttin' away."

"You're a hard man, Preacher."

"I know it. Goodbye, Clower."

"Oh, God—God, it hurts so much."

Preacher watched silently until Clower gave up his spirit. Then he collected the weapons, loosely tied the surviving vagabond, and took their horses with him. He'd use them to carry meat back to the valley.

Preacher sensed their disapproval the moment he rode up to the busy center of activity. All it had taken was for the missionary folk to count the number of horses he led. They didn't give a hoot about the meat he had brought in. They could count, and they knew he had taken only one packhorse with him. As expected, Reverend Thornton Bookworthy expressed their disapproval.

"What happened to the men who owned these horses?" the rotund cleric demanded.

"They sort of suddenly got dead. An' they pro'lly didn't own them. More likely they stole 'em," Preacher answered him.

Reverend Bookworthy chose not to listen and believe. "That doesn't bother you at all?"

Preacher pulled out his coat to illustrate his point. "Yes, it does. One of them put a couple of holes in a perfectly good coat. They worked for Pease, who—unless you've forgot—is tryin' mighty hard to kill me."

That registered on the good reverend. "Do . . . his men know about this valley?"

"Not likely," Preacher answered lightly, coming off his prod. "I left one alive and afoot, to carry a message back to Pease. Told him I was comin' after him. Then I rode out, headin' north. By the time that feller gets to the pass and finds another horse, all sign of where I really went will be wiped out.

Bookworthy looked at the string of heavy-laden animals. "We're—ah—appreciative of the meat. The—er—smokehouse was completed in your absence and is already working."

"Humm," Preacher responded. "Smoked venison or elk haunch is right tasty. But I'd eat the thinner parts fresh, and right fast."

Reverend Bookworthy seemed bemused. "Yes—yes. I'll see to it right away." He wandered off, leaving Preacher with his load of meat.

Only scant minutes passed before men from among the missionaries came to relieve him of his burden. Preacher put Thunder in his private corral, the one he had built for the previous winter, and placed the others in the common pen. A barn had been laid out next to that, and framing for one wall already stood tall, raw and proud. *Civilization,* Preacher thought uncharitably.

His mood improved an hour later when Nighthawk came in with both of his horses complaining under enormous loads. The news the Delaware brought quickly restored Preacher's dark outlook.

"There is a large party of white men to the west. I cut their sign three days ago." He did not need to mention that as the reason he had come in late.

Preacher spoke through his scowl. "The bunch jumped me worked for Pease."

Nighthawk raised an eyebrow. "Oh? I won't ask why it is you have a whole skin."

"Thank you, Nighthawk. But my coat didn't fare near so good. Five of 'em. An' one told me before he expired, that they worked for Pease. Things, they is a heatin' up, ol' hoss."

"I'm inclined to agree. What do we do about it?" Nighthawk prompted.

"Nothin' for the time bein'. We got these pilgrims to edjicate," Preacher said with a snort.

Preacher heard more about his treatment of his would-be murderers after Reverend Bookworthy spread the story through his congregation. Cora Ames and several of the good women of the mission flock came to him to demand if he had provided proper Christian burial.

"What for?" he asked, clearly not understanding the reason for the question.

"I would assume that after brutally murdering five men . . . ," Patience Bookworthy ranted at him.

"Four. It was four men. I left one alive," Preacher defended himself.

"Four men, then. The least you could have done was to give them proper Christian burial."

Preacher could not believe what he had heard. "Waall, hell, ma'am, if you'll pardon the language, them fellers had just tried to kill me. Jumped me when my back was turned. Now, do you think that's a proper Christian thing to do? D'you think they had even a speakin' acquaintance with the moral way of doing things? Or that I owed them anything for their efforts?"

Patience must have bitten down on something sour from the look that came on her face. "Oooh, you're an abomination," she forced out. "You have a way of twisting everything a person says."

"Not at all, ma'am. Just pointin' out which way the wind blows."

To his astonishment, Cora Ames backed his stand. "He's right, you know. This isn't Philadelphia, or Boston, or New York. Life is harsh out here. Didn't those Indian attacks teach you anything?" A sudden, stricken expression washed over her. "Oh, I am so sorry. I shouldn't have spoken so harshly. I . . ."

Preacher found himself defending her. "No, you didn't, Miss Cora. Right to the point, I'd say."

"You would," Patience Bookworthy snapped, then stalked off.

With a more contrite tone, Preacher offered his amends. "I'm afraid my bullheadedness has gotten you on her bad side. Only thing is I didn't have a choice in how I handled them fellers. I did have with how I used my mouth."

Mischief lighted Cora's eyes. "If I'm in Patience's book of bad girls I think I'm in good company, Preacher. I'm glad you weren't injured."

Dumbstruck, Preacher watched, with mouth agape, as she walked to where the other women worked to prepare a meal for the laboring men of the new community.

With a week of construction and meat curing behind them, half of the missionary men and all of the boys over ten were attending a special school. It would be learning that could mean life or death in the isolated village that sprang up faster each day. The instructor was Preacher. His classroom the meadow and forested hills that surrounded the valley. He held a yellowish-white bulb in his hand and waved it under the noses of the more curious youths.

"This here is wild onion. An' no, it don't taste 'zactly like a regular one. But it'll do in a pinch. Some of you who've et with me an' the boys have tasted it in stew. They grow in clumps like you see here. Notice that the tops are flat, rather than round. There's another plant like 'em only with round tops an' whiter bulbs. Stay shy of those. They'll poison ya right terrible. Now, let's move on. There's wild turnips growin' here, along the bank of that crick. We'll look at them next."

An attentive audience accompanied Preacher to his next stop. He took the blade of his knife and dug up a round, flattened tuber with lacy green fronds above ground. "Is that a turnip?" young Nick chirped.

"Sure is. They's stronger flavored than the ones you can grow from seed next year. When you boil 'em up with a slab of that smoked elk and some onions an' yucca' root they'll make you full an' warm."

"What's yucca?" Nick asked, a frown creasing his forehead and button nose.

"That's them spiky, dark green leaves you see stickin' up in the sandy places. Later on they'll have waxy white blossoms on a stalk. They grow big, fat roots to store water for dry spells. Sweet as a yam," Preacher unveiled, pleased with his role as teacher. He pointed to a shadowed gulley across the creek.

"Them long vines with the stickers are wild blackberries. They'll bloom in early May, put on dark fruit and be ready to eat in mid-August an' all September. That is if the bears don't get at 'em first."

"Bears?" a mousey missionary squeaked.

"Oh, sure. An' if you see any out here, don't dispute their claim to the blackberries."

"I'd shoot him an' put him in the smokehouse," young Chris declared.

Preacher made a face. "Bear meat's sorta strong, and greasy. Sometimes tastes of fish, only fish that's gone bad. And you got to cook bear meat through and through."

"Ugh!" several of the missionary boys chorused.

"That's about it for now. We'll look into pine nuts and woodsy things tomorrow. Now I've got to help the ladies learn to jerk venison."

A loner all of his life, Preacher often felt ill at ease around groups of people. Yet, he had a high old time when he spent hours with the women of the camp in the task of preserving food. He worked at their side, and took them through each step in the process of cutting, seasoning, and drying strips of venison and elk. The only thing that kept it from being a total delight was that they chattered all the time. About woman things, at that.

His cheeks flamed frequently when the subject of corsets and petticoats came up. At such times, he retreated into conjecture on the problem that kept gnawing on him. Ezra Pease and his dealings with the Indians always came to the forefront of Preacher's thoughts. At last he had to take his gleanings to his companions.

Preacher sat aside his plate and licked his lips in satisfaction. "Elk ham makes a man's day, it rightly do," he declared. "Now, I've got something eatin' at me that we need to worry over together."

"Pease," Nighthawk said simply.

"That's right. What do you reckon we ought to do about it?"

"We've been tied down here for better than a week," Beartooth stated the obvious. "Who knows where Pease is now?"

"That's the point," Preacher seized on it. "He could be lookin' right down on us this minute. And who knows what mischief he's up to. We got this here little town off to a good start. I think it's time to go out and hunt down Pease and settle his hash once and for all."

"These gospel-shouters have ten thumbs when it comes to any real work," Beartooth complained, contradicting his earlier statement. "Someone has to stay with them to make sure their houses don't fall down when they finish 'em."

Preacher cocked a brow. "You ain't the world's greatest carpenter either, Beartooth."

"But I can hit the pegs with the hammer, not my thumb."

"Then yer elected," Preacher said simply. "Fact is, if there's no objection, I think you all should stay on to get the job done right, whilst I go hunt down Pease. I can clear out in two days' time, find him, then come back for the rest of you. Then we can clean out that nest of rattlers."

BOOK TWO

1

Ten of Stone Drum's Dog Soldiers crouched in the choke-cherry bushes at the crest of the rim that surrounded the hidden valley occupied by the hated whites. The oldest among them, a smooth-muscled man in his mid-thirties, father of three boys and two girls, nodded, his hawk-beak nose pointing out the crude shelters erected by Pease's men. Although a quarter-mile away, he spoke softly.

"We must find Falling Horse. One of you go to the camp of Stone Drum. Our chief must know of this also."

"They cave moved close to the land of the Blackfeet," a younger brave observed.

Good Sky nodded again and a flicker of smile lighted his face. "That is why when we attack we must do it swiftly, with all our warriors. None must escape to tell their friends the Blackfeet." He looked around at the men with him. "Young Bear, you are lightest, can move fast without tiring your pony. Go to Stone Drum. Ottar, you go to Falling Horse. The rest will stay here, keep watch, guide our Dog Soldier brothers to this valley."

Young Bear's chest swelled. "We are strong enough to take them now."

"I think not. It is better that we wait," Good Sky ruled.

That wait lasted three days. Young Bear and Ottar rounded up all of the roving Dog Soldiers who had been searching for the whites and brought them to the valley. There, Falling Horse laid his plans for the attack. He saw at once that some of the whites would no doubt break free of their initial charge and escape the camp that had been established. Yet, he wanted to cause what damage they could.

"We are not enough in numbers to close off both ends of the valley," he instructed the eager warriors. "We can come from both sides, to increase their confusion. It is best after that to ride to where we can join forces and fight our way back through one side."

Wiser heads nodded agreement. "To be quiet and surprise them is important," Falling Horse cautioned.

Without further discussion, the Cheyenne set out to make ready for war. Many of the Dog Soldiers painted themselves and their ponies for the event. Others made up in soft tones of brown and green, in order to sneak up close on the unsuspecting whites before the signal was given to charge. When everyone had reached his proper place, a ruby-throated warbler call advised Falling Horse of this. The time had come.

Suddenly the peaceful atmosphere of the camp shattered at the sharp-edged war cries of the hundred Cheyenne. Arrows rained from the sky and made a pin cushion of one hard case. His wails and shrieks of agony joined the battle sounds of the Dog Soldiers. Ponies at a gallop, they thundered toward the assortment of tents and brush shelters from upstream and down.

"B'god it's Injuns!" Two Thumbs Buehler shouted in astonishment. His hands darted toward his rifle.

Ezra Pease jolted from his folding camp stool and rushed to the open flap of his tent. Spurts of smoke jetted skyward as the Cheyenne opened up. Belatedly, some of his own men returned fire.

"Hold tight," Pease shouted. "We out-gun them."

"How do you know?" came a nervous challenge. "There could be hunnerds of them."

"You dolt! *We're* the ones selling the guns," Ezra Pease snapped, wondering how he had come to have so many lamebrains in the gang.

It soon became clear that the Indians advanced in a two-pronged attack. With them they brought firebrands, which they threw into the brush shelters. Flames licked high in scant seconds. A screaming man staggered out of one, his body engulfed by fire. Terrified by this, several of the thugs made a run for the brushy slope of the basin. Fire from London-made fusils erupted in their faces. One man caught two arrows from so short a range that only the fletchings protruded from his shirtfront. The captive boys still with Pease wailed in confusion, uncertain as to where their safety lay. For all their superiority in firepower, Ezra Pease soon saw they had no choice but to make a run for it.

"Harness the teams," he bellowed, regretting the inevitable loss of his stout tent.

Then, totally unexpected, when the two wings of the charge met near the middle of camp, the hostiles turned in one direction and dashed out of the encircling white men. Although not before they had snatched up a case of rifles, two kegs of powder and one of bullets packed in layers of sawdust. Three, who had been able to understand the pleas of the captive white boys, had youngsters behind them on their ponies. Pease roared his anger after them.

"Damn them! Damn them all. They think they can come in here and take what they want, eh? Then run like whipped dogs. They'll not get away with it." Still contemptuous of Indians in general, Ezra Pease made yet another mistake. "There can't be more than forty of them. Everyone mount up. I want them hunted down and killed, every last one."

Two wagons ambled into the missionaries' valley late the next afternoon. They presented a sorry sight. Both wagons had broken down repeatedly on the rough trail north of Trout Crick Pass. Silas Phipps suffered from withdrawal from alcohol and his orphans all appeared sickly. They stumbled around like walking corpses and all of the missionaries agreed that they needed considerable care.

"Our supplies ran out two days ago," Helen informed the concerned mission folk. "We haven't had anything to eat since then. Peter has a fever. Please, can you help us?" she appealed to a compassionate committee of women.

"Oh, you poor dears. We'll get you fed right away. Where is the sick boy?"

"In the front wagon," Helen told Patience Bookworthy.

"Now, you keep yer hands off that boy," Silas Phipps growled. "He's just faking being sick to get out of work."

Preacher didn't like the cut of the man at first sight. He had a meanness about his mouth and little, squinty eyes, that darted from place to place, as though assessing the value of everything in sight. His lack of concern for the children didn't sit right, either. It was this that made Preacher decide to step in.

"Are you a doctor?" the mountain man demanded.

"No, I ain't. An' it's none of your concern," Phipps snapped.

Preacher produced a grim smile, a sure warning sign to any who knew him. "Since you're not a doctor, you don't know any more about how sick that boy is than I do. Let the women take care of him."

Phipps had time by then to gauge the size and metal of the man confronting him. Coward that he was, he backed down a little. "They can ply him with some soup, and maybe some medicine. We could all use something to eat. But mind, they're not to touch him or take him out of those clothes."

Preacher wondered on that throughout the day and into the next. Peter responded to the ministrations of the missionary women and roused out of his fevered state by mid-afternoon. Once the affliction had left him, he ate ravenously. Talk went around the new settlement about asking the wanderers to remain in the valley. Preacher objected to that, but withheld comment.

On their second full day in the valley, the children had lost some of their listlessness and befriended children among the missionaries and refugees, in spite of the efforts of Silas Phipps to prevent that. When several of the boys, including young Peter, went downstream to take a bath, Preacher went along to stand guard.

When the lads had undressed, little Nick stared at Peter, eyes wide with wonder. "Jehoshephat! What happened to you?" he blurted.

"It's . . . nothin'," Peter responded quietly, his face aflame with humiliation.

"Don't tell me that," Nick persisted. "Someone whomped on you real fierce."

"NO! No one did it. I—I . . . fell. Fell off the wagon," Peter invented in desperation.

Made curious by the anxious tone in Peter's voice, Preacher cut his eyes to where the boys stood naked and knee-deep in the chill creek. His eyes widened and turned as hard as high quality flint when he saw all the scars on Peter's back. Fresh purple welts criss-crossed the boys shoulders, the small of his back and his skinny buttocks. It brought a flash of fury.

Then Preacher recovered his go-easy, mountain man outlook. Not his business, he decided. Some kids needed more rough handling to be brought up right. Might be that Phipps feller told the truth. Then he recalled that the Indians raised some mighty fine youngsters without ever laying a hand on them. Small wonder Phipps didn't want the women to see Peter's back.

Preacher dismissed his immediate concern. They'd spend only another day and a night in the valley, resupply what they could and then Phipps would be told to move on. He'd point the way back to Trout Crick Pass to Phipps and bid him good luck. These youngin's weren't his to be worrying over, Preacher allowed. He turned back to his guard duties.

With Preacher keeping watch for predators of the two and four-legged varieties, the boys splashed and played with the lye soap bar until they turned a bit blue around the lips and shivered violently. Only then would they admit that the water might be a bit chilly. They climbed from the stream and toweled dry. Then Nick, who was small for his age, and a size with Peter, presented the latter boy with a fresh change of clothes. Tears of gratitude and affection filled Peter's' eyes and he turned away to hide them from the other lads. When they had all dressed, Preacher marched them back to the settlement.

There he found Cora Ames all atither over the condition of the older girls. "There's something very wrong in the lives of these children," she announced sternly.

"Such as?" Preacher prodded, the knowledge of Peter's frequent beatings clear in his mind.

"They won't say anything, in fact they deny that something . . . unpleasant has been going on."

"Only you don't think that's the truth?"

Cora cut her big, blue, troubled eyes to him. "Oh, Preacher, all I have are suspicions. But they seem to be in absolute terror of that Mr. Phipps."

"We'll have to keep an eye on Phipps, for as long as they're here with us then," Preacher offered.

"Will you, Preacher? It's all I can ask, I suppose. And, tell the others, too. Beartooth, Dupre, and Nighthawk?"

"Sure, Miss Cora. Done without sayin'. Ain't none of us cottons to the man. I reckon it was him who gave Peter a powerful beatin'. More than one, at that."

Cora's hand flew to her mouth to cover her astonishment. "How badly was the boy injured?"

"I reckon it's what gave him that fever. Some of them stripes was deep, could have festered."

"Why, that's monstrous."

"May seem so to you an' me, Miss Cora. But if they belong to him, it ain't again' the law. He can do whatever he wants with 'em, short of actual killin' one."

Stubborn anger colored Cora's next words. "Not if he's doing what I think he's done to those girls."

Preacher lost any doubt about her concerns. His lips thinned into a hard line. "So, it's that way, huh? Might be I should have a little talk with Phipps."

"I'm afraid that might make things worse for them all," Cora pleaded for restraint.

"Not until he got off his back and outta the splints I'd be puttin' him in," Preacher rumbled.

Preacher thought at first he was dreaming of a wounded rabbit. Yet, the pitiful cries had more volume than the squeak of a hurt animal. He came fully awake when they changed to outright screams.

"No! Please, no! I won't let you. It hurts. I won't!" a child's voice penetrated the haze in Preacher's head.

A short distance away, Nighthawk roused from sleep also. "That's a child," the Delaware stated thickly.

"Yep. An' I got an idee where it's comin' from." Preacher slipped into moccasins, drew up his buckskin trousers and padded off into the darkness. Nighthawk followed him to the source of the sounds of anguish and humiliation.

Preacher sprang up onto the lip at the base of the tailgate to the second wagon that belonged to Silas Phipps. He had been guided there by the soft, dim glow of a candle burning inside. He was the first among the occupants of the valley to see Silas at his evil pleasure.

Phipps had pulled the thin dress off the skinny, naked form of little Gertha, the ten-year-old. Gertha wretchedly, hot trails of tears coursing down her cheeks. Feebly she batted at the pawing hands of Phipps.

With a roar, Preacher bent inward and grabbed the perverted vermin by the back of his collarless shirt and scruff of his neck. With no more seeming effort than jerking a fly clear off a square of sticky paper, Preacher yanked Silas Phipps out of his wagon and hurled him onto the ground. Nighthawk stood over the astonished Phipps.

"Not even the filthy buzzard-puke that rides for Dirty Dan Frazier would do a low-down thing like that, you bastard!" Preacher roared.

"Them orphans mine. I can do with them what I want," Phipps wailed in his defense. "Besides, she likes it. Purrs like a li'l kitten she does."

That set Preacher's control boiling over. "Move over, Nighthawk. This'uns got him a powerful whuppin' comin'. Git up, you sick son of a bitch."

Phipps cowered, arms up and curled around his head for protection. "Don't you touch me. I didn't do no harm."

Fire burned in Preacher's eyes as he reached down and dragged Phipps to his boots. "How many o' them little girls have you pestered?" he grated through his fury.

"Only the older ones. Them that's nine or over," came a whimpered reply.

"What about what you done to Peter?" Preacher prodded, his vision filled with the purple welts on the skin of the boy's pale back.

"Yeah—yeah, him, too, a couple of times. An' Billy, too."

Shocked to stupefication by this disgusting revelation, Preacher responded with his fists. His big knuckles mashed into Phipps' lips, pulped his nose, split the skin under one eye. Phipps bleated in terror, twisted and pulled in an attempt to escape this terrible punishment. Preacher gave him no slack.

When Phipps wilted in Preacher's grip, the mountain man brought up one knee smartly and smashed into the pervert's crotch. Then he went to work on the soft belly and vulnerable ribs. The disturbance awakened everyone in the settlement. Lamps bloomed with light and people began to gather. In the forefront, black frock coat draped over nightshirt, came the Reverend Thornton Bookworthy.

"Enough!" he thundered. "Desist at once. You'll kill that man."

Preacher ceased his pounding and looked at the minister from his anger. "You're right. I allow as how any man forcing himself on a woman, and in particular a child, has committed a hanging offense. I say that's what we do with this rotten trash."

Despite the closeness of their earlier conversation, Cora Ames flared at Preacher also. "You can't do that without a trial. This man is entitled to the protection of the law. Everyone is presumed innocent until proven guilty."

Preacher noted the fervor with which she had made her statements and it only fanned the flames higher. "Well, hell, Miss Cora, if you'll pardon my sayin' it, I caught him in the act, with his britches down around his knees like they are now. That ain't no sportin' house girl in there, that's a ten-year-old child."

Gertha's small, pale face appeared over the tailgate. "Hit him again, Mr. Preacher. Hit him for me."

Reverend Bookworthy had gathered more steam. "We can't hang him. Why, it's—it's *uncivilized.*"

"That's right," Patience Bookworthy rallied behind her husband. "Everyone knows that hanging people is no deterrent to crime."

Preacher eyed her like a creature from another planet. "I beg to point out that hangin' is a sure-fire way to deter the feller from doin' it. Any rapist, once hung, sure as ol' Nick himself, won't ever rape another."

Asa Pettibone stepped forward. "I agree with Preacher. If we are establishing a community here, then we're responsible for enforcing the laws. As I recall, rape is a capital crime. I say we select a jury, from among our drivers and ourselves. Did you see what went on?" he asked Nighthawk.

"I only saw Preacher drag this wretch out of his wagon."

"Good. Then you can be prosecutor, Nighthawk. Beartooth can be bailiff, Dupre can be judge. And, Thornton, if you feel so strongly against the death penalty for such scum as Phipps, you can damn well defend the low-life trash."

More lanterns were brought, the fire built up, and everyone gathered around. Only the children were barred from witnessing the events that transpired. When summoned, Beartooth escorted each of the orphans forward to testify. Each one sobbed out their face-reddening, humiliating evidence. Through it all, Silas Phipps grew more surly.

"Yer a lyin' whelp," he snarled at Billy when the boy told between gulps of fear and loathing what Phipps had done to him.

"It—it's the truth, an' you know it," the eight-year-old boy accused. "I swore to myself I'd never tell a soul. The shame would kill me. But if it will free us all of you, I'm glad to answer what they want to know."

Peter told of the many beatings, and of the dark, degrading, secret things Phipps had compelled him to do. Several of the missionary women swooned dead away, others erupted in fits of tears and hysteria.

"Yer a liar, same as the others, you miserable brat. Next time, I'll whip the life out of you."

Preacher could no longer restrain himself. "I don't reckon yer gonna get a 'next time.' "

Dupre rapped a pistol butt on the barrel head that served as his bench. "Let's not get out of line, *mon ami*. You'll have your chance to give testimony in a little while."

"What's wrong with now?" Preacher growled.

"I seem to recall something about establishing a link between the accused and his crimes. Mr. Pettibone was kind enough to instruct me in this custom of law. So we need to start in the past and bring it up to the events of this evening. Then we can hang this *batard* right legal and proper," he added, a cold fire in his black eyes. "Proceed, Mr. Prosecutor."

"What happened after the last beating, Peter?"

"He—uh—he smeared me with axle grease. He was real tender about it, especially my ba-backside. I just knew what he wanted."

Phipps came to his feet, hands fisted, eyes wild. "Shut up, you dirty little liar."

Dupre cut his eyes to Beartooth. "Bailiff, please restrain the defendant."

Beartooth gave a curt nod, walked to where he faced Phipps, at a little less than arm's length, and biffed the blustering pervert in the mouth. "That good enough, Judge Dupre?"

"Fine as frog fur, Beartooth. Once again, please continue."

Peter did. Then Preacher was called, he related being awakened, recognizing the cries to be those of a child and following the sound to the second wagon of Phipps. At that point he became ill at ease, shrugged and shuffled his feet, until he at last turned to Dupre.

"Frenchy, uh, Judge, can we ask the ladies be excused before I say what it is I found inside that wagon?"

"Considering the circumstances, I find that a reasonable request," Nighthawk supported Preacher's position.

Realizing that if Preacher revealed all the gruesome details, the client forced upon him would surely hang, Reverend Bookworthy protested. "The Constitution guarantees a speedy and public trial. The Lord knows this is speedy enough. If the womenfolk are excused it will not be entirely public."

"Now, hold on a minute there, *Pere* Bookworthy. I've never been in a real court but once," Dupre challenged. "But the one I was in didn't allow women to witness the trial. I'm going to rule that the women be excused."

After they had gone, Preacher described what he had seen. When he concluded with the pounding he had given Phipps, rumbles of angry discontent swept through the long gap in testimony. Dupre rapped again and brought silence.

"Do you wish to call anyone else?" he asked Nighthawk.

"Yes. The victim, little Gertha."

After her account of what had gone on, several among the jury had to be restrained by Beartooth. Dupre turned to Reverend Bookworthy. "Do you have anything to offer in defense?"

"I call Silas Phipps."

Phipps took the oath, then slumped on the barrel used as a witness chair. "I might have done some bad things in my life. But it weren't my fault. I had an awful childhood. My parents beat me, they didn't love me. I had an uncle, my pa's brother, who pestered me when I was little," he recited his list of imaginary woes. "I was shunned by the other children because we were poor. I went hungry most every day . . ." He went on and on with the usual purile snivel about his past life.

When he finished, the jury took only one minute to reach a verdict. "Guilty," Buck the foreman announced.

"But it ain't my fault. I can't help myself," Silas Phipps whined, squealed, and sobbed out.

"Having been found guilty as charged, I sentence you to be hanged by your neck until you are dead, dead, dead. And may *le bon dieu* have mercy on your soul," Dupre pronounced in a sepulchral voice.

Phipps squealed like a pig. He struggled and fought with the four men who wrestled to restrain him. He thrashed and howled all the way to the tall fir tree with long, thick lower branches. There his hands and feet were tied and a hastily fashioned rope fitted around his neck.

He was still shrieking when the rope went suddenly taut and hauled him off his feet. No one wanted to break the silence that followed that.

2

War talk resumed among the Cheyenne. Many of the younger warriors and war chiefs had grown highly discontented with the failure to settle decisively with Pease. Their representatives on the council made their position known. The debate turned even more serious.

"It is foolish to make war on the whites. Unless we kill all of these men, others will come to avenge them. Think of our women, our children," Running Bear appealed to reason.

"While we spend our days chasing after them, the Blackfeet are making up for war," Wind Rider reminded the assembled chiefs. "We cannot fight them, and all the whites, too."

"No. It is the white men who sell guns and whiskey we must kill," Gray Cloud rose to speak his thoughts. "When we do, the Blackfeet will have to take counsel again about fighting us."

Falling Horse rose next, a brief smile flickering on his wide, handsome face. "I do not think the whites think well of these men who sell guns and whiskey to our people. I have met with the one they call Preacher. He and three friends are hunting this man called Pease. They mean to stop him."

"What can four men do against all those who ride with Pease?" Gray Cloud demanded scornfully.

"That is not the point, old friend. What we must do is find Pease first and finish off his fighting men. With Preacher opposed to what Pease is doing, he will speak in our favor to his kind. I believe that no other white men will seek to punish us if we kill Pease."

Little Mountain rose to add his sentiments. "Falling Horse is right. This Pease rides like a mighty chief across our lands. He and his warriors are crowding up our open spaces, selling rotten whiskey to those who would drink it, and being troublesome in many ways."

"Yes. The white boy-child I took from their camp told how the men with Pease killed his parents, and many other whites in a rolling lodge train and took them captive," Falling Horse informed them. "This is also why I say the whites will not care who it is that ends the days for Pease."

"It is known that they are the ones who sold guns to the Blackfeet," White Bow added in mounting anger. "We are agreed to fight the Blackfeet if they come into our land. I say we take the battle to them. Attack their villages. Punish them for trading guns with the whites."

"But first we must make Pease pay for what he has done," Falling Horse urged.

Running Bear sighed and shook his graying head. "Your words are good, Falling Horse. Yet, we must take counsel in what is true, and not give in to being guided by what we wish could be done. I say it is to be moon-struck to decide for a general uprising. Look at the power of the Blackfeet, their great numbers. And the endless stream of whites. Do you forget their Tall Hats* who keep the log wall villages?"

Falling Horse had to admit the wisdom of that argument. Although few in number, and widely spread over the high plains, the forts provided a constant thorn to irritate the Cheyenne. After much wrangling, the council decided not to

*Dragoons.

change their initial decision. They would first hunt the whites who had killed Little Knife and his warriors and destroyed the village of Black Hand. More than half the number of braves able to fight would be needed to protect their villages from any surprise attack by the Blackfeet, while the rest went in pursuit of Pease. They would discuss widening the fight later. Falling Horse had the last word.

"I will lead the Dog Soldiers, if you approve," he told the council. None objected.

Cora Ames was not speaking to Preacher after the drumhead trial and hanging of Silas Phipps. That pleased Preacher mightily. He decided to set off on another hunting sweep, then see to finding Pease. To his surprise, young Peter and Billy overcame their ordeal enough to share their skill in setting snares for smaller game with the boys of the village. Before Preacher departed, the youngsters were out in the woods to trap rabbits, squirrels, and other edible, fur-bearing critters. Preacher used a big hand to cover his satisfied smile.

"You will be back when?" Nighthawk asked.

"Before the first game I shoot spoils," Preacher answered.

"The one who has her eyes set for you is angry, I gather."

Preacher sighed, more in relief than regret. "That she is. I'll never understand wimmin. Cool as ol' Jim Beckworth, she was when it came to shootin' Injuns. Wouldn't abide hangin' that rotten trash. Oh, well, I reckon the Almighty will sort out whatever, if any, was good about Silas Phipps. Be seein' you, Nighthawk."

Preacher took similar leave from the other pair, along with some ribald advice about how to rewarm the cockles of Cora's heart. That, he told himself, he didn't need. In the meanwhile, Cora had found herself a new distraction. Over coffee and sweet cakes, she conferred with Lidia Pettibone, Sue Landry and, of course, Patience Bookworthy.

"These orphans are truly alone now," she began her campaign.

Lidia Pettibone gave a shudder. "Better that than the life they had."

Cora sipped from her cup and eyed Lidia over the rim. "What I'm getting at is they can hardly strike out from here all alone."

"Certainly not," Patience Bookworthy gave her opinion. "Yet, they have been so degraded, so shamed, that they are hardly fit for ordinary society, let alone to live among the righteous."

"I would expect that, comin' from you," Flora Sanders said as she bustled up, fists on hips. "I am so tired of hearing how righteous you folk are. Wasn't it the Pharisees and Sudducees who were considered the most righteous among the Jews? And didn't Jesus tell them that he was of his father and they were of theirs, 'who was a liar and a murderer and a thief from the beginning of time?' "

In a huff, Patience sprang from her rocking chair. "Why, I never . . ."

"Nope. Don't reckon you ever did think about that. You been too busy being righteous. Now, dear," Flora directed to Cora, "what was it you had in mind?"

Pleased and inwardly warmed by this show of support, Cora carefully framed her reply. "These children need homes, and parents to love and care for them. Surely there are those among our group who could open their hearts to these waifs?"

"I'd say so. I'm not too old to be a mother hen," Flora volunteered. "I'd be right pleased to take in that little girl, Gertha, and perhaps Billy."

Cora turned to the others. "There you are. That leaves only ten more to be comforted. And, another thing, we should start thinking toward a school. Our own children are running wild, without the education they need. Twelve more only add to the importance of schooling."

"I agree," Lidia Pettibone offered. "Our Jason is becoming more like those mountain men every day. He even wants a set of buckskins to wear."

Patience Bookworthy recovered from her snit enough to

be scandalized. "That goes to show you. We must be shut of those uncouth hooligans as quickly as possible. They are a bad influence on the children."

Cora had another view of the issue. "I think buckskins make a lot of sense . . . out here. We have no ready supply of cloth, tailormade clothing cost dearly, if any is available. With animals in ample supply, we can have an endless quantity of clothing. Preacher . . ." She stumbled over the name, then recovered her composure. "Preacher says we can even trade with the friendly Indians for ready-made buckskin clothes."

Sue Landry joined Patience in her objections. "Just the thought of that animal skin against my—my person, makes me cringe."

"And rightly so, dear," Patience supported in prim disapproval.

Not to be put off, Cora made a sweeping gesture with one arm to the stacks of hump-backed trunks outside each nearly completed cabin. "Judging from what we brought along, we women would not be subjected to that for a long time. Perhaps never, if the land is settled as quickly as our mountain men guides seem to think. Yet, it would certainly stretch our husbands' and sons' meeting house clothes a lot longer. It does no harm for boys and men to wear clothing made from animal skins. Not if they are decorated as attractively as those of Pre—er—that man."

Patience would not let it go. She felt her control of the women slipping away. "Well enough for you to say, with neither man nor child to care for."

That struck home, though Cora vowed not to let it show. "Yes," she said sweetly. "But that's of my choosing, not for any lack of suitors."

Squelched, Patience let it go without challenge. Talk returned to the proposed school while the level in the coffee pot lowered steadily. Lidia Pettibone offered to teach the lower grades, and her husband would provide instruction in music. Martha Yates, recovered from her fright over Johnny, offered to teach the older children. Patience Bookworthy, naturally, stated that she would teach religion.

"But not all of us are of your persuasion," Falicity Jones reminded the officious minister's wife.

To her surprise, Cora found herself on the side of Patience. "True enough, yet we all worship the same God. The moral truths of religious belief are the best guidelines children can have when growing up. Take the Ten Commandments out of the schools and we'll raise up a nation of heathen savages more benighted than the Indians."

Patience Bookworthy shot Cora Ames a gimlet eye before accepting the reality of what the younger woman had said. "I heartily agree. The Ten Commandments were not the Ten Suggestions or Hints. They represent the absolute distillation of moral law. Without them, where would civilization be?"

Their talk went on until the women realized with a start that they would have to scurry to prepare the noon meal for their laboring men. They set off in a flutter of skirts and hair in disarray. It would have pleased Preacher mightily, Cora Ames thought.

Cord Dickson cut his eyes to the ugly features of Grant Ferris. The bucktoothed Ferris had the unsightly habit of picking his nose in the presence of others. Had Cord Dickson not been a knife artist, who gloried in gutting his victims, it would have turned his stomach. He and Seth Branson had been partnered with Grant Ferris for nine days now, searching for any sign of Preacher.

They had gone to the trading post at Trout Crick Pass three times in those days. All with negative results. If anyone knew anything, they sure didn't share it with the scruffy trio of hard cases. Now Dickson, the nominal leader, wanted a unanimous decision from his companions. His hard look made Ferris uncomfortable.

"Whaddayasay, Ferris? I'm for trailin' north an' west of

here. Odds are, that's where Preacher went. He sure'n hell ain't to the south of the pass."

"Right you are, Cord," Grant Ferris agreed readily. "Only I for one ain't all that eager to catch up to him."

"Why not?" Cord Dickson need not have asked. He had his own doubts about the advisability of confronting the legendary mountain man.

"You know what's happened to all them others what ran afoul of Preacher," Ferris clarified his response. "Well, I don't aim to become the next."

Dickson tried to reason with his man. "All we have to do is find him. See where he's holed up, an' then go get the rest to finish him off."

"Sounds simple enough," Seth Branson agreed. "Only we've seen enough to know Preacher is a sudden man. He might not let us just walk away."

"He will if he don't know we've seen him," Dickson let his over-confidence say for him.

"It might be easier to let an Injun not know we've seen him," Ferris offered.

Dickson's eyes narrowed. "Sometimes, Ferris, I think you've got a yeller streak wide as my hand runnin' clear down your spine."

"No I ain't!" Ferris barked at the insult. "Only, I think through somethin' before I act on it."

Ferris turned away in his saddle to gaze behind them at the steep trail they had just descended. "I'm hongry. What say we stop here and chew on something?"

"Good enough," Dickson agreed. "So long as we head northwest when we leave."

Preacher had been following Dickson, Ferris, and Branson for half a day when he made his decision. He had been in close enough to learn their names, and their business, from their careless conversation on the trail. These flatlander highwaymen who had come so recently to the High Lonesome had yet to learn the value of noise control in the mountains.

Soft breezes and the deadening of hoof falls on mats of pine needles gave the false impression that voices would not carry far. In truth, the high granite walls of the canyons, valleys, and hills became natural channels to convey sound a long ways. Too bad these three would not live long enough to learn that lesson, Preacher mused as he edged Thunder down the sharp decline, through thickly growing fir, beech, and aspen.

He had judged that they had come entirely too close to the protected valley where his ration of pilgrims worked to build a home. His hunting would have to wait. Already he had four plump stags tied high in trees to keep away hungry scavengers. He would take care of these three, then round up his kills and head back. His sharp ears picked up the whiney voice of the one called Ferris.

"I say we've gone far enough. Not a sign of Preacher anywhere."

There had been, Preacher thought with contempt. They had cut his trail three times only they were too stupid to know that.

"Look at it this way," Branson, the calculating one of the trio suggested. "When we get done with this, we'll know more about this country than near anybody."

Not likely by a damn far shot, Preacher refuted. "What good's that?" Ferris asked.

"Well, if we ever decide to break off with Mr. Pease, we can lead folks in here and collect good, hard gold for it. We'll be the best guides around."

"You will like hell," Preacher muttered aloud as he came down out of the trees and onto the trail ahead of the three louts.

Dickson, Ferris, and Branson rounded a bend in the trail and came face-to-face with Preacher. Dickson and Branson filled their hands. Ferris gaped . . . and filled his drawers.

Dragged along by their momentum, Ferris charged with the other two. It did them little good. Preacher had both of his four-shot pistols out and ready.

He let one bang when less than fifty feet separated him from the trio of lowlife trash. One of the balls from the double-shotted load went over the left shoulder of Ferris. The second smacked meatily into his shoulder. He kicked free of his mount with a yowl and hit hard on the granite surface of the trail.

Rolling to one side, Ferris careened down the bank and into the icy little stream that cut through the canyon. At least that washed away the foulness his fear had created. Above him, Dickson fired wildly with a .60 caliber pistol. His ball didn't hit the target, Ferris noted when a loud, flat blast followed the discharge of Dickson's gun.

Dickson's ball put another pair of holes in Preacher's coat. "That's about enough," Preacher roared and fired another barrel.

He took the hat from Dickson's head. By then Grant Ferris had scrambled to the lip of the bank and looked on as both of his friends fired again. That emptied their supply of pistols. They rode on past Preacher, giving him a wide berth, and he held his fire, loath to shoot them in the back. That gave them time to reload one pistol each.

Preacher waited for them when they turned about. He had dismissed any threat from the downed Ferris. That slip nearly cost him his life. Grant Ferris found one of his pistols sound, and the powder dry, when he triggered a load at Preacher's back. Hastily fired, the ball went low and struck the cantle of Preacher's saddle. The stout, fibrous oak of the saddle tree absorbed the energy of the ball, so that it burst through much slower and with far less force. It still punched through the wide leather belt beneath the sash Preacher wore and gave him a painful, stinging bruise in the small of his back.

He repaid Ferris's kindness by swiveling in his seat and plunking a ball between the cowardly thug's eyes. That still left the other two to deal with. Preacher faced front again, in time to see both their weapons discharge. This time he went to the ground, to avoid a fatal collision with hot lead.

"I got him! I got him!" Seth Branson shouted gleefully.

"No you ain't, he's jist duckin'," Cord Dickson corrected his overjoyed companion.

Preacher proved him right a moment later when he put a ball in Branson's belly. A mournful howl came from the bearded throat of the St. Louis grifter and he wavered in the saddle. Seth Dickson grabbed for the rifle scabbarded behind his stirrup fender. Preacher shot Dickson through the back of his hand. The ball also wounded Dickson's horse, which stumbled at the impact and threw its rider face first in the sharp-edged sand. Skin shredded in dozens of places by the decomposed granite, Cord Dickson shrieked as he rolled over and over along the trail. He ended up near Thunder's forehooves.

Gasping, Dickson raised his head to Preacher. "You— you've gotta be out of loads by now." His good hand slid toward the big butcher knife at his left side.

"You think you're lucky? Did you count right while the shooting went on? Ready to try it? It'd really please me. I don't cotton to killing an unarmed man."

"Jist let me go. I'll not do you any harm."

Preacher chuckled. "Oh, I'm sure you wouldn't. It's for what you've already done that I'm gonna send you off to see yer Maker. Go on, try it," Preacher taunted again.

Cord Dickson did. Which made it three-for-three for Preacher when the four-shot in his left hand blammed again and sent two balls into the chest of Cord Dickson. While he looked down on the dying man, Preacher reflected on what he had learned from them before this encounter. He had become a marked man. No doubt of how serious Pease was about having Preacher killed.

"Things are gettin' right interesting," he spoke aloud to Dickson. "If I had a scrap of paper and a stub of lead, I'd leave a note for ol' Ezra Pease. But, chances are it would never be found." He frowned down at the foamy, red ooze that billowed from Dickson's chest. "I done shot yer lights out, Dickson. If you're so inclined, I'd say you best make your peace with your Maker."

"Go . . . to . . . hell, Preacher."

"Most likely, it's you's headed that way, and right sudden, I'd say."

With that, Preacher turned away and picked up the arms of the other two, returning to Dickson after the man expired. The folks in the valley were getting right well outfitted with weapons, courtesy of Ezra Pease, Preacher considered as he led away the dead men's horses.

3

Preacher soon found out that a message would have been received. Not three miles along the trail that led to the quartered deer waiting him, a dozen more of Pease's hard cases thundered along in pursuit and struck from the rear. Preacher had wisely reloaded, and took the first three out of their saddles with fast work on the trigger mechanism. Quickly he exchanged the pistol with only a single shot for the second one. Then he turned to face the others.

They had wisely taken cover in the boulders along the side of the road and poured heavy fire toward Preacher. He let go of the captured horses, which ran off in the direction their noses pointed. In a smooth motion he slid from Thunder's saddle and snagged up his pair of rifles. He laid the pistol aside and nuzzled the Hawken to his shoulder, after he had hunkered down behind a large boulder before any of the rattled gunhawks could recover enough to take careful aim.

At once he saw motion beyond a fallen pine, the thick trunk of which provided protection for Preacher on his right flank. Some fool was charging him. He gave a .54 caliber ball from his Hawken to the ignorant lout and reached for the French rifle. Only the crown of a head and an eyeball showed above the curving surface of a boulder at extreme range behind the dying outlaw. Preacher steadied his own breathing enough to take careful aim.

Finely engraved, the barrel heated up as the conical bullet sped down its length. It emerged at tremendous velocity, speeding true to the target. A chunk of the exposed head exploded in a shower of scarlet. Preacher grunted in satisfaction. A lull came as all who were left ran out of loaded weapons.

Preacher took the time to reload while his enemies did the same. One of the swifter of Pease's men opened the dance again with a ball that screamed off the top of the boulder that sheltered Preacher. Preacher responded with another kill and the nasty vermin grew more cautious. Muttered words reached Preacher where he waited out their plan of attack, while he reloaded his first pistol.

"You, Trump, make a careful count of how many shots he's popped off. That was the fifth. You saw those funny-lookin' pistols. Four shots each, so keep that in mind."

"Gotcha, boss," Trump replied louder than necessary.

More than good, Preacher thought as he methodically reloaded the Hawken. A rattle of gunfire got his head down low. Two more made a rush along the trail. Preacher put the Hawken aside, the ramrod still down the barrel, and drew a pistol. His first round set one target to dancing a jittery death waltz.

Preacher turned from the fallen tree to engage the second thug, who charged the blind side of the boulder. A head and shoulder appeared around the mound of granite, followed by the barrel of a pistol. Preacher triggered his four-barrel and fanned his free arm at the cloud of smoke that quickly filled the space between him and his attacker.

When he could see again, Preacher noted a splash of blood on the gray surface of the boulder. A low groan came from the ground beyond the rock. Three mounted bits of trash spurred forward. Preacher moved to the open side of his stone fortress and downed two of them with the last pair of loads.

Switching pistols, he emptied the third saddle and rotated the barrels. From the screen of brush beyond the downed pine, he heard the voice of the man named Trump.

"That's five more shots. He can't have had time to reload his rifles and he sure can't carry more than those two pistols."

The boss apparently agreed with that, because Preacher heard some indistinct mutters in the chokecherry and the rustle of inexperienced booted feet moving through fallen leaves. Four men came at him at once, from three directions. Preacher sighted in on the nearest one and doubled the thug over with a double-shotted load to the gut.

Quickly he picked another target while the first gunrunner sagged to his knees and fell forward to remain in a folded position, his head against the ground. Preacher's next round shattered the right shoulder joint of a pasty-faced lout with a mouthful of crooked teeth. Howling, the wounded man tripped over his feet and rolled to the bottom of the slope.

By then, the other two had gotten dangerously close. Both fired at once and showers of lead fragments and granite went flying around Preacher's head. Blood trickled from several cuts on his face. Preacher fired and missed. He worked the tricky trigger again and scored with both balls high in the chest and neck. It knocked the hapless vermin over onto his back.

Preacher didn't slow down as he stuffed the empty pistol into its holster and reached for his Hawken. A cap went into place on the nipple and he eared back the hammer. As he brought the weapon up he started to turn toward the fourth gunman. Hot pain burst in the under side of his left upper arm. The trashy whiskey peddler had shot him.

Without thinking about the ramrod, Preacher blazed away. He received a tremendous recoil as the brass-tipped hickory rammer retarded the expansion of gas in the barrel. It shot out, however, ahead of the ball it had seated. It struck the target and, like a slender lance, drove three quarters of its length through the chest of the boss a fraction of an inch above his heart. In seconds the attacker bled to death internally from a punctured aorta.

"D'ja see that?" Trump blurted from his concealed position.

Someone made a gagging sound and began to run downhill toward the horses. "I'm gettin' outta here," he wailed.

Preacher tied a paisley kerchief around the bullet hole through his arm and hastily reloaded the French rifle. He stepped from his cover and easily downed the nervous one as the latter stepped into his stirrup. Only Trump remained and he took a hasty shot at Preacher before bolting for his mount. Preacher grabbed a .60 caliber Hayes pistol from the brace of holsters on Thunder's saddle and took a deep, steadying breath.

Trump died a second later with a look of total horror on his face. Preacher winced at the various pains that racked his body and lowered the smoking Hayes. "Gonna be one hell of a bruise," he muttered over the throbbing in his shoulder.

Businesslike, Preacher gathered up the weapons and other possessions of the outlaw scum who had jumped him. Then he located the proper type of moss and stuffed his wound with it. That accomplished, he rounded up the horses and started off for camp.

Those among the denizens of the High Lonesome who had chosen to spend at least part of the spring around Bent's Fort didn't know what to make of him. He dressed much like an Easterner, in tight black britches and a distinctly military tunic, sort of like the Dragoons, only without all the fancy colored piping and brass. He wore a fine, store-made white linen shirt, with a plain, black stock that fluttered in the constant breeze.

A hard-faced man, with close-set eyes, and a brace of pistols in his waistband, he arrived at the Fort in early April. After tending to his horse, he went directly to the trading post and began showing around sketches. Without any explanation, he asked if anyone had seen the children, or the man who might be with them.

"What business might that be of yours?" Jake Talltrees asked pugnaciously.

"I'm a United States Marshal. Ruben Talbot is my name. This man," he lifted the sketch, "is Silas Phipps. He is supposed to be in the company of a band of orphans who have raped, murdered, and robbed all the way across the country from Pennsylvania."

His disbelieving onlookers held a different opinion. Black Powder Harris put it to words. "No, sir. I don't believe those youngsters to be capable of any sort of mischief. I runned into them on the Injun trail north of here. That one dickered with me for a jug of whiskey. He's a drunk, an' poison mean, I'd wager. But those youngin's looked too skeert to do evil."

Marshal Talbot ran the back of one hand across his brow. "We all have our opinions, stranger. I allow as how you're entitled to yours. But, these warrants I have say different. How long ago did you encounter them?"

"Oh, better than a week." He meant more than two.

Talbot thought on that a moment. "I'd be obliged to stay the night. Then I'll be headin' north after them."

Ezra Pease stomped across the bare ground of the campsite. He stopped on the far side of the fire to confer with Titus Vickers and Hashknife. "We should be headed north, not southwest."

"Not if we want to stay shut of the Cheyenne," Vickers opined.

"Titus is correct, Mr. Pease. The men I sent out to search

for Preacher haven't returned as yet. Perhaps when they do, they will have useful information."

Pease considered that a while. "That leaves us with no option but to poke along their trail."

"The easier to consolidate our force when the time comes," Hashknife suggested.

Pease nodded curtly. "You're right, both of you. Now, when we run Preacher to ground, and we are going to, I guarantee you that, I want to deal with him myself. I've been thinking on this and nothing else will give as much satisfaction as seeing genuine fear on that ugly face of his."

"Might be he won't be so easy to contain," Vickers offered. "He could force us to kill him from long range."

Pease's face got a testy look. "Well, you'll just have to see to it that he does not. I want to feel my fingers around his throat, crushing the life out of him. Oh, yes, Preacher is going to be mine, all mine. And you two are going to see that it happens that way."

John Dancer came to knowing that he had been bad hurt. Shot through the side and bled a lot. He could remember how it happened and falling from his horse. Then, everything had gone blank. Who and how many had jumped them? He had a flash of a tall, broad-chested man, clad in buckskins, who held a strange-looking pistol that spouted flame four times before being empty. Surely not one man.

Pain knifed through his side, an inch or two above his hip bone. Dancer wanted very much to survive. He also wanted a drink of water in the worst way. His mouth felt like a sawdust box. Slowly he roused himself and inched his way through his agony toward the sound of a rippling stream. He saw no sign of his horse, or any others. All his eyes took in were the bodies of the men who had ridden with him.

Again he saw the flickering image of the wild-looking man with the odd gun. Preacher? The name taunted Dancer as he eased his way down the embankment to touch a fever-ish hand to icy water. They had been sent out to find Preacher. The three men he had ordered forward to scout had been gunned down, they had all heard the shouts and came on fast. Yeah, that was it. They rounded a bend and there he was, bigger than life and twice as deadly.

From there on everything went to hell in a handbasket. Preacher fought like a cornered wildcat. In no time he had the upper hand. And he showed no mercy. That young pup, Trump, must have miscounted the shots, Dancer reasoned. Because at the exact moment he thought they had regained the initiative, Preacher opened up with another hail of lead. Shooting the boss with that ramrod had been the final bit needed to spook those who remained.

Even he had been shot trying to flee from the demon in buckskin, Dancer thought ruefully. He lowered his head and drank deeply. After that he wiped at his wound and took stock. At least he didn't have any guts pokin' out. If he took care of himself, he might survive after all. But miles from nowhere, without a horse or eats?

The prospect of it gave him a fit of the cold shudders.

Back at the settlement in the valley, Cora Ames ignored the welcome addition of more meat in her excitement over Preacher's wound. Over his objections, she led him by one hand to her recently completed cabin.

"I'm tending to that personally," she insisted.

Preacher grumbled and complained, then had to admit that these Eastern feather-heads had toughened up as he watched Cora remove his makeshift bandage and the poul-tice of moss, then clean and dress the through-and-through bullet holes. She made the new binding as neat as any school-taught doctor, the mountain man saw with satisfaction.

"There, all done. I will want to see it again tomorrow. And the day after. We don't want it to fester."

"Dang right, that's why I'm gonna fix me some willer bark an' some other stuff to pack in the holes," Preacher told her with a straight face.

Quickly fading, the glow of accomplishment left Cora's face. "Don't you dare. Why, who knows what that would cause?"

"It'll cause it to heal, that's what," Preacher's stubbornness dictated. "Besides, I ain't got three days. I'm takin' Nighthawk an' Buck and startin' out tomorrow mornin' while the trail of the men who jumped me is still fresh. We can track 'em right back to Ezra Pease."

Horrified by this, Cora clapped both hands to her cheeks and spluttered her objections in rapid fire. "Why, you can't. You would be risking the loss of that arm. I won't allow it. I'll talk to your friends."

"There's nothin' you can do. An' the boys'll tell you that these Injun cures work right good on gunshot wounds."

Cora tried another tack. "You lost a lot of blood. You're too weak for such goings on."

Preacher nodded thoughtfully. "Fact is, I do feel a bit peaked. Nothin' a big chunk of elk steak won't fix."

Cora Ames blinked in dismay. "Preacher, Preacher, you are impossible," she gave in, albeit with only a slight return of good humor.

Early the next day, Preacher set out with Nighthawk and the driver, Buck. They rode in companionable silence for long hours. After crossing the spine of the Sierra Madre by way of Rabbit Ear Pass, they entered a wide, sweeping highland prairie. As the hours and miles went by, Preacher began to notice something that mightily displeased him.

"Lookit over there," he addressed to Nighthawk and Buck. "See them smoke trails on the horizon? Over the past fifty miles, I've seen more than a dozen of them, scattered out where none existed last year a-tall."

"It's called progress, Preacher," Buck said lightly. "Folks are moving West."

"I call it a disaster. This keeps up, 'fore long there'll be so many that the cabins will be cluttered up near to every couple of miles. Now, we're right close to where I took my last deer. Over in those mountains to the east. If we move out at a little smarter pace we can make it there first thing in the morning."

"That suits me fine," Buck commented.

"You weren't far from there when you had your run-in with Pease's hooligans?" Nighthawk probed.

"Right you are. That's when the work begins."

Mid-morning found them well past the large tree where Preacher had hung his last kill. In fact, they had been on the trail of the men sent by Pease for better than an hour. It led constantly north and east. Preacher topped a small saddle draw that marked the access to yet another mountain highland valley. A string of dark objects, moving determinedly westward caught his eye.

"I got me a bad feelin' about this," he told his companions as he took the spyglass from his saddlebag.

With the brass tubes pulled to full-length, Preacher focused in on the far off blobs. One by one he counted thirty of them. His mouth twisted in a grimace of dislike.

"Wagh! They's comin' like flies to a dung heap," he spat his disgust.

"They're what I think they are?" Nighthawk asked.

"Sure enough. More greenhorn pilgrims headed west. Odds say they don't have the least idea where they are or where they're going. I tell you, boys, I've had more than my fill of 'em. I'd like to run this bunch clear the hell outta these mountains."

"But you won't do that," Nighthawk tweaked Preacher.

"Nope. Onliest thing we can do is ignore them an' hope they don't see us. Well, let's ride. This trail ain't gettin' any newer."

"What are we going to do when we find this Pease?" Buck asked.

"Go back for the rest of the boys an' wipe Pease out lock, stock, and barrel," Preacher pronounced carefully. The hot glow in his eyes verified that his annoyance with the corrupt trader had changed into implacable anger.

4

Falling Horse and Little Mountain still led their Dog Soldiers south and west toward the suspected location of Ezra Pease. One of the advance guards sent out by Falling Horse came back to the column of warriors with exciting news shortly after midday.

"We think we have found them. Six of the rolling lodges, some men, women, a few children."

"Yes. Pease took children from a white man's traveling lodges," Little Mountain declared.

"I know this to be true, we took three of them from the camp when we raided it," Falling Horse verified. "Even if they are not with Pease, it will be good to eliminate some of these wiggling white worms that invade us."

"We ride there now?" Little Mountain asked eagerly.

Falling Horse nodded to the scout. "Show us the way."

What the Cheyenne found were six stragglers who had become separated from the wagon train spotted by Preacher and his companions. Quickly the Dog Soldiers spread out to launch their attack on the unwanted visitors. Cries of alarm from the whites soon reached their ears and the wagons began to circle. Little Mountain led his braves to the south to close around the lumbering vehicles, while Falling Horse took his warriors above the hastily formed laager. They opened fire at a range of fifty yards.

Two pilgrims exchanged frightened glances. "My God, where'd those Injuns come from? I never saw a one," the burly one with a gray-streaked beard blurted.

"We made a mistake in stopping to fix that harness on the Kilmer wagon, Caleb."

"Now you know we couldn't have left them there all alone, Stub. They'd of been sitting ducks."

"Now all six of us are sitting ducks, Caleb. Watch yerself, they're gettin' close." Stub discharged both barrels of his shotgun in his nervous excitement. The recoil of the ten gauge nearly dislocated his shoulder. Pellets struck several braves and their ponies. It didn't put them out of the fight. They came on, whooping and howling.

Three small, tow-headed youngsters in Caleb's wagon added to their war cries. In a flash it seemed to be over. The Cheyenne broke off their charge and began to circle the wagons. An arrow thudded into one thick, oak side. Bullets moaned and cracked overhead. It soon became clear that the settlers would be going nowhere and the Indians had no intention of breaking off.

"We're all going to die out here," Caleb's frantic wife screamed from the rear of the wagon.

"Hush up, woman, and get to loading."

A flurry of shots blasted the hot, dry afternoon air. Dust rose in smothering clouds from the skiddery livestock. Once again, the Cheyenne wheeled their mounts a quarter way around and charged the wagons. Rifles and shotguns in the hands of men and women alike roared in defiance. When the heavy curtain of powder smoke cleared, the Indians were seen to have ridden a short ways off.

"There seems to be some sort of palaver goin' on," Caleb observed.

"Figgerin' who gets whose scalp most likely," Stub complained. He had reloaded his shotgun and now worked on the second of three rifles close at hand. What he disliked most was not that possibility, but that only three Indians lay on the ground beyond the circled wagons. While the whites recharged their weapons, even that changed as six warriors broke from the Indian position and rode out to recover their fallen friends.

When they returned to the lines, another charge began. They were doing well this time, when Preacher, Nighthawk, and Buck showed up over the rise to the west. The increased volume of fire startled the Cheyenne. They broke off the circle on the west side and turned to confront the men who rode to the relief of the settlers.

When the three white men drew nearer, Falling Horse identified Preacher. These two had sworn repeatedly not to make war on one another and, knowing that, Falling Horse called off the assault on the wagons. He came forward, making his identity clear to Preacher. Tension held for a while, during which the men from two worlds talked. Then Preacher walked Thunder toward the huddled immigrants.

"Git them wagons straightened out and set the mules off lickety-split. Don't spare 'em none, either. I can't hold these braves here for very long. Your other folks is about two hours ahead of you on the trail."

"You saved our lives," Caleb stated wonderingly. "We're eternally grateful."

"If you was smart as well as grateful, you wouldn't be here in the first place," Preacher growled back. "I don't know where you think yer goin', an' I don't care. But, sure's Hades is hot, you are in the wrong place now. Tell your wagon boss to cut north beyond the Bighorn Mountains if he's bound for Oregon. Now, step it up or you'll be the guests of honor at a scalpin' party."

After the last wagon trundled over the ridge to the west, Falling Horse came to where Preacher stood beside Thunder. "Where do you go that you are this far away from where we met you last?" the Cheyenne chief asked.

"Like I told you then, Falling Horse, we're out to get that no-account scoundrel, Pease."

"Then, once again we seek the same man, Preacher. This time it might not be wise for you to get to the whiskey peddler first."

Preacher cocked an eyebrow at his Cheyenne friend and grunted. He ignored the implied threat when he made reply. "Ride with the wind, Falling Horse."

"May the rain not take the strength from your bow, Preacher," the Cheyenne chief replied politely.

Then the two parties turned their separate ways and headed off on the trails they had been following.

Walt Hayward peered over the top of his half-spectacles at the sheets of vellum art paper. Yes, he'd seen these faces before. One big, callused hand stroked his beard in characteristic fashion. Them woeful-looking kids and that sneak-thief looking feller with them. After they had left, he'd discovered his storehouse to be shy of three gallon jugs of whiskey, a small keg of powder, and a gunnysack of potatoes.

"Yep. They passed through here better than a week ago. This one," Walt hefted the drawing of Phipps, "was a shifty-eyed little rat. Sticky-fingered, too, I'm thinkin'."

"How's that?" Marshal Talbot asked, alert to any news of the wanted band.

"Right after they took off up north, I came up short three jugs of whiskey. The good stuff, too," Walt added grumpily.

"I gather they haven't been back?" the lawman inquired.

"Nope. Nary hide nor hair. And good riddance to them. Though I feel sorry for those youngins, headed the way they are. The Blackfeet an' Cheyenne are cookin' up a war."

"Might be I'll catch up to them before that."

Curiosity put a light in the eyes of Walt Hayward. He'd never heard of anything important enough for a man to walk directly into an Injun war. "You plannin' on keepin' company with them?"

"No. They are wanted for a scad of crimes all the way back East. I'm here to arrest them."

Hayward didn't like the sound of that. "The kids, too?"

"That's what the warrants say."

"Well, Marshal, I'm right sorry to hear that. Those youngsters all seemed too scared of this-here Phipps to do anything lest he yelled at 'em to do it."

"That may be true, but it's not mitigating circumstances under the law," Talbot replied stiffly.

Walt Hayward reared his head back and eyed the marshal with obvious distaste. "You know, you're the first real lawman we've seen out here. They might do it that way back where you come from, but out here we take more store in fairness and justice than in whatever the law says. Find them good homes, with folks who'll love them, and they'll never give you another minute's trouble."

Marshal Talbot cleared his throat, emptied his tin cup of raw whiskey, and licked his lips. "I'll certainly take that under consideration, innkeeper. Now, I would appreciate a room for the night."

"A *room!*" Walt Hayward bellowed through a stout guffaw. "Marshal, I got *a* room, out back, with twelve rope-strung beds in it. He'p yerself."

For the past hour, as they rode on northeast, Preacher had grown uneasy over the weather. There had been that freak snowstorm three weeks back, and now clouds had started to pile up to the west. Already the highest peaks were lost in dirty gray mantles. Fat white bellies spilled down the wrinkles of the slopes. The air remained mild, almost balmy, so Preacher shrugged off his premonition and kept a wary eye on the buildup.

After an hour more, the impending change could no longer be ignored. "We've got us a storm brewin', Nighthawk."

"I can feel it in my bones, Preacher," the Delaware replied.

"What? No scientific double-talk to tell us what's happenin'?"

"It's the rhumatiz, Preacher, from those long days in the cold water. Don't tell me that's not what tipped you off."

Preacher snorted in merriment. When he recovered, he made a swift decision. "We'd best be lookin' for some place to shelter. It could be a bad one."

"I've spotted several places already," Nighthawk answered smugly.

"Why, you ol' coot," Preacher barked.

"It's him, all right," Titus Vickers remarked as he lowered the spy-glass. "Preacher, in the flesh."

Delphus Plunkett, one of the eight men with Titus Vickers, crawled up beside him and spoke softly into the outlaw leader's ear. "Think we could take him right here an' now?"

"There's two more with him," Vickers pointed out the obvious.

"Yeah, but there's nine of us. That means we outnumber them—uh—uh—three—or is it four?— to one."

"Haven't you learned as yet that three to one means nothing to Preacher?" Vickers snapped. "We'll wait a while longer. There's a storm brewing. What we'll do is move in on Preacher's backtrail and then close on them when the storm reduces visibility."

Ahead of them, the air split open with eye-searing light and a calamitous roar. Tremendous peals of thunder shook the ground and startled a flock of pigeons out of the trees. The pungent scent of ozone surrounded Preacher as he reached behind him for his poncho-like capote. The first drops of an icy rain fell around them as he whipped his hat from his head and draped the garment over his shoulders. At either side, Nighthawk and Buck sought similar protection from the elements.

With a seething hiss, the downpour increased, sped along in nearly horizontal sheets by a lashing wind that bent the tops of the fir and pine trees and wildly whipped the limber aspens.

"D'you have one of those places you saw in mind now?" Preacher drolly asked Nighthawk.

"I cannot see the nose of my horse, how can I be expected to find shelter?" the Delaware answered calmly.

"Well, I got a spot in mind," Preacher answered. "We're gonna get wet aplenty before we reach it."

"Then don't sit here jawing about it in this deluge," Nighthawk ripped out.

Preacher took the lead. He kept to the trail, that led up a steep incline. Water quickly gathered and ran in freshets along the sides of the course they followed. The constant booming of celestial artillery prevented conversation and each man retreated into his private thoughts.

Unaware of the crusade by Cora Ames to find homes among the missionary families, Preacher mulled over what to do with the orphans. Clearly, they had been handed some of life's rougher portions. From what they revealed at the trial of Silas Phipps, he had made every day, or at least the nights, pure hell for them. Considering the holier-than-thou attitude of most people, Preacher reflected, who would ever take to their hearts children who had suffered such perversions?

A grunt silenced Preacher's ruminations. He had more important things to think about. The way his mind wandered, he sounded as maudlin as those schoolmarms and gospelshouters that kept insisting on moving out here. Take, for instance, Ezra Pease. Preacher had heard nothing more about Pease after running the renegade out of the High Lonesome. Yet, Pease obviously kept him in mind. He'd spent enough time trying to bring an end to Preacher. Somehow that didn't add up. Not with the youngins Pease's men had taken from that wagon train. The trash riding for him might use kids in a bad way, but Pease didn't strike Preacher as being the Silas Phipps type. So, what were they for?

When Preacher saw the overhang, a blacker smudge against the darkness of the storm, he forgot about everything else, save getting out of the wet and cold. He touched Nighthawk on one shoulder.

"Over there, across the crick."

"I see it. A good place," Nighthawk answered.

Buck, with his flatlander's perceptions, stared right at it and had to have the arch of soil and boulders pointed out to him. "Oh, yeah. What'er we waitin' for?"

They found branches and twigs enough for a small fire under the lip that shielded them from the tempest. Preacher built it and then all three tended diligently to their horses, wiping them down and slipping nosebags on to feed the tired animals. "Coffee next," Preacher announced, producing a small, battered tin pot.

Along toward nightfall, with the rain still in blinding sheets, Preacher spoke the obvious. "We'll not be havin' any trail to follow when this is over."

"Only too true," Nighthawk agreed.

"Even I'm smart enough to know that," Buck added. "What do we do next?"

Preacher didn't even blink. "We figger out some other way to get to where Pease is holed up."

Beyond the other two, who hunkered with Preacher around the small fire that gave scant warmth, he saw flickers of movement against the grayish walls of water that dropped from the sky. Dark figures cut through the tortured aspens and moaning pines. Preacher had one of his four-shot pistols yanked free even before he spoke again.

"By gum, we've been jumped by more of them carrion-eaters."

Decent, law-abiding men didn't sneak up on a camp. They let everyone know of their presence loud and clear. Not these fellows. Preacher saw that right off and made the wisest move. Those with him flattened themselves on the rock shelf and he fired one .50 caliber barrel through the space previously occupied by Buck.

None too soon, because answering fire had already started on the way. Not as accurate as the ball sent by Preacher, the incoming lead smacked into and moaned off the back wall of the open-sided cave. Preacher's round found meat in the chest of one charging hard case. He flipped onto his back and gave up his life in a terrible groan.

Preacher now occupied a prone position beside his friends and they sent a heavy volume of fire toward the dimly seen figures. A horrendous flash of lightning illuminated the scene long enough for aim to be adjusted. Preacher sent another pile of trash off on the long trail of eternity with a double-shotted load to chest and gut.

Nighthawk winged a man who screamed his agony to the weeping sky. Buck gave a soft grunt and clapped his free hand to his upper arm. "Damn, got me in the shoulder."

"You all right?" Preacher asked.

"Burns like the fires of Hades, but I'll manage." To prove it, Buck downed a third of the craven bushwhackers.

Preacher put out such a volume of fire for a single man that the reports of his companions' weapons got lost in the repeated blasts. The next crash of lightning and thunder revealed the cowardly vermin in full flight.

"They're gone," Buck pronounced with relief.

"For now, maybe. An' maybe they've runned off to bring more of their kind," Preacher opined. "Might be that ray of hope we were lookin' for. Saddle up, we'll follow them."

"Jehosephat, that man has eyes like an eagle," Delphus Plunkett gulped after he steadied his heaving chest enough to speak.

"Weren't by accident," Titus Vickers allowed. "I'm beginin' to believe that Preacher ain't human."

"Whatever that means, what do we do now?" Plunkett bleated.

"Head back. They won't get far as long as this storm continues. We can lead Mr. Pease and all the gang right to their camp. That way, Preacher won't be pullin' any irons out of the fire so easily."

5

Preacher and his companions made poor headway, faced into the brunt of the storm. The heavenly outrage continued into a second day. Soaked until the pads of their fingers turned white and wrinkled, they pressed on. Preacher caught a fleeting glance of their quarry, only to lose them in a thick cloud that lowered to fill the canyon through which he, Nighthawk, and Buck walked their horses. Buck's wound had given him a lot of pain, yet Preacher knew that it would be certain death to send the man back alone.

Instead, he treated it frequently with moss and a few drops of whiskey from a small, gourd flask tied to Thunder's saddle. Preacher's own arm throbbed from the earlier gunshot and made any quick movement of his left side out of the question. They all held up well, confident the fleeing outlaws would lead them to Pease. Their expectations were nearly dashed when they made camp for the night.

A hastily constructed lean-to, covered with pine boughs, provided relief from the constant rain well enough to allow a hat-sized fire. While they dried themselves as best they could, another wave of the stalled-out front swung into place overhead. The first enormous clap of thunder shook them until their teeth rattled.

"This one ain't gonna be fun, fellers," Preacher advised.

"Have any of them been?" Nighthawk asked tartly.

"Not so's you'd notice, no," Preacher agreed dryly.

Jerky and stale, now soggy biscuits provided supper. The men munched in silence while nature raged around them. Preacher chewed purposefully, his senses tuned to the elements. A palpable intensity built within the disturbed air as Preacher opened his mouth to speak.

"I think . . ." He got no further.

A cascade of sound ripped at them. A man asleep under the mouth of a twenty-pounder cannon could not have been punished more. The world washed stark, actinic white, the air sizzled and crackled and stung their nostrils with ammonia, as a bolt of lightning struck a tall pine close to where they had secured the horses by ground anchor.

Nighthawk's mount, Sundance, and Buck's ex-outlaw plug panicked. Already weakened by the thorough soaking, the ground gave way around the corkscrew shaped anchors and the beasts bolted into the night. Only Thunder remained behind a second later. The sturdy animal had picked up his head, whinnied as though in pain, shook his big head and then trotted about nervously at the far extent of his tether. Preacher pulled on moccasins, draped himself with his capote and ran to comfort the nervous stallion.

"Easy there, Thunder. Easy, boy. I'm gonna bring you closer to us," Preacher crooned.

When he released the anchor and led Thunder up beside the lean-to, the anxious faces of Nighthawk and Buck popped out of the low shelter. "What about our horses?" Buck asked, shaken.

"Doubt they'll go far," Preacher opined, water dripping from the brim of his hat and the fringed hem of the capote. "An' this can't last forever. Come mornin', I'll set out after them. Now'd be a good time to grab some sleep."

"After that?" Buck asked with a nod toward the blazing pine. "I got jarred hard enough to loosen every tooth in my jaw."

"You chew on enough jerky an' they'll tighten up again," Preacher teased.

Buck threw his hands in the air. "Lord spare me from such humor."

By first light, the maelstrom had subsided to a drizzle. Preacher downed coffee, another stale biscuit, and saddled Thunder for the search. Nighthawk and Buck wished him good luck and set about drying everything they could put over their stingy fire.

At noon the sky showed patches of blue, large enough, as Preacher's father had used to put it, to make a Dutchman a pair of pants. It meant a clearing trend for certain. He also found smudged hoofprints that soon led him to Sundance. The Delaware's pony wickered a greeting to Thunder and allowed itself to be led peacefully along on the continuing search.

It seemed the odds had turned against him, Preacher reasoned as the trail remained illusive. Here and there he caught the marks of a riderless horse, yet never near enough to see the missing animal. He pushed on through the afternoon. Along toward what Preacher reckoned to be five o'clock, he developed a tightness and itch between his shoulder blades. He could swear someone had put eyes on him.

Then the sensation went away. The birds warbled their usual sweet music and insects hummed accompaniment as they recovered from the past two liquidy days. Preacher shrugged off the premonition, yet remained watchfully alert.

From the moment he heard hoof falls on the trail below, Delphus Plunkett knew his stock would surely rise in the outfit. His eyes narrowed to cold slits, when the man came into view, then widened when he recognized it to be Preacher. Thoroughly disabused of any ideas of bravado by past experience, Delphus wisely selected to keep watch and then report back to Vickers. It soon became obvious to Delphus Plunkett why Preacher was alone.

From his vantage point in a thick stand of fir, Delphus kept Preacher in sight until the wiley mountain man made a solitary camp and settled in for the night. Then Delphus took the reins of his horse and led it quietly away. Excitement charged his pale, watery blue eyes when he reported to Titus Vickers.

"It's Preacher, shore enough, alone, and not an hour's ride from here. He's got another horse with him, that gold one the Injun was ridin'."

"The storm must have driven off their mounts, scattered them through the mountains," Vickers surmised aloud.

"That's how I figgered it," Delphus prompted. "What do we do now? We gonna go back for Mr. Pease?"

"I don't think so. It's six to one now," Vickers savored his expected triumph. "Besides, he don't know we know where he is."

"He didn't the last time," Delphus reminded Vickers. It earned him a hard scowl.

"We'll wait until just before dark, then move in on him," Vickers planned the attack in low, heated tones. "We take him from three sides. But, you boys be careful to not overshoot the target. No sense in killin' each other."

Delphus Plunkett didn't think he liked the sound of that, though Vickers was boss of this search party. He went off to talk with some of the others.

Titus Vickers called them together. He reviewed his plan again and they mounted up. A mile short of the camp, with the eastern horizon turning dark purple, they halted and muffled the hooves of their horses with strips of gunnysack. Satisfied after a quick inspection, Vickers spread his men out and they made straight for where Preacher had bedded down for the night.

* * *

They came out of the stuff of his dreams. Mind still foggy from sleep and visions of the lovely movement of the backside of Miss Cora Ames, Preacher's body took over at the first sound of a bootsole scuffing ground. He rolled free of his blankets with a big four-shot in each hand. Muzzle flashes came from left and right so he swung his arms wide, wincing at the stab of pain in his left one, and triggered each of the big guns.

He had no expectation of hitting flesh, only sought to confuse and jangle his enemies. One of them, partly blinded by the boom of his own and Preacher's pistol stumbled into the fire ring. Sparks from the hot ashes and buried coals swarmed up his trouser leg. The stench of smoldering hair and burned flesh formed a cloud around him. Howling, he hobbled away from the resurrected blaze and directly into the flight path of a bullet fired by Titus Vickers.

"Son of a bitch!" Vickers blurted when he saw the fatal collision.

Preacher cycled the barrels of his right-hand pistol and took aim this time. Before the glow from burning gases dimmed, he had moved, cat quick, to a low boulder that protruded like a giant potato from a mound of earth. Not a hell of a lot in the way of protection, but it would have to do, Preacher decided.

"Where'd he go?"

"What happened?"

Preacher had gotten his way about the confusion. Already one of the attackers had been shot by another. Maybe he could improve the score, the crafty mountain man decided as he tried to recover his night vision enough to find a target. It proved easier than it would have an hour later.

Darkness lay in shadow pools in the meadow where Preacher had camped, yet above, long bars of magenta and crimson still streaked the western sky. It intruded enough, though weakly, for Preacher to take stock of his enemy. One man stood dumbstruck at the side of the fire, his attention riveted on the fallen thug. Preacher used that one's lack of motion to sight in a perfect shot.

Trailing sparks of partly burned powder, the conical ball in that barrel sped to the chest of the hapless man. The soft lead ball, thirty-eight to the pound, opened out to over .75 caliber on impact with the breastbone of the vicious lout, who made not a sound as he fell face first into the fire pit. Two down, how many to go? Preacher wondered as he rapidly shifted his gaze in order not to miss any opportunity for another shot. In the darkness, the best way to lose an object, Preacher knew, was to stare directly at it.

A flicker of something darker, moving against the night shadows, drew his attention. He fired the fourth and final load in that pistol, only to discover that it missed. Three yellow-white bursts in the blackness revealed as many opponents. They fired high and wide of the intended target. Preacher patted his buckskin-clad chest in search of the powder horn and ball pouch he had come away with.

Once located, rather than go to his second pistol, he set about reloading the first. Patches came from a recess behind the hinged butt-plate, and caps from the wooden capblock at his waist. He had three barrels reloaded before his assailants recovered enough of their wits to determine the location of one another. He rammed the fourth home a moment before they tried a concerted rush on his position.

They came at a rush, bent low, as Preacher raised his unwieldy pistol and fired at the nearest. A high, thin cry advised him of success. Like nearly everyone, Preacher knew that night shooting presented some tricky problems. Not the least of which was being able to see your target. Preacher relied on a simple technique. His first shot drew their fire, which positioned them for him. He dumped two more with the next three rounds, then changed for the loaded pistol.

"Get in there, get going," a harsh voice prodded from the darkness.

Preacher tried to find that voice with a bullet. He missed and counted muzzle flashes from three weapons. Taking care to aim slightly to the left and an inch lower than one muzzle bloom, he triggered another round. A sobbing voice followed thrashing in the underbrush.

"Oh, Lordy, Lordy, I'm hit bad."

The gravel voice came again. "Where are you shot, Delphus?"

"Through my right lung, Mr. Vickers. I ain't long for this world."

Vickers didn't bother to answer. Instead, he directed his last man forward. He could not believe Preacher could be so lucky. Lucky, because no man could be that good. He and John Dancer stepped into the open at the same time. Preacher's pistol banged again and Dancer grunted softly before he fell face first on the ground. Vickers fired at the muzzle flash. Then he bent and retrieved Dancer's pair of pistols.

No time to reload, Preacher realized. He drifted off to one side in the thicket of hemlock, eyes at work to locate the enemy still out there. The crackle of a dry twig pointed Preacher the right way. He could take the risk of reloading in the dark, yet discarded that idea for something a lot surer. Ears searching for him, Preacher continued to edge closer to where Vickers likewise stalked him. A hidden depression in the ground caused Preacher to stumble and set the brush to rattling to his left side.

At once, Vickers fired. Muzzle bloom illuminated his face, a mask of rage, which quickly faded out. Preacher moved away.

"Preacher, you hear me?" Vickers called out. "I'm supposed to bring you in alive. Ezra Pease wants to deal with you up close and personal. For my own part, I'd as soon kill you quick and leave you for the scavengers."

Preacher refrained from making any reply. Instead, he wormed his way between two stunted fir trees and glided downslope toward the sound of the voice. Gradually, the last scudding clouds cleared away and pale starlight spread downward. Preacher saw his man then.

Down on one knee, Titus Vickers swung the muzzle of his

second pistol in an arc. He didn't see Preacher, who advanced. Embolden by the silence, some night creature that had hunkered down at the outbreak of gunfire bolted through the underbrush. Vickers fired wildly in its direction. Realization struck Vickers that he had fired his last weapon. At once his hand went to his powder horn. He worked desperately to load a pistol, as Preacher advanced to a spot within arm's reach behind the outlaw leader.

"Vickers, is it?" Preacher spoke softly. "I'm right behind you."

In panicked reaction, Vickers whirled and fired the reloaded pistol. The ball passed within an inch of Preacher's head. Vickers reversed the smoking weapon and came up at Preacher. The butt whizzed through the air, a wicked sound, and missed the mark. Preacher sidestepped and swung at Vickers's head with his tomahawk. At the last instant, Vickers blocked the blow with his improvised club. Both men grappled for a moment and Vickers reached his free hand for the knife in his belt sheath.

With a grunt, they broke away. Vickers flailed with the clubbed pistol and Preacher blocked it. This time, when the tomahawk checked the momentum, Preacher rolled the shaft of his war hawk and swung in a horizontal slash. The keen edge cut through the clothing Vickers wore and made a shallow cut on his upper chest. It burned like hot coals and Vickers bit his lip to keep from crying out. He whipped the pistol across in front of him, and aimed at Preacher's temple.

Preacher ducked away from the deadly blow and gave an overhand swing with the 'hawk. It buried deep in the meaty portion of Vickers's right shoulder. The pistol fell from his grip. His knife flashed in the starlight and Preacher decided to end it right there. Another hefty swatch with the tomahawk and the skull of Vickers gave off a ripe mellon *thock!* as steel sank deeply through bone into the brain.

Eyes already glazed, Vickers went down, nearly dragging Preacher with him. His mouth worked, yet no sound came out. Short-circuited, his brain no longer commanded his body. Preacher looked down on Vickers without any show of emotion.

"Yer the best Pease has sent so far," Preacher provided an epitaph for the dead man.

With ten horses in tow, Preacher set out the next morning to locate the last missing mount. For all the rain, he was surprised to see how clear a trail had been left. A sore stiffness in his left arm reminded him of the previous night's activity. No matter how he figured it, he could not be more than thirty-five or thirty-seven years old at most. Yet, he sensed a slowing down. Wounds took longer to heal, prolonged hard activity left tight, aching muscles where none had lingered before. He had known of fellers in the High Lonesome who had not seen their fortieth birthday, and not from carelessness. The energy just seemed to drain out of them and they were found along the trail or in their cabin, frozen like a block of ice.

Taking stock, Preacher vowed that it would not happen to him. So far he managed to keep on going. So long as he didn't give in to the increased twinges and aches, he reckoned he could continue that way. He'd let time decide for how long. His ruminations over the state of his health brought him to near midday. Dismounting, he set the horses to graze and retrieved the last of his biscuits and brewed coffee. He would soften the rock-hard bread in a cup and have it with jerky. He looked up from his tasks to see his Appaloosa horse watching him.

"It's jist you an' me, Thunder. With a good hoss like you, a man can do anything." The big, gray, spotted-rump animal raised its massive head and twitched ears inquisitively. A moment later it whinnied in greeting.

"What you pickin' up out there, Thunder?" Preacher asked.

For an answer, the Appaloosa whinnied again and snorted a horselaugh as Buck's strayed mount ambled into the meadow and lined out for Thunder. Preacher shook his head in mystified amusement. "Ain't that somethin'. Go out to find these critters an' one of them winds up findin' me."

Thunder nickered softly beside Preacher's ear. Quickly the mountain man gathered in the stray horse, rigged the string and headed back for the overhang where Nighthawk and Buck waited. His thoughts turned right away to the lovely Miss Cora Ames. A woman like that could just about domesticate an old tomcat like him, Preacher decided after due reflection.

Nice turn of ankle—he'd caught a flash during the first encounter with Indians—good lookin' legs, too. Good bone structure—as though he evaluated a horse for purchase. A heart-melting smile. If only—if only she weren't one of those gospel-spouting mission folk. Got on a feller's nerves, rightly enough. Enough so that he didn't harbor any romantic notions . . . or so he told himself. His mind turned to other matters.

Get these horses back. Distribute them and the guns. Then get on after Ezra Pease. He had spent enough time thinking about it. Buck had taken a ball in his shoulder. Maybe send him back alone with the animals. Sure. That shined. The days left to Ezra Pease would be that much shorter.

6

Nighthawk and Buck greeted Preacher upon his return. Buck expressed his disapproval of the plan Preacher outlined even before the mountain man had the last words out of his mouth.

"I don't like the sound of that, Preacher. I don't mean I'm worried about makin' it back by myself. I'm thinkin' of what might happen if you run across the whole body of those scum."

"I did in a dozen of them jist yesterday, didn't I?" Preacher challenged, an eyebrow cocked.

"And I still don't know how," Buck shot back. "This wound smarts some, but I can carry my load."

"Don't doubt you can, ol' son. But we'd be slowed down with all these horses, the guns, and powder. This way everyone can keep in touch."

That ended the argument. With a good six hours of daylight left, they set off at once. Preacher easily picked up the backtrail of Vickers and his gunmen. It led northwestward, which set off a tingle of premonition along Preacher's spine. He knew the mountains well in this area. If pushed by the

Cheyenne, Pease and his band would no doubt flee south-ward. Following the most accessible route, it would take them, eventually, to the valley where the helpless pilgrims had settled. He expressed his concern to Nighthawk while the sun slanted well down on their shirt fronts.

"We'd best turn west some. I've an idee where they went. We want to be able to cut them off from runnin' south if the Injuns hit them again."

Nighthawk frowned. "We're getting close to Rabbit Ear Pass. If Pease has moved camp beyond there, going south would put them right in among our nest of pilgrims."

"Just so," Preacher allowed. "Dang if I shouldn't have thought of that before Buck took off. He could have carried a warnin' to those folks."

Nighthawk scowled and shook his head. "They wouldn't listen. You know that."

A snort came from Preacher's nostrils, fluttering the long, soft hairs of his mustache. "Damned if I don't think you're right. Those gospel-shouters can be the most one-way crit-ters I've ever done seen. We'd best be findin' a place to stop. We'll hit the pass tomorrow."

Hashknife rode into camp at twilight. A worried frown creased his brow. He left his mount with young Vern Beevis and strode to where a pole and brush hut had been outfitted for Ezra Pease. He found the land grabber downing a stiff shot of bourbon.

"No sign of Preacher anywhere," he reported.

Pease produced an ugly expression. "Where is he? Worse, Titus Vickers has not returned. I'm relying on you to come up with some answers." With that, he gestured to the small keg of good Tennessee sour mash.

Their talk went long into the night. A pug-nosed thug brought them food, which they consumed untasted. Hashknife felt relieved to get away at last. He headed for his own lean-to, intending to clean the brace of brand new .44 Walker Colt he wore around his lean hips. Those six-shooters were the envy of everyone in camp.

An improvement to the Colt Patent Firearms Co. revolver, Model of 1838, designed by Colonel Walker of the Texas Rangers, the new sidearms featured a trigger guard and fixed trigger, instead of the open, folding trigger that made the original revolver so dangerous to carry in heavy brush. It also had a lighter cylinder and an improved barrel wedge. Six nipples, protected by a recoil plate, allowed the weapon to be carried fully loaded and ready for business. Although a smart man wore it with the hammer down on an empty chamber. A hinged rammer, affixed under the barrel, allowed for reloading while on a moving horse. Hashknife knew full well that about half of the lowlife scum in camp would have gladly killed to possess the pair he owned.

Except, of course, that he was so much more accurate a shot, and could deliver such devastating firepower so much faster than any of them that they didn't have a chance. Hashknife truly believed the astonishing weapons had saved his life several times before, and felt confident they would again.

His head a bit muzzy from all the liquor, Hashknife swung by the central campfire for a cup of coffee He arrived in the midst of an ongoing conversation.

Vern Beevis steadily whanged the ear of Two Thumbs Buehler with his whiney voice. "Now, I tell you, an' I've seen him up close, that Preacher ain't human. He's part wolf, I swear it. No human man can sneak up so close to a body without bein' heard. An' another thing . . ."

Two Thumbs raised his disfigured hand to silence the stream. "You don't think I've seen him in action? Well, hell, boy, he's human enough. Jist good. Damn' good. Way I hear it, he's been in these mountains since he was a little tad. Growed up knowin' ever' nook an' cranny, the twist an' turn of ever' canyon an' trail."

"Well, don't that sound like a lobo-wolf to you?" Beevis persisted.

"No it don't," Two Thumbs snapped. "All that has to be done to get rid of Preacher is to catch him out in the open an' . . . *Whang!* blast him with a rifle." He gave Beevis a "so there" look.

Hashknife could not resist. "The problem is getting him in the open."

Both of the Missouri trash looked up at the tall, slender outlaw with the powerful six-guns. Beevis started to speak, then thought better of it. Two Thumbs Buehler gave him a lopsided grin.

"I suppose you've got the way to do that?"

Hashknife produced a grim smile. "I might. And if what I suspect is right and Titus Vickers doesn't return, I'll have a chance to prove it."

"Why ain't Vickers comin' back?" Beevis blurted.

"I think Preacher has gotten them all."

"That ain't possible, Hashknife. Vickers had a dozen men with him."

"Fifteen actually," the cultured voice of Hashknife corrected. "Our poor Titus insisted on searching the area where we know Preacher to have been roaming. Given his unusual properties, it takes little imagination to envision Titus running afoul of the mountain man. We know he's not alone," Hashknife went on, repeating the substance of his talk with Ezra Pease. "He has at least three of his scruffy type with him. And, even when we've found bodies, they have been stripped of weapons and ammunition. Their horses taken. Preacher is taking those for someone to use. What I don't know is who."

"Does Mr. Pease know all this?"

"We talked about it. Half the night, in fact." Hashknife yawned and stretched. "If Preacher found Vickers, he can backtrack him to us. Were I you, I'd get all the rest I could. Things are going to get rather hot around here, quite soon."

* * *

Preacher wanted to ride ahead and see what lay beyond a big bend in the trail they followed. So, he was alone when five of the fresh ruffians jumped him. The first shot caught him by surprise. For some reason his notions weren't prodding him like usual. The ball cracked past his head and he spotted a puff of smoke in some gorse at the base of the treeline on his left.

His Hawken came to his shoulder in a smooth, swift motion and he had the hammer back before another round could be fired. He sent the double ball load a bit to the left of the white puff, then lowered his weapon and slid the French rifle from its saddle scabbard. Another of the lowlifes fired an instant before the LeFever roared.

By then, a yell told him his first shot had counted. Sitting atop a horse, like a thumb poked up from a fist, made too good a target, Preacher realized and slid from the saddle. He ground-reined Thunder and moved away toward a rotting tree that lay at an odd angle to the slope.

"Those fellers up there ain't got the good sense to give it up and make a run," Preacher surmised aloud. And they wouldn't give him time to reload, he reasoned as he lay the French rifle aside.

"Right on both counts," Preacher congratulated himself a moment later when the remaining four thugs broke clear of the underbrush and ran downhill toward him, firing as they came.

Preacher eased one of his big pistols from its holster and cocked the hammer. A little bit closer, he estimated. Hold it. That's the way. One of them critters runs a bit faster than the rest. He'll get his reward for it. The four-barrel cracked. Dust and cloth formed a plume at the center of the chest of the man nearest to Preacher. He went over backward. The others suddenly discovered they had emptied their rifles.

One brought forth a pistol as they scrambled for whatever scant cover they could find. He fired wildly behind Preacher.

His bullet passed over the tree trunk. Preacher didn't even blink. Instead, he rotated the barrels and fired again.

"My leg!" a bucktoothed bit of slime shrieked. "Oh, God, he done shot me through the leg."

"Crawl over here, you idiot," snarled another of the trash.

The third lout raised up from behind a rock and popped a round in Preacher's direction. The ball thudded into the wood of the deadfall. Preacher readied the third barrel. Blood, hair, and a slouchy, black felt hat flew into the air and the ambusher slumped over the small boulder. That left two; the wounded man and the one with the bad attitude, Preacher kept score.

"C'mon, Hank, help me," the leg-shot villain whined.

"Think I'm gonna show myself, yer crazy," grumbled his companion.

Preacher tried a new gambit. "Hey, Hank, don't you reckon you bit off more'n you can chew?"

"Go to hell, Preacher," Hank shouted back.

His answer came in the form of rock chips in the face and dust in his eyes. Cursing, Hank moved to one side and exposed a wedge of his thick back. Preacher changed pistols and fired at that slim target. He missed, but sent Hank scurrying on hands and knees for a more secure position.

"Ain't neither of you leavin' here alive," Preacher taunted.

"I'm bad hurt. You wouldn't kill a helpless man, would you?" the whiner bleated.

"Damn betcha. At least one o' your kind."

"Jesus, you're a hard man, Preacher."

"Got to be." Preacher sensed movement off to his right and turned that direction.

Hank came at him with a pistol in both hands. Preacher snapped off a round and fought the complexity of his weapon's mechanism. Hank closed ground swiftly. He fired blindly and showered Preacher with decomposing bark. Preacher shot back. Another miss. With a triumphant grin on his face, Hank loomed over his intended victim and fired his second pistol.

His ball burned a hot line across the top of Preacher's left shoulder. Preacher loosed his last round. It grazed Hank's rib cage. Undeterred, Preacher came to his feet, his tomahawk in his left hand. He swung at the astonished Hank and received a yelp of surprise as reward. Hank backpeddled and holstered one pistol. The other he used, clublike, to batter at Preacher's head while he drew a long, slender knife.

Their action had not gone unnoticed by the wounded slime. "Kill 'im, Hank, kill him for me."

"You'd best be thinkin' about yourself, Hank, not him," Preacher advised, as he and his adversary circled. "Turn tail now and we'll be even."

"Not a chance. I ain't never turned tail in my life," Hank growled, still in his black mood.

"It's your funeral," Preacher observed dispassionately.

Then he struck. Swift as lightning, the tomahawk whuffled through the air, and sank into the extended left forearm of Hank. Howling, Hank released the knife and backed up. Preacher wrenched his 'hawk free and swung it backhand. The pointed knob on the rear smacked into Hank's ribs. He grunted and whipped the clubbed pistol toward Preacher's head.

Preacher ducked and brought his own knife from the sheath. It glinted in the high altitude sunlight, the edge a wicked blue fire. Hank cut his eyes to it; a bird fascinated by the snake. Too late he realized his mistake. The tomahawk descended in a whistling arc that ended with the blade buried to the heft in the top of his skull.

"Unnngh." The soft sound came from blood-frothed lips as Hank sank to his knees.

Preacher forced the axe head free and bent to wipe it on the shirt Hank wore. That's when he discovered that the wounded man had taken the interim to reload. A .60 caliber pistol ball moaned past Preacher's right ear. A second one was due to follow from another pistol, only Preacher acted too soon. He leaped to one side and did a shoulder roll.

Coming up on one knee, he raised his arm in a saluting gesture and let the 'hawk fly. It struck true and split the breast bone of the injured trash. Reflexively, his pistol discharged into the ground. Preacher came to his moccasins.

"Wouldn't leave it alone, would you? Jist wouldn't leave it alone."

He walked over and retrieved his bloodied tomahawk from the dying man's chest. Lips worked into a grimace of pain as the ruffian struggled to speak.

"B'God, ya killed me, Preacher."

"I know that. Didn't have to be."

"No," the swiftly expiring drifter corrected. "Weren't no other way. You or us. Th-there's more. They be comin' any time."

Preacher pursed his lips. "I reckoned that. But, thank you for doin' the decent thing. When it's over, I'll see that you're buried proper like."

"Won't be time for that."

"I mean after I'm done with them," Preacher explained grimly.

"Oh . . . yes . . . I see." Then he gave a shudder and died.

Quickly, Preacher began to reload. His own weapons first, then those of the dead men. Almost with no time to spare, eight more of the two-legged beasts rushed through the twilight effect of the tree-shaded glen on foam-flecked horses. Preacher reasoned that his first pick had been a good one, and returned to the dead pine to take up position. Only two of the outlaw weapons had not been loaded. He could stand them off for a while.

He had heard the very first shots. No reason not to, they hadn't been that far away. At once Bart Haskel shouted to the men with him and put spurs to the flanks of his mount. The horses reached for distance as one. A long, uphill grade sweated their skins in no time. Over in the next valley, Bart told himself. The boys he had sent ahead had run onto something. He had a good idea what. They crested the ridge line and reined in.

Far below in the meadow they saw dark, crumpled figures sprawled in the grass. A single man stood over them, working to load a rifle. "Gawdamn, it's Preacher," Bart bellowed. No one else, he knew, could have taken out five able gunmen like that.

"We've got him now," King Skuyler boasted.

"Only if we keep our heads," Haskel responded "Spread out as we go down hill. We have to hit him from different places and all at once."

It didn't work that way, and in less than three minutes Bart Haskel regretted it bitterly. Preacher heard them coming and skittered behind a fallen tree. With the terrain a blur from the movement of their horses, the outlaws could not see a trace of the buckskin-clad Preacher when he melted from sight behind the deadfall. Preacher could see them, though, and in a moment, proved it.

A puff of white smoke spurted from the tree and, a second later, the ball made a meaty smack as it struck flesh. One of Haskel's men cried out sharply and fell across the neck of his mount as blood flowed freely from one shoulder.

"Awh, crap," Haskel spat. Then the fight was on in earnest.

Preacher waited long enough to insure that any failings of the strange weapons did not effect his marksmanship, then he opened up. A hit on the first shot smacked of good medicine. He had made a quick count and knew he faced eight men alone. Oh, well, he'd had worse, and against some fighting mad Blackfeet, too. He exchanged rifles and popped another cap.

He winced with regret as the ball shot low and struck a horse full in the breast. The animal shrieked and its front legs collapsed. That vaulted the rider over the neck and head and landed him on the crown of his balding pate. Even at that distance, Preacher could hear the crisp snap of bone in spine and skull. Time for another rifle.

Preacher selected his French LeFever. Some of the enemy began to hold back in the face of his deadly accurate fusillade. The hammer fell and a thin, blue spurt of smoke came from the cap. The rifle recoiled solidly and projected the conical ball into the grinning face of a lout with a brow so low Preacher swore the man could wrap his lower lip over it. Now the odds looked a little better. Back to five on one.

"What say, Thunder?" he called out as he selected another long gun. "This is turnin' out to be one hell of a day, ain't it?"

Bart Haskel wisely decided on a change of tactics. He waved an arm over his head and signaled for the rest to follow him. With a hard pressure on the right rein, and a tug on the left, he sent his horse diagonally across Preacher's field of fire. Without realizing it, he lined out directly toward the trees where the five dead men had begun. Preacher sent two more balls after them, then turned his attention to the ridgeline above.

Four more scruffy derelicts had shown up. With only a slight pause to take in the situation, they angled downhill to join up with the rest of their misbegotten kind. Preacher slapped the stock of his Hawken.

"Be damned if I ain't worser off than before," he spat.

Time dragged after the fighting dwindled to an occasional shot. That suited Preacher right fine. He used the lull to reload. Then he started taking potshots at those who wanted his head so badly. One of the vermin climbed a tree to try to get a clear angle on Preacher. His first shot gave away his position. Preacher drew a fine bead.

An ongoing shriek of pain and terror answered his efforts. When the wounded man could make himself coherent, the reason became clear. "He s-s-shot me low!" he screamed.

Pitiful wails and sobs of despair continued for a while. But no one came to help the groin-shot brigand.

"Miserable bastards, they won't even help their own,"

Preacher grumbled aloud. Then he stiffened. He had seen ghostlike movements from the corner of one eye.

Preacher turned his head slightly and cut a hard look at the spot where he had noticed the rustle of a sumac branch. Nighthawk, sure's God made green apples, Preacher reckoned. Darkness had begun to fall and it appeared as though the opponents had stalemated. Well, things would start to heat up a mite once Nighthawk managed to drift in beside him. Together they could cook up a real nasty stew. Might be fun after all, Preacher decided, a grin cutting his face.

7

Moonset came at a few minutes after eleven o'clock that night. Preacher slipped away from his friend, to circle around the remaining outlaws. They had discussed the matter and concluded that it would be best for Preacher to go alone. If any of the human garbage made a break in that direction, Nighthawk's gunfire would serve to confuse them even more, convincing them that Preacher remained where last they had seen him.

A heady aroma rose from the dew-damp sage and lupine through which Preacher forged on foot. His moccasins made such slight whispers they could not be heard more than a couple of feet away. Each tread, he planted the edge of his foot first, tested the ground, then rolled inward to the ball, his heel never touching the ground unless he came to a full halt. Bent low, he avoided low-hanging branches which would brush noisily against his buckskins. After a half hour of circling approach, Preacher came in close enough to hear low, murmured conversation around a tiny fire. All of the men, strangers to this country, sat with their backs to the outside world, he noticed when he edged in close enough to see.

"Dang it, this sure'n hell ain't my idea of how to track a feller down," Goose Parker complained.

"How you propose to go about it?" Rupe Killian challenged. "You figger to go out there in the dark and jump on Preacher whilst he sleeps?"

Goose defended his stance. "It could be done."

"Sure, by a ghost," Killian scoffed.

Delphus Plunkett blanched. "Don't go talkin' about ghosts," he pleaded. "You ask me, that Preacher acts 'nuff like one to give us all nightmares."

Preacher smiled in the darkness. From the sound of it, they were doing half his work for him. He moved silently on to another vantage point. He wanted to find their horses before the fun began.

When Preacher reached the horses, he found with them a little pug-faced lout, barely out of his teens, if that much. Preacher sidled up behind him without giving a modicum of warning. His big, steely arm snaked around the punk's neck and tightened to the hardness of a vise. Preacher put his lips close to the ear of the bug-eyed youth and whispered softly.

"You fancy meetin' your Maker tonight?" He released his grip enough for the kid to make a reply.

"N-no—ooooh, noooo," came a soft, sincere reply.

"Then I suggest you cut your losses right fast. Pick your horse and walk him real quiet out of here and ride for the main trail, then head south."

"M-my—my saddle an' gear?" came a plaintive appeal.

"You got the things you need most; your bridle, your gun, your horse, and . . . your life. Was I you, I'd be grateful for that and haul outta here."

That didn't take much thinking on, especially when the young ruffian felt the cold edge of Preacher's knife against his throat. "Yes—yessir, I surely will."

"That's a good boy. I reckon your momma will be glad to see you back home and safe. Now get along and do it."

With the guard out of the way, Preacher swiftly arranged

for the second act of his little drama. He released three of the horses and left the rest. Then he worked his way back in close to the collection of scum that hunkered around the fire. Using the advantage of the steep mountain sides that surrounded their campsite, he gave off a series of wolf howls.

He could almost feel the chills that gathered along the spines of the tenderfoot brigands. Their conversation died off at the first mournful yowl. Then, breathless, barely more than a whisper, the questions began.

"What's that?"

"What's going on?"

"Ned, you out there with the horses?" A pause, then, "Ned? You hear me?"

Another wolf howl, longer this time and sounding closer. *"Ned! Answer me!"* came a frightened demand.

Preacher gave them the cough and hiss of a puma. Low, soft moans followed, like the tortured soul of a damned man. Then Preacher threw back his head to take advantage of the natural sound chamber.

"He's comin' to get you, too. He'll carve out your hearts and eat your livers," he drawled out in ghostly voice.

"Awh, Lordy—Lord, it ain't human. Somethin's done got Ned and it's comin' for us."

"Shut up, you idjit!" Rupe Killian snapped.

Another panther caterwaul and the loose horses broke into shrill whinnies as they thundered away from the picket line. "B'God, the horses!" Rupe shouted.

"I'm gettin' outta here," Goose wailed.

"Yeah, yeah, we'll do that, right after we get them horses," Killian agreed, his own spine having a spell of icy shivers. "Goddamn you, Preacher!" he bellowed, certain the mountain man was behind this, but unable to quell his own terror.

Preacher spooked off through the underbrush, his lips pulled back in a pleased smile, a chuckle only partly repressed as his chest heaved. That bunch would live to fight another day, but it didn't really matter. In their fright, they'd lead him right to Ezra Pease. And about time.

* * *

Rosy morning light showed a clear trail left by men in a total panic. Nighthawk nodded to the scuffled ground.

"Looks like they left in a hurry."

"Somethin' must have upset 'em durin' the night, 'Hawk. What you reckon?"

"Ghosts, perhaps? It's said these mountains are haunted by the spirits of the Arapaho ancestors. Funny, I thought I heard a cougar not far off last night."

"Mayhaps you did," Preacher replied with a twinkle in his eyes. "Reckon we just oughtta follow these fellers an' see where they've gone."

"I don't imagine it will be a long trail," Nighthawk opined.

"How's that?"

"The way they are running those horses," the Delaware went on as they rode along the clearly marked escape route, "they won't last long."

Preacher gave a dry chuckle. "You're learnin' right fast, Nighthawk."

Nighthawk put on a show of affront. "'Learnin' is it? Why, I forgot more than you know about the High Lonesome before you were out of knee-britches."

Preacher joined in with his own barb. "You ain't that old. I ain't either, for that matter. We're headed for some right interestin' valley over Elk Crick way. If Pease is anywhere around, we should be cuttin' more sign any time now."

Within an hour, Preacher's prediction came true. The tracks they followed became swallowed up in a heavily traveled stretch of trail. That decided them to press on a little faster. Preacher admitted he had developed a considerable itch to come face to face with Ezra Pease.

Back in his not-so-secure valley, harmony and tranquility fled for Ezra Pease the moment the survivors returned. "This can't be happening!" he railed. "I send out twenty of you and you fourteen come back, your tails between your legs, whining about wild animals working in concert with Preacher."

Hat in hand, Rupe Killian tried to explain. "It's true, Mr. Pease. There was wolves an' some sort of lion, we all heard its chillin' cry. Somethin' done et young Ned Morton. Not a sign of him anywhere."

"No blood? No intestines on the ground?" Pease asked sarcastically. "All of you," he assailed the gathered trash, the possibility that his planning was flawed never occurring to him. "You disappoint me terribly. At every turn you fail. I thought I had brought along men of intelligence, of perspicuity, instead, it seems I have recruited a company of poltroons."

His eyes narrowed as his mood changed again. "This is all Preacher's fault. His doing, and his alone." Then he deflated, realizing that it was indeed his men who had failed. For a moment he cast his eyes heavenward. "Why am I surrounded by incompetents, fools, and cowards?" he pleaded. Then his own cunning provided a solution. "You are all cut one third of what you've been promised. It will be divided equally among any of the rest of you who can stand up to Preacher and bring him to me. That is, if any of you think you're man enough to face an army of wild animals to get to him." His contempt vibrated in the mocking words.

Hashknife stepped forward. "I'd like a chance at that."

Pease beamed and clapped the Easterner on one shoulder. "Good. Now, here's a man who knows how to seize the advantage. Hashknife, select the men you want and make ready to go back with whichever of these cowards will guide you to where they ran into Preacher. Trail him, track him to his lair, and then send back someone to guide the rest of us there. He's overplayed his hand this time. There will have to be some signs left to lead you to him. This time, Preacher will be surrounded and cut down like the dog he is."

*   *   *

Unknown to Ezra Pease, Preacher and Nighthawk lay be-hind a low screen of young spruce, low on the slope of the mountainside overlooking the camp. They had worked their way into hearing range, at least of the shouted tirade of the outlaw leader.

Preacher had to cover his mouth to stifle a chuckle when Pease laid the blame at the mountain man's feet. The way Preacher saw it, Pease refused to see his own weaknesses. He probably couldn't plan a trip to an outhouse without mis-hap. When the camp grew busy with activity as men made ready to go with the man named Hashknife, Preacher and Nighthawk silently withdrew.

Far enough away that their voices would not carry, Preacher rubbed his jaw and expressed a niggling curiosity about the new manhunter sent after him. "That feller Pease called Hashknife. There's somethin' mighty familiar about him. The cut of his jaw, his hair . . . somethin' says I should know him."

"You have seen him before?" asked Nighthawk.

"No. Not that I recall. More like I've seen his pappy, or someone in the family. There's . . . jist a touch of some-thing."

Nighthawk clapped him on the shoulder. "It will come to you. Now do we go back for enough men to finish this?"

"You do, I'm gonna stay, make sure they don't all get out of here and disappear again."

Nighthawk frowned. "Even for you, that could be quite a job."

"I know, ol' hoss. Don't reckon on takin' 'em on all alone. If they move, I go along an' leave a trail."

Nighthawk nodded. "Then good luck. I should be back in three days. Near as I can judge, you were right about this lo-cation is due north of the new settlement. Should be easy."

Preacher struck Nighthawk gently on the shoulder. "Ride with the wind, Nighthawk."

"Be sure of it."

Preacher saw his friend off, then settled in to keep track

of the outlaw band. Then he set about preparing some unpleasant surprises for anyone who wished to get out of the
valley. He started on the trail to the south.

There he located some springy aspen saplings and bent
half a dozen on each side in arcs away from the trail. These
he secured while he fashioned some pencil-sized twigs into
sharp-pointed spikes, which he secured with rawhide thongs
along the saplings, pointed toward the trail. Then he rigged
trip lines that crossed the roadway at the proper distance
from the deadly traps and eased the tension of the deadly
flails into their strain. Satisfied, Preacher moved on.

Silently he wished he had a dozen men with sharp spades
to dig some pits. Then, thought of injury to innocent horses
changed his mind. With spare ropes and thongs left with him
by Nighthawk, he rigged a spike-bristling deadfall to swing
out of concealment among low branches and knock at least
two men off their mounts. Some tough vines and a smoothly
grooved rock provided a huge snare that could yank yet another piece of vermin from the saddle.

Preacher kept up his work throughout the day and most of
the next. When he finished, he had some most unpleasant
surprises rigged for any of Pease's men who tried to ride out.
The only way into or out of the valley he left untouched was
one he felt certain the bunglers with Pease knew nothing
about. Then all he had to do was settle in on the south end of
the valley and wait for reinforcements to arrive. Chuckling
over the expected reaction of the walking filth, he rode off in
that direction, tired and sore, but hugely pleased with himself. He decided on a little snooze to help pass the time.

While Preacher waited for his volunteer force of fighting
men to arrive, Falling Horse and his Cheyenne Dog Soldiers
came on from the northeast, following the sign of some of
the less skilled among Pease's fighters. When the Cheyenne
chief realized where those tracks led them, he called for a
halt.

"I know of where these men go. It is a nice, wide valley, much grass, good water. Many ways in and out. But there is one that the white men would never find. It is narrow and dark, and we must move slowly. We can use it and not be found. Our surprise will be total."

Several older, wiser heads nodded in agreement. The more restless among the younger warriors offered their opinion in the form of questions. "Why don't we take the faster way?"

"Yes," another agreed. "They may escape."

"The known paths will be watched. We would lose our surprise," Falling Horse explained. A cold smile lifted his lips. "And I want them to be surprised."

Without further discussion, the Cheyenne war party turned away and followed Falling Horse's lead toward the hidden entrance. They soon found the progress slower than expected. Trees attacked by insects and others struck by lightning littered the way, reducing forward movement to a dragging walk. At points they had to stop and drag limbs clear of the narrow, meandering trail that followed a tiny stream.

It took the Cheyenne the rest of the day to make it halfway through the steep canyon. They made camp and talked quietly among themselves. Some of the more enterprising among them produced small buffalo paunch pots, into which they put jerked bison meat and water. When the meat softened, they shredded it with fingernails then added cornmeal, ground nuts, and salt. It made a nourishing, if not savory, stew, which they shared with the others, then all rolled into blankets and slept soundly.

Up before dawn, they advanced on their enemy. At midday, Falling Horse halted the column and pointed to the south. A wedge of blue sky showed ahead. They had little distance to go. Each warrior muffled the muzzle of his mount, to quiet any whinny of recognition when the animals scented the presence of the white men's horses. An hour later, the Cheyenne came into the clear. Falling Horse used silent signals to direct his war party into line for an attack.

Every Dog Soldier mounted and readied his weapons.

Many smiled broadly, the prospect of scalps and plenty of coups energized them. Falling Horse let his ebony eyes cut along the double line of warriors and knew satisfaction. Every man had at least two weapons at the ready. Their first sweep would be a bloody one. He nodded his approval and raised his feather-decorated rifle over his head.

When it came down, the Cheyenne charged into the valley. They had covered more than half the distance to the white camp before the first shouts of alarm rose from their enemy.

Preacher came out of a light doze with a jerk. His eyes focused on a distant haze of dust. "Waugh! It's the danged Cheyenne," he grunted aloud.

White plumes rose and the reports of discharging rifles reached Preacher's ears. He didn't expect the reinforcements much before mid-afternoon. That crafty devil, Falling Horse, had followed the careless flatlanders right to their nest and now he was bringing them a whole world of grief. Preacher longed to be in there, mixing it up with Ezra Pease and his rabble. He crawled, crablike, to his saddle and reached into one of the leather bags for his spy glass. When the brass tubes had been extended, he focused in on a wild scramble of outlaw trash, as they sought to form up to give resistance.

The bright circle of light steadied on a knot of a half-dozen vermin who stood back to back and poured out a steady stream of fire into the milling ranks of Cheyenne. The Dog Soldiers rallied around this strong point, hooted and yipped, and swarmed over them in a single rush. Only writhing, blood-smeared forms remained when they rode on. Preacher heard some angry shouts off to the left and swung the glass to pin the action in place.

Seven harried bits of human slime raced their horses toward the southern outlet to the valley. Ten Dog Soldiers pursued them. Both parties exchanged shots, which went wild, and the race continued. A tight smirk formed on Preacher's face. Those fellers would soon find out what losers they were. The first one disappeared into the open mouth of the passage and Preacher sighed with satisfaction over his fore-thought.

Two long minutes passed and then a hideous scream, magnified by the echo effect, rose from beyond where the thugs had disappeared. The one in the lead must have found the first of his unpleasant gifts. More shrieks followed rapidly. Then a spatter of gunfire. Silence returned to the cut through the hills. After a short pause, the Cheyenne warriors trotted back to the area of the main battle. Preacher could hardly contain himself. He wanted so badly to be a part of this. He had a deep, burning need to get his hands on the throat of Ezra Pease and slowly squeeze the life out of him. That might not happen, he realized.

A lull came in the fighting as both sides exhausted their loaded weapons. Typically, the Cheyenne pulled off to pre-pare for another charge. That gave Pease time to rally his men. Faintly, a commanding voice drifted to Preacher's ears.

"Load up everything you can. Forget the wagons. We've got to save ourselves."

"What about the powder and guns?" a frightened voice demanded.

"Blow them up. Set a long fuse and let's ride for our lives."

Typical yellow-belly, Preacher thought. Pease showed his yellow streak more than ten years ago, and now he did it again. Let them go, he decided. That would give him another swing at them. Which way would they head? Preacher pon-dered that until the panicked horses had been calmed enough to saddle and the men mounted. With the Cheyenne whoop-ing it up for a second charge, Preacher focused his glass on his nemesis at last.

Pease sat before a roughly formed column of twos. He seemed to be haranguing them with some inspiring words, unheard over the drum of galloping hooves as the Cheyenne bore down on them again. Preacher's lips curled in disgust and contempt as he gazed at the bushy brows and matching carroty hair on a balding head, the thin, bloodless lips, and snaggled, yellowed teeth of Ezra Pease. Watery, pale blue eyes glittered with malevolence even at this distance, enlarged by the spy glass. At the last possible moment, Pease gave the command, whirled his mount and the outlaw trash sprinted away to the south.

"Well, damn," Preacher cursed aloud, then had a different view of circumstances. "Maybe we can catch them between us," he speculated.

He looked back at the battlefield to find only men too badly wounded to sit a horse receive the attentions of the blood-lusting Cheyenne. Those who had been trapped offered no resistance. Even so, Preacher noted grimly, most of them died very slowly.

8

Whiskey splashed high in the air, as a barrel head shattered under the powerful blows of three Cheyenne warriors. Flames crackled among the abandoned tents of the white trash that had fled from the valley. When a river of rotgut washed into these, a great whoosh resulted that sent a ball of fire high in the air. When the fuse set by the minions of Ezra Pease reached the powder magazine, the resulting explosion had put most of the Dog Soldiers on the ground from the shock wave, knocking several unconscious, Preacher noted.

He still fumed impatiently from his lookout on the steep slope of the eastern side of the valley. The orgy of destruction went on into the afternoon. So involved were the Cheyenne that they failed to notice when Nighthawk, Buck Dempsey, and Kent Foster slipped into place next to Preacher. Awed by the destructiveness of the Indians, Buck and Kent gaped at the smoldering ruin. Preacher nudged Buck in the ribs.

"Now you got an idee what Falling Horse meant when he said it would be better if we did not get to Pease and his nest of vipers first. Wouldn't want them Dog Soldiers takin' out their mad on us, now would ya?"

Sobered by the display of ruthlessness, Buck answered

softly. "No. It's not the sort of thing Mrs. Dempsey's little boy would like to get mixed up in."

Preacher stirred himself. "I reckon it would be a mistake to wait until things quiet down. How far off did you say the rest were waitin'?"

"Two hours ride from here," Nighthawk informed him.

"To the south?" Preacher asked with a grimace. "Chances are that Pease an' his buzzard-pukes rode right through them."

Nighthawk sighed. "They are reluctant to fight. At least without direction. I doubt that Beartooth is enough to inspire them to great effort."

"So am I," Preacher acknowledged. "Well, we're wastin' daylight. Either the Cheyenne will chase after Pease, or more likely head for home with their fresh scalps to do some celebratin'. Whichever, it should keep them busy long enough for us and what help we've got to round up that pack of reprobates."

Preacher's uneasiness increased during the day it took for the small company to rest men and horses and make repairs on equipment. He wore an outright scowl by evening. Lookouts he had posted came in to report that the Cheyenne pulled out to the northwest.

"That's good news," Preacher answered. The prospect of being between Pease and the Cheyenne had troubled him greatly. "We can move out in the morning. Best chance is to split up and follow the scattered trails. They will have to meet up somewhere. From then on it should be easy."

Early morning light saw the expedition on its various ways. Preacher and Buck rode together with nine men. At first the trail was easy to follow. Frightened by the prospect of Indian justice, those they sought made no effort to cover their tracks. Preacher pointed that out to his contingent of greenhorns and took the lead.

After a while the signs grew scarcer. Preacher took to dismounting and studying what scant evidence they came upon.

At one such point, he poked a finger into a green and brown road apple and a hopeful expression brightened his face.

"Can't be more'n two, three hours old. Still warm. And rookie there. Ain't seen that spade shoe print before. Some others joinin' up, I'd say."

"How do you know that?" one of the more militant among the missionary group asked.

Preacher cocked his head and gave the young man a quizzical glance. "Don't nobody keep a spade shoe on a horse that's not got a tender frog. If that horse had been with the ones we been followin', we'd have seen sign of it before now."

Chagrinned, the husband of one of the gospel-shouters swallowed hard. "Oh, yes. I see now."

"We keep goin', we'll catch sight of them 'fore long," Preacher advised.

"Is that wise?" a nervous carpenter asked.

"Hell, they's eleven of us. Way these boys been rode hard and put up wet, we should be able to handle however many there are. Won't be the whole bunch, I can guarantee that."

Reassured, though not possessed of Preacher's confidence, the young man nodded and they rode on.

Night brought little rest to Ezra Pease. From the height of his success he had plummeted to an all-time low. Almost as low as when he had been savagely beaten by Preacher and run out of the Rocky Mountains. He lay on the ground, sheltered by the crudest of lean-tos, uncomfortable in blankets, every pebble, twig, or irregularity in the ground a source of fiery discomfort. He groaned and rolled onto another side for the hundredth time.

Images of war-painted Cheyennes haunted him. They screamed literally right in his face and awakened thoughts of how close he had come to death. Where would they go? Where could they hide? Bathed in sweat, Ezra Pease cried out in the darkness and sat bolt upright. Forgotten was the compact he had made with the Eastern businessmen. Vanished, the visions of mountains of gold. Only the enraged, contorted, coppery faces of the savages who had attacked them without warning remained.

"They drove us out. Drove me out," he whispered to himself. "Drove *me* out." Humiliation burned hotly on his face.

In those long hours of the moonless night, his resolve weakened. Groggily, Pease recognized the figure of Hashknife squatting beside the fire, where he sipped from a tin cup of coffee. Pease shrugged on his trousers and slid long, narrow, unnaturally white feet into boots and walked to join his only remaining subordinate leader.

"I couldn't sleep, either," Pease remarked with what he hoped would sound casual.

"I've been thinking about . . ." Hashknife gestured behind them, toward the valley of their defeat.

"So have I." Pease agonized over taking this mysterious gunman into his complete confidence. Reluctantly he admitted he needed someone to confide in, to solicit for advice. "There is something you should know."

Hashknife tilted his head, cocked a brow. "Before deciding to cut and run?"

"Uh—yes. Or something very like that. What I wanted to tell you is that I'm not alone in this. I have . . . partners. Influential men back East. For a while today, I have debated throwing over the whole thing. I could head for California, or somewhere I'm not known. Leave the whole land grab up to my partners."

Hashknife's brow furrowed. "That might prove quite unwise," he prompted.

"I know that. But then I think, what the hell have they done to help?" His expression changed to chagrin. "Of course, the answer is, they have bankrolled the whole enterprise. I am obligated to them for that."

Hashknife relaxed somewhat. "I'm glad to hear you consider that. You see, I was steered to your organization by the very men you are discussing." Ezra Pease felt a cold chill run up his spine at the words Hashknife spoke. "Obviously you wanted a second opinion before you decided what to do."

"Yes, I did. What do you feel we should do next?" Pease appealed.

"Certainly we cannot stay here. We would be better off closer to the Blackfeet."

"I can see that," Pease allowed. "So we move northwest. And first thing tomorrow, I would say."

"Not . . . quite so soon," Hashknife cautioned. "It would be wiser to go south a ways further. To—ah—throw off pursuers. Also to let the men regain some of their composure."

Ezra Pease considered this, coming as it did from an underling he considered only another passable gunman, albeit a failed gentleman. "You have a strong grasp of strategy, sir. And, you couch your words in the phrases of a military man."

"I—ah—was. Until an unfortunate incident separated me from the Army. But, speculation on my past is a waste of time under the circumstances. What we need is a sound plan. One that takes advantage of the terrain, our own condition, and the enemy's situation."

A new light shone in the eyes of Ezra Pease. "Yes, yes, I was right in promoting you in this enterprise. Go ahead. At this point, I am open to any reasonable suggestion."

Hashknife gave him a wintry smile. "I would be glad to, for . . . shall we say a fifty-fifty split?"

Anger and greed flashed across the face of Ezra Pease. "Rather ambitious, aren't you?" he fired hotly. Then recognition of their perilous status modified his outlook. "Although I must say that a successful outcome would be worth it and then some. I'll stand by my original request."

Hashknife quickly outlined what he had in mind. It met with the full approval of Ezra Pease. The cashiered officer, for that's what Pease was certain Hashknife was, concluded with a summary of their end goal. "We managed to bring away enough of the boys and youths to conduct the initial mining operation as you outlined it. Once we reach the Blackfeet, they will welcome us, especially if we give them a few more rifles and ammunition to insure their good will. Yet, the most important thing is to forget about Preacher and to get far away from the Cheyenne. After that, raids on passing wagon trains will insure a steady supply of labor."

Beaming now, Ezra Pease rose and clapped Hashknife on one shoulder. "I like it. We'll do it that way. Make sure the men are informed of all they need to know and are ready to move out first thing in the morning."

Preacher went ahead on a lone scout. He felt certain that Pease and his remaining outlaw band could not be far ahead of them. Sign of their presence had decreased, yet remained enough to lead the way. His steady, watchful pace put him far ahead of the remaining force of volunteers by the time the sun began to slant rapidly toward the western horizon.

The whinny of a startled horse, borne faintly on the breeze, alerted Preacher of his nearness to those he sought. This was almost too easy, he reasoned. Not too much so, he amended when he had dismounted from Thunder and wormed his way to the crest of a low ridge. Beyond he picked out some twenty of Pease's hard cases, settled into a scattered camp by a stream.

"Fools," Preacher muttered to himself. "Anybody worth his salt knows enough not to camp right beside a body of moving water. The noise it makes muffles any sounds of someone tryin' to sneak up on the camp." A short distance away, Thunder nodded his big, gray, Appaloosa head as though in agreement. It brought a fleeting smile to Preacher's lips. "Even m'horse knows that."

Preacher continued to watch until three hours after nightfall. Then he slipped away to a safe distance, mounted Thunder and headed back for the small company of avengers. He reached there shortly after midnight.

"There's nigh onto twenty-two of 'em there," he told

Nighthawk, Dupre, and Beartooth. "I rec'nized Pease amongst them. What I want you to do is lay low for a day and a night. On the way back here, I got some plans I want to put to use on this group up ahead. It ain't all of them, but we got to start somewhere."

Preacher picked his positions well, and in advance. As he had expected the cavalcade of carrion eaters continued south through the next day. That, he definitely wanted to put a stop to. So he picked a likely campsite and settled in to wait for them to come to him.

Now he slithered on his belly, the LeFever rifle cradled in the crook of his elbows, headed into the first of his several sniping locations. He reached it undetected, a "V" notch slightly off-center in a split boulder, and settled in. Easing the muzzle and first six inches of barrel on the French rifle through the opening, he adjusted his position and sighted in. The first thing he lined up on was a coffee pot.

His imagination supplied the heady aroma of boiling grounds, the anticipation of men tired from hard travel and residual fear. Gently, he squeezed the trigger. The recoil had hardly ceased when he went into motion again, crawling toward his second spot. It took fifty of Preacher's slow, unlabored heartbeats before the flatlander trash below reacted. At that extreme range, their bullets struck ground a hundred yards short of the rock he had used as cover. Preacher made a note of that; he'd come back later for another go-around.

At rest, in an easy position behind a tall pine, he let its shade mask his presence while he reloaded and took a look at the camp. The coffee pot, holed through-and-through lay on its side, the former contents formed a puddle around the blue-gray granite utensil. Coldly amused by this, he glanced around for the inevitable one or two louts with duller minds who would not have taken proper precautions.

He found them almost at once. "Yep," he muttered. "This is gettin' to be entirely too easy."

Preacher shot the heel of one boot, and the human one inside it, off of a thug who had thoughtlessly sprawled behind a saddle. A yell of agony reached him a second after the report of his LeFever rolled across the camp. Then a voice that rang with authority rose above the disorganized encampment.

"Some of you get out there and stop that."

"Naw, sir, Hashknife. Ain't gonna do it. We're sittin' ducks as it is."

"You'll do it or I'll shoot you where you lay," Hashknife barked.

"Pease is gettin' smarter," Preacher mused aloud. "He's makin' use of someone who knows how to deal with the scum of the earth. Might make this job a tad more difficult."

He refrained from moving this time. Preacher wanted to encourage those beneath him to waste their advance on a place he would soon abandon. Reloaded again, he took aim on an exposed shoulder near the single wagon that had been whisked out of the fight with the Cheyenne. The LeFever barked and bucked and when the smoke blew away, a man writhed on the ground, right hand clutching his left shoulder. Only then, did Preacher eel his way to his third chosen spot.

From there he watched the cautious movement of three men, who came on foot out of the camp, rifles at the ready. They spread out and swung wide of the ancient pine, so as to put the brow of the hillside between them and their intended target. Grinning, Preacher made a half-turn and waited. The first one to show himself over the rise took a ball smack between his eyes. He went down like a stone and his two companions scurried back toward safety.

"Keep going, goddamnit!" Hashknife bellowed.

Preacher noticed a blur of brightly colored cloth from the corner of one eye as a heavy-set thug darted for the back of the wagon. Preacher left the ramrod for the LeFever on the ground as he took quick aim. The conical ball smashed the big bone in the fatty's right thigh and he plowed ground with his nose and chin.

"It's the Cheyenne. They've caught up with us." Preacher recognized the voice of Ezra Pease, for all its quaver of fear.

"If it was Indians, they would be attacking us by now," Hashknife differed.

"No—no, it's them. No one else was anywhere close to us," Pease insisted.

Preacher returned his attention to the two men flanking him. At once he caught sight of the braver of the pair. He ran flat out toward the screen of wild blackberry bushes, behind which Preacher crouched. Too close for a rifle shot, Preacher quickly laid aside the LeFever and drew one of his brace of .60 caliber Hayes, single-barrels.

"A little more," he coaxed. "That's right, come to poppa."

The Hayes discharged and smeared the sky with smoke. Preacher peered beyond it and saw his target drop onto wobbly knees. Both hands clasped over his belly, the worthless scum looked first at his wound, then cut his eyes upward in a final appeal to his Maker for mercy.

Appeal denied, Preacher thought as the hulking brute toppled face-first into the grass. All but too late, Preacher exchanged the empty pistol for the LeFever and brought it to bear on the chest of the more reluctant enemy. Loping along, bent low as though that would protect him from a frontal shot, the Boston rag bag took the ball in the top of his bald pate, which released a shower of blood and tissue. Impact stunned him to a momentary stop. Then his booted feet drummed frantically in place until his body drained of impulses and he flopped on his side in silent death.

"Not bad for an afternoon's work," Preacher congratulated himself in a hoarse whisper. Then he faded away, at an angle uphill. He'd come back later and reopen the dance.

Preacher had no need of his vocal tricks that night. From a mountaintop overlooking the nervous camp of wastrels and slime, came the haunting yowl of a prairie wolf. The amorous coyote sought a mate in the waning moonlight. In another turn of the earth, it would be the dark of the moon. Far off, an answer wavered toward the frosting of stars. Preacher had worked in close enough to hear the quavery voices of the men he stalked.

"Lordy, is that thing for real? Or is it . . . Preacher?" a crack-voiced youth asked.

"Best pray it's for real," came a growl from the far side of the fire.

Preacher grinned over that so hard it became a smirk. Like a wraith he crept in closer. All at once he overstepped his bounds.

"Who's that over there?" a tense voice challenged.

"It's nothin', jist me," Preacher responded. A new, wild, impossible idea had entered his head and it tickled him like a certain peacock feather in the hands of a buxom bawd he had sported with one time as a youngster of tender years.

"Well, then, come on over an' have some coffee," the gravel-voiced one rumbled.

With a shrug, Preacher removed his tell-tale four-shot pistols and laid them aside, then stepped into the light. He settled in between two of the younger hard cases and accepted a cup of steaming brew. He sipped while they talked. Time passed in a dumb lull. They talked of the fight with the Cheyenne. Preacher allowed as how it had plum upset him a lot. He refrained from saying why. While they rambled on, Preacher eased a hand into the possibles bag hung at his waist and removed a paper twist filled with pale yellowish crystals. The ease generated by the moment vanished when a loud rustling came from the brush close at hand.

Preacher seized his chance. Widening his eyes, he pointed into the darkness and blurted an alarming, if false, discovery. "B'God, it's a bear!"

Everyone looked where he pointed, while Preacher deftly emptied the salts of cpccac into the coffee pot. He was in a crouch, half-standing when the first of the scum looked back. Preacher gave a nervous grin and waggled an empty hand at the man.

"At least I thought it was a bear. Musta been a deer, frightened by all us people around."

"Yeah. Could be."

"Yep. Well, best be gettin' back where I belong. Gonna be a short night," Preacher excused himself as he drifted toward the darkness again.

No one thought to stop him. He had retrieved his favorite pistols, snugged them in place and covered about fifty yards when the first sounds of vomiting reached his ears. Suppressing a chuckle, he glided on through the frosty starlight to do more mischief.

9

Early the next morning brush flew from the leading edge of the lean-to roof that sheltered Ezra Pease. He came up with a start and a yelp that chilled the already unsettled hard cases. "It's the Cheyenne!" he bellowed.

Preacher's gunshot echoed over the ground. By the time the sound reached the camp he had the LeFever nearly reloaded. His second round split the breastbone of an incautious gawker who had foolishly remained at the fire, sipping coffee. He dropped his cup a moment before his face hit the coals.

"See, I told you it was Indians," Pease shouted, the words tumbling over one another.

"No, it's not," Hashknife growled from where he hugged the ground. "It's Preacher. He snuck in here last night and put something in the coffee that made several men seriously ill."

"I want proof of that," a terribly agitated Pease demanded.

Hashknife glanced up at the sound of approaching hoofbeats. Two of his men came toward the center of camp, a captive tied to a horse between them. "I think I can provide that in a short while. By the way, have you noticed the shooting has stopped. If it were the Cheyenne, they would be whooping down on us by now."

Hashknife went to the prisoner and roughly yanked him to the ground. He stood over him, legs widespread, and bent until his face hovered inches from the hapless man.

"Who are you?"

"I—I'm a hired d-driver."

"A driver? For whom?"

"There's—ah—there's a band of psalm-singers not far from here. I went off yesterday to hunt for meat. Got lost."

"How far are these missionaries?" Hashknife demanded.

"T-two valleys over, to the south," the gutless driver readily offered.

"Hummmm." It came from the chest of Hashknife as a sound of contentment, rather than a sign of resignation.

"We have to break camp at once," Ezra Pease broke into the interrogation. "Head west at once. We can outdistance Preacher or the Cheyenne. I know we can."

"Be quiet a minute," Hashknife snapped, then changed his command into a request, "If you please, sir." To the driver, "Does the name Preacher mean anything to you?"

"Yes—yes, he's the one who led us to the valley."

Purring like a cream-stuffed cat, Hashknife turned to Ezra Pease. "I think we have solved both of our problems. This man can lead us to some people who are enjoying the protection of Preacher. He'll have to come after us and we'll have his proteges as hostages. Preacher will have to surrender or see them all killed one-by-one."

Terror fled from Ezra Pease and he beamed at Hashknife. "I like your dirty, devious little mind, Hashknife. That's a splendid idea. Damn the black heart of Preacher into the hottest corner of hell. We've got him now."

Starting shortly after the impassioned speech of Ezra Pease, more of the disorganized vermin began to drift into camp. Observed in secret by Preacher, their presence did nothing to lighten the mood of the mountain man. He had managed to reduce their number to some fifteen, now twenty more gathered around cookfires and talked out their nervousness. Preacher chafed as he accepted that he must stay longer, to determine how many men Pease would have.

He took careful note when five of the thugs, cleaner in appearance and better dressed than most, rode out of the meadow where Pease had made camp. Preacher longed to follow them, learn their destination. Yet, he had to know the enemy strength. He would wait overnight and see what the morning brought, then set out to advise the others, and to follow the mysterious quintet that had parted with the rest.

Morning brought a crushing blow for Preacher. Twenty-three Blackfoot warriors rode into camp. From what Preacher could make out through his spy glass, their war leader spoke only his own tongue, while another made sign talk and translated into English. The signs revealed that they had come to help their old friends and to get fresh Cheyenne scalps. Pease replied that they had surely come to the right place. Nothing could be worse, Preacher reckoned. Quietly, he crawled from his observation place and, mounted on Thunder, rode off to bring the latest to his band of volunteers.

The mountain men among the small company received his news with grim expressions. Yet, they agreed among themselves, they still had to destroy Pease or a summer of intertribal fighting could turn into a long campaign, with white against Indian.

"They are not making it easy for us," Nighthawk observed.

"You are even more correct than usual, *mon ami*," Dupre admitted.

"It ain't impossible," Preacher insisted. "Thing is we can no longer take the fight to them. We must make them come to us and be ready with every nasty trick we know. If only I could stir up some trouble between them Blackfeet and Pease . . ." Preacher mused into silence.

* * *

Late the next afternoon, five presentably dressed strangers rode into the hidden valley and stopped before the largest structure in the new settlement, the church. Their leader was well-spoken and Reverend Bookworthy greeted them effusively.

"You are welcome, brothers, so long as your intentions are peaceful. If you haven't provisions or shelter, we can accommodate you. Would you— ah—be staying long?"

"No, not for long, sir. I must say I am heartened to find a House of God in this benighted wilderness," Hashknife purred softly.

A gaggle of children had swarmed forward and followed them through the meadow and into the clearing. They frolicked now around the legs of the horses and their shrill voices rose in a deafening chorus. Reverend Bookworthy rounded on them with a hint of heat in his voice.

"Here, now, that's enough. Shouldn't you be in school?"

"No, Reverend," Nick chirped. "It's Saturday."

"Then you should be working for your parents. Go along now. Make yourselves busy at something useful." He turned to the visitors. "Children. You understand, I'm sure."

"Of course." Like his men, Hashknife's eyes had picked out the abundance of young women among the settlers and he appraised them with a hungry gaze.

One among them, who had drawn closer darted a hand to her face to conceal her shock. Although many years had passed, enough that Cora Ames could not be certain, yet she felt almost sure, that the one speaking to Reverend Bookworthy was Quincey. She spoke the name softly, giving it the New England pronunciation of Quinzie. And she knew it was so.

After several minutes more of conversation between the missionary minister and Quincey, it became apparent that recognition had not gone both ways. Cora Ames turned away thoughtfully and hurried from the presence of the enigmatic young man. Her mind was awhirl with conflicting emotions.

Whatever could he be doing here? How had he come to find them? Had he—had he . . . changed?

Part of her didn't want the answers to those questions, while another yearned to know. Perhaps to be able to . . . to give an alarm? Foolishness, her practical side mocked her. It couldn't possibly be him.

Cora spent a troubled night and nearly swooned with relief the next morning after breakfast when she saw two of the men with Quincey making preparations to saddle up and presumably ride out. Bony fingers of ice clutched her heart a few minutes later when it became clear that Quincey and two of his companions would remain behind. What might that signify? Cora Ames dreaded the answer.

Only, having kept silent so long, she knew she had to keep her terrible secret to herself. It tormented her throughout the day as she kept a respectable distance between herself and the visitors.

Two more days had gone by while Preacher waited with his small force of dedicated fighters. During that time he made plans and prepared weapons to try his mischief and break the alliance with the Blackfeet. To further that, he was watching the camp when two of the dandies who rode out three days earlier returned. They held a brief conference with Ezra Pease. At once orders were bellowed to break camp and make ready to move out.

"What the hell now?" Preacher grumbled to himself.

He returned quickly to the waiting company of amateur fighters and advised them of the changed situation. "All we can do is follow along and see where they lead," he concluded.

They, too, broke camp at once.

By mid-morning the next day, Preacher had a haunting, uneasy feeling that he knew exactly where Pease's vultures were headed. Also why five of them had ridden out dressed to the nines. The High Lonesome held only one attraction for the foul scavengers of Ezra Pease that lay due south. His little settlement of pilgrims.

A cold blast of arctic air seemed to wash over Preacher and down his back. They would be totally helpless. And not even Pease and whatever men would stand with him could hold back the Blackfeet when they rushed in among the white women and children. Sickened by memories of past such slaughters, Preacher gnawed at the inside of his cheek to try to shake loose an idea. It took him until nightfall to decide what to do.

Preacher took Nighthawk along. Together they moved in on the night camp of Ezra Pease. A hundred yards short of the lookouts posted to secure the area, they separated and went their various ways. Preacher scouted his sector before making a move.

Fixed in his mind was the location of the Blackfeet. He intended to end up there. But first, the sentries had to be taken out. After placing each of them, he closed on the first. The chinless lout had time to utter a sharp "Huuh!" before Preacher's tomahawk split his skull and he crumpled to the ground.

Silently, without a backward look, Preacher moved on. He found that one of the guards had moved, out of loneliness and inexperience. Young, dreadfully young, Preacher noted as his intended target talked in a low murmur to the one who had left his post. Preacher gave it a moment's consideration and decided on a risky course of action. With ease, he crept up to within arm's reach, then spoke softly.

"If both of you want to keep on living, don't make a sound."

"Preacher?" the younger thug gasped.

"None other. Now, what you are going to do is ease them pistols and your belts and lay 'em on the ground. Put your rifles alongside them. Then back up to me."

Without protest, they complied. When they stood inches

from Preacher's chest, he tapped each youth on a shoulder. "Now, we can do this two ways. I can knock you out and tie you up. That way, maybe you'll be found an' maybe not. Or . . ."

"Or what? Don't torment us, Preacher," the older lad whispered harshly.

"Or you can give me your word that you are going to take off walkin' and get clear the hell an' gone from anywhere near Ezra Pease. I won't hurt you and I won't come after you. But if I ever see either of you in the High Lonesome again, I'll kill you on sight."

"I believe you," they chorused.

"Well, then, which will it be?"

"We're gone," the younger blurted. "We ain't ever been here."

Preacher smiled in the dark. "Now that's fine. That's sensible, boys. Whenever you're ready, jist start walkin'."

"Can we—can we go back an' change our drawers first?" the older lad bleated.

Preacher could have fallen down and rolled around laughing if he hadn't kept a tight rein on himself. "No. Jist scoot."

They scooted. Preacher moved on. Another sentry died, which cleared his sector and gave him access to the Blackfeet. Ready in position, Preacher lighted fuses on some of his gourd bombs and hurled them in among the small war trail lodges of the Blackfeet. Almost at once they began to go off with tremendous roars. Smoke, dust, and rock chips filled the air. Preacher heard the wild whinnies of horses from the far side of the camp. Nighthawk had reached his objective also.

Preacher found the Blackfeet ponies too well guarded to risk stampeding them, so he glided away into the night. What they had done might not bring a complete break, but from now on the Blackfeet would look with distrust at their white allies. It had been a good night's work.

* * *

"They are moving on to the south," Nighthawk informed Preacher when he awakened him from a light snooze an hour after sunrise.

"Dang it. That's the very thing I wanted to discourage." The crafty mountain man considered the implications of this. He had to accept that no way existed for his small force to get around the larger band of trash and slime led by Ezra Pease. Without being able to pose themselves between the brigands and the helpless folk in the valley, all they could do was snip away at the rear and flanks of the column. He quickly outlined his ideas to that effect.

This harassment got under way almost at once. Some stragglers remained in the camp Pease had established, still loading packsaddles and gathering their personal gear. From the concealment of trees and brush, Preacher and his men opened up with a withering fire. Hot lead scythed down seven of the human dregs in an instant. The others panicked and abandoned their supplies to race off on loudly protesting horses.

"That's doin' it, boys!" Preacher shouted his approval. "Now, split up in your groups. Nighthawk, Dupre, an' Beartooth will lead you. You know what to do."

And they proved it within less than an hour. The dull thud of rifle fire drifted back northward as the small bands struck at Pease and his trash. Preacher took his group, including Buck and Kent, the most capable of the driver volunteers, and set off along the eastern flank. His goal was to get close to the head of the column before engaging the enemy. With luck he might even get a shot at Ezra Pease.

Their torment of Pease and his vermin continued throughout the day. Then, shortly before Preacher estimated Pease would make camp for the night, the other three well-dressed outlaws rode up the trail from the south. With them they brought four captives. A cold knot formed in Preacher's stomach when he recognized young Chris from the ravaged wagon train, the boy Peter who had come with Silas Phipps and with him the girl, Helen. Worst of all, he had no trouble recognizing Cora Ames. The apparent leader of this group met briefly with Ezra Pease and summoned more men.

These, along with Pease rode a short ways off from the column of vandals. Pease rose in his saddle and bellowed his demands loudly, turning all ways and repeating them, to be certain he was understood.

"Preacher! Do you hear me? We've found your precious garbage. I have men already in that valley of yours. Back off or these will be only the first to die." Pease paused, then began to rant again. "Make no mistake. If you and those with you do not give us free rein, I will not hesitate to kill every one of those helpless grubs. I'll start with these and believe me, their deaths will be slow and painful. Now, back off, and let me hear you agree to it."

Preacher chewed at his lower lip. He had never given his word falsely and didn't intend to now. Yet, too many lives depended upon what he did. Even his hesitation proved to be the wrong thing to do. Pease made a gesture and two of his sub-human fiends yanked young Peter from the horse he rode.

They ripped the clothes from the boy's body and began to make small, shallow cuts on his chest and belly. His screams slashed through Preacher as though he were under the knife instead. Sudden fury washed away his indecision. He had had enough. Taking his LeFever rifle, Preacher rode out into the open, still well out of ordinary rifle range.

"Pease! You back-end of a polecat, hear me! We can end this without harm to any more. Face me, man to man, we'll fight it out. Winner goes his own way. You have my word on it."

Pease made a show of considering this offer, while his henchmen continued to slice into Peter's body and the boy screamed in agony. "What about the others with you?" Pease asked tauntingly, toying with Preacher. "Will they abide by what you say?"

"They will."

"I don't think so," Pease mocked him. "To give you time

to secure their promises to leave us in peace, I'm going to let these gentlemen finish with this boy here, and then we are going to ride on into your little paradise. If any more shots are fired while we do, I will have the other children killed, one by one, and then the woman. I'll allow my men to have their way with the females before they dispatch them, naturally."

That did it for Preacher. He snapped the French rifle to his shoulder and shot at Pease. A nervous twitch from Thunder sent the ball off course and put it through the meaty part of Pease's left shoulder.

"That's the last shot fired, Pease," Preacher roared. "We will abide by your terms. No one will fire on the column while you ride to the valley. When you get there, we'll face off man to man. And . . . I'll see you put in hell."

10

Terror-stricken, the residents of the valley ran before the onslaught of the advancing human debris led by Ezra Pease. A few of the remaining missionary men tried to resist and were cut down in a storm of lead. Pease had pushed his company of worthless trash on through the night, which caught Preacher by surprise. Now he pressed his advantage as the much smaller force with Preacher closed in from behind. Once they had driven all the way to the center of the settlement, Ezra Pease called a halt in front of the raw planks that walled the church. Again, he turned back to harangue Preacher with threats.

"Leave off! There is nothing you can do to stop us. If you persist, we will start killing the residents."

With the mutilated body of Peter, which they had recovered and brought along, fresh in his mind, Preacher had no doubt that Pease meant what he said. Reluctantly he gave the signal to break off and draw back. He had never felt so low in his life. Preacher blamed no one else for what had happened. He was the one who had led these innocents to this terrible end. His face hidden from the others, he led the way out of the valley.

Once inside the screening trees, Preacher called a halt. "There is nothing we can do tonight, but come nightfall, it's another story."

"What can we do then?" one of the drivers asked.

"We're gonna raise hob with 'em, hoss," Preacher assured him. Quickly he outlined his idea. It had everything to do with their familiarity of the valley and Pease's lack of it.

During the long, difficult day, Preacher came to a grudging admission that so far Ezra Pease had kept his word. Outside of being frightened, no harm had come to the residents of the valley. When twilight purpled the sky, Preacher called his stalwart band together.

"They'll be edgy tonight, so we'll wait until it gets near to mornin'. That's the best time to hit. I've heard say it's the last hours before dawn that a man sleeps soundest. Even the ones on guard will begin to droop. That's what gives us a chance."

"What if we get caught by daylight?" an uncertain evangelist asked.

"Then we keep on fightin'," Preacher explained. "Now, ever'body get somethin' to eat and rest up. You'll be told when it's time."

"You have sunken to a new low, Quincey," Cora Ames spat. "When you first arrived in the valley, I had the misapprehension that perhaps you had reformed your ways. I regret that I could be so mistaken."

"You should be pleased for me. I have found the way to a vast fortune, to power and respect and a good life," Hashknife responded, disconcerted to see that Cora gazed past his shoulder and out the window of her small cabin toward the distant trees where those infernal fighting men with Preacher had disappeared.

"What you've found," Cora snapped, "is a cold, shallow grave once Preacher gets done with you." Her anger rose to choke off further threats. "I'm ashamed that I ever knew you, let alone . . ."

A smirk lifted the lips of Hashknife. "Ah-ha! That of which we never speak, eh, my dear? Never mind. I have grown quite used to rejection. The years have not been kind to me, but no matter. Ezra Pease has made me an equal partner in his enterprise. There are literally millions to be made."

Cora produced her own, knowing, self-satisfied expression. "Provided he doesn't dispose of you once your usefulness to him is at an end. Oh, Quincey, Quincey, it could have been so different, so much better. If only . . ."

Hashknife raised a hand to stem the flood of her words. "Enough. I have no need of a lecture from you, let alone another sermon from that self-righteous hypocrite. I see you are in no mood for cordial conversation, so I will leave you now. Have no fear, none of these smelly louts dares to touch you." He patted the holster that contained his right-hand Colt Walker. Turning on one boot heel, he stomped out before Cora Ames could make another caustic reply.

Preacher gave his neophyte warriors more than enough time to get into position. Then he slowly advanced. Spread around with the fumbling, stumbling missionaries, he had positioned the drivers, and his mountain man friends, to lead. To his surprise, shortly after darkness fell, a number of the more peace-loving among the male gospel-shouters had risked sure death to sneak out of the cordon set up by Ezra Pease. They begged for the chance to take up arms and defend their families.

"Those aren't men, they're animals. The lewd looks they cast on our wives and daughters. It's unspeakable," Art Landry spoke for them all. "If I can shoot Indians in self-defense, I can strike out at savage filth like those."

A chorus of "Me, too" ran through the men with him.

Their number increased the thin ranks to forty strong. Preacher knew gratitude for their offer, though he doubted how useful the newcomers would be. He would soon find out, Preacher acknowledged as he came within fifty feet of the picket line set out by Pease and his able lieutenant.

That man who called himself Hashknife still troubled Preacher. Why did his features seem so familiar? Obviously he had intelligence. Most likely far beyond that of Ezra Pease. He remained cool during the worst of the fighting. And his auburn hair haunted Preacher's memory as much as his close resemblance to . . . someone. His study ended at the sound of a foot tread on a fallen twig, only three yards ahead. Preacher tensed himself.

The blamed fool came directly toward him. Preacher couldn't understand it until the man spoke in a harsh whisper. "You come to relieve me? I can sure use it. M'eyelids is droopin' somethin' awful."

Darkness had confused the man, Preacher realized. He thought he walked toward the settlement, not away from it. Preacher didn't give him time to learn of his error. A swift swing of the billet of wood in his hand sent the lookout off to a different starfield than the one that twinkled above. The wrist-sized stick made a hollow sound when it struck the side of the man's head. Preacher leaped forward and eased the sentry to the ground. Then he turned to his right, as he had instructed all of the men to do, and set off to roll up the others close at hand.

Two more out of the way left a pie-shaped sector open in which Preacher could work his mischief. Bent low, he covered ground rapidly. The hunk of wood he held had been frazzled at one end and dipped in tallow to serve as a torch when the situation called for it. Preacher paused within pistol shot of the settlement's cabins and fished out his tinder box. He was about to strike a spark and ignite his makeshift flambeau when all hell broke loose.

Jolted out of their deepest slumber by a ragged fusillade, the sub-human detritus with Ezra Pease had little chance of organizing a resistance. Firing as they came, their shrill yells electrifying the night, the men of the settlement charged in among the cabins. Torches aflame, they set fire to tents and bedrolls. Hard cases who still remained in some of the latter began to scream as the flames licked at their bodies.

Preacher struck flint to steel and blew to life his milk-weed down, which lighted a sulphur-tipped sliver. It blazed and ignited his torch. Then he joined the others. He dodged around a drowsy man who had only come to his feet and smacked him in the ribs with the firebrand. Howling, the thug spun away and fell to roll in the dirt. Preacher changed hands and drew one of his big four-barrel pistols. Two thick-chested, reckless louts reared up to block his path. Preacher coolly shot one, the other ran. In fact, Preacher noticed a whole lot of the buzzard-pukes deserting their cause.

Initially it seemed a stunning victory. Worn down by end-less days on the trail, the fierce fighting, first against the Cheyenne, then Preacher and his band, nerves jangled by the harassing fire on their column, many had no heart for more battle. Even as they hunted for their horses, Ezra Pease and Hashknife sought desperately to organize some resistance.

"Stand fast. Hold on, there. We outnumber them, you fools," Pease bellowed.

"Alone you can be picked off and left for buzzard bait," Hashknife assured the men.

Gradually their words took effect. The panic fled. Scum and filth they may be, but they saw the wisdom of strength in unity. Here and there knots gathered and began to return fire. A couple of the psalm-singers went down. One of the drivers threw hands in the air and fell, shot through the head. Preacher watched the effect as the initial shock wore off and muttered a curse. Without a means of direct control, he could not coor-dinate a sustained attack against these strong points.

Within no time, the contenders had pulled back from one another. Firing slackened and Preacher knew he had to do something to prevent Pease from carrying out his revenge against the helpless women and children. He tossed his torch into the midst of a group of Pease's vicious swine and began a swift, long run around the perimeter of the besiegers. When he came to the individual clusters, he paused long enough to give new orders. After leaving each group, he heard his new plan being carried out as men fired alternately, keeping up a steady stream of lead into the defensive positions taken by the outlaws.

That way, he knew, it might be possible to prevent them from moving from the small parcels of ground they presently held. If it worked, it would keep them away from the residents. He reached the last batch and Beartooth greeted him with a big hug.

"We got them out in the open now," the burly mountain man brayed.

"Thing is to keep them there," Preacher replied and explained the purpose he had in mind.

Beartooth put his charges to it at once. Then he turned to Preacher. "What do you reckon on doin' now?"

"I want to move in on that big cluster out there where Pease has taken command. Cut the head off a snake and the body dies."

Beartooth nodded solemnly. Preacher glided off from shadow to shadow to avoid the bright areas created by flickering fires. He had no way of knowing it, but his plan would work exceedingly well.

It came to him when the first pale band of gray appeared in the east. Pease and his cohorts had been fought to a standstill. With improved light, the marksmanship of Preacher's volunteers would improve. So, too, would that of the tenacious gunmen with Ezra Pease. A quick count through the round field of his spy-glass told Preacher that numbers no longer counted that much. Maybe the time for a charge had come. Pick one cluster of scum at a time and roll over them?

It appealed until Preacher heard the distant rumble of pounding hooves. One thing he knew for certain. It could not possibly be reinforcements for his side.

*   *   *

Several times during the long, pre-dawn hours, most of the underlings committed to the cause of Ezra Pease lost heart and thought of making a break. The hail of bullets from their invisible opponents convinced them otherwise. Now they congratulated themselves on standing fast. New hope came bearing down on them out of the sunrise.

"Lookie over there," Vern Beevis shouted, a grubby finger pointing at the shapes resolving out of the low ground mist.

Bart Haskel came thundering through the thin line of besiegers with a dozen hard-faced, gun-bristling men in his wake. They made for the largest cluster of their comrades, some who still crouched behind hastily dug breastworks. Relief at the eleventh hour! A ragged cheer rose.

"Well, I'll be damned," Beartooth drawled.

"We may well all be, Beartooth," Preacher answered sadly.

The words hardly out of his mouth, Preacher put hand to one of his revolving four-barrel pistols as the enemy swirled out of their defensive positions and launched a wild, screaming attack. Only a steady rate of fire slowed them at last. The final man to fall lay only ten feet from where Preacher crouched behind the stump of a fir that had been logged out for housing.

While the renegade whites regrouped, Preacher marked furtive movement to one side of the main enemy force. The man called Hashknife broke clear of the men around him and started off at a lope toward one of the cabins. The one that belonged to Cora Ames, Preacher noted with a sudden flash of anger and apprehension.

With a roar, Pease's scum charged again. Preacher had to put away his concern for Cora. This time the fighting became clouded in dust and powder smoke, men determined to triumph at whatever cost pushed on with empty weapons, to club and smash with their rifles and stab with knives. The fighting degenerated into a wild hand-to-hand melee. Preacher saw his amateur fighters waver and then begin to give ground. A sense of helplessness washed over him. How could he have been so blind, so proud as to believe they had a chance?

Then, with all lost, another, distant sound blew new hope through the momentary fog of defeat. He cast off his dejection and turned to verify what his ears told him.

"Ki-ki-ki-yi-yi-yiiiiii!"

Hoofbeats pounding, the Cheyenne Dog Soldiers of Falling Horse thundered into the valley. Preacher broke away from those around him and hopped up and down, waving both arms over his head to attract the attention of his old friend. Falling Horse cut his pony to the left and rushed down on Preacher.

"We thought they had finished them," the Cheyenne chief said through a smile. "It is good we did not go home."

"That it is. Now have your braves give some new spine to those gospel-shouters of mine," Preacher replied, his voice thick with emotion. Preacher had his own agenda.

Falling Horse spun away and directed his men toward the Blackfeet, who had so far not partaken in the battle. White men fighting white men was a novelty to them. Now, in the presence of their traditional enemy, they had a sudden change of heart about allegiance to Ezra Pease. Beartooth and Dupre led their men against the Indians also, hurling explosive gourds as they advanced.

Loud blasts and whizzing pieces of scrap metal and gourd shards shattered their nerve entirely. Howling in consternation, convinced their medicine had deserted them, the Blackfeet broke from their separate camp and streamed wildly across the meadow toward an opening in the valley walls.

Dog Soldiers hooted and shouted vulgar insults at the Blackfeet. They also pursued them with wild abandon. Thirsty for Blackfoot blood, hungry for their scalps, the Cheyenne ignored what went on among the warring whites to settle old scores with the fleeing warriors.

"Now that shines," Preacher exclaimed. "I was plum worried about what those Blackfeet would take it in mind to do."

"So was I," Nighthawk admitted at Preacher's side. He cut his eyes to a struggle that went on on a small rise, outside one of the cabins. "Oh-ho, my friend. It appears the woman who hungers after you is in need of assistance."

Preacher had seen it, also. He already started that way. He had to batter two brawny hard cases out of his way, shoot another and kick a fourth between the legs before a clear path lay between him and Hashknife, who held Cora Ames roughly by one arm, half-dragging her toward where Ezra Pease had taken his last stand.

By that time, Hashknife had closed the distance between Cora's cabin and his leader. He shoved Cora into the arms of Ezra Pease. All around, the fighting dwindled to an end as men stopped to stare at the bizarre scene going on atop the little knoll. Hashknife turned to face the cause of their downfall. For Hashknife had not the least shred of doubt that their end had come. Yet, he determined to take the cause of their failure with him. He pointed a long, spatulate finger at Preacher and roared his despair.

"I'm going to kill you, Preacher!"

"No, you're not," Preacher answered calmly.

"I am, I swear it. You have single-handedly undone us. For that you must pay."

Preacher kept a wary eye on the desperate man while he canted his head to the side and thumped with his left palm above the ear. "Am I hearing right?" he asked. "Them's fancy words for a man about to die."

"Don't toy with me!" Hashknife shrieked, on the edge of losing his grasp on sanity. "Fill a hand with one of those fancy pistols of yours. Before you can fire twice, I'll pump six bullets into you," he raved on, oblivious to the silence that hung around him.

"You'd best get started then," Preacher invited as he whipped out one of the four-shooters and eared back the hammer in one smooth move.

Hashknife had hardly touched the butt grip of his Walker Colt when the hammer fell and the pistol bucked in Preacher's hand. The .56 caliber ball took Hashknife square in the middle of his forehead. His back arched in a spasm and he slowly leaned further back, until he toppled over and landed on his shoulders and heels.

Astonished gasps rose from the witnesses. Before anyone could react, the voice of Ezra Pease cut raspingly through the murmurs of surprise. "It ends here, Preacher. I've got the girl. One wrong move and I spread her brains all over the ground. Get me a horse and I'll be gone. Don't come after me, or the girl dies."

He had to get Cora clear enough for a clean shot, Preacher knew. Without it he would have a tragedy on his hands. Warily, he shifted to one side. Pease moved to keep Cora between himself and Preacher. Blocked again. Preacher sought another diversion and found he did not need it. Cora Ames took care of clearing the target for him. When Pease shifted his weight to one leg, she gave a sharp, swift upraise of her boot heel into her captor's crotch.

At once, Ezra Pease let out a howl, his face turned a beet-red, and he released his grip enough for Cora Ames to break away. His face ashen now, Pease fought to suck in the air he had so rapidly wheezed away. Much to Preacher's surprise, rather than scurry to safety, Cora dashed to the fallen body of Hashknife.

"Don't make it too quick for him," she called over one shoulder to Preacher.

Preacher obliged her. He took time and fined his aim so that his next ball shattered the left kneecap of Ezra Pease. Pease shot wild as he went to one knee, and put a ball across Preacher's shoulder close to his ear. Preacher fired again. He put a hole in the unwounded shoulder of Pease. Pease groaned and dropped his Herrison Arsenel .50, double-barrel pistol. With his previously injured arm, he reached for the second two-shot handgun. Preacher waited.

Pease cocked both barrels and took slow, painful aim. Standing spread-legged, arms akimbo, Preacher still waited. When the black holes of the muzzle came level with his eyes, Preacher fired again. His hammer fell on an empty nipple. At once, Pease emptied his last barrel. The slug tore a hot, ragged trough across the top of Preacher's right shoulder. By only a fraction of an inch it missed his collarbone. Preacher winced, but covered it quickly.

Then he holstered his empty pistol and advanced steadily on the kneeling Pease. "It don't have to be this way, Pease," Preacher offered the olive branch again.

"Goddamn you, Preacher," the renegade wailed. "I . . . want . . . you . . . dead." With that, he gingerly fished a knife from its belt scabbard.

Preacher marched up to him, kicked the knife from the hand of Ezra Pease and punched him solidly in the mouth. "I want this one to hang," he announced, then turned and walked away.

11

Preacher stopped beside the prostrate figure of Cora Ames. She lay across the chest of the dead man named Hashknife. Gently Preacher bent down and raised her. Tears streaked her face. Preacher's puzzled expression asked the question for him.

"Th-they called him Hashknife," Cora gulped. "Hi-his— his real name was Quincey Ames. He is— was—my oldest brother."

That took Preacher like a sucker punch. He had words of scorn for any man who would mistreat a woman, yet her revelation sucked them out of his mouth. How could he tell her to dry her eyes and not grieve over such a lowlife, when it was her own brother. Well, by dang, all considered, she shouldn't waste tears over him, Preacher bristled at last. He bucked up and tried another approach.

"From the first time I saw him, I was thinkin' there was somethin' familiar about his looks. His face that is. I never imagined. Can you tell me what brought him here with Ezra Pease?"

"I—don't know all of it. He was my idol when I was little. Then, when he was around fifteen . . . something . . . went wrong. He changed. Grew rebellious against Father. He held religion to scorn, despised every decent emotion. He started running with some rowdy boys from the other side of town. Then one day, the bank was robbed and Quincey disappeared along with several of his hooligan friends. Father saw him once or twice after that, but it always upset him so, he never talked about their meetings. His name appeared in the Boston newspapers several times and then . . . he seemed to have disappeared off the face of the earth. Now, he is here . . . and he is dead."

"And I killed him. I won't say that I am sorry. He made that choice, not I. I'll leave you now, Miss Cora. Only I'm gonna leave a bit of good advice. Don't grieve for him too much. He weren't worth it."

A week passed in the valley, the missionaries busy burying the dead, the drivers nursing their wounds. Cora Ames remained distant from Preacher throughout the long days of ripe spring. Then, late on Friday afternoon, a stranger ambled his mount down into the settlement. Preacher and his friends slouched over to inspect the newcomer.

"Howdy, folks," the stranger greeted. "I didn't know there was a settlement here."

"Well, now you know," Preacher challenged, his wounds making him testy. Cora's avoidance had something to do with it too, Dupre suspected.

"So I do." The stranger cut narrowed eyes to Preacher. After a long moment of inspection, he gave a small negative shake of his head. "You're not the one, but I am looking for a man. I am U.S. Marshal Ruben Talbot." For the hundredth time, he produced the sketches of Silas Phipps and the orphan children. "They are wanted for robbery, murder, and flim-flam games all over the East."

When the likeness of Phipps reached Preacher he wrinkled his nose and gave a short. "Yup. We seen this one. Hanged him for the unnatural things he done to them kids."

"You've seen the children, then? I have warrants for their arrest. Tell me where they are, if you please."

Cora Ames pushed her way through the crowd that had gathered as Preacher spoke out forcefully. "An' if I don't please?"

"What's all of this about?" Cora demanded before an explosion could erupt between Preacher and this menacing-looking man.

"This uppity twerp of a You-nited States Marshal says those youngins with Phipps are wanted for a whole lot of crimes," Preacher summarized.

"That's not possible," Cora blurted. Then she went on to describe Silas Phipps and how he treated the youngsters. After a breathless pause, following her passionate defense of the children, she concluded a bit defensively, "If they did participate in any crimes, you can be sure they were forced into it. I've told you how Phipps beat them, nearly starved them. Here they will have good, Christian homes and lives.

"Several couples are childless and will, no doubt, make the effort, once they have settled in, to adopt them," she concluded.

Marshal Talbot muttered to himself, garrumphed and grumbled somewhat. "The law's the law; ma'am. I ain't judge and jury. All I do is bring 'em in."

"We have a judge, and enough men to make a jury. We've used them already," Cora came back perkily.

Marshal Talbot looked startled, recalling what he had been told happened to Phipps. He took a long, good look at Preacher, saw the coiled, barely restrained power and fury there, and made his decision. "I suppose what you would do is convene this court and dismiss the charges on the children and designate them as wards of the court, in the custody of those who have presently taken them in?"

"If we had to," Cora responded, her chin thrust defiantly forward.

"An' me an' my friends would back it up," Preacher announced. Beartooth, Dupre, and Nighthawk pushed through to the front of the onlookers.

Talbot took them in, swallowed hard. "I've no doubt that you would. Well, then, I see no solution but to allow them to stay." With that, the marshal extracted the warrants from an inner coat pocket and made a show of tearing them in half across the middle. "I'd be obliged if one of you would show me a place where I can take the night, then I'll be on my way."

"No problem," Art Pettibone piped up. "We have a spare room in our cabin. Mrs. Pettibone is expecting our first child."

"Obliged, indeed," the marshal responded, relaxing in this fresh, cordial atmosphere.

After he had departed, taken in tow by Art Pettibone, Cora turned to Preacher and spoke to him for the first time since he had killed her brother. "Thank you for standing up for the children."

"Weren't nothin', Miss Cora. They ain't bad, considerin' they're still kids."

"Oh, Preacher, you are still impossible," she replied, the wry twinkle back in her eyes. "I hear that you are planning to leave soon."

"Yep."

"Well, then, with Pease dead and the Cheyenne at peace again, I see no reason why you can't lead us on to the villages of the Indians."

"Oh, yes, there is."

Cora pouted a moment, then changed her tack. "At least there's no reason why you cannot stay in the valley for the summer. Perhaps take winter here and then lead us to our golden land of promise."

All at once, Preacher could hear wedding bells ringing inside his head, and see a vine-covered cottage in Cora's eyes. He had to think fast. "But there is. I have to go weltering a bit to visit the soldier-boys at the small fort on the Yellowstone. They need to know about the guns on the loose and see to gettin' them all back from the Blackfoot and Cheyenne. Otherwise, there won't be any place safe in the High Lonesome for years to come."

Beartooth slapped a big hand against a hamlike thigh. "Whoo-boy, Preacher that's the biggest mouthful of words I done ever heard out of you."

"Hush up, dang you, Beartooth. Just hush up," Preacher protested.

Disappointment decorated Cora's face. She considered the lives of these rough and ready men and the tales she had heard, sighed and took one of Preacher's hands in both of hers. "Well, if I can't prevail on you to do what's reasonable, the least I can do is part without hard feelings between us. I've never thanked you for saving my life. I want to do so now. Also, there is something I want to give to you before you leave."

"No call for that, ma' . . . er, Miss Cora."

"Yes, there is. I'm sure you are the one who would most appreciate this gift."

"I'll be heading out early tomorrow morning."

"I will rise promptly and see you off," Cora promised.

A thin, silver band, tinged with pink hung over the mountains to the east when Preacher completed his preparation. He had been right sprightly in packing his gear and loading his packhorse. While he had worked the evening before, Beartooth and Nighthawk came to him.

"Now, we've been talkin' this over, an' we allow as how we might just stay the summer and help these good folks over the next winter," Beartooth offered.

Preacher made no effort to hide his amusement. "I reckon as how it might be a good idea, at least for Dupre and Nighthawk here, seein' as how there's some of those gospel-spouter gals that are single. But, you, Beartooth, you're a married man."

"Only in the Cheyenne way. Besides, I wouldn't be untrue to my woman nohow. It's only . . . these folks are so darn thick-headed about so many things. Like be they'd wind up croaked come spring without help. An' you gotta get the Army to settle down the tribes before it's safe to venture that way."

"Promise me one thing?" Preacher prodded, eyes glittering a zealous fire.

"What's that?" Nighthawk asked.

"That under no conditions, no way, no how, you guide them soul-savers north to the Cheyenne. It could mean the ruination of ever'thing that's good about this country."

Laughing, they struck a bond on that. Now, Preacher tightened the cinch strap on the packsaddle a second time as a soft footfall came to his ear. He turned to see Cora. She held her hands behind him.

"I've come to say goodbye," she offered simply. "I brought you these. As I said, I'm sure you'd be the one to most appreciate them."

She brought from behind her the two cartridge belts and holsters that held the .44 Colt Walker revolvers owned by her brother, whom Preacher had known as Hashknife. His eyes went wide and he blinked to conceal the moisture that formed in them.

"Why, that's mighty nice of you, Miss Cora. It's too fine a gift for the likes of me."

"No it isn't. You explained to me why you adapted yourself to those outlandish four-barreled contraptions. I figure you'd be glad to have the convenience of these."

"Darned if I wouldn't." He reached hesitantly for them, then unbuckled the jury-rigged outfit he had for his multibarrels pistols. "They are fine as frog's hair. I heard about them for sometime now, never seen one before . . . until I faced one. I'll just fit these big ol' things across the pommel of my saddle and wear the Walkers. I can't find words grand enough to thank you, Miss Cora."

"No need to, Preacher." With that, she took three quick

steps forward and was in his arms. On tiptoe she pressed her sweet lips to his weathered ones, and kissed him long, deep, and passionately.

When their lengthy embrace ended, Preacher coughed to cover his embarrassment, then gruffly said, "Goodbye, Miss Cora," and swung into the saddle. Twenty minutes later, he still smelled hearts-and-flowers as he rode swiftly out of the valley and off to add more exploits into the pages of history—a lot of it as yet unwritten.